MW01092396

DOC SAVAGE

The Wild Adventures of Doc Savage

Please visit www.adventuresinbronze.com for
more information on titles you may have missed.

PYTHON ISLE
WHITE EYES
THE WHISTLING WRAITH
THE FORGOTTEN REALM
THE DESERT DEMONS
HORROR IN GOLD
THE INFERNAL BUDDHA
DEATH'S DARK DOMAIN
SKULL ISLAND
THE MIRACLE MENACE
THE ICE GENIUS
THE WAR MAKERS

Coming in 2015: THE SINISTER SHADOW

THE ICE GENIUS

A DOC SAVAGE ADVENTURE

BY WILL MURRAY & LESTER DENT

WRITING AS KENNETH ROBESON

COVER BY JOE DeVITO

ALTUS PRESS • 2014

First Edition — September 2014

DESIGNED BY

Matthew Moring/Altus Press

SPECIAL THANKS TO

*James Bama, Jerry Birenz, Condé Nast, Jeff Deischer, Norma Dent,
Dafydd Neal Dyar, Dave McDonnell, Lohr McKinstry,
Matthew Moring, Brian Pruitt, Ray Riethmeier, Howard Wright,
The State Historical Society of Missouri, and last but not least,
the Heirs of Norma Dent—James Valbracht, John Valbracht,
Wayne Valbracht, Shirley Dungan and Doris Leimkuehler.*

COVER ILLUSTRATION COMMISSIONED BY

Bob Gasparini

Like us on Facebook: "The Wild Adventures of Doc Savage"

Printed in the United States of America

Set in Caslon.

For Marc Jaffe—

The visionary Bantam Books editor
who had the foresight to revive the
Man of Bronze fifty years ago in 1964.

The Ice Genius

Chapter I

COLD CAVERN

THE MOST MOMENTOUS discoveries are sometimes made by accident, so history tells us.

The navigator Christopher Columbus, considered a great man today, set out to discover a short cut to the East Indies, and stumbled upon the New World, hitherto unknown.

It was an accident. Ignorance of the world's true geography resulted in the great discovery. That Columbus died in abject poverty matters not a whit. The world changed forever because of him.

The scientist Sir Isaac Newton, resting beneath a fruit tree, discovered the mysterious force called gravity because a common apple chanced to collide with his skull.

The European continent, it is said, was on the verge of being conquered by the Mongol warlord, Sabatoi, when word of the death of his chieftain, the fearsome Genghis Khan, reached his ears. Sabatoi Khan promptly turned his horde around and Europe was spared horrors undreamed.

A few centuries later, Europe was scourged by plague—the direct result, historians claim, of a lack of hungry cats to keep the flea-bearing rodent population in check. Superstitious belief that cats were in league with the Devil had brought about their unfortunate downfall. Without cats, the rats thrived. Plague-bearing fleas enjoyed free reign. And for the lack of tabby cats, humanity suffered greatly.

More recently, an Austrian nobleman's touring car happened to take a wrong turn. This detour brought the nobleman into the sights of his assassin. And his death became the spark that plunged the modern world into the bloody fuss called the World War, in which ten millions died.

Accidents. Mistakes. Happenstance. By such freakish gyrations do the wheels of history sometimes turn.

So it was with William Harper Littlejohn, the eminent archeologist and geologist. The history book publishers had already set aside a barrel of ink with which to enter the prodigious accomplishments of Professor Littlejohn in future tomes, as well as a roll of the finest paper the size of a box car to print the laudatory words upon, when William Harper Littlejohn made the most amazing discovery of his remarkable career.

It was, as it turned out, the most terrible one, as well. Great fame would attach itself to the renowned archeologist because of it, and great sorrow, too. By the time the world learned of it all, William Harper Littlejohn had reached the dark place in his soul wherein he would have gladly swapped his discovery for the peace of mind he had enjoyed before he found the strange cave on the arid steppes of Mongolia.

Ironically, William Harper Littlejohn had come to the rough land in search of bones. Human bones to be exact. Pre-historic human bones, to be absolutely clear about it.

The scientific world was in a frame of mind that caused them to think that early man, primitive man, had first come into this sorry world in Mongolia. The theory was not exactly new, but with the Japanese gobbling up parts of Asia at an alarming rate, the world's archeologists were concerned that any discovery of proof that man came forth in the Gobi wastes would be lost forever—or at least delayed many generations—should Mongolia be consumed by spreading war before any prehistoric bones were found.

So a great many archeologists representing the finest universities all over the world piled into chartered aircraft and picked spots for their digging. William Harper Littlejohn just happened to be one of the many.

Still, it was an accident, the horrible thing that happened.

For a land reputed to be the birthplace of Adam and Eve—if the paleontologists were correct in their surmises—Mongolia was no Garden of Eden.

The area outside the few cities the great sprawling country boasted consisted mainly of snow-capped red-brown mountains and flat, endless steppes. Cold, bitter, barren land, barely able to support the wandering nomads who moved with the seasons, seeking the tough scrub grass that sustained their sheep and shaggy ponies.

And there were bandits.

Most of the bandits had come up from the Manchurian border, fleeing Japanese occupation. They were cruel devils, accustomed to bloodshed. Their trade was pillage, but bandits on ponies were no match for Japanese warplanes and armor-plated tanks. Besides, there was no money in fighting Japanese. Only sudden death.

This particular band of brigands had ranged up into the south of Mongolia, where they lived off the land by pillaging the tiny camps of Mongol sheep herders. By reputation, Mongols are fierce fighters, and after four or five months of this activity, each member of the bandit band could boast of owning two fine ponies—the original owners of the riderless ponies having succumbed to Mongol blunderbusses.

So it was decided one howling night around a feeble campfire that in the future more worthy victims would be selected. This decision was arrived at after three days' argument and many flagons of sour *kumis*—fermented mare's milk—had been quaffed.

When their minds cleared, the bandit group shoved assorted knives and pistols into the sashes of their voluminous robe-like coats, mounted their ponies and, waving rifles in the air, set out in search of more suitable victims. Ones that did not shoot back, was the unspoken assumption.

They rode like wild Indians. The war cries they offered the impossibly blue sky would have done credit to Cochise.

When they appeared on a ridge overlooking the archeological site where William Harper Littlejohn was doing his excavating, silhouetted against the setting sun, they looked remarkably like Comanches—minus the eagle feathers.

"An equestrian calamity impends," muttered William Harper Littlejohn, who had been speaking the Mongolian tongue for so many weeks now he had all but forgotten his English.

Despite having held the Natural Science chair in a prominent American university in his past, William Harper Littlejohn was currently affiliated with no particular seat of learning. Thus, he had no white helpers. Only Mongols willing to do the hard, dusty work for which he paid them in good American greenbacks.

Hearing William Harper Littlejohn's tone of voice, the Mongol helpers looked in the direction he was staring.

And their chins began trembling.

"Bandits!" a man hissed.

Then, as if the hissed word had carried all the way up the ridge, the bandits let out a whoop and their ponies plunged down, kicking up dirt and grass.

They were a blood-curdling sight.

NOW, digging for fossil bone is not unlike drilling for oil. Locations do not advertise themselves. To the untrained eye, one great patch of inhospitable land looks much like another.

Johnny Littlejohn—they called him Johnny, never William or Bill—had selected this particular patch of ground for two reasons, both having to do with the great ridge which the setting sun threw into shadow. First, the ridge kept the prevailing winds from burying the stretch with bone-covering soil. Second, it also cut the bitter winds so prevalent this time of year.

Johnny dropped a short-handled shovel and sifting tray that might have been used to pan for gold at one time, and unfolded his wonderfully bony length in the direction of a duffel bag with alacrity.

The duffel bag was something he kept at hand at all times. The gangling geologist was not, like some college products, ignorant of the perils of Mongolia.

As his helpers dived for the protection of the pit they had been excavating, Johnny fished out a remarkable weapon from the bag. It resembled an ordinary automatic of foreign manufacture. But it was very large for an automatic. There was a drum mounted before the trigger guard and Johnny yanked this off. He fumbled in the bag for another as the bandits continued negotiating their difficult way down the ridge.

The spectacle was not unlike a semi-organized avalanche.

"I'll be superamalgamated!" declared Johnny in his native tongue, which was a brand of English not ordinarily encountered during common conversation. He had found the drum he was looking for. It had a dab of red paint on it for identification purposes.

The drum was hastily clipped into place, the safety latched off, and the bony archaeologist lifted the weapon. He was, for a moment, a ludicrous sight. Johnny Littlejohn was an elongated articulation of bones and skin—with only the skin keeping him from looking like something dug out of the pit after burying. A white pith helmet sat on his long skull like an inverted bowl precariously balanced on the shaggy end of a mop. Tied to the lapel of his jacket was a monocle too thick to be used as such.

No man with a pistol can hope to overcome a wall of hard-riding bandits—even if the pistol is equipped with an ammunition drum packed with bullets.

Then, a long linkage of skin-wrapped bone that was Johnny's trigger finger pulled back the firing lever. The weapon's performance was remarkable. It hooted. An ear-splitting bawl of sound accompanied the furious shuttling of the mechanism, and bullets poured out of the smoking muzzle at a frightful rate. Quantities of brass cartridges dribbled from the breech.

The sound, although loud, was probably lost upon the scrambling bandits, who were preoccupied with making frightful noises of their own.

The commotion that directly followed the striking of the bullets in a line several hundred feet above and behind the line of bandits was impossible to ignore, however.

First, there came a procession of noticeable explosions, spaced fractional seconds apart. The top of the ridge came apart, seemed to fly in all directions at once, and suddenly—gravity exerting its inexorable pull—plunged downward, returning to its former place.

The weight of the returning earth was too much for the broken ridge top. A rumbling landslide commenced.

That was the sound that really got the attention of the bandits. They had already begun throwing open-mouthed glances over their shoulders—neglecting to pilot their mounts would have been dangerous under the circumstances—and these glances rapidly changed character. Surprise followed shock, and shock came hard on the heels of utter terror.

An avalanche was descending on the human avalanche!

All thought of form was thrown to the winds at that point. The riders urged their mounts in whatever direction blind panic dictated. Some broke left. Others right. The riders in the exact center of the skirmish line, predictably enough, got tangled up, trying to cross one another. They fought to keep their mounts from stumbling and lashed them madly to flee.

The avalanche—the real one—took some time to gather itself. It was really roaring along by the time the bandits reached the foot of the ridge.

Thereafter, all effort went into utter flight.

By the time the collapsing top finished its contribution to the base of the ridge, the bandits were a distant pounding of hooves and boil of dust. All fight had been spooked out of them. They would not return.

The Mongol helpers poked their broad stunned faces out of the pit after they felt it safe to do so.

They looked for their boss.

He was calmly returning his mighty weapon to the duffel bag and closing its zipper. A tiny padlock snapped into place.

More than one Mongol gave thought to stealing away with the bag in the dark of the coming night.

None of them ever got the chance. For William Harper Littlejohn was about to make his great discovery—the one he was forever to regret.

Johnny was looking at the change he had wrought in the ridge with his tiny weapon. It had fired explosive bullets, obviously. The ridge stood obscured by settling dust. But behind the dust loomed a dark shape. A darkness inside the shadow that was the shape of the ridge.

The hollow-faced archeologist blinked. His other specialty was geology. Something had been exposed to the light, after how many centuries no one could guess. Abruptly, Johnny hastened to approach, even though the dirt was still settling and there was danger of tumbling rock and loose clumps of red-brown earth.

The hanging-in-the-air dust commenced to thin.

The dark shape was beginning to resolve itself.

"I'll be superamalgamated," muttered Johnny Littlejohn. "A chthonic orifice!"

Which, had there been a scholar with a dictionary at hand to translate, meant that Johnny had spied the mouth of a cave, newly revealed.

He was running now. The Mongols were pounding after him, certain that he had gone crazy from the awful noise. It is not wise to leap into the aftermath of an avalanche. One landslide often sets up the circumstances for another and the ridge had looked none too stable from the start.

Oblivious to the shouting and warning cries ringing in the dusty air, Johnny scrambled up the loose side of the ridge, his incredibly long legs sinking up to his knees in the shifting earth. He lost his pith helmet. A boot, after extracting a stuck foot from a soft section of earth, came loose.

Johnny gained the cave mouth with the awkward-looking agility of a granddaddy longlegs spider, which he rather resembled. He stood at the edge of the cave mouth. It looked deep. Very deep. The air coming out had a strange, cold dead smell to it. The dust in the air did not add any pleasantness to the smell, either.

He entered anyway.

ANCIENT man sometimes inhabited caves, Johnny knew. True, most such caves were found in Europe, but there was no reason that a cave man might not inhabit a Mongolian cave. It was not unheard of. Just never known.

From a pocket, Johnny produced a tiny flashlight. He gave its crank a brisk winding, thumbed the thing on—and the interior of the cave sprang into sudden brilliance!

At first, it looked as if the cave were lined in volcanic obsidian, the kind of glassy black stuff that lava makes when it cools.

Johnny touched an outcropping, fully expected to be cut. Obsidian is so sharp it can be chipped into vicious black blades.

It was not obsidian. It was ice. This was an ice cave—a natural ice cave. This was not unheard of, either. Many ice caves had been discovered. Again, usually in Europe, for some reason.

Johnny continued walking along. He knew the cave could not been very deep. The ridge was not very deep at its deepest part.

At the end of the cave, there was a wall. It was black. The skeletal geologist felt of it. The black came away on his fingertips. Dirt. And behind it, ice. Ancient ice.

Bringing up the bright cone of his flash ray, Johnny twisted the lens and the beam thinned noticeably, seeming to become brighter and more penetrating.

Johnny played the beam against the expanse of ice, endeavoring to see how thick it was. Perhaps to see if there might be cave paintings on the wall—as was sometimes discovered in European caves where primitive humans once dwelt. That was all. He did not mean to set so many heads rolling off so many shoulders by his actions.

What Johnny saw made him gasp instead.

It was something chiseled in the ice. A squiggle, it seemed to be. Mongol, or a related tongue. His heart sank. Although an old language, Mongol is not prehistoric. As far as science knew, Mongol script writing got started about the time of Genghis Khan, the bloodthirsty war chieftain who conquered great portions of Europe and Asia six or seven centuries previous to our own age. This was not a prehistoric cave, probably. Humans had been here in recent centuries.

Then, Johnny came upon a second squiggle and put the two together.

Johnny Littlejohn reached down to his bootless foot and pulled off his sock. He used it to rub at the ice. And so it would later be recorded by the historians, after all was said and done, that by employing nothing more glamorous than a sock, Johnny Littlejohn made his momentous discovery.

He rubbed more squiggles into the light. Mongol script writing, without a doubt.

He read along, mouthing the English translation of the Mongol lines.

" 'If I Still Lived, Mankind Would Tremble,' " he murmured.

Johnny Littlejohn blinked. Then he became very agitated. Furiously, he started rubbing more dirt off the ice with his sock. When it was too dirty to be of further use, he shed his other boot and used that sock.

William Harper Littlejohn had ruined his tweed jacket by the time he got a large patch of the very smooth ice face uncovered. Then he stepped back and employed his flash to full effect.

There was a shape beyond the ice. It was tall, but not taller than he. But Johnny Littlejohn stood nearly seven feet in height, so that was not much of a slight. It was also quite broad at its thickest part.

It stood—if that was the term—not terribly deep in the ice. In fact, it floated in the ice. Johnny could see an impossibly large—compared to the rest of it—head. There were limbs. That was clear. There were fingers, of a sort. It was difficult to quite see because the ice was rippled and this distorted the thing's darksome outlines.

The flash picked out two eyes—and that was what sent Johnny stumbling back into the dying light of the greatest day of his entire life.

"Bring shovels—pick axes—any tools you can!" he shouted.

The Mongols looked up at him with blank, moon faces.

Then he remembered himself and switched to their native tongue. "Hurry!" he exhorted.

The tools were brought. The Mongols, curious, but moving with fear in every step, filed in, wonderment on their faces.

They laid the tools at Johnny's bare feet. Then they saw the shape behind the wall of ice. It might have been the shape—more probably it was the Mongol inscription cut into the ice—that made them bolt from the cave.

They simply ran, leaped from the cave mouth and went rolling and stumbling down in a slide of red-brown earth. That nearly precipitated another avalanche.

Johnny Littlejohn seemed unperturbed by the desertion of his hired hands. Murmuring, "The indigenous aborigines are without exception pusillanimous," he took up a pick axe in painfully fleshless fingers and went to work on the ice with a will.

The sounds of chopping continued far into the night, without cease.

Chapter II

EXPEDITION

BRIGADIER GENERAL THEODORE MARLEY "HAM" BROOKS was addressing a class in a Manhattan law school that night when he was called to the telephone.

"We are leaving for Mongolia at once," said a voice. It was deep, cultured and remarkably toned. It also had a compelling power that promised things.

"Why?" exploded Ham.

"Call it research."

"Research into what?"

"Catalepsy, or suspended animation, as it is sometimes called."

Ham said, "Something important?"

"Perhaps very important. Perhaps nothing at all."

"I don't understand this," Ham declared. "What—"

"The possible explanation might sound absurd just now," said the voice. "In fact, the thing is so fantastic that discussion had better await proof. If you wish to go to Mongolia without knowing any more than that, you might get down here in a hurry."

"Do Monk and the others know?"

"You might," the speaker said, "give them a call."

The speaker then hung up.

Ham ran for his innocent looking cane and his impeccable silk hat.

The voice on the telephone had belonged to the man whom the world was beginning to consider possibly the most remarkable fellow who had ever lived—Doc Savage.

Ham the lawyer occupied a rather strange position in the world. He was one of a group of five men who were following a very unusual profession. The aforementioned Monk was one of the five. Johnny Littlejohn was another. There were two more, an electrical wizard, and an engineer, who were busy following their professions. These five men, all experts in their particular lines, worked with and for Doc Savage. They drew no salaries. They were free to quit any time they chose. It was a safe bet that any one of the five would as soon have been shot as quit. They loved excitement. With Doc Savage, they got it.

Doc Savage, individual of mystery and achievement, was engaged in probably the most unique career ever pursued by man. He went to the ends of the earth, righting wrongs, punishing evildoers, aiding the oppressed. The five were his assistants.

It was difficult to describe what sort of a fellow was Clark Savage, Jr., who was best known to the world as Doc Savage. Some considered him to be the greatest scientist of the day. Newspapers called him a champion of humanity and explorer of the cosmos—this last was on the grandiose side, for Doc had never actually left the planet. He was a man of deep knowledge, yet despite his profound contributions to astronomy, anthropology, medicine and other disciplines, his chief reputation was as a philanthropist.

The philanthropy of Doc Savage was of an unusual nature. He did not disburse funds to worthy charities as his main line. Instead, he held forth in an office at the top of the highest skyscraper in midtown Manhattan, where persons with troubles bigger and more complex than anything lawful authorities might handle could appeal. If you had a problem, you took it to Doc Savage. Many were turned away or referred to other agencies. But if a seeker's troubles were big enough—or interesting enough—for Doc Savage to tackle, he undertook it. Without pay. That was where the philanthropic part came in.

Doc Savage was a combination of Sir Galahad, Sherlock Holmes, Tarzan of the Apes and Albert Einstein. It sounded ridiculous in cold print, but a lifetime of intensive study in all worldly disciples, along with a physical development that was breathtaking, had produced a Twentieth Century superman who was destined to be remembered as one of the great men in human history.

JUST now, Ham Brooks was rushing downtown to the Wall Street sector of Manhattan, where Monk maintained a swanky penthouse laboratory.

An elevator whisked the dapper lawyer up to the vestibule of the combination laboratory and living quarters. Ham strode to the door of the former, and pushed open the unlocked portal.

The interior was modernistic, the furnishings a little too sumptuous to be exactly tasteful.

The inhabitant of the place was a sight to behold. A clever artist had created a popular comic strip featuring an amiable caveman. Lieutenant Colonel Andrew Blodgett "Monk" Mayfair greatly resembled that cartoon character. He was as wide as he was tall, boasted of a blunt head that was sunk between near neckless shoulders. Overlong arms hung on either side of his barrel chest. His entire body was furred with rusty red hair as coarse as shingle nails.

Right now, most of that fur was encased in a full tuxedo that had to have been a tailor's nightmare to custom fit.

"Are you giving a speech somewhere?" blurted out Ham.

"Naw," snorted Monk. "Got a date tonight."

A door cracked open, and out of another room poked a long snout that was followed by the homeliest pig in creation. It was a runt, skinny of leg and long of ear. It trotted out and sat down to observe Ham with suspicious eyes like black buttons.

"What the devil is that—that insect doing in there?" snapped Ham. "Shouldn't he be in his own suite?"

"It's bein' remodeled," homely Monk replied in his normal squeaky voice. "I'm puttin' in a row of health-ray lamps for his mud wallow. Habeas is lookin' kinda pale lately."

"A very good idea," sniffed the dapper lawyer. "Perhaps some cooked bacon will result the next time he oversleeps."

The ungainly shoat seemed to comprehend the word bacon, for he trotted up to Ham and began nibbling at the ferrule of his neat black cane. A tug of war ensued, with the immediate result that the elegant barrister had to fight for possession of his stick.

"I hope whatever Doc has in mind," Ham said angrily, "is interesting enough to make up for the trouble of collecting you."

"What's up?" Monk asked, beetling brows working.

"I do not know. But it involves a trip to Mongolia. And if you care to accompany us, I would advise you to climb out of that monkey suit—a term I would never resort to except for the fact that a tuxedo on you is precisely that."

Hastily stripping off his soup-and-fish, Monk ducked into another room to change. When he returned, he was wearing a shapeless coat of hideous pattern. It elicited a groan of sartorial horror from the elegantly-dressed attorney.

Eyeing Monk's suit critically, Ham remarked, "That coat of yours has insomnia, hasn't it?"

"Whatcha mean?" Monk growled. "Insomnia means you can't sleep."

"That coat hasn't had a nap for years," Ham said. "That's what I meant."

"Don't ride me, shyster. I ain't in the mood," growled Monk.

Turning, Monk told the porker, "Habeas, fetch me that missin' wristwatch of mine."

The homely pig obediently rooted around the floor with his long, inquiring snout.

"That infernal hog thinks it is a dog," Ham said unkindly. "But he will never find that watch."

"You watch, shyster."

After a single trotting turn about the room, Habeas went rooting under the cushions of a leather sofa with his inquisitive snout. He emerged bearing an expensive wristwatch in his tusk-like teeth. This he deposited into Monk's outstretched paw.

Donning the timepiece, Monk beamed proudly. "He's as handy to have around as a pot hound."

Ham sneered acidly, "Bacon is the only thing that pest is good for." He gave his dark cane a twist. It separated, disclosing it to be in reality a sword cane forged of excellent steel. He eyed the ungainly shoat as if contemplating a dissection. This seemed to bother the hairy chemist not at all, as his next words indicated.

"You call Long Tom and I'll try an' hunt up Renny," Monk suggested.

MAJOR THOMAS J. ROBERTS was nothing much to contemplate. He was called Long Tom by his friends, a nickname that hardly described him. He was on the short side of average height, wore his sallow skin as if it were loose, and evinced a perpetually pinched expression, when it wasn't sour.

Long Tom possessed three distinctions. As an electrical engineer he was destined for the hall of fame. Few were his equal in his chosen field. As an fighter, he could lick just about any man he met, and then whip his three brothers to add insult to injury. This despite looking as sickly and frail as if he were a chest cold away from a hospital stay. Lastly, he was an associate of the renowned Doc Savage, which was a distinction that sometimes outweighed the other two.

Long Tom was puttering around his personal cave of a cellar workshop. The place was a cluttered electrical experimental laboratory that in the days before Repeal had served as a dank maze of wine cellars. Long Tom had acquired it very cheaply, which was another of his dominant traits. The puny electrical wizard was exceedingly tight-fisted.

A phone rang and Long Tom ignored it, so deeply was he engrossed in the device he was working on, changing out minute vacuum tubes. It continued ringing. Finally, he scrounged around for the receiver. The instrument was buried amid apparatus.

"What is it?" Long Tom snapped. He had a temper.

"Busy?" asked Ham Brooks.

"I am engaged in an important new experiment in television."

"Then I take it you are not interested in a trip to Mongolia?" drawled Ham.

Long Tom straightened up on his stool. "What's in Mongolia?"

"Doc did not say, but we leave within the hour."

"Do not leave without me," Long Tom said sharply, and flung down the receiver.

NOT many minutes later, a number of vehicles converged on a sprawling brick warehouse situated on a Hudson River pier. The warehouse had a general air of age and disuse. There was a sign at the pier end. It read:

HIDALGO TRADING CO.

The concern existed only as a sign. In reality, the warehouse was a gigantic aircraft hangar and boathouse, which became apparent whenever one of the arriving cars pulled up to the landward doors, which rolled open, disclosing its cavernous interior and the armada of ultra-modern aircraft reposing within.

Doc Savage was there to meet them. The press had hung many names on this awesome individual over the course of his astonishing career—the Man of Mystery, the Mental Marvel and other superlatives. The one that stuck was the Man of Bronze.

Beholding Doc Savage, one could fully understand why. If future scientists ever discover a process to transform cold metal into a living simulacrum of life, the product might very much resemble Doc. He was a powerful example of manhood, standing considerably over six feet in stature, and possessed a fabulous set of muscles that were not much concealed by the clothing he wore.

His fine-textured skin was the hue of bronze. The hair on his head was a darker continuation of that skin, and resembled a metallic skullcap. Most arresting of all, however, were the bronze man's eyes. Perhaps no one in human history ever owned such optics. Not bronze, but a more precious metal seemed to inhabit those orbs. Gold flakes swirled continuously in their aureate depths, as if tiny winds continually stirred them.

The entire effect was that of a man created by some alchemical spell. But the truth was far stranger. Doc Savage was a scientific product. When very young, his father had placed him in the hands of a seemingly unlimited procession of scientists, physical culture experts and other notables. They reared Doc into the man he was now. The entire audacious experiment was designed to fit the bronze giant for the work he did. It had more than succeeded.

"We will depart very soon," Doc told them in a voice vibrant with restrained power.

Toting a large case that normally contained a wonderfully compact portable chemical laboratory, homely Monk asked, "What's up, Doc?"

"Johnny has uncovered something of interest in Mongolia," the bronze man explained. That was all he would say. But that was enough for the four adventurers. If Johnny found something which Doc considered interesting, then it was nothing for them to circumnavigate the globe to see how interesting it might be.

Doc selected the largest aerial conveyance in the combination boathouse-hangar, a four-engine flying boat, capable of crossing the Pacific in one hop. It was very similar to the big Pacific clippers presently carrying passengers to the Orient.

Settling into the pilot's seat, Doc took the control wheel. His hands were long, bronze, perfectly shaped—but they looked hard as alloy steel. The visible tendons were like cables of piano wire.

Once under power, the big bird eased down the ramp into the Hudson's choppy grayness. It moved up river, turned into the wind, and Doc opened the throttles.

The gigantic aircraft took to the sky with a thunder that scattered pigeons off Jersey rooftops and brought heads turning as far away as Staten Island as it sought high altitude.

In the electrically-warmed cabin, Monk Mayfair was heard to say, "Sure hope this is worth my time. I was all set for a night at the opera before this shindig came along."

Ham looked puzzled. "Opera? You?"

"Sure. Lova is an opera buff."

Ham moaned. "Lova? Not my Lova? What are you doing with my girl?"

Monk grinned his widest. "I think she got tired of you."

Chapter III

STOPOVER

FLYING FROM NEW YORK to Mongolia in the heart of Asia was not something undertaken lightly, under ordinary circumstances. With the world consumed by spreading war, it was decidedly more difficult an undertaking than it would have been just a few short years before.

Transiting the Atlantic Ocean and overflying Europe was out of the question. Likewise, crossing the vast Pacific Ocean direct route to Asia—although perfectly practical in the big flying boat—was not wise. The growing Japanese influence in Asia made that flight plan a risky proposition.

This unhappy reality was uppermost in the minds of Doc Savage's men as the big bird volleyed north.

Homely Monk voiced the question on everyone's mind. "Say, Doc, how are we gettin' to Mongolia?"

"There is no safe route," admitted the bronze man. "Obtaining permission to overfly most nations in that part of the world would be difficult, if not impossible, at best."

Ham murmured, "I fail to see how we can get around the problem."

Doc explained, "I have received late word from Renny Renwick, who is going to meet us at the College."

"What's he doin' there?" wondered Monk.

Doc replied, "Renny was investigating a rather shady group of war-profiteers. He managed to capture them all, and transported them to the College for processing."

This "College" was an unusual institution which the bronze man maintained in the wilderness section of upstate New York. In the course of his adventures, Doc often came into possession of individuals whose crimes either could not be prosecuted by duly constituted authorities, or whose trespasses against society were so hideous they would earn the death penalty in a court of law. Doc did not believe in prisons or killing. So he devised a curious method of dealing with wrongdoers who constituted a menace to society. They were spirited away to his private sanitorium, where they were made to forget their crooked pasts through delicate brain surgery, and then reeducated for a new life in society, after being taught to hate crime.

This was a facility known only to the bronze man's inner circle. No doubt had this place become public, there would ensue cries to abolish the institution and turn over its graduates to the proper authorities. In Doc's mind, the rehabilitation and return to society of formerly crooked men justified this radical approach to the problem of crime.

Long Tom said, "I didn't realize that Renny was doing any undercover work."

"This was something Renny stumbled upon on his own," explained Doc.

In considerably less than an hour they landed at the secret institution, which was a cluster of low buildings surrounded by several fences and made to look to the outside world as if this was a private sanitarium. Few ventured into this rugged, out-of-the-way place, so its secrets had remained uncovered for many years now.

The airfield which serviced the institution had not been built for aircraft as large as the four-motored flying boat. Yet Doc Savage slanted the lumbering leviathan in for a landing as if the runway was long enough to accommodate the mighty ship.

Dropping the flaps, Doc slammed the big plane down as quickly as he could, and through an ingenious breaking mechanism brought the plane to a shuddering halt.

When the props ceased their spinning, Monk flung open the plane door and everyone piled out, Doc Savage emerging last.

A strange figure stepped out of a small building to greet them.

Hardly more than four feet tall, it proved to be a perfect little gem of a man. At the sight of Doc Savage stepping off the plane, the minute individual broke out into a great big grin. He hurried forward.

When the small person saw the bronze giant, he all but saluted him.

"Everything's shipshape," reported the little man in a voice that made one think of a happy hound dog.

Doc Savage was not one for smiling without good reason. His training had given him a poker face. But the bronze man bestowed upon the little man a pleasant smile.

"How are you, Monzingo?"

"Spiffy," said the agreeable little man. "Staying long?"

"Just a stopover," replied Doc.

Together, they walked toward the main building. Doc's men acknowledged the tiny Monzingo with stiff gestures and half-hearted smiles.

Doc Savage rarely made idle conversation, but in this case he made a point of it.

"You seem to have adjusted remarkably well to your new life."

The little fellow beamed. "I like it just fine here. They feed me good. And the people are nice." A bit of a catch came into the small man's hound voice.

"You seem hesitant," prompted Doc.

The man screwed up his tiny face, and admitted reluctantly, "I make a lot of friends here, but after a while they always move on."

"That is the nature of this hospital," reassured Doc. "The men who come here do so to be cured of their ills. Once they are cured, they are free to go."

"Don't get me wrong," the midget said hurriedly. "The staff treat me just great. But sometimes I would like my friends to stay here."

"That is understandable," said Doc quietly.

Doc Savage's men were silent during this exchange, but they glanced at one another uneasily.

For the little man who was barely four feet tall was not originally known as Monzingo Baldwin—the name by which he currently went. In years gone by, he had been one of their most dangerous foes, a wealthy schemer named Cadwiller Olden. Olden had seemingly perished during the course of their first encounter, but as they discovered to their surprise a year or so after that, he had survived, but with the loss of his memory.[*]

Having come into possession of the murderous mite a second time, Doc Savage decided that it would be best to place him in the College. Due to his memory loss, and the diminutive size of his brain, it was considered unwise to perform the delicate brain surgery that would wipe his memory clean. So Doc attempted to erase his tragic past through clinical hypnosis. This had seemingly worked, and the former Cadwiller Olden had become a trustee in the secret College, and its only permanent resident.

While this had temporarily solved the problem of what to do with the minute man, it had not led to a permanent solution. Doc Savage was wary of releasing Olden back into society, without assurances that his memory might not return. So instead he remained.

Reaching the main entrance, Doc entered first, and soon found Renny.

.

---

[*] *Repel* & *The Miracle Menace*

Colonel John Renwick was a raw tower of humanity. He was also one of the foremost civil engineers in the world today. A severe countenance and a formidable pair of fists that could hardly fit into maple syrup pails were his outstanding physical characteristics.

The big-fisted engineer looked miserable. He wore rather a gloomy expression that lent itself to the profession of funeral mourner, had there been such a thing. Conversely, this meant that Renny was well pleased with life.

Frowning deeply, Renny strode up to Doc and boomed out in a bull-like voice, "What's this about trouble for us?"

"Trouble may not be the correct word for it," Doc returned. "This is more in the nature of scientific expedition. We are going to Mongolia. Do you wish to come along?"

"Wouldn't miss it for all the tea in China," thumped Renny. "You could throw in all the coffee in Java, too."

Monk offered, "Johnny found somethin' out there. Somethin' mighty interestin'."

The former Cadwiller Olden was an interested listener to all this. During the course of his institutionalization at the College, he had been reading about Doc Savage in the newspapers. Consequently, he had become a big fan of the bronze giant. It would not be too much exaggeration to say he was now an ardent admirer of Doc Savage.

Listening to this exchange, he piped up. "Can I come along?"

The question caught everyone off-guard. They looked down at the little man, features slightly frozen.

The midget took this to be hesitation, when in fact it was a species of horror. The thought of Cadwiller Olden being loose in the world once more made their marrow congeal.

"I won't be any trouble," he bayed. "Honest."

"This could be dangerous," Doc Savage told him gently. "It would be no place for someone not used to the hardships of the places we intend to visit."

The former Cadwiller Olden made a brave face, and one might suspect that he was fighting back tears of disappointment.

Doc Savage said gently, "Perhaps another time."

The midget brightened. Such was his faith in the big bronze fellow that he did not perceive that this was nothing more than a polite white lie.

"Why don't you run along?" Doc suggested. "No doubt you have a great deal of important work to do."

"Sure. Sure, I do. We got a new load of patients in. They are going to be mighty confused. I can help cheer them up. I've done it a million times before."

"You do that," encouraged Doc.

The diminutive fellow went scampering away, and rounded a corner.

THIS left Doc Savage alone with his men. The bronze man immediately got down to business.

"There is no safe route to the Gobi," he told his men frankly. "But my thinking is that we fly north, across the Arctic Circle, and enter Mongolia by traversing Russia."

Long Tom tugged at one oversized ear. He did this when he was concerned.

"The Germans have Moscow under siege," he reminded. "Not likely to cotton to us dropping in on them, even if we are headed for Inner Mongolia."

"The route I have in mind is far east of the fighting, and sparsely settled. If we are careful, we should be able to make it without being challenged, or shot down."

"Then let's get going!" Renny thundered.

Doc halted the general rush to depart with a sentence. "There is one matter to clear up before we depart."

"What's 'at?" Monk wanted to know.

"Since we are traveling north, a stop at my Fortress of Solitude is in order. We can refuel up there, and while doing so, I have a new radio transceiver on the plane that I wish to drop off there. The old set has become outmoded."

Doc Savage's men looked impressed. The bronze giant maintained a fabulous laboratory-workshop near the North Pole, and a few of them had visited there once, years ago. But not all. It was a rare thing to see the Fortress of Solitude. So they looked forward to the opportunity.

Doc took a few moments to speak with the chief surgeon who had charge of the surgical wing of the College.

"The men Renny dropped off should be processed as soon as practical," Doc told the man.

"Of course," the medico replied. "Have you given further thought to the disposition of the fellow we are calling Monzingo Baldwin?"

Doc Savage looked slightly uncertain. "Continually," he admitted. "Hope for the final disposition so far has eluded me."

"If Mr. Baldwin should regain his memory and discover that he has been kept here under false pretenses, it will be a very terrible turn of events. He is coming to a position of trust, and while I am not disagreeing with your decision to make him a trustee, it is just the nature of this institution not to retain prisoners any longer than necessary."

Doc nodded. "This matter concerns me as much as it does you. But the risk of release is greater than the dangers you describe. For if Cadwiller Olden—to employ his real name— should recover his memory, the damage to our operations will be just as grave if he is out in the world as if he remained here. At least here, we can monitor him. As well as take steps should he have a relapse of any type."

"I do not need to remind you that in addition to the issue of his memory," the surgeon continued, "his crime gland has not been attended to. His tendency toward criminal behavior remains present without that additional surgery."

Again Doc Savage made an expression that slightly indicated concern. "We are accustomed to operating on the brains of normal-sized individuals. Even with special miniaturized tools, to operate on his brain entails more risk than usual."

"Nevertheless, I would like to try," said the chief surgeon earnestly.

Doc Savage seemed to give the matter considerable thought. He was very silent until the wall clock advanced with a click, and it was the top of the hour.

At last, Doc said, "If it is your professional opinion that the surgery can be done successfully, you have my permission to undertake it."

"Thank you."

"But operate on the gland only," cautioned Doc. "We will not attempt to erase his memory surgically. At least, not at present."

"Very well. I will give the man some excuse so that he will submit to the operation."

Doc Savage added, "My men and I will be away, possibly for weeks. But radio us your results. It would be a load off our minds to know that this matter has been advanced toward a permanent solution."

With that, Doc Savage turned to go.

He stepped out into the hallway and moved swiftly to rejoin his men waiting in the outer lobby.

Neither the bronze giant nor his chief surgeon noticed that around the corner, the tiny fellow who had been Cadwiller Olden had been huddled inside a wastebasket.

The basket appeared full, although it was not. After Doc had departed, and the door to the chief surgeon's office closed, the pile of crumpled papers which had crowned the wastebasket fell away, exposing a small but perfectly formed man's head.

Monzingo Baldwin, alias Cadwiller Olden, lifted his head out of the paper debris. His dark eyes were very open, and very, very stark. He had overheard everything. And from the expression on his features, the knowledge he obtained had shaken him to his very core.

Hastily, the midget extracted himself from the wastebasket and carefully replaced every scrap of paper.

Then, he went running out of sight as fast as his little legs could carry him. The expression on his tiny features was terrible to see. It was as if the little man were struggling to keep from bawling his eyes out.

Chapter IV

STRANGE SILENCE

WHEN DOC SAVAGE rejoined his men in the lobby, he found Monk and Ham engaged in one of their routine rows.

Renny Renwick eyed Doc Savage and asked gloomily, "Want me to knock their blocks off? I'm not up to hearing them squabbling all the way to Mongolia."

Monk glowered at the big-fisted engineer and growled, "Any time you're feelin' lucky, big fists."

Ham Brooks, for a miracle, took Monk's part. "If you want to wring his thick neck, you will have to get past me first."

Renny grunted, "When did you fall in love with him?"

Ham gave his sword cane a flourish in the homely chemist's direction. "I have been looking to brain Monk Mayfair since we first met," he said loftily. "And I will not be cheated out of the pleasure."

Apart from this muscular exchange, Long Tom Roberts was staring out a window. Like all of the windows of the strange installation, this one was made of very thick glass reinforced by chicken-wire. The stuff made it difficult to see the grounds outside with clarity.

"Pipe down!" the puny electrical wizard grumbled. "I think I see a fox prowling around our plane."

Ham bleated, "We left the door open! Better look into this."

They made a concerted rush for the plane.

All seemed normal when they reached the big leviathan.

Monk came to a stop by the aircraft, commenced exploring it with his pocket flashlight.

Doc Savage remained under the wings, and was scrutinizing the ground with his acute golden eyes.

Then he climbed aboard.

"No fox tracks," he told the others. "Just those of our party, and Monzingo Baldwin, from our arrival."

Long Tom said sourly, "Well, through that chicken glass, it was hard to tell."

Still, Doc Savage made a tour of the interior and discovered nothing amiss.

The bronze giant, hardened by years of negotiating peril, overlooked nothing where the safety of his men was concerned.

Monk joined him in the rear, and asked, "Is that the big radio you were talkin' about?"

Doc nodded. The radio was mounted upon caster-type wheels. Straps affixed to the bulkheads held it in place, preventing it from rolling around and damaging itself during flight.

Doc was examining the straps to make sure they still held properly.

As he did so, the bronze man discovered a short-handled screwdriver which lay on the metal floor. He picked it up.

"Did any of you use this?" he asked.

None of his men admitted to having dug out the screwdriver for any reason.

Doc Savage felt of the screwdriver. The handle was cool to the touch. But it was a very cool night.

Replacing the screwdriver in a tool box, the bronze man went forward and took the control bucket.

Doc and his men were accustomed to taking long flights to faraway points on the globe. Each had their assigned places on such ventures. Monk slid in the co-pilot's seat, next to Doc. Renny dropped his big bulk into the navigator's station. Long Tom took over the radio cubicle, and placed a radio headset over his oversized ears.

Lastly, Ham Brooks closed the plane door, then took a comfortable seat. He had brought along a law book to read. Over time, he would spell Monk or Long Tom at their stations. But for the moment he had nothing to do.

While Doc Savage warmed up the four radial motors, Ham said to no one in particular, "It is a distinct pleasure not to have that infernal hog along for a long trip."

No one said anything to that, and Ham cocked one ear to capture any piggy sounds in the cabin. There was a tiny rattle that made him suspicious.

"Do not tell me that pig is on board!" he flared.

Monk called, "You know I hadda leave him behind in New York."

"Yes," sniffed Ham. "But you have promised that before, yet managed to smuggle that infernal pest along."

Ham continued listening, thought he detected something. Glowering, he rushed to the back of the cabin, waving his cane around like a pig-sticker. But his violent sweeps failed to stir any pig that might be present.

Half-satisfied, the dapper lawyer returned to his seat, and complained, "I thought I heard something rattling back there."

"It was your tiny brain rattlin' around in your narrow skull," goaded Monk.

Ham's sharp retort was lost in the thunder of the four mighty engines as the air giant lurched ahead.

The flying boat began traveling, eating up the short runway at an alarming pace. Doc lifted the plane into the air. He pointed the howling motors north, and then settled down for the long hop to the Fortress of Solitude.

AS the big flying boat passed over Canada, curiosity over what Johnny Littlejohn discovered in Mongolia had reached the boiling point among the bronze man's aides.

Long Tom was the first to broach the matter. The puny electrical wizard was probably the most temperamental of Doc

Savage's men, with the possible exception of the excitable Ham. Also, he had very little to do at the radio.

"Will someone fill me in on why we're charging off to Mongolia in the middle of a world war?"

Doc Savage was a naturally reticent person. He was not given to long conversations, or broaching theories before he had all the facts at hand.

Still, it was going to be a very long flight, and no doubt boring if they were lucky. The bronze man knew he would have to reveal what motivated him to leave in such a hurry.

"Johnny was digging for prehistoric human bones on the Mongolian steppes," he began. "During the course of this, his party was attacked by bandits. There was a fight. Johnny had to unloose explosive shells from his supermachine pistol, and in doing so exposed an ice cave of unknown age."

"Sounds interesting," rumbled Renny. "But where's the blamed fire?"

"That's what I want to know," said Long Tom sourly.

"In this ice cave, Johnny discovered a body entirely encapsulated by ice."

"Like those mastodons—or were they woolly mammoths?—that were discovered frozen in ice a few years back?" grunted Renny.

"Exactly."

"They defrosted those big boogers, and fed the sled dogs the cooked meat. They said it tasted pretty fresh."

Monk's squeaky voice exploded, "Blazes! You don't suppose that man in the ice could still be alive?"

Doc Savage was a long time in replying.

"There have been incidents in which creatures have been extracted from ice, and revived, restored to life. There was one unexplained incident in which a rock was broken open. A small toad emerged as healthy as the day he was entombed countless generations ago. In another, a desert snail affixed to an Egyptian tablet kept under glass in the British Museum came to life after four years of immobility."

"Is that what you meant by suspended animation?" wondered Ham.

"It is premature to consider such a thing in this instance," Doc returned. "For there has never been in recorded history a circumstance when a living human was entombed in ice and then later revived."

Monk muttered, "In the olden days, didn't they sometimes bury people they thought was dead, only to discover that they had not died?"

Doc nodded. "The problem of premature burial is one that has been solved by science. But in the days when people ate off lead plates, some fell into comas that were not recognized as such. These unfortunate persons were buried alive, although some managed to escape their predicament by luck."

No one spoke much after that. The thought of being entombed alive, and awakening in one's own coffin buried several feet underground, had a chilling effect upon conversation.

After a while, Ham Brooks found his tongue. "What I fail to follow," he admitted, "is why the finding of this man in ice should produce such an urgent response."

Doc Savage seemed hesitant about responding to that assertion. When he did, all that he would say was, "According to Johnny, there were signs that this may not be an ordinary man."

"Holy cow!" boomed Renny. "What do you mean by that?"

"I would rather not say," replied the bronze man quietly.

"Holy cow! Now my curiosity is really out of the barn," muttered Renny.

THE HOURS passed and they approached the area of the Arctic Circle west of Greenland where the Fortress of Solitude lay, supported by an ice-bound island, far from civilization, unsuspected by man.

By this time, Doc's men were growing excited about the prospect of visiting the strange spot. Renny the engineer was particularly interested in the place. He had never been there, while the others had.

"I'm mighty interested in checking out this place," he admitted. "It sounds like an engineer's dream."

Monk offered, "It looks kinda like an Eskimo Paul Bunyan built an igloo out of some kinda blue glass, as big as a football stadium."

Ham declared, "This boastful baboon is, as usual, exaggerating. Slightly. But the Fortress is an impressive structural achievement, I will admit."

Indeed it was, for the bronze man had built it out of a superconducting material of his own invention. The outer skin, Monk and Ham agreed, resembled highly polished blue agate. But the substance was actually a glassy metal that could be welded so that no seams showed.

By the time they approached the place where the Fortress stood, it was day. But Arctic winter had arrived, and with it the perpetual polar twilight. Anticipation was high.

Doc Savage dropped the air giant out of the clouds, and sent the ship skimming over the ice-choked seas.

"There it is," he told them. "Look off to starboard."

It was a rush to the starboard windows, and every man pressed his nose against any available window. Disappointment rode their faces.

"Where is it?" demanded Renny, voice flavored with disappointment.

"Squatting on that island," directed Doc.

"I don't see any blue dome," Renny grumbled. "All I spy is a kind of glacier sitting on an island of ice."

"That is it," Doc said quietly.

Doc Savage dropped the plane toward the water, and made an extremely careful, if dangerous, landing inasmuch as the wintery waters were filled with ice chunks.

Doc ran the big aircraft up to the edge of the island, and drove the ship up onto a natural ramp that had been smoothed out of one stony side of the isle.

Shutting down the motors, Doc directed that the hatch door be opened. Ham took care of that, and quickly stepped back, driven backward by a blast of cold air.

They all donned parkas from a storage locker aft.

Stepping out, they approached the strange glacier.

Doc Savage explained for his befuddled men what had become of the Fortress of Solitude that they knew or had heard about.

"You will recall that after the unfortunate affair in which John Sunlight discovered this place, it was necessary to relocate the Fortress to an even more remote location. With the world at war, military air traffic over the Arctic has been increasing to the point that an air patrol discovering the dome was all but inevitable. Thus I felt compelled to remodel it, so that it resembled a natural glacier. But it is not a glacier, for the construction is of a special plastic I have devised that resembles glacial ice."*

The men clustered around the Fortress, and touched its icy surface with tentative fingers. The weird material was cool to the touch, and slick in a way that ice is not slick. It was too dry. The outer surface, with its facets and diamond-sharp projections, looked as if it were transparent. But peering into the ice that was not ice showed absolutely nothing at all.

Taking a tour around the perimeter, Renny finished his circuit and remarked, "This wouldn't fool anyone who landed here. You can tell it's not really a glacier."

Doc nodded. "From the air, it is indistinguishable from a so-called blue growler, and unlikely to attract the attention of a pilot willing to land in such an inhospitable place."

Renny grunted, satisfied that Doc Savage's remodeling of his Fortress of Solitude would long go unnoticed. The Arctic

---

* *Fortress of Solitude*

was not exactly a tourist spot. And military floatplanes overflying this area were always on missions that required them reaching their destination efficiently. This Arctic zone was not currently being explored. Doc's secret was safe, barring the unforeseen.

From a pocket, Doc Savage removed what proved to be a small magnet, which he placed against the curved side of the Fortress. He touched several flat planes in a specific sequence.

Two amazing things happened. First, a man-size hatch heaved upward, permitting them to enter. There had been no sign of any door prior to this manifestation.

On another side of the great diamond-like structure, two doors parted revealing a cavity that was nothing less than a hangar for aircraft. There was already a gyroplane therein, as well as a small two-engine aircraft equipped with an ingenious arrangement of floats that doubled as skis.

"We will not tarry long enough to hangar our plane," said Doc. "But we do need to refuel for the next leg of our flight. And I must get that radio inside."

While Doc Savage's men split up—Renny to take a quick tour of the interior of the Fortress of Solitude while Monk and Long Tom unreeled a great hose that fed off underground aviation fuel tanks in the hangar space—the bronze man located a stainless steel sled that was obviously oversized and used to move heavy equipment over the ice.

Doc pulled this down to the waiting plane, and single-handedly unstrapped and then jockeyed the big radio out of the plane and deposited it on the sled without damaging it.

He towed this back with one hand, and only then was it apparent how immensely strong the big Hercules of a fellow actually was. His muscular development was so symmetrical that Doc Savage did not seem over-muscled, when wearing ordinary garb. The casual ease with which he jockeyed the radio around showed that he was prodigiously strong.

Reaching the entrance, Doc Savage set the radio in one corner, and warmed it up. He wished to test the set before departing.

It was not a portable set, and it was very powerful. Doc started the generator, spun the dials, watching the various meters. It was in perfect working order.

He waited. The air was still in the radio room. The place was amazingly soundproofed, as well as perfectly insulated against the cold.

Then the radio made noise. It sputtered, popped. Bright blue electric flame spurted. Odor of burned insulation arose.

Doc Savage whipped to one side, changing position. He snapped a light on, the better to see. There was an inspection window back of the radio apparatus, and he expected to see that open. But it was closed.

Taking up a flashlight, Doc roved the flash beam. He stabbed the ray over the rest of the apparatus, shifted to the immediate surroundings, flake-gold eyes scrutinizing. No one in sight. He went back to the radio.

The apparatus had been short-circuited by thrusting some metallic object into the wiring. Certain essential parts had burned out, rendering it useless.

The damage, although complete, was such that it would escape the eye of one who did not know much about radio transmitters. A wooden-handled screwdriver—it lay on the floor below—had been placed across two contacts under and at the rear of the main power panel.

Doc Savage scrutinized the terminals which had been shorted. It was easy to discern their location, down near the corner of the board. They were prominent. He tried to reach them. He could not, without removing certain braces.

After a moment, the bronze man's fantastic trilling note, his small peculiar sound which always denoted surprise or some form of intense mental activity, came into evidence. The sound filled the radio room like a chorus produced by unearthly crickets.

It was manifestly impossible for a man to have reached in to those terminals with the screwdriver. This was a fact, incredible as it seemed.

THE others came running from other parts of the structure.

"What's wrong?" demanded Ham, waving his sword cane excitedly.

Doc Savage did not immediately reply.

Instead, he wheeled the radio into a laboratory so fabulous that it shamed anything else in the world, including the great wizard's workshop at his skyscraper headquarters, which was believed to be the most well-equipped in the world.

Doc Savage moved the radio behind a large fluoroscopic machine. He turned the latter on, and watched the screen intently.

The device showed the complicated innards of the radio and Doc Savage traced the tubes and bundles of wires and other elements until he discovered something out of place.

Directing the attention of his men to a lower quadrant of what was revealed, he signaled them to be ready.

"You may come out now, Monzingo," invited Doc.

There was an interval of silence, followed by a rodent-like rattling. Then, Doc repeated his request in a louder voice.

A panel dropped down in the back, and out crawled an uninvited stowaway.

"Holy cow!" Renny roared. "What's *he* doing up here?"

"Obviously stowing away," spat Long Tom. "I'll bet that's my fox."

"Explain yourself," Doc instructed. No trace of fire flared in his resonant voice. But deep in his flake-gold eyes, there was an angry sparkle.

Monzingo Baldwin shuffled feet like a little child. He refused to meet their accusing eyes.

Finally, he stammered, "I—I thought I'd tag along. I only wanted to have s-some fun."

"That is out of the question," stated Doc Savage. "This expedition is too dangerous for an outsider."

"Blazes!" bellowed Monk. "We can't turn back now!"

Doc Savage said simply, "We cannot take him along."

"I won't be any trouble—honest," Monzingo Baldwin promised.

Doc Savage studied the miniature man intently. "Out of the question," he repeated.

There ensued a kind of argument that rarely overtook Doc Savage and his personal brain trust.

LONG years of association, first in war, and then as peacetime adventurers, carried with it a strong deference to the judgment of the Man of Bronze. Although independent fellows, Doc's aides understood the value of following orders. When Doc Savage directed them to do something, they invariably complied.

Here, they were voicing a natural desire to get on with the expedition, and not turn back without good reason.

The fact that the former Cadwiller Olden had managed to stow away this far was more than alarming. Countering that was their reasonable expectation that their old foe had been rendered harmless. But the collective memories of his murderous former life were not greatly diminished.

The sight of the reformed master criminal in Doc Savage's holy of holies was distressing in the extreme.

Despite all that, there was a strong, unanimous feeling that they needed to get on with the expedition to Mongolia.

Doc Savage was not persuaded. He was a man of extreme caution. He left little to chance. That they were flying into danger, there was no doubt. The additional risk of this new passenger greatly added to that danger, even if the calculation was inexact.

Doc Savage decided to check in with Johnny Littlejohn by radio before taking off. It was his hope that his men would settle down and see the wisdom of his decision.

Returning to the radio room in one corner of the lab, Doc Savage warmed up the old set and attempted to raise the archeologist.

"Doc Savage to Johnny Littlejohn. Come in, Johnny."

But the big-worded geologist did not respond.

Doc Savage decided to give the matter another hour to settle.

During that interval, the bronze man let his men talk themselves through the situation. He did not attempt to persuade them, but simply allowed them to work out their concerns.

The strategy appeared to be bearing fruit. After some forty minutes, Renny began to argue for a swift return in order to avoid dangerous complications.

Most of them agreed with this. Monk was for getting on with it. Ham predictably took the opposite view, but impatient Long Tom also wanted to get going in the direction of Mongolia.

What finally decided the matter was Johnny Littlejohn's voice crackling from the radio excitedly.

"Johnny to Doc! Johnny to Doc! Come in, Doc Savage."

The bronze man seized the microphone. "Doc here."

"Doc! Trouble is brewing! I don't know if I can hold out much longer."

Doc's voice leapt out, "Hold out from what?"

Johnny Littlejohn began to reply, then his words got mixed up, and the deafening racket of his supermachine pistol came over the ether to fill the cavernous laboratory of the Fortress of Solitude.

After that, Johnny's voice was heard no more. There followed a great deal of background noise, assorted commotion, and then a species of unpleasant silence.

Doc Savage turned to his men, his voice edged with a metallic bite. "We have no choice in the matter now. We must press on as quickly as possible."

At one quadrant of the lab, the former Cadwiller Olden grew frightened when he heard these words. He clapped his small hands together like a small boy. It was such a childish display that it actually allayed much of their fears.

No one noticed the cunning gleam that came into the tiny eyes of the mischievous midget.

Chapter V

THE LONG FLIGHT

FLYING ACROSS THE Arctic region, although it has been accomplished many times over recent years, remains an unusual and perilous enterprise.

Doc Savage relied on the big airplane's robot pilot to guide them for much of the way over the great barren wasteland of ice and snow. Despite the presence of their diminutive stowaway, the boredom of the long hours of monotonous flying fast became tedious. The depressingly endless Arctic twilight did not help their mood, either.

The cabin interior was electrically warmed, so they had a great deal of comfort despite the inhospitable environment through which they hammered. Too, the silencers Doc Savage had installed in the four great motors kept the cabin relatively quiet, otherwise the relentless racket of the great engines would eventually have driven them to distraction.

They did not expect to encounter any military aircraft above the Arctic Circle, and they were not surprised by the fact that they remained unchallenged for much of the journey. For they flew over the polar ice cap—that being the most direct route to their destination.

Two days into the flight, they had to put down to again refuel. They did so in Siberia, at a military landing field, far west of the fighting. They had radioed ahead to avoid being shot down.

When asked as to their ultimate destination, Doc Savage politely said, "Mongolia."

The Russian authorities were not satisfied by that. So Doc had to reveal that his archaeologist friend, Johnny Littlejohn, had encountered difficulty with bandits and had radioed for assistance.

"We are aware that your comrade is in Mongolia," Doc was told. Evidently, the Soviet security apparatus had been keeping close tabs on the gangling archeologist, for the official added, "He has been calling himself Ichabod Sprain."

"Johnny knew that if he traveled under his real name, enemies of ours might seek him out," explained Doc.

"*Da.* So he informed us."

Since the bronze man's story checked out, he was allowed to proceed.

Relations between the United States and the Soviet Union, long cool, had warmed somewhat since the German invasion of Russia the previous summer. American aid was helping prop up the Soviet government. So Doc Savage was not looked upon with undue suspicion. In fact, in years past he had rendered an important service to the Soviet government, and this had not been forgotten.

Still, the Red officials warned him, "We cannot guarantee your safety at any point in the journey that lies before you."

"Understood," Doc Savage replied tightly. "Thank you."

They took off, driving south into the inhospitable Gobi region of Mongolia.

During the trip, Monzingo Baldwin tried to make himself useful. He was not a bad cook, but some of them—especially Monk—examined his food carefully before eating.

"Since when did you become a picky eater?" asked Long Tom querulously.

"Not picky. Just making sure we're not bein' poisoned."

After that remark, they all investigated their food nervously. But the meal proved satisfactory, with no complaints, gastric or otherwise, afterward.

Basking in the approval of his culinary skills, Monzingo Baldwin beamed, saying, "If this works out, maybe I can join the team permanently."

Ham Brooks almost spat out his water when he heard that.

The others made polite noises, remaining noncommittal.

Renny was the only one who made a remark of substance. "Once you see the kind of scrapes we charge into, you might experience a change of heart."

"I hope not," Monzingo Baldwin said carefully. "I like to have fun and see new places. But I don't think I would care to be shot at."

"In this crowd," Long Tom told him, "being shot at is as regular as a rainy day."

Hearing that, the former Cadwiller Olden sat down in his seat and was very quiet for a very long time.

Monk shifted alongside of Long Tom and undertoned, "Good thinkin'. I think you banked his fire."

The big flying boat thundered across the great steppes of eastern Russia and down into Inner Mongolia, which had managed to avoid being gobbled up by encroaching Japanese legions after several border skirmishes resolved by treaty.

"I can't remember the last time I was out here," Monk muttered, peering out one window.

"Nor I," admitted Ham. "It has been quite some while."

"Reminds me of the most desolate parts of Wyoming," muttered Long Tom. "I would hate to have to make a forced landing out here. Nothing but monotony for hundreds of miles in any direction."

Passing over the Russia-Mongolia border, having traversed the expanse of the Russian steppes, they began to relax. Mongolia was not at war with anyone, and they didn't have much of an Air Force.

Still, danger existed. They were flying an unmarked aircraft over a sovereign nation in a time of global war.

In past years, Doc Savage had painted his planes a uniform bronze color as a way of identifying them to foreign nations over which he flew. Now, with the world dividing itself into armed camps, the sight of a bronze plane no longer meant merely the world-famous adventurer, Doc Savage, but symbolically the United States of America. Although not formally at war, the U.S. had sided with certain of the warring parties against others. This had all but erased United States neutrality.

Thus it was that Doc had started painting his planes silver, and they remained unmarked. While that meant his flying boat would not be targeted as a United States aircraft straying into foreign skies, an unmarked plane was always a suspicious thing.

Despite those theoretical complications, the big silvery flying boat passed over Mongolia without attracting trouble or anti-aircraft fire.

Doc had elected not to alert the local Mongolian authorities that he was coming. This was a calculated risk, but one which he thought prudent to make. The bronze man suspected that Russian officials had slipped word of his coming to their Mongolian compatriots, however. Mongolia was a vassal state of the U.S.S.R.

IN the navigation compartment, big-fisted Renny Renwick suddenly rumbled, "If my calculations are on the money, we're getting close to the spot where Johnny was doing his digging."

Hunkered in the co-pilot bucket, Monk Mayfair gazed down at the desolate wilderness unrolling below. "How can you tell? It's all dirt and dead yellow grass."

Bored, Ham Brooks said sharply, "By navigating, you nitwit!"

Monk growled out, "In a place this big, all anybody can do is pick out a general spot. Finding Johnny's camp ain't gonna be easy."

Doc Savage interrupted, "With any luck, Johnny will have provided a beacon."

"Beacon?" muttered Monk. "It's broad daylight. How are we gonna spot any beacon?"

Doc Savage did not reply. The bronze man was intent upon his flying. He dropped the leviathan flying boat closer to the flat endless Gobi, which was a desert unlike any other on earth, for it was not comprised of sand dunes, but arid steppeland.

This caused everyone on board to become concerned. It was one thing to fly high over Mongolia, quite another to drop closer to the ground. It was true that the great expanse of snow-dusted scrubland lying below was sparsely inhabited. And there were few land radios. That did not mean there were none.

Before long, a trio of airplanes came charging up to greet them.

Monk grabbed for his binoculars and examined them.

"Russian-style fighters," he said. "Old jobs. Two of them are biplanes."

Doc cautioned, "They will be armed with machine guns regardless. Best to take them seriously."

The bronze man got on the radio, and dialed around until he found the frequency on which the Mongolian Arat Air Squadron operated.

He spoke in the Mongolian tongue, one he knew very well. Doc Savage was a master of many languages. This was but a small part of his intensive training.

The exchange was brief, and pointed. Before long the three fighter planes had them surrounded.

Doc Savage continued speaking to the pilots, and after a period of silence they broke away in different directions, returning to their desert base.

"What did you tell them?" rumbled Renny.

"The truth," said Doc. "We are on a rescue mission for a missing associate. They accepted my story."

Ham Brooks said carefully, "Word will get out that we're here."

Doc nodded. "That may or may not complicate our mission."

After a short period of time, Renny remarked, "I'm pretty sure we're about where Johnny last reported his position."

By this time, Doc Savage had dropped the plane to about one thousand feet, and throttled back the engines.

Everyone had their binoculars out now, including Monzingo Baldwin. He seemed very eager to help.

It was late in the Fall season, and nomadic Mongol herdsmen had already moved to their winter pasturage. So there were a few visible felt tents of the type called yurts dotting the grasslands. Here and there, small lakes stood out like dull mirrors, reflecting the gray skies overhead. It was one of the reasons they had taken the flying boat, the other being that the Fortress of Solitude was accessible only by amphibious aircraft.

Doc flew in a wide, sweeping circle, golden eyes alert.

"Johnny spoke of an ice cave that he had uncovered. We are looking for such a feature, which will have a lot of dirt stirred up and around its location."

Long Tom, scanning the terrain below through strong binocular lenses, remarked, "One thing is for sure. We won't have much trouble landing out here. I can't remember the last time I saw such a flat wasteland."

A line of forms moving majestically along drew their attention. But when Ham studied the procession, he reported, "Just camels."

Monk asked, "One hump, or two?"

"What difference does it make?" snapped Ham, turning.

Monk eyed the ceiling innocently. "Two humps means twice as ornery."

"You are making that up!"

"Knock it off!" yelled Renny and Long Tom in unison.

Doc piloted the big leviathan about, seeking the exposed ice cave of Johnny's radio report.

From time to time as they had traversed Mongolia, they had attempted to raise the missing archaeologist on the radio. But either Johnny's set was out of commission, or he was unable to reach it. All entreaties had failed to elicit a response.

This worried them all, for the silence portended poorly as to Johnny's fate. The extraordinarily long flight caused them to grow impatient, as well. But nothing could be done about the situation, except to fly as quickly as was prudent to do so.

Suddenly, Monzingo Baldwin piped up, saying, "I think I see it!" He sounded very excited.

The little man was pointing to port. Doc Savage's gaze lanced in that direction.

There was a ridge, and one face of it, pointing south, had collapsed into a rubble of rock and dirt.

The exposed hole was very dark and impenetrable to sight.

It took only seconds for the bronze man to scrutinize the landmark and come to a decision.

"We will land here," Doc announced.

Chapter VI

THE THING IN THE ICE

THE LANDING WENT very smoothly, except for the rock.

Doc Savage had dragged the long flat section of steppe twice before he felt confident about setting down the air giant. The others assisted in this process, scanning the ground with their binoculars.

Trees were sparse out here in the Gobi, so their main concern was rocks and boulders and similar obstructions. The area was hilly and rugged, but there were great flat stretches, too, as well as depressed bowls many miles wide.

One by one, Doc's men called from their positions to report that the rough landing strip was clear of obstructions.

"Looks good," Renny rumbled.

"I don't spot anything that spells trouble," added Long Tom. Ham agreed.

The last to report was Monzingo Baldwin, the former Cad-willer Olden.

"I don't see anything rocky," he reported, smiling broadly.

At the control yoke, Doc Savage had spotted nothing dangerous in his planned landing path. Bringing the great four-motored aircraft around one more time, the bronze man dropped the wheels electrically, and started his approach.

It was a very bumpy landing. They expected as much. The steppe was tufted with dying grass, and was cracked and corrugated by rough weather.

So they were not greatly surprised after the wheels touched down, and the big plane began vibrating alarmingly, jarring its way toward touchdown.

Doc Savage spotted the rock. He flung the control wheel to starboard, and managed to avoid it. This sent the aircraft careening toward the second rock. The second stone, like the first, had been covered in the dust and dirt of the season, and did not stand out by shape or hue.

Still, it was rather large and should have cast a warning shadow.

The port wheel glanced off it, and the big plane gave an abrupt jump like a bucking bronco.

No one said a word. They just hung onto their seats for dear life.

Doc Savage was one of the most accomplished pilots in the world. Further, he had executed dangerous landings onto rough terrain and bad weather all over the globe. There was little he had not encountered in the way of an aviation emergency.

The bronze man cut the engines, having decided in a split second that jumping back into the air was imprudent. Moreover, it was likely to cause them to do a violent ground loop.

Wrestling the hurtling bird, Doc let the plane run out momentum until he felt it safe to throw the wheel brakes. The powerful hydraulic brakes took hold. The sky giant commenced screeching and complaining at every joint and rivet. A frightening series of noises accompanied the last part of the landing.

Fortunately, the natural runway Doc had chosen was much larger than was needed to land the big plane. Doc maintained control over the hurtling leviathan, until finally it shuddered to a final stop, motors blooping and belching exhaust smoke.

Only then did someone speak.

"What a man!" Monzingo Baldwin breathed in awe.

Jumping out of his seat, Long Tom Roberts sprang for the little man whose job it was to watch for rocks on the port side of the plane.

"You said there were no rocks!" snarled the puny electrical wizard.

In his oversized seat, the little man recoiled in horror at the sight of Long Tom's mallet-hard fists.

"I didn't see anything! Honest, I didn't!" The midget sounded terrified.

From the cockpit, Doc Savage called back a warning, "Long Tom, the rocks are covered in dust and dirt, and difficult to see."

Knuckles white with anger, his sour face crimson with repressed fury, Long Tom Roberts ground his teeth audibly and reluctantly returned to his seat.

Another minute passed before anyone stirred. They were getting a grip on their frayed nerves.

It had been one of the most arduous landings they had ever experienced. A crash out here, a thousand miles from any civilized settlement, would have put them in a bad spot.

Coming out of his seat, Doc Savage went to the cabin door and flung it open. He carried with him a pair of goggles of unusual construction.

Outside, Doc Savage gave rapid instructions.

"Long Tom, you remain here and guard the plane from bandits. The others follow me."

"What about me?" asked Monzingo Baldwin.

Doc Savage told him, "Best that you remain here with Long Tom."

The little man gave a sideways glance in the direction of the pallid electrical expert. "But I—I'm afraid of him," he quavered.

"Very well. You may accompany us. But stick close."

Monzingo Baldwin gave the big bronze man an angelic smile. But the look he bestowed upon Long Tom Roberts was dark.

They set off on foot, Monk, Ham and Renny brandishing supermachine pistols. Doc Savage did not carry one of the intricate weapons, preferring from longtime experience to rely on his wits rather than become dependent on firearms.

They were a fair distance from the cave; it took them more than a half hour to reach the spot.

There they found Johnny's camp, abandoned.

Doc Savage picked through the remnants of the camp, and said simply, "Johnny's camp lantern is missing."

Renny grunted, "Bandits probably made off with it."

Doc said nothing, but led them toward the ice cave.

They entered by scrambling over tumbled rock and dirt. It was a testament to the power of the explosive bullets Johnny's supermachine pistol had disgorged that so much natural debris had been ripped loose from the side of the ridge that it formed a small hill by itself.

By this time it was becoming dusk. They found it necessary to produce their special flashlights, which operated on a spring-generator system. Simply by winding a small crank on the barrel, current was generated that would last several minutes.

They entered, Doc Savage leading the way.

THE place appeared to be a natural cavern. Even though it was cool outside, it was much colder within. The reason was the interior walls of the cave were rippled with ancient ice. The stuff had a dark greenish quality, as if it were not natural ice.

Monk and Renny rubbed at the ice with their sleeves, removing the grime of centuries. Beneath, ordinary-looking ice was revealed. The stuff was striated and not very transparent.

Doc Savage spoke up, "Natural ice caves such as this one have been found in other parts of the world. They are rare, but not terribly unusual."

The bronze giant pointed his flashlight at the ceiling. Suspended overhead were great icicle-like stalactites that resembled icy fangs. Some of these were quite large. A few had been broken by the explosion that had revealed the cave, and were lying in great conical sections on the dirt floor.

As they worked their way deeper into the cavern, Doc Savage found a pick axe that had been carelessly tossed aside. It was a special tool machined with fangs and a pike extension at the top.

"Johnny's, no doubt," he said. Then the bronze man's ever-active golden eyes went to the wall of ice by the pick axe.

It was clear that the bony archaeologist had been attempting to excavate something from the ice. He had done a great deal of chipping in one spot, then in another section several feet away.

In the center, framed by these vertical excavations, something shadowy loomed within the deep greenish ice.

Doc Savage directed the beam of his flashlight toward this shadowy shape.

The others crowded around.

Renny boomed, "Looks like a man stuck in there."

"Jove!" added Ham. "He appears to have been entombed in ice."

Monk asked, "Did the old Mongols bury their dead this way?"

Doc Savage shook his head. "Not according to history."

Then the bronze man's golden eyes saw the script.

It was excusable that he did not notice this at first glance. The ice was wonderfully rippled, and cloudy within, having veins and occlusions. This was not pellucid ice, such as covers a frozen pond in winter.

The script writing on the wall stood high up, above the shadowy form entombed within.

In the eerie silence of the place, with their breaths showing cold, the sound of Doc Savage's trilling came as a sudden shock.

They were used to this, for Doc Savage had displayed this habit for as long as they had known him. Perhaps it was the dank atmosphere of the place. Possibly the flavor of the sound this time was different.

Whatever the truth, Doc Savage's trilling manifested as a low melody, which impinged upon their ears and carried throughout the ice cave, as it mounted the musical scale in its characteristically tuneless yet melodic fashion. Its ventriloquial quality was also very marked in the cave confines. It seemed to be coming from nowhere yet everywhere, saturating the cold confines of the cavern.

Often, Doc's trilling swelled from a subtle sound to a more awesome cadence. But in this instance, the sound climbed only so high and lingered at that pitch, wandering about like an insect lost in a barn.

It took a long time to trail off. This meant that Doc was so struck by what he saw that the bronze giant failed to notice that he was issuing the trilling. It was a habit he picked up in the Orient, and it always embarrassed him. So naturally, Doc stifled it whenever he realized he was emitting the strange susurration.

Ham demanded, "What is it, Doc?"

Doc Savage was slow in replying. "The writing is in the old Mongol script of long-ago," he said quietly.

"Is that so?" squeaked Monk. "What does it say?"

" 'If I still lived, mankind would tremble.' "

"Holy cow!" thumped Renny. "What's trapped in that ice? A blamed monster?"

"Yes," said Doc Savage steadily. "One of the worst monsters in recorded history."

Doc Savage's straightforward response stunned them for a moment. The bronze man was not given to exaggeration, or hyperbole. Nor did he joke about serious matters.

It was abundantly clear to all of them that Doc was very grave indeed.

Renny rumbled, "Well, let's hear it."

Doc Savage did not reply. He stepped close to the wall of ice, which had been wiped clean of all grime and dust.

The bronze giant's eerie flake-gold eyes were peering deep into the matrix of ice.

The figure there looked human enough, although very squat and broad of build. The skull of the thing seem larger than it should, and its outlines were grotesque and defied comprehension. It looked human, but in a general way. That is, it possessed the requisite limbs in their proper places and proportions.

The thing in the ice was possibly only a foot and a half deep into the block of frozen matter.

Doc's flashlight shifted its intense beam, attempting to illuminate it.

The others watched, crowding close. They were very curious.

The penetrating ray of Doc's flashlight found the eyes of the creature within. They were a pale yellow color—as yellow as a cur's eyes. But these were not canine orbs. They looked human.

These sulfurous orbs seem to be staring back, as if the thing within yet lived.

It was unnerving, and made some of them shiver in spite of themselves.

Monk spoke up. "Blazes! It's like he's lookin' right at us."

"Nonsense," snapped Ham. "Whoever or whatever that thing is, it has been dead for very long time."

Others looked to Doc Savage for confirmation of that bold assertion.

Doc Savage only said, "It appears as if Johnny was trying to remove the block of ice single-handed, but ceased or was interrupted."

"Why would he do that?" asked Ham. "Why not expose the body, if he was so interested in it?"

"To preserve it for posterity," replied Doc. "Or possibly it was because he was afraid to unearth the being entombed in the ice."

The gravity of Doc's words held them all in a momentary silence.

It was then that the earsplitting hooting of one of Doc Savage's supermachine pistols split the gathering night.

"That's Long Tom!" howled Monk. "He's in trouble!"

Chapter VII

THE DEVIL IS A DWARF

DOC SAVAGE AND his men made a concerted rush for the mouth of the uncanny ice cavern.

Plunging outside, they were met by a deepening dusk under a rising moon. For the afternoon had grown long during their exploration of the cavern.

The lunar orb happened to be full, climbing in a sky scoured clear of clouds. Sufficient illumination poured down from the open sky to show Long Tom Roberts perched on the folding steps of the big flying boat, firing his supermachine pistol at an oncoming horde.

"Bandits, blast them!" roared Monk.

Evidently, a knot of horsemen had come galloping down from the hills, alerted by the sight of Doc Savage's landing plane.

Now they were thundering toward the aircraft, their ponies picking up speed.

Pistols and rifles boomed and cannonaded. Tufts of grass and dirt clods kicked up under the plane's broad wings.

Long Tom was hosing the onrushing bandits with the supermachine pistol. He was doing a good job of knocking horseman off their steeds, but an unfortunate consequence of the efficiency of the rapid-firing pistols was that the ammunition drum tended to empty in an amazingly short amount of time, forcing Long Tom to have to change canisters in order to resume firing. In these intervals, he was exposed and vulnerable.

Seeing his predicament, Doc and his men charged for the plane.

They immediately attracted bullets.

A rifleman who was either an expert shot or plain lucky, selected the largest target, who was Renny Renwick. He fired once, and Renny was hurtled backward as if kicked by an invisible mule.

Ham halted, and knelt beside him, aristocratic features dark with concern.

"How badly are you hurt?" the dapper lawyer demanded anxiously.

"Not as badly as that bird when I get hold of his neck," rumbled Renny, climbing to his feet. He commenced coughing, but was otherwise unhurt. His bulletproof undervest had turned the slug.

They raced to catch up with the others.

By this time, Monk was sounding as if he were waging a one-man war against the bandits, who were now pulling their horses to a stop, dismounting with alacrity.

The bandits were well-drilled, for they did a remarkable thing. They pushed their horses into a prone position, and dug in behind them, using their steeds as living sandbags.

From these novel defensive positions, the raiders lay down and started firing over the sleek, sweat-lathered sides of their horses.

Apish Monk was methodically hosing these positions while emitting a bloodcurdling yell that would normally have struck fear into any ordinary foe. But the hairy chemist's war whoops seemed only to encourage the Mongols to return fire more rapidly.

The barrage of answering bullets was remarkable, considering that the weapons employed were not the most modern. A few even qualified as blunderbusses. Some were muzzleloaders. No doubt many of the whizzing slugs that sought human occupancy were hand-poured.

Doc Savage was the first to reach the aircraft, as Long Tom got his machine pistol back into operation. The puny electrical expert managed to put a few of his foes to sleep, but seemed to knock out more horses than men.

Doc urged Long Tom into the plane, whose sides were bulletproof. The bronze man pulled from his person several small items which he armed, then pitched them in the direction of their foes.

These devices ranged from smoke bombs to compact tear-gas generators. Doc hurled them overhand, and they begin detonating among the men behind the whinnying horses. The pyrotechnics seemed to have more effect on the horses than their riders, because the horses abruptly struggled to their feet, exhibiting signs of a growing panic. Prior to this they had been remarkably nerveless, which showed that they had been trained for this sort of raid.

Even through the growing smoke and the choking, swirling, moonlit gas, bullets continued to snap in the direction of Doc Savage and his men. But these were necessarily going wilder than before.

Monk, Ham and Renny reached the aircraft unscathed, and clambered aboard. The last to climb in was the big-fisted engineer, who slammed the cabin door shut. It drummed and vibrated in its frame as arriving bullets pounded it relentlessly.

Monk grinned broadly. "Made it! For a while there I wasn't so sure that we would."

It was then that an awful realization came to them.

Oddly, it was Long Tom Roberts who noticed it first.

"Where is that fool midget?" he barked.

They looked around wildly, then realized that Monzingo Baldwin had not followed them out of the ice cave.

"What do we do about this?" demanded Ham Brooks.

Doc Savage said, "He will have to wait. Too dangerous to fetch him now."

It was a strange sensation they felt at that moment. Through the long hours of the flight to Mongolia they had not become accustomed to the company of the little man who had been the cause of so much trouble in the past. Now that he was in imminent peril, some of them felt a little queasy about the matter.

Doc Savage moved briskly to the cockpit and reclaimed the control wheel. But he had no intention of taking off just yet. It was just that the cockpit afforded him the best view of the besieging band of bandits.

Sepia smoke mixed with whitish tear gas was swirling around the broad, moon-washed steppe. Horses, whinnying madly, were breaking in all directions. Well-armed bandits were rushing to recapture them. It was not exactly a rout, but it was a remarkable break from the former iron discipline of the Mongol attackers.

Doc Savage watched this panic for some time, counting the number of foes, tabulating their weapons and considering options.

A few Mongols lay scattered about like so many fur-trimmed rag dolls, attesting to Long Tom's marksmanship. He might have done better, except the sheer numbers of attackers had motivated him to unleash mercy bullets in great streams. Had he set the weapon to discharge single shots, conceivably the slender electrical genius might have actually downed more foes. But he was counting on the deafening bullfiddle roar of the tiny weapons to have a psychological impact upon the attackers.

Bustling up to the control cockpit, Monk Mayfair wanted to know, "They don't look like they scare easy."

"Mongols have a reputation for fierceness and courage," remarked Doc Savage.

"What say Renny and me slip out the trap-door hatch in back and try to pick them off from a good spot?"

Doc Savage shook his head slowly. "We will see what they do. It is possible they will retreat once they realize they cannot harm us."

Monk made a disappointed gorilla face. Invariably, he preferred to take direct action even if a problem showed signs of solving itself without force. Monk loved action. He thrived upon it.

Soon enough, night breezes tore the billowing clouds of smoke and tear gas into rags and dispersed them.

The Mongol bandit band struggled to reassemble themselves. They held council. The tallest among them, a man with a Russian fur cap and a costume that suggested a Mongolian Cossack, seem to be in charge. There was a great deal of arm waving and other excited gesticulations.

Horses were checked for signs of wounds and those that could not be awoken, because they had succumbed to Doc Savage's mercy bullets, were kicked savagely and then abandoned.

AFTER a time, the Mongols settled down and the tall leader led his men past the flying boat in the direction of the ice cave.

They seemed unafraid of an ambush. As they walked along in their felt boots trimmed in wolf fur, some of them kept a wary eye on the plane hatch, in case it should pop open and disgorge shooting foes.

These men disappeared into the cave, leaving two pickets behind to stand guard. They were in there quite a long time, inasmuch as they possessed no light by which to search.

When they emerged, the party dragged Monzingo Baldwin out rather roughly. The little man had been lifted up by one leg and carried like a chicken being taken to the tree stump where the farmer's axe stood waiting.

"They got him!" Renny boomed out.

"Probably gonna shoot him dead," said Monk, as if the prospect was not unappealing.

Sounding grave of voice, Doc Savage said, "We cannot let him be executed."

"Can't we?" rumbled Renny. "The little squirt tagged along without our permission. He may just have earned himself a bullet."

Doc Savage said nothing. He was not as hard-boiled as some of his men, who believed that mercy should be tempered by justice, and not the other way around.

Kicking and squawling, Monzingo Baldwin was dragged toward the flying boat, and made to kneel in the dirt. His face was twisted something awful. It looked as if tears were streaming down his small squeezing eyes.

The tall Mongol placed the muzzle of his rifle against the back of the midget's head, and looked up at the faces peering out at him from the cabin windows.

He called out in his own language.

"What's he saying?" asked Long Tom.

Doc translated, "The bandit chieftain is warning if we don't come out with our hands in the air, he will shoot Baldwin dead before our eyes."

Ham said, "We can't very well surrender to spare the life of that confounded scamp, can we?"

Doc Savage was silent. His golden eyes were molten.

"If we do not, they will slay him for a certainty," he said at last.

Renny rumbled, "What's to say if we do, they won't scrag us all anyway?"

That prospect, obviously, was what was making the bronze man hesitate.

Doc Savage is not a foolish individual. Although he valued life, he also understood calculated risk. To simply surrender, might or might not preserve Monzingo Baldwin's skin. It was impossible to tell. Probably it would not. But neither did Doc Savage want to be the cause of the little man's demise.

While the tall Mongol chieftain once more exhorted them to surrender, matters took a strange new direction.

Out of the East came reinforcements.

Another batch of Mongol riders were coming hard. Possibly, they had held back to see which way the warlike winds ended

up blowing, with the intention of stepping in, and turning the tide of combat if the battle went against their brethren.

Among the riders was an unusually tall and thin man with a shaggy mop of hair.

Doc Savage, possessing extraordinary visual acuity, was the first to recognize him.

"They are bringing Johnny along," Doc told his men.

Ham produced a pair of binoculars, and trained them on the oncoming riders.

"Johnny, all right. And he looks like he's been roughed up pretty bad."

"Wonder he wasn't killed," grunted Renny.

Ham studied the archeologist's bony frame. There was not much to Johnny but bones.

"He looks more brittle than usual," he commented.

The new arrivals piled up to the scene, brought their charging ponies to a dusty halt, then dismounted, fists bristling with firearms, ready for battle.

One strode up to the tall chieftain who was holding Monzingo Baldwin at his mercy. A vigorous conversation ensued.

Then the new arrival went back and hauled Johnny off his pony, parading him about for all to see.

The gangling archaeologist was made to kneel beside the blubbering midget.

A long-barreled pistol was placed against his temple, and all eyes went to the watchers at the plane windows.

"We're in for it now!" moaned Renny.

Doc Savage told them grimly, "Now, we have no choice but to surrender."

The bronze men's unequivocal pronouncement caused their tongues to freeze in their mouths. No one questioned their leader's order. If any of them had been in Johnny's position, the others would have risked anything and everything to ransom his life. They would perforce surrender, and take their chances, hoping to turn the situation back to their advantage.

Doc Savage went first, flinging open the door.

Stepping out, he began treating with the bandit chieftain in his own language.

The Mongol leader almost fainted from surprise. He did not expect a white man, even one as bronzed as Doc Savage was, to speak his native tongue as fluently as himself.

A short exchange ensued, after which Doc Savage came down the stairs with his hands held high.

The size of the bronze giant impressed the assembled Mongols most profoundly. They trained their weapons on him, and actually looked somewhat awestruck in their impassive way.

Monk and the others soon followed, their hands also held in the air.

They were roughly searched at gunpoint, and relieved of any small items on their possession. They had naturally left their supermachine pistols behind, locked in storage, not wanting them to immediately fall into the hands of their enemies.

The Mongols showed no signs of boarding the plane in order to loot it. At least, not just yet. They seemed more interested in knowing what the big bronze man's business was in Mongolia.

In their own language, Doc Savage told them. He spoke the truth. He repeated himself often, emphasizing certain points. He made it very clear that his only interest was in rescuing his colleague, Johnny Littlejohn, who was present.

"You are all now my prisoners," proclaimed the Mongol war chief, who gave his name as Chinua. It meant wolf. His mother had named him well. He had a wild, windy face.

Chinua laughed rather roughly when he said this. His sheepskin-clad men joined in.

While they were convulsing in their triumphant laughter, strong bronze hands whipped out like lightning, and seized Chinua's rifle from his fingers.

Swapping the weapon in his hands, Doc pointed the long muzzle directly at Chinua's chest. It was an unnerving move, and so uncharacteristic of Doc Savage that even his men were taken aback.

Every rifle muzzle swept in the bronze man's direction. Hammers were rocked back, pistols cocked.

"You should have held onto this," said Doc Savage plainly.

The Mongol, his mouth frozen in mid-laugh, looked a little sick. Then, as the reality of his predicament sank in, he resumed whooping, this time uproariously.

Doc Savage, uncharacteristically, joined in the laughter.

Soon, all the bandit clan were cracking up.

Monk joined in, and gave Ham a sharp elbow to prod him into doing the same thing. Long Tom and Renny added to the raucous merriment. Renny's booming guffaws caused several Mongols to examine the night sky for the lightning that was certain to follow this strange thunder. This hilarity went on for a few minutes, then naturally subsided.

When quiet returned, Doc Savage informed the Mongol chief that he had something of great value to offer.

"Offer?" returned Chinua.

"Consider it a ransom for our freedom," said Doc Savage.

Chinua liked the sound of that. Since Doc Savage was holding him at gunpoint, it suggested that he was being respected. And not a mere prisoner.

"What is this treasure you offer, foreign bronze devil?" demanded Chinua.

"Frozen in ice, in that cave yonder, we have discovered a great thing," intoned Doc.

"What is the name of this great thing?" wondered Chinua.

"The great thing," explained Doc Savage, "is named Timur."

Chinua looked blank. His flat face was like a brass gong that had been beaten flat and pitted by the harsh elements of the Gobi.

"Timur?"

"Emir Timur," stated Doc Savage.

Strange, wistful expressions crossed the faces of the Mongol bandits, as if a ghostly wind had swept by, touching their hardy souls.

They looked to one another in confusion, wonder, and uncertainty.

"He lies buried in Samarkand," insisted Chinua. "Every Mongol knows this."

Doc Savage shook his head somberly. "In that cave lies entombed in ice a man, and written on the face of the wall of protective ice are these words: 'If I still lived, mankind would tremble.'"

These words struck Chinua like a whiplash. His wind-weathered face quirked strangely, his brown eyes narrowing.

With the ripping volley of words, he sent his second-in-command to investigate.

This Mongol aide raced into the cave and was therein a very short period of time.

He stepped out, waving his arms over his head excitedly, shouting, crying, "The bronze devil speaks the truth. It is true. Timur lies within!"

A mighty shout erupted from the throats of the Mongol bandit horde. It seemed to shake the very stars.

Chapter VIII

"IF I STILL LIVED—"

STRANGE SOUNDS EMERGED from the pulsing throats of the Mongol bandits. Weird, excited cries. Ululations. They filled the bitterly cold night.

Chinua tore his gaze from his excited comrade and met the hypnotic flake-gold orbs of Doc Savage. "I must see this with my own eyes," he said, his voice thickened by hoarse emotion.

Doc nodded. He escorted the Mongol to the cave entrance at rifle point.

Chinua's troops were strangely passive. They appeared absorbed in their unreal surroundings.

Monzingo Baldwin and Johnny Littlejohn were permitted to stand up and accompany the group. Because the latter wore his hair in what was sometimes styled scholastic length, the rail-thin archeologist looked like a well-used mop draped in an ill-fitting suit of clothes. His normally narrow features were more hollow than usual.

Johnny undertoned to Doc, "I have been a prisoner since our last communication. They have been trying to force me to divulge my reasons for being here. I refused to tell them, because of what is in the cave."

Doc nodded, said nothing.

"What lies in the cave is too precious and too dangerous to fall into their hands," hissed Johnny urgently.

Doc said, "Your lives are also of value, and must be preserved at all costs."

Johnny said nothing. He appeared to be torn.

They slipped into the cave, and Doc's men produced flashlights. The Mongol who first entered the cave had a box of wooden matches, and this he had been using to illuminate the way. Now he threw his flaring match away as unnecessary. It sizzled when it struck the icy floor.

Chinua marched toward the wall of ice, with its dark, shadowy shape floating within. He studied it, wonder becoming a gleam in his brown, curious eyes.

Doc Savage directed his blazing flashlight beam at the Mongol script carved in the rime centuries ago. It seemed to shimmer, as if written in lightning.

No sooner did Chinua read this, than he sank to his knees as if prostrating himself before an idol he worshipped.

Finally, he found his feet, turned stiffly and faced the Man of Bronze.

"It is done. The deal has been struck. You are free to go your own way."

"Thank you," said Doc Savage.

Johnny objected, "Doc! This is one of the greatest discoveries of all time! We can't just turn it over to them."

"We have no choice in the matter," returned Doc Savage calmly. "This is their country, and their heritage. We have no legal right to a claim."

Chinua ignored this argument, which he could not understand since it was in English, and issued barking instructions, as if the white Americans were no longer present.

He picked up the discarded pick axe, while others drew daggers, knives and even short swords. They commenced hacking away at the fractured outlines that Johnny Littlejohn had begun several days before.

The long-worded archeologist became practically apoplectic. "Doc," he pleaded. "If they drag the ice out of the cave, it will begin melting."

Doc Savage said firmly, "There is no stopping what has begun. We will have to allow events to take their course."

But the stork-like geologist would have none of it. He attempted to interfere by stepping up to Chinua and seizing the swinging pick axe.

Snarling, the Mongol chieftain pushed him back and resumed his frantic work.

Doc pulled Johnny back, and they stood watching.

An hour of forceful toil produced a block of ice that could be removed. It was quite large, and very rough around the edges. Some of the Mongols carried short knives and curved swords. Several of these were severely bent or broken during the operation to pry loose the core of ice.

Once the chunk containing the body had fallen forward and was no longer part of the ice wall, Chinua gave rapid instructions to haul it out of the cave.

Ropes were brought and the ponies led up to the mouth of the cave. Strangely, the horses snorted and whinnied nervously, all but refusing to enter the cave itself.

By carefully chopping crude eyelets into the ice, they were able to loop rawhide ropes into the holes and tie them into knots. In this fashion, the Mongols were able to haul the big block of ice out into the open air.

Johnny Littlejohn watched this operation with haunted eyes, his fists skeletal knobs in which the knuckles were ivory chips.

"Supercalamitous," he said angrily.

Monk muttered, "I don't get this. What's so important about the dead guy in the ice?"

Johnny told him flatly, "That is no ordinary person in there. Unless I am gravely mistaken, the body entombed in that cave is no less than the terrible Asian warlord, Tamerlane."

"Tamerlane?" Ham protested. "He was one of the most feared conquerors to follow in the war boots of Genghis Khan."

"Are you sure it's him?" demanded Long Tom skeptically.

Doc Savage answered that. "The inscription on the ice, 'If I still lived, mankind would tremble,' is identical to the one inscribed upon the supposed tomb of Tamerlane."

"What do you mean, supposed?" grunted Renny.

Johnny vouchsafed that reply. "The tomb of Tamerlane exists in the city of Samarkand, with that very same inscription upon it."

"Then this is some other stiff, right?" Monk put in.

Johnny shook his shaggy head. "According to history, Tamerlane died during a long winter's march to conquer China. He is said to have been buried in Samarkand, but the evidence in this ice cave suggests that account was a hoax. Instead, he was entombed in ice far from his home city."

"Why would they do that?" wondered Ham. "Why would Mongols bury a great leader in ice?"

"Perhaps," suggested Johnny, "because he was not actually deceased when they entombed him."

Ham's aristocratic face worked in horror. "Do you mean to suggest that Tamerlane was deliberately fixed in ice before his death?"

"The correct term is vivisepulchure," returned Johnny. "And there are many possible theories for this situation. Perhaps Tamerlane himself ordered this, in the hope that the ice would preserve him long enough to fetch doctors from faraway Samarkand. Or perhaps his own warriors turned against him for some reason, and entombed him rather than put him to death, out of respect for his high station in life."

Monk muttered, "Either way you slice it, he's still dead, ain't he?"

Neither Doc Savage nor Johnny Littlejohn replied to that rather ominous question.

"Ain't he?" repeated Monk.

It was dapper Ham Brooks who offered an answer to that inquiry. "Perhaps we will all know once the ice completely melts."

DOC SAVAGE was very thoughtful as he watched the Mongol bandit band haul off the block of ice containing one of the world's most cruel former despots. Golden flakes continuously stirred in his eyes, although more briskly than normal. There was a strangeness in those eyes, as if for one of the few times in his life, the big bronze fellow was fixed by indecision.

Doc Savage caught up with Chinua, and addressed him in his own language.

"What are your plans for that body?"

Chinua paused, and regarded the bronze giant in a questioning manner.

"This is the body of the revered Emir Timur," he replied firmly. "We will take him back to camp, and a council will be held over the question."

Doc Savage told him, "It is not cold enough for that ice to remain frozen. What if it melts?"

The bandit Mongol seemed taken aback by the question. "If it melts, it is the will of the sky god, Tengri."

"Animals that have been frozen in ice," cautioned Doc, "have sometimes been revived. Are you prepared for that eventuality?"

The thought had apparently not occurred to the big Mongol. His flat brass face brightened instantly.

"It would," he said fervently, "be a glorious day should that occur."

"Or a terrible day," suggested Doc.

"Terrible?"

"Tamerlane was a cruel man, whose cavalry swept across Asia and the Middle East. He slew many innocent people, in addition to conquering formidable armies. What if he still lived? Would he not pick up where he left off?"

This notion seemed to stagger the Mongol.

"If that were the case," he said frankly, "I would be proud to follow such a warrior."

A flicker of disappointment crossed Doc Savage's impassive features. He had not expected this response.

Hovering nearby, Johnny Littlejohn had absorbed the tense exchange and understood it. In the Mongol language, he inserted a thought. "You are the chieftain of your band, correct?"

"I am the warlord of my band. I am Chinua," the Mongol said proudly.

"If Tamerlane lived, you would be reduced to a mere captain—provided he let you live."

The expression on the Mongol's wind-whipped face told clearly that this thought, too, had not crossed his mind.

At last, he intoned, "I would rather be a captain under Emir Timur than a general in Heaven."

Johnny's puckered face fell. He considered himself something of a psychologist, but he, too, had failed to undermine the Mongol's brutish intentions.

Chinua turned, and resumed the push to convey the icy chunk to the waiting ponies. There was some little difficulty in breaching the tumble of earth and stone that partially blocked the cave mouth. Rocks were flung aside and dirt smoothed by blades and tamped down by booted feet, until a rough ramp was formed.

The cube of ice began sliding downward, got away from the Mongols, who chased it with frantic cries. It cracked upon stopping, but did not shatter.

Wind-burned hands seized the rawhide ropes and the Mongols commenced hauling it along flat ground.

Finally, they reached the animals and the loose ends of the ropes were affixed to the saddles, which were colorful constructions of good wood, painted and decorated with silver. Then the ponies were urged on, dragging the ice block behind them.

In English, Johnny addressed Doc Savage and asked plaintively, "What do we do?"

Doc Savage said, "Let me try something else."

Catching up to the Mongol, Doc Savage said, "Many of your horses are asleep. I can rouse them."

Without turning, Chinua muttered, "That would be most welcome if you did."

With his men trailing behind him, and a quaking Monzingo Baldwin taking up the rear, Doc Savage followed the procession to the main body of horses, many of whom still slumbered.

From a vest of many pockets, the bronze man produced a hypodermic syringe and charged it with a stimulant. This was an antidote to the potent chemical solution with which his mercy bullets were filled.

Doc Savage went among the sleeping horses, administered this antidote. It was not long before the horses shook their heads, and with assistance, climbed unsteadily to their feet. Their liquid eyes were very strange, as if they had returned from another world.

Chinua grinned broadly and tossed the bronze man a curt salute of gratitude.

It was at this point the Doc Savage made a new suggestion.

"I am a doctor," he said. "If the man in the ice should emerge from his long slumber, he may need medical attention, if he is to survive."

Chinua said, "There are doctors among my men, as well. They know great medicine."

Doc nodded, thinking that the Mongol probably referred to the local shaman.

"As you can see, my medicine is very powerful," Doc pointed out, indicating the revived horses.

Chinua ignored the comment as he and his men conferred over how best to ferry the frozen block back to the Mongol camp.

Monk muttered, "Looks to me like that block is gettin' a little round around the edges. I think the friction of dragging it is causin' it to melt."

Johnny said urgently, "We must do something."

Doc Savage replied, "We *will* do something. We will depart at once."

Johnny's eyes flew wide. He looked as wobbly as a scarecrow in a stiff breeze.

"We are getting nowhere with these hillmen," Doc explained. "We will take off, and pretend to fly away."

A visible relief crossed Johnny's long, drawn face.

Saying rough farewells, they made their way back to the flying boat and climbed aboard.

The last to step inside was the little man they were calling Monzingo Baldwin.

When he stepped into the cabin, he made a peculiar remark.

"Did you see the muscles on that fellow?"

"Which fellow?" asked Monk.

"The one in the ice. He was the most incredible specimen of manhood I ever saw."

Everyone looked at Monzingo Baldwin in a strange way.

Finally, Renny rumbled, "You better sit down for the take-off. You're so small you might bounce around the cabin like a basketball. Wouldn't that be too durn bad?"

Chapter IX

BLACK-LIGHT BEACON

DOC SAVAGE THREW the big flying boat back into the air with a skill that took the breath away.

The air leviathan showed no signs of damage, despite the previous difficult landing. Landing-gear wheels cranked up into their wells without difficulty.

Doc Savage turned the plane north, and looked down over the moon-washed steppe. It was possible to discern the caravan of Mongols, riding their ponies back to camp. They had managed to tie the chunk of ice to the saddles of two sturdy ponies, who were pulling the block along, leaving behind a trail of moisture that the moonlight made into a shining snail track.

Doc Savage called back to Johnny, "Where is your special camp lantern?"

"The Mongols have it."

"At their camp?"

"Yes. And I know what your next question is. Yes, I left it on as a beacon."

Doc nodded, satisfied.

Long Tom turned to Johnny and asked, "Is that one of the camp lanterns that has an ultra-violet bulb?"

Johnny said, "Indubitably," a little of his professorial composure returning now that he was safely in the air.

Doc Savage said, "We will use that as our beacon to the Mongol camp."

Donning a pair of special goggles, which were mechanical in nature, the dark eyepieces being extraordinarily thick, the bronze man flipped the switch on the side which permitted him to see the terrain below through fluoroscopic apparatus.

Johnny cautioned, "I do not know where the lantern is. It might be inside a tent."

Monk was in the co-pilot seat as usual. He overheard all this and asked Doc Savage, "What's your plan, Doc?"

"We will find the camp by air, and land quietly."

"Gonna set up an ambush?"

Doc nodded. "Something like that." He did not elaborate. The bronze man never liked to reveal his plans before he was ready to execute them. Possibly, he was still formulating them.

As they volleyed through the night, Johnny Littlejohn talked. He was a man known for his elaborate sentences and jaw-breaking linkages of words. It was one of his trademarks, along with the monocle that he wore affixed to the lapel of his now-disheveled tweed coat. The latter was no longer necessary as an eyepiece, Doc Savage having years before operated on the geologist's bad eye, restoring it with his surgical wizardry.

The bony archeologist still carried the lens as a magnifying glass with which to study potsherds and other rare finds encountered in his field work. He fiddled with it as he fidgeted in his seat. Johnny seemed to have lost his appetite for long words.

"Tamerlane," he expounded, as if delivering a lecture, "was one of the last of the successful Mongol conquerors. He started life as little more than a bandit, growing up near the city of Samarkand. In later life, he claimed to be a descendant of the terrible Genghis Khan, but this was a fable he wrapped around himself in order to achieve legitimacy among the peoples over which he ruled."

Ham asked, "How far back does he go?"

"He is reliably reported to have died in the year 1404. He was then 76 years of age. The remarkable thing about Tamerlane is that he did not begin his campaign of conquest until the age of 40. In his time, he swept over Asia Minor, Afghanistan, invaded India, sacking Delhi, as well as other famous seats of antiquity."

Long Tom remarked sourly, "If he didn't descend from Genghis Khan, he sure learned plenty from him."

From the back, Monzingo Baldwin piped up, "He sounds like an ambitious fellow."

No response to that impertinent remark was offered.

Johnny continued, "Near the end of his life, Tamerlane captured Baghdad and Damascus, after which he set his sights on what he envisioned as his greatest campaign of all. For he wished to conquer all of China."

Renny rumbled, "But you say he didn't get far?"

Johnny shook his leonine head. "He died on the march, according to surviving records, having succumbed to a fever."

Ham Brooks regarded the shiny head of his cane and mused, "It is reasonable to assume that his warriors and generals, seeing him falling victim to a fever, might attempt to break the fever by bringing him into a cave of ice."

"A sound theory," admitted Johnny. "But that is only supposition. For it clearly did not work."

"What was that word you used back in the cave?" asked Monk.

"Vivisepulchure. It means to be entombed alive."

Monk grumbled, "You're thinkin' that his soldiers packed him in ice, hopin' it would save his hide?"

"It is a theory," Johnny said, brittle-voiced. "Nothing more."

"Then why didn't they come back for him?" wondered Long Tom.

"Perhaps they never intended to. Perhaps rather than let him perish, they consigned him to the ice in the hope that he would be preserved for future generations, who might devise a method to restore their emir to life."

Monk turned to Doc Savage. "What do you think?"

The bronze man replied, "The simple fact that they carved a warning to posterity on the face of the ice wall suggests that Tamerlane's followers anticipated a future resurrection of some sort."

Monk grunted, "How likely is that?"

"Unlikely, I'd say!" thumped Renny. "It's been more than five hundred years that he's been cooling in that icebox."

Ham shivered. "I get the chills just thinking about it."

They flew on in silence for a time, until Monk thought of a question.

"How brutal was he back in his day?"

Johnny hesitated to reply. Perhaps he was reflecting on the fact that he had, although inadvertently, been the mortal instrument by which the long-deceased Mongol conqueror might be restored to an earthly state.

"It was said," he said slowly, "that Tamerlane's soldiers would sack a city, then remove the heads of most of the inhabitants, stacking them in ghoulish pyramids. But that was not the worst of the atrocities."

"Yeah?" said Monk.

Johnny nodded somberly. "Tamerlane's armies often carried the men and women off into slavery, forcing them to abandon their babies and children to starve to death. Prisoners were sometimes flayed alive. And there was one infamous instance when the captives of one conquered city were flung into wet plaster, and raised into a human tower that rose and struggled helplessly until they finally expired."

A great silence greeted these gruesome descriptions.

Monk remarked, "Well, let's hope he's croaked for good—and stays that way."

Doc Savage did not contribute anything to this discourse, as he was giving his full attention to his flying and the speeding terrain below. His men realized the bronze giant had discovered something only when the plane banked sharply to port, and

Doc was looking out the side window. He was wearing his mechanical goggles.

"Find what you want?" murmured Monk.

Doc nodded. "Johnny's lantern. It is admitting an ultra-violet shine."

Johnny jumped into the cockpit and looked down, studying the moonlit terrain.

"I was a prisoner in sand hills just like these. I believe this is the locus of my incarceration."

Monk muttered, "No good place to land out here."

"Take the controls, Monk," Doc Savage directed. He left his seat.

GOING to the back of the plane, the bronze man donned a parachute rig, and gave every indication that he was going to exit the plane.

Seeing this, Renny rumbled, "Want some company?"

Doc Savage shook his head.

Johnny protested, "I insist upon accompanying you. After all, I initiated the events that brought about this calamity."

Long Tom barked, "Why do you call it that? It's not as if Tamerlane is going to sit up in his icy coffin and begin issuing orders to conquer the world."

"Do you know he will not?" snapped the bony archeologist.

The vehemence with which Johnny spat those words caused the ever-irritable Long Tom Roberts to bite his tongue.

Johnny continued his plea, imploring Doc, "I speak the Mongol language almost as well as you do. I know the camp. I can be of assistance."

Not helping matters any, Monzingo Baldwin popped up in his seat and said, "Take me along, too. I could be useful."

"We have no parachute that would fit you," Doc Savage told him.

Frowning, the little man smacked down in his seat, folding his babyish arms angrily. He looked like a spoiled brat.

Then Monk Mayfair made a fateful comment.

"There's a spare chute that we use for Habeas Corpus. It might fit the little runt."

"I resent being called a runt," fumed Baldwin. "But thanks for the tip."

"Too dangerous," said Doc Savage. To Johnny, he said, "You might be useful at that. If you are up to it after your ordeal."

"I have been through worse," said Johnny stiffly. He began wriggling a parachute pack onto his gangling frame. Even after he had tightly buckled every harness strap, it looked ill-fitting.

Monk Mayfair had the ultra-violet scanning goggles now and was using it to pinpoint the bandit camp as he swung the big plane around.

When he was approaching the spot, the homely chemist called back and warned, "This is it! Good luck!"

Doc Savage flung open the door and threw his great frame out into space. Johnny hesitated only momentarily to tuck his lapel monocle magnifying glass into the safety of a coat pocket, then he too launched himself out into the night, long hair flying.

Reaching out with his big fists, Renny pulled the door shut and said to no one in particular, "This has got to be one of the craziest durn undertakings we have ever been pulled into. Looking to rescue a five-hundred-year-old dead man."

"If he's really dead," remarked Ham Brooks without a trace of humor.

"Don't you start that kind of ghoul talk, too!" Long Tom complained.

"Johnny knows dead things the way I know torts and writs," mused Ham. "Mark my words. If he thinks that fellow in the ice might not be fully deceased, it is an opinion to take seriously."

Chapter X

RUSE

DOC SAVAGE LANDED first.

The bronze giant pulled his ripcord late in his plunge, choosing to do so to minimize any chance of a lone sentry spying his parachute bell floating down in the night sky.

Doc had selected a chute that was dark in color, rather than the regulation white, but with a full moon riding high in a cloudless sky, it made little difference.

Johnny followed suit, and the elongated archaeologist followed him down to earth.

Scrutinizing the terrain, the bronze man pulled on his shroud lines, steering himself to the top of a low hill. Johnny did likewise, but landed on an adjoining hill.

Once they got themselves organized, they gathered up their shrouds and the folds of the silken canopies, and set about to bury them. This was easily done, for the hills were very sandy.

The two hills were too far apart for comfortable voice communication, so Doc Savage produced one of his spring-generator flashlights and pointed the lens in the direction of Johnny's hill. Capping the glass with one hand to muffle its harsh glow, he flashed a simple message in Morse code.

O.-K.?

Y-e-s, Johnny signaled back.

They doused their lights, and settled down to watch for activity below.

The moon bathed a cluster of round felt tents, rather like small editions of circus big tops, about which no one appeared to stir. There were a few spare warhorses picketed in one spot, grazing on the tough grass left over from the summer.

The Mongol camp appeared to be unguarded, but Doc Savage knew that appearances could easily be deceiving. The big tents might well have been occupied by malingering Mongols, with rifles ready at hand.

From his equipment vest Doc Savage produced a slim black tube which was an optical instrument he had long carried. It was a remarkable device, for simply by changing the arrangement of tubes and lenses, it could be transformed from a telescope to periscope and even, in a pinch, a simple breathing tube.

Doc employed the gadget as a telescope, and used it to scan the horizon in the direction of the exposed ice cave many miles distant.

There was no sign of the approaching caravan, but he had not expected there to be. Pack horses are no match for a modern airplane tearing across open sky.

So Doc and Johnny waited as the evening hours stretched into the dead of night.

The surrounding steppe was remarkably barren of life. Few animals dwelled here, owing to the tough terrain, and birds were all but nonexistent.

It was a tribute to the nomadic Mongols that they could live off such arid, inhospitable grassland. But they have been doing it for centuries, and no doubt would continue so subsisting for centuries far into the future.

After an hour of waiting and watching, Doc Savage decided to investigate the camp. He signaled to Johnny on the adjoining hill, and the archeologist sent back a simple response.

B-e c-a-r-e-f-u-l.

Doc went down the back side of the hill, using great caution and seeming to melt into the shadows. Had there been any sentry posted, he might have spied the bronze man when he first detached himself from the top of the hill, but as the metallic giant progressed further, he became all but invisible.

MOONLIGHT picked him out approaching an outlying tent. Doc paused at the flap entrance, listening intently, and using his acutely sensitive sense of smell.

Detecting no occupants, he stepped within. When he emerged, not long after, the bronze man was attired in a Mongol costume that barely fit him, but helped disguise his true identity. Doc applied a combination of coppery make-up and dirt to his features, and did other things that gave his eyes an Oriental cast. His distinctive golden orbs were masked by glass shells the color of black smoke.

So attired, Doc moved from tent to tent, seeking anyone who might be left behind. It was a discouraging search, but at last he discovered a rather small individual sleeping on a *kang*—an ingenious kind of Mongol bed, which was a shelf constructed over a brick stove. This construct allowed the hardy Mongols to sleep comfortably even in the depths of winter.

Slipping up to the man, Doc Savage discovered a short sword—a curved Mongolian *kilij* sabre—and appropriated it, slipping it into the sash of his colorful costume.

Shaking the man awake, he hissed, "Awaken! I bring amazing tidings."

A round-faced Mongol snapped awake, one hand instinctively going for his sabre. He failed to find the familiar handle.

"Who are you?" he demanded of Doc.

"I am called Batu," Doc told him in fluent Mongol. "Chinua sent me ahead."

The man jumped out of bed, demanding, "I do not know you!"

"You will know me well enough in time. Chinua is marching back with the devil he is captured in ice."

"Devil?"

"A very terrible devil," Doc assured the man. "This devil has been encased in ice for over five hundred years. Chinua is trying to get him here before the ice melts, and unleashes his devil upon the world."

The Mongol's eyes grew as round as silver dollars. "Why is he bringing it here?"

"It is Chinua's intention to keep the demon trapped in the ice. He has sent me ahead to order all the fires put out, and all fire-making matter disposed of, or rendered useless."

"Everything?"

"Down to the last flint striker and wooden match," assured Doc Savage.

"I will see to it at once!" the other breathed. "If that is what Chinua commands."

"Chinua commands that this be done instantly," intoned Doc Savage. "If it is not done properly, swift punishment will follow."

The Mongol immediately went to a bucket of water, and flung it under his shelf bed where it doused the coal fire. A great quantity of gray-black smoke erupted upward and disappeared out a hole in the top of the felt tent, which was for ventilation purposes.

Rushing out of the yurt, the Mongol exclaimed, "Help me do this. Help me get this important task done."

Doc told him, "You douse the tent fires. Tell me where to find all the fire-making material."

The Mongol was only too happy to comply, so great was his fear of the devil encased in ice that was being towed back to the Mongol camp.

Between the two of them, Doc and the other managed to put out every fire, and destroy or bury every instrument for making fire or warmth the Mongol camp harbored.

When the deed was done, Doc Savage told the round-faced Mongol sentry, "I will now go to meet with Chinua and tell him it is safe to bring the frozen devil to the camp."

"Very good," said the other. "I will await you here."

Before the quaking man could return to his sleeping tent, Doc arrested him with a metallic hand. "Do not sleep. You will be needed. While you await Chinua's return, double-check every tent. Make sure there remains nothing that can produce fire."

The Mongol looked disappointed, for he had not slept very long before being aroused. But he did as the strange new Mongol bid him, for he believed it was the command of his chieftain.

That matter settled, Doc Savage walked off into the steppe, and was soon lost from sight. Satisfied that he was not being watched, the bronze giant doubled around and made his way back up to the top of the hill where he had earlier landed.

Doc waved to Johnny. Johnny waved back in recognition of his return.

Then they hunkered down to await the return of Chinua and his bandit band, and the terrible thing dragging behind his train.

Chapter XI

SOLEMN PROCESSION

CHINUA THE BANDIT chieftain was leading his men in song. It was an old Mongolian song about a young bowman in love with a beautiful maiden.

Every man knew this song, so when Chinua started to sing, his followers quickly joined in.

It was necessary to sing their way through the night, for the going was slow and arduous, with only two shaggy ponies pulling the cumbersome chunk of ice in which was imprisoned one of the greatest Mongol chieftains in recorded history.

The song helped them trudge along, lightening their load—even if it did not increase the pace of the horses, who could only go as fast as the slowest pack ponies.

From time to time, Chinua—that was the only name by which he was known, since Mongols did not give their children last names—wheeled his horse around to examine the cube of ice as it was being sledged across the dry steppe.

Despite the coolness of the night, friction was taking its toll on the underside of the frigid block. Pieces of chipped ice from the rough edges had been scraped off, further eroding the icy extrusion.

Chinua frowned. If this kept up, he knew, the translucent cube might break or be sundered by the monotonous punishment it was receiving. He did not wish for this to happen. Chinua wanted only to bring the great warlord Timur back to his camp, there to discuss the disposition of the find. It was possible that authorities in the capital of Ulan Bator would pay a handsome ransom for this find. Or perhaps the leaders in Samarkand would pay more. Chinua envisioned an important auction for this great prize.

He called a temporary halt to the caravan, and his men dismounted as they gathered around the great frosty block.

The figure deep within the rippled frozen matrix had remained intact. They examined him from all angles, attempting to see the entombed individual more clearly. This was impossible, due to the roughness of the ice. It obscured most details.

Yet, touched by moonlight, pale yellow eyes could be perceived. Chinua again looked into them, and felt the chill deep into the marrow of every bone in his sturdy skeleton.

These were the eyes of Tamerlane the Great. Chinua had no doubt of this. Although every Mongol knew Tamerlane was entombed under a slab of black jade in an impressive temple in faraway Samarkand, the warning inscribed upon the ice block told a different story.

IF I STILL LIVED, MANKIND WOULD TREMBLE

"Is it really him?" murmured one Mongol.

Chinua nodded firmly. "It is him. The Great Champion, the Iron of Samarkand. He was found in a spot not far from where Emir Timur is said to have perished on the march to China."

This was a lie, for they were many miles from that faraway spot west of Mongolia.

But Chinua's uneducated followers did not know this.

That simple logic was enough for the Mongol nomads. That this was a great Mongol conqueror, they had no doubt. It was an amazing, miraculous thing. And looking into the canine yellow eyes of the long-dead conqueror, they started to suspect that he was not so dead after all.

"Might he yet live?" asked another Mongol.

"Reindeer meat when it is frozen, tastes fresh after it is thawed," replied Chinua sagely. "It might be so with a man, if he did not completely die."

"If true, then it is a wondrous thing," breathed another bandit.

Chinua strode about the chunk of ice with his sharp *kilij* sabre, and used it to chip away at some of the roughest spots, smoothing them out. The others joined him in this work. Unhitching the ropes from the pack ponies, they turned the block over twice, smoothing out every rough spot with the edges of their keen blades.

When Chinua was satisfied, the ropes were reattached to the wooden saddles, and the caravan continued its solemn march.

This time, the chunk of ice scraped along more smoothly, and ceased to lose jutting shards of loose ice.

"We will reach camp by dawn," predicted Chinua.

"Dawn," mused one man. "Will not the rising sun cause this block of ice to melt?"

"If it does," replied Chinua calmly, "then it is meant to be."

"If it is meant to be, it is meant to be," intoned another Mongol fatalistically.

As they trudged along, swaying in their ornate wooden saddles, Chinua led them in song again.

"This song was old when Timur was a mere boy," stated a bandit. "I wonder if he should live again, will he join us in our singing?"

"Not join," corrected Chinua. "But lead. He will lead us in song. Song—and much, much more."

Chapter XII

THE BAIL OUT

DAWN WAS STILL more than an hour off when Monk Mayfair turned the big flying boat around, sending it in a sweeping circle to the south.

The apish chemist had found a spot that was sheltered by low mountains and set down there to conserve precious fuel while Doc Savage and Johnny performed their reconnoiter of the ground. Now he was back in the air.

Boredom having seized them once more, Monk and Ham had fallen into their perpetual "quarrel."

Monk was berating Ham for his choice of profession.

"You are the most shystery excuse for a lawyer ever to come out of Harvard. And, believe me, that's sayin' a lot."

"Do not disparage my alma mater," warned Ham, separating his cane into two sections, revealing the keen blade of Damascus steel.

"Or what?" growled Monk.

"Or I will trim every bit of rust from your hide to show the world what a hairless baboon you truly are."

"Try it and I'll wrap that blade around your throat so many times people will think you're wearing an old-fashioned starched collar."

Renny was in the control bucket next to Monk, and quickly grew tired of the overloud exchange.

"Knock it off, you two!" he thundered. "It's times like this when I wish you both had brought your durn pets, if only to keep you out of our hair."

"I did not think it wise to bring along my Chemistry," sniffed Ham.

Chemistry was a small ape the barrister had collected on an adventure long ago. Ham had adopted the unclassified creature due to its remarkable resemblance to Monk Mayfair, but in miniature. The ape was subject to becoming airsick, so Ham rarely included him on long trips.

"That reminds me," muttered Monk. "Habeas should be wakin' up by now."

"What!" howled Ham.

"Don't listen to him," Long Tom barked. "He's just trying to get Ham's goat. That pig is nowhere on this crate."

"Hey, Habeas!" called back Monk. "Are you awake yet?"

A snuffling grunt, very much muffled, could be heard from in back of the plane.

Long Tom plunged from his seat to investigate. He located the source of the sound. It was Monk's portable chemical laboratory. He undid the latches, flung up the lid.

Out bounded Habeas the pig, shaking his long-eared, narrow-snouted head. He rushed up to the aisle and joined Monk in the cockpit, where the shoat received a vigorous scratching.

"You smuggled him on board!" Renny exploded. "How'd you manage that?"

"Aw, I knew that he wouldn't stand the long flight none too well, so I fed him some food laced with a sleeping preparation. This way he'd be in a better humor when we got here. It was due to wear off about now."

Fuming in his seat, Ham Brooks looked like a man who had bet his farm on a nag who didn't place. He was without words.

Monk grinned. "I'm sure glad I brought Habeas along."

"So am I," said Ham waspishly.

They all looked at him with incredulous eyes.

"It will give me something to do, slicing that runty hog into thin strips of bacon," snapped the dapper lawyer, reassembling his dark cane.

That got Monk riled up again, and he launched into a continuous assault on Ham's character, or lack thereof.

In an effort to change the subject, Long Tom returned to his seat and favored Monzingo Baldwin with a pale, suspicious eye.

"I've been meaning to ask, but how is it that you got left behind in that cave that time?"

Monzingo Baldwin shrugged negligently. "I don't know," he said petulantly. "It just happened."

Renny put in, "I've been wondering about that myself."

"Yeah," said Long Tom. "Seems to me that you had something up your sleeve."

Monzingo Baldwin rolled up his sleeves to show that there was nothing in them other than his tiny well-formed arms.

"What does that prove?" demanded Long Tom peevishly.

Baldwin shrugged. "I don't know. But it was all I could think to do."

There was a brief silence as this comment was absorbed and digested.

Monzingo Baldwin filled the silence by saying, "I know you fellows didn't want me along, but I wish you would treat me better. I am just trying to be helpful."

No one said anything to that. Their memories of the midget's old life as Cadwiller Olden were too vivid. Too, while Doc Savage's men did not as a rule hold any personal grudge against any graduate from their criminal-curing College, Olden had not undergone the entire course of training, nor had his memory been expunged in the customary manner. He was not, therefore, cured of his evil. The possibility that the malevolent little man might recover his old personality haunted their thoughts.

"Sure wish I knew what you fellas had against me," Baldwin added.

No one commented on that either. The silence grew very uncomfortable in the plane cabin.

To cover for that, Monk said suddenly, "While it's still dark. I think I'll run the ship over the spot where we dropped Doc and Johnny. Maybe by now something is poppin'."

Monk sent the big plane barreling further south, while Renny drew on the special goggles that would reveal the eerie glow of Johnny's ultra-violet camp lantern.

BEFORE too long, they were flying high over the camp.

Everyone kept their eyes glued to a window and, while they were preoccupied, Monzingo Baldwin slipped to the rear of the aircraft cabin and rummaged around as quietly as he could. In a locker, he found a miniature parachute pack that had been constructed with Habeas the pig in mind.

Sending guilty glances forward at intervals, the minute man struggled to fit his small body into the harness. Since that contraption was designed for a pig, not a human being no matter how small, it was hardly a perfect fit.

So the midget removed his belt, and used it to help secure the complicated web harness in place.

When he was satisfied, Baldwin slipped cautiously ahead, until he located the cabin door.

Baldwin had to stand on tip toe in order to reach the latch, but when he did, he threw his entire weight of less than a hundred pounds against the door.

Came a windy rush of cold air. The cabin was suddenly alive with swirling paper and everyone all but jumped out of their seats.

"What just happened back there?" Monk called out.

Long Tom bolted out of his seat, yelling, "That infernal midget jumped!"

"Jumped!" yelled Ham Brooks. "He wasn't wearing a parachute!"

Struggling to get the door safely closed, Long Tom managed to latch it with a little help from Monk, who tilted the plane so that gravity exerted its proper pull on the door.

That threw everybody into confusion and about in their seats. But the hatch slammed shut.

Renny's bull-throated voice made the four engines sound like distant thunder in comparison. "Holy cow! Doc won't like it when he hears about this flub."

Bustling into the rear, Long Tom went for the parachute locker, a suspicious cast on his face. It wasn't long before he came back, face red with flushed fury.

"Monk, your pig's parachute is missing."

That made everybody rush to the nearest window.

Monk hauled the moaning plane into a careful circle to assist in their search.

A small white parachute popped into view off to starboard.

"That canopy," murmured Ham, "is undoubtedly his."

"What the heck does that tricky runt have in mind?" Monk complained.

"If I didn't know better," Long Tom said suspiciously, "I'd say his memory is coming back."

That thought made the chill in the cabin seem warm by comparison.

Chapter XIII
THE DEMON ARRIVES

CHINUA AND HIS bandit horde were still punishing the air with song when the Mongol chieftain spied the tiny white parachute floating down from the sky.

Chinua carried tied to his stout saddle a collapsible antique telescope, which he pulled open and employed to track the falling white bell. He could make out the parachute itself. What it was conveying to the ground was impossible to discern. Even by moonlight.

Barking out a sharp command, the bandit chief sent two riders to retrieve whatever hung off the shrouds of the parachute.

The riders' horses kicked up a great deal of dirt charging in the direction of the falling object. It was soon lost to sight behind a hill, which the racing horsemen rapidly rounded. They rode with great determination.

When they returned, one brigand carried an unusual individual in the crook of one arm.

Riding up to his chieftain, he presented his prize with both hands. "For you, sire."

Chinua took the limp figure. Holding the face up to the moonlight, he saw that it was the remarkably tiny midget who had been in the company of the foreigner with the bronze skin and golden eyes.

There was a lump on the little man's head, and his blunted nose was bloody.

Chinua snapped to his men, "I did not tell you to beat him, only to retrieve him."

"We discovered him in this condition," one Mongol protested vigorously.

Another Mongol added, "He landed hard, striking his head on stones. He was unconscious when we found him."

The Mongol pair assumed innocent expressions, for in truth they had discovered the tiny man running for his life and, for the cruel sport of it, they rode him down, knocking him about with the flat sides of their broad blades until he moved no more.

This false testimony seemed to mollify the Mongol chieftain. He and his clansmen had been searching the sky since the appearance of the parachute, but could see little. By this time, clouds had moved over the moon, plunging the steppe into unrelieved darkness.

They knew enough about modern flying to understand what a parachute was. They also were familiar with the types of sounds modern airplane motors make when passing overhead. So the absence of engine noises puzzled them greatly.

They did not understand, of course, that Doc Savage's flying boat was equipped with special silencers that reduced engine noise to a low hissing, which was virtually inaudible when the plane was cruising at higher altitudes.

Unable to satisfy their curiosity, the Mongol troop resumed their march, and their lusty singing once again lifted into the night.

Chinua rode with Monzingo Baldwin stretched out on his stomach on the front of his saddle. The midget was out cold, and showed no signs of reviving.

DAWN was breaking as they filtered between the outlying hills that ringed their sheltered cluster of round tents.

The clouds were still packed tight overhead, so the rising sun provided little warmth.

The round-faced Mongol who had been left in charge of the camp came running out to greet them, waving his arms excitedly.

"Mighty Chinua," he shouted. "I have done all that was asked of me. There is no shred of fire left in the camp."

Chinua heard the excited man, and it was as if a thundercloud crossed over his windy, weatherbeaten face.

"What is this you speak of?" he demanded harshly. "I gave no such orders."

The Mongol wrenched to a halt, and started protesting in an excited voice. "The new man brought your orders to me."

"What new man is this?" growled Chinua. "There is no new man."

Now the round-faced sentry was completely nonplussed. He suddenly shivered, for he knew that discipline in the bandit camp was as firm and ferocious as that of any Khanate army of ancient times.

"He said his name was Batu," protested the other. "He arrived in the middle of the night, proclaiming you had sent him on ahead."

"What else did he say?" asked Chinua, dismounting.

The nervous Mongol pointed toward the great frozen block taking up the rear of the caravan. "Batu said you had captured a demon in ice, and it was urgent that this demon remain in the ice."

"Go on," said Chinua, unsheathing his curved *kilij* sabre.

The Mongol swallowed hard. He seemed to be searching for the proper words to speak. His watery eyes kept glancing toward the blade.

"Batu said to destroy all fire, and all apparatus for producing flame, so that the camp would be cold enough to keep the demon fast and preserve him in ice until you decided what to do about him."

Chinua's bleak eyes narrowed, as he thought speedily.

"What did this Batu look like?" asked Chinua in a low, quavering voice.

Measuring an imaginary man with one upraised hand, the sentry said, "A giant, with dark, smoky eyes. He was the tallest Mongol I have ever beheld."

Chinua's eyes narrowed further. An awful expression plucked at his brassy features.

At length, he muttered, "That was no Mongol. That was a foreign devil masquerading as a Mongol. I sent you no such man, and those orders contradict my plans."

The plump little Mongol swallowed hard.

"Is that not a demon in ice?" he bleated.

"Why don't you see for yourself?" invited Chinua.

Thinking that he was absolved of all blame, the intrigued man floated up to the chuck of ice and begin scrutinizing the shadowy shape within from all angles. He came to the inscription carved into the uppermost surface, and his fattish jaw dropped, watery eyes all but popping out of his head like grapes being squeezed.

"This—this—"

He never got the word out. A bright blade flashed in the early dawn and severed his head from his rounded shoulders with a sound that was as swift as it was unforgettable.

The body collapsed instantly, the head landing in the crook of the man's elbow, as if he had contrived to capture it in death.

"That," said Chinua, turning to his men while shaking amazingly few crimson blood drops off his blade, "is how Timur the Terrible disposed of fools. Do not be a fool. I will suffer no fools under me."

Murmurs of ascent came from every Mongol mouth.

With a sweep of his blood-streaked blade, Chinua commanded the great block of ice be dragged into the camp, while the headless body was left as carrion for the wolves.

As they rode, Chinua said to one man, "Keep your eyes sharp. Watch for spies. The bronze devil has not departed."

The other nodded solemnly. "What does he want?"

Chinua gave a toss of his head to the rear and said, "He wants Timur. He will never have him. Mark my words. Over my dead body will the foreign devil take this illustrious ancestor from me."

The other grunted, "Over all our dead bodies. This is our history. No one else's."

They rode into camp as dawn broke, suspiciously scanning the colorful tents sides flapping in the soft cool breeze, with the warming light changing the shadows on the hilltops. Particularly did Chinua pay attention to the hilltops. He knew that, if there were any ambushers, it was where they would lurk.

Chapter XIV

THE DANGEROUS ONE

DOC SAVAGE WAS not unaware of what was transpiring among the Mongol horde of the bandit chief, Chinua.

The bronze man had seen the tiny parachute come down, although the darkness had prevented him from making out what hung at the end of the parachute shrouds. He recognized that the parachute was one specially designed for Habeas Corpus, the pig. It was too small to support a full-grown man. That suggested only one conclusion, either his aides were dropping a package of some sort, or Monzingo Baldwin had for some reason evacuated the plane.

All things being equal, Doc could conceive of no reason his men would drop a package unannounced, and even if they had, to leave his hilltop perch to retrieve it would have exposed him to the Mongols on their approach march.

Employing his tiny telescope, Doc observed the byplay that took place when Chinua marched into the wind-blown encampment.

The Mongol sentry whom Doc Savage had tricked into snuffing out all fires had naturally gone to greet his master. Doc observed the decapitation of this bearer of bad news, and a flicker of distaste crossed his normally impassive bronze features.

Doc had not expected that result. But it had transpired, and there was nothing to be done about it now.

The bronze man had not seen the riders retrieve the figure who descended by parachute, nor Chinua take possession of the midget.

So as the bandit band drew closer, Doc at first did not perceive Monzingo Baldwin draped across Chinua's saddle. The horse's head and tossing mane blocked that small figure from view.

Only after Chinua and his warriors dismounted and hobbled their horses, did the truth became apparent.

Chinua lifted Baldwin off the saddle and flung him over to a lieutenant as if the insensate midget were a sack of booty.

Doc Savage could not tell if the little man was still alive or not.

It was now light enough that Doc and Johnny could see one another clearly. Using their flashlights as heliographs would no longer be effective. So the bronze man caught Johnny's attention and began forming finger signs that were of a type similar to those used by the deaf-and-dumb.

"C-h-i-n-u-a h-a-s B-a-l-d-w-i-n," Doc signaled.

"U-n-f-o-r-t-u-n-a-t-e," returned Johnny. "W-h-a-t d-o w-e d-o a-b-o-u-t i-t?"

"W-a-i-t."

Below, Chinua's men got busy going from tent to tent, seeking signs of spies or lurkers. They came out with soggy bushels of ashes, testifying that every fire in the camp had been extinguished in such a way that none could be relit.

Mongol profanity rolled up and around the hills. There was a lot of it. Chinua's band had ridden all night, and they were cold, chilled to the bone. A warm fire and hot food was their deepest desire at this point. Neither was possible, thanks to Doc Savage.

Having no recourse for comfort, Chinua ordered his men to move the crude cube of ice into an upright position in the center of the camp.

This was done very easily, for virtually every man wanted the privilege of standing the great Mongol warrior and general, Tamerlane, on his feet once again.

In the sharp-elbowed bustle for the privilege, a few fights broke out. Fists and knives came into play. Blood was spilt.

Had this been America, no doubt a bloody brawl would resulted, and the police called to quell the riot. But among these lawless Mongols, breaking another man's nose or inflicting a non-fatal stab wound was considered a kind of roughhouse sport.

Chinua allowed this high-spirited horseplay to run its course, and soon enough the frosty lump of ice stood upright, and the yellow eyes of the long-deceased Tamerlane gazed down upon them through icy striations.

They stood about in a circle, marveling at the semi-shapeless form in the ice. A reverential silence attended this solemn ceremony. No one spoke.

Doc Savage saw that the block had been shaved and shaped during its arduous transportation. Although fractured, it was largely intact, and the figure within well encapsulated.

In the cloudy dawn, the icy bier showed no signs of melting. This was a relief, but of course it was only temporary. Doc's subterfuge had simply forestalled what was probably inevitable.

Johnny caught Doc's eye, and began signing.

W-h-a-t i-f i-t b-e-g-i-n-s t-o m-e-l-t?

Doc Savage hesitated long enough for Johnny to realize that the bronze man had not yet formulated an overall plan to deal with the situation. He had bought them time in the best way he knew how, but that was all that the bronze giant had accomplished.

Finally, Doc signed back: I-f t-h-e i-c-e s-t-a-r-t-s t-o m-e-l-t, w-e w-i-l-l h-a-v-e t-o t-a-k-e a h-a-n-d.

O-u-t-n-u-m-b-e-r-e-d, Johnny pointed out.

Doc did not reply to that. The prospect of taking on the Mongol clan was not an inviting one.

So they waited. Behind the clouds, the sun rose, and there was the faintest warmth suffusing the chilly morning air. How much warmer the day was going to get would be up to the cloud cover. Winter was not many weeks off.

Doc cast his eerie golden gaze in all directions. The Mongolian sky was normally a brilliant blue during the day. The country was famous for its open skies. Rank after rank of clouds marched along, thus spoiling that pleasurable vista. But here and there, Doc perceived breaks in these clouds.

Knowing that time was not on his side, Doc signaled to Johnny: A-m g-o-i-n-g t-o t-r-y s-o-m-e-t-h-i-n-g.

W-h-a-t-?

D-a-n-g-e-r-o-u-s, signaled Doc.

That was all the bony archaeologist could get out of him. Moving low, Doc started down the hill, slipping around to the side opposite of the encampment. Johnny tracked him with eager eyes, but the bronze giant was soon lost from sight. It was a remarkable thing, for Johnny had been with the bronze man for many years now, and even in broad daylight his stealthy ways still managed to fool the eye. Even the prepared eye.

Moving cautiously, Doc Savage found the base of the hill, and commenced making a circuit of the sheltering hills. Plainly, he was looking for something. But what it was could not be guessed by any observer, had there been any such.

DURING his careful observation, Doc Savage had seen one of Chinua's men carry Monzingo Baldwin into the Mongol warlord's personal tent. It was obviously the bandit chieftain's tent because it was the largest and most sumptuous of all. Also, Doc had been inside it and seen by its lavishness that it clearly belonged to the leader of the Mongols.

Doc's firm intention was to reclaim the little man while Baldwin was still unconscious, or if dead, to ascertain that fact.

Doc slipped along, moving from tent to tent, being careful to pause behind shelter every so often, so that his movements did not attract the attention of the sharp-eyed Mongols.

Reaching the yurt, Doc produced a clasp knife from his gadget vest, opened it, and used it to slice a long vertical slit in the rear of the thing. Once this gap was made, it was possible to slip within the tent, unseen by the Mongol warriors gathered outside of its entrance.

Giving his golden eyes a moment to adjust to the dim light, Doc soon found Monzingo Baldwin splayed on a heap of sheepskins like a discarded doll.

At first, it appeared as if the midget were deceased. Doc moved to his side and laid a metallic hand upon his incredibly small chest. The slow rhythm of respiration, combined with the warmth of breath emerging from the tiny man's mouth and nostrils, told Doc that Monzingo Baldwin still lived. It was a strange species of relief. The bronze man might have been equally relieved to discover his old Nemesis to be dead.

Making a careful check for injuries, Doc found the tiny man's limbs to be intact and unbroken, but there was a significant lump on the miniature forehead, which told Doc that Baldwin had either been blackjacked and tossed out the plane, or had struck his head upon landing.

Doc could not envision his men, even at their most disagreeable, doing the former. So he concluded it was the latter eventuality that had produced unconsciousness in the midget. He was nearly correct.

Reaching into his vest, Doc took out a hypodermic syringe, and charged it with a stimulant. On second thought, Doc reconsidered the needle, having decided that the stimulant might be too potent for this little man. Restoring it to his vest, he brought out an ampule containing a chemical restorative of his own devising, similar to but more powerful than the common smelling salts.

Clamping one hand over the midget's minuscule mouth to stifle any sudden outburst, Doc broke the ampule with the other, and waved the potent stuff under Baldwin's nose.

Fractions of a second later, tiny eyes snapped open, grew round, and focused on the bronze man in horror.

His voice muted, Doc related, "You are a prisoner of the Mongols. You must be quiet so I can get you out of here safely."

Doc gave the little man time to absorb these words. "Do you understand?" he pressed.

Cadwiller Olden shook his head in the affirmative very vigorously.

Satisfied, Doc removed the hand that had been keeping the midget's mouth shut. As soon as he had done so, Olden opened his mouth to its widest, and shrieked out in a girlish voice.

"He's in here! Doc Savage is here!"

Doc's trilling was yanked out of him in spite of himself. It was rare that he forgot himself so, but this was one such time.

Wrapping up the midget, Doc plunged for the escape slit.

Olden attempted to scream his lungs out. Most of it was inarticulate. Some of it was understandable words.

"Save me! Save me!"

Doc Savage got out through the slit just fine, his head whipping in all directions, seeking the best route of escape.

Behind him, he could hear Mongols charging into the tent. There was a moment of confused yelling and searching. Then they spotted the slit, and rushed for it, assorted weapons brandished high.

Bullets started slamming through the felt fabric of the tent. Mongols were firing blind, and lead snapped through the air all around the bronze man.

Dropping suddenly, Doc Savage flattened himself atop the midget, silencing his outcries. Reaching into his vest, he brought out several metallic cartridges, primed them, and threw the devices here and there.

Black smoke was the first to erupt, but mixed with that was teargas and other noxious gases. The fumes might not help, given the tightness of his situation.

The bronze man had already drawn a simple gas mask over his own head, to protect him from his own fumes. It consisted of a cellophane-like transparent hood, to which was affixed a cartridge which chemically purified the air.

There were a few times in his life where Doc Savage regretted not carrying a supermachine pistol; this was one of them.

Bullets were snarling overhead with alarming regularity. It was impossible to stand up, without risking death.

Then it became a moot point.

THE entire camp was aroused. Hollering Mongols came streaming from all directions. When their bullets started cutting down their own fellows, Chinua's voice ripped out, ordering them to employ blades alone.

That gave Doc Savage confidence that he could stand up. He did so, but his situation was not greatly improved. The bronze giant could not see in the sepia pall, but knew that he was under attack by the close-by swishing of Mongol blades probing for his vitals.

Doc Savage's senses were probably the most remarkable of any human who had ever lived. He could not see in the weird murk, however—although his training was such that he could operate amid utter blackness where another man would be paralyzed by sightlessness.

The point of a blade struck him in the back.

Doc pivoted, measuring the probable place in which the head of the man wielding the blade must stand, and metallic knuckles collided with the side of the other's face, knocking the swordsman out of his boots.

Edge of another blade slashed down and the angry swish of it before it cut into his shoulder made Doc think for a moment that he had lost an ear. The edge dug into the chain mesh undergarment he wore. Like the sword tip that had done no great harm, it failed to penetrate flesh.

Doc threw himself backward, and landed on that swordsman, his over two hundred pounds of muscle, bone and sinew causing the air to rush out from the grunting Mongol's stunned lungs.

Springing to his feet once more, Doc crouched low and reached out for moving legs. As swords clashed and collided over his ducking head, terrible bronze fingers dug into the flesh of thighs and shins. Doc yanked, upsetting more Mongols.

In the swirling blackness, it appeared that he was doing more than holding his own, when the flat of a blade came out of nowhere, colliding with his left temple.

Doc was briefly staggered, but spared mortal injury due to the fact that he wore over his natural hair a sheet-steel skullcap, to the outer surface of which was affixed a realistic semblance of his own close-cropped bronze hair.

Doc swung more wildly than he intended, and so failed to connect with anything.

Another blade drove in for his back; still another sought his vitals.

The powerful voice of Chinua, the bandit chieftain, was bellowing out harsh orders.

"Take the foreign devil alive!" he roared.

That was all well and good, but his minions had been getting the worst of it, and now their anger was impelling their actions.

"He fights like a demon!" one Mongol barked.

"We need him alive!" Chinua insisted.

This made no sense, of course, but orders were orders and the Mongols did their level best.

There was hardly any wind, only a little breeze between the hills. So the rolling dragon of black smoke simply spread outward and did not thin appreciably. Fighting in this disagreeable murk became next to impossible.

True, there was a lot of hacking, slashing and kicking—not to mention other strenuous activity—but Doc Savage was like a formidable phantom in the midst of it.

Weaving this way and that, ducking frequently, he managed to avoid any decisive blow.

His frustrated foes, redoubling their efforts, chopped off pieces of their fellows, unwittingly. This only added to the general chaos in the ferocity of the fight.

Mongols howled as they lost fingers, pieces of scalp. In one case an unfortunate man's sword hand, still clutching its weapon, dropped lifelessly to the dirt.

ABOVE the fray, Johnny Littlejohn watched as Doc Savage was swallowed by the oily smoke and fierce Mongols. He could not see what was happening. For all he knew, Doc Savage was being chopped to pieces.

Face twisting with fury, Johnny rose up to his full scarecrow height, and sprayed the sepia stuff with his supermachine pistol. Its bullfiddle moan swelled and reverberated, as the tiny weapon spat out innumerable mercy capsules, while ejecting streams of brass empties from the receiver. In operation, the intricate weapon seemed to be trying to shake itself apart.

Having nothing to guide him but rank guesswork, the bony archaeologist sprayed mercy slugs into the coiling dragon of impenetrability.

Doc Savage was well armored against the tiny slugs, which were after all only hollow capsules filled with a potent potion. But Johnny full well understood that Doc was exposed to their fury, at least so far as his face and hands were concerned.

There was nothing that could be done for it. If the skeletal archeologist happened to bring down the bronze man, so long as he quelled Doc's murderous foes at the same time, it was worth the risk.

So Johnny Littlejohn pulled back on the firing lever, emptied his drum, reloading as rapidly as possible in an effort to probe the swirling dark mass.

When he was entirely out of bullets, the human beanpole stood erect and tried to peer down into the spreading pall.

So intent was he upon discerning the fate of Doc Savage that Johnny failed to see Chinua rush out of his colorful tent with a traditional Mongol composite bow and quiver of arrows hanging off one hard shoulder.

Withdrawing one shaft, he nocked it, aimed at the bony archaeologist, then let fly.

The iron tip of the shaft struck Johnny in the left shoulder, and would have inflicted a severe wound, possibly leading to the inevitable amputation of that shoulder, except that Johnny also wore his armored union-suit underwear.

As it was, he was knocked backward, separated from his now-empty weapon, and generally stunned. He went rolling down the sandy hill, stopping only when he encountered a stony obstruction.

Johnny lost consciousness shortly after that.

Chapter XV

JOHNNY'S CALAMITY

WHEN JOHNNY LITTLEJOHN awoke, he felt cold in a very strange way.

Blinking baffled eyes, he rotated his shaggy head, and attempted to ascertain his situation.

Flat blank brassy faces regarded him without warmth or friendliness.

Johnny attempted to move, and saw that he was pinioned by coils of heavy rope. He appeared to be on his back, but atop something very high off the ground, because even though he was lying prone, he hung above eye level of the surrounding Mongols.

The bony archaeologist gave out a groan of miserable defeat. Shaking his elongated body, he attempted to test his bonds, and in doing so discovered that Doc Savage was tied at his back, also a prisoner.

Unlike Johnny, Doc was in chains. Evidently, the frame of the mighty bronze man had caused the Mongols to take that extra precaution.

To all appearances, the bronze man was unconscious. Glancing over his titanic form, Johnny saw no signs of significant blood, but the back of one hand was red and swollen, and Johnny recognized at once that several mercy bullets had struck Doc Savage there.

These wounds were not deep, nor had they bled very much. The design of the small capsules was engineered so that they broke on impact with the outer skin, introducing the powerful anesthetic into surface blood vessels. Doc Savage no doubt had succumbed immediately. The stuff was amazingly fast acting.

Again, Johnny gave out an awful groan that made his lathy ribs ache.

But there was worse yet to come.

"What are you going to do with us?" he demanded of Chinua in the latter's own language.

The bandit chieftain grumbled, "We have found a use for you."

"Use?"

"We have no fire, no matches—no method of making heat."

Talk of heat caused Johnny's eyes to gaze skyward, and he saw that the sun was approaching the noon hour, and while there were stratocumulus clouds in the sky, they were also breaking up.

The solar rays are beaming down upon them. This caused Johnny to remember the sturdy block of ice in which the Mongol conqueror known to the west as Tamerlane stood imprisoned.

Frantically, Johnny glanced about, looking for that icy extrusion. He could not locate it, which puzzled him. It had been very near this spot only recently.

Then the skeletal geologist remembered how cold his back felt. A fresh chill overtook him. This impelled him to wrench himself around in his thick, ropy web and look downward.

Only then did Johnny discover the missing chunk of ice. It was not missing. He and Doc Savage were tied to the top of it!

A LOOK of utter horror washed over Johnny's long, drawn features. This brought hearty laughter from the throat of Chinua the Mongol. His bandit tribe joined in the full-bodied hilarity.

Johnny blinked furiously as the awfulness of his position dawned on him.

"The heat of your circulating blood will be the stove that frees the Terrible One," confirmed Chinua.

"Doc! Doc!" yelled Johnny excitedly. "Wake up! Please, wake up!"

But the mighty bronze man appeared dead to the world.

To add insult to injury, Monzingo Baldwin then bustled up, and caught Johnny's gaze. The look in the midget's eyes was very wise.

"What are you doing here?" Johnny demanded hotly.

"Wouldn't you like to know?" the midget snarled.

The sneering vehemence of the small man's words took Johnny entirely aback.

"What has come over to you, Baldwin?" he demanded.

"Don't call me that." He drew himself up to his full, if rather ridiculous, height. "My name is Cadwiller Olden."

This was the final blow. Johnny lay back, shut his hollow eyes, and seemed at a loss for words—or even the strength to respond.

"My memory came back," Olden said unnecessarily. "I got suspicious back at that hospital when I overheard that damned Doc Savage talking about my case. He wanted to do a brain operation on me. I thought he was my friend. But now I know he's my enemy. Now that I remember who I am, thanks to these bandits banging me up after I landed, I know for sure he's my enemy. I remember everything. Everything. Get me?"

None of this exchange appeared decipherable by the Mongol tribe, since none of them appeared to speak English. But they seemed to tolerate the presence of the angry little man. Johnny decided to do something about that.

Turning his head to address Chinua, he began speaking the man's own lingo.

"This truncated man is an awful criminal. He has done great evil. It is dangerous to have him around."

Chinua looked interested. "You say he is a bad man?"

"The very worst," assured Johnny.

"Good!" exploded the Mongol leader. "I need such men in my band."

The other Mongols broke into raucous laughter. Cadwiller Olden joined in, although the conversation thus far was lost on him.

Johnny was at a loss for words. He said nothing. He tried to shake himself free of his ropes. What the gangling archaeologist expected to do if he succeeded, surrounded as he was by well-armed Mongol warriors, was impossible to say.

But Johnny gave it his all. He used his teeth, tried to chew on the heavy rope over his left shoulder. He managed to chip a front tooth in his ferocity.

This evoked more ribald laughter from the circle of Mongols surrounding the block of ice that contained one of the most terrible human beings ever to have lived.

It was as the uncouth hilarity was dying down that Doc Savage roused back to consciousness.

Chapter XVI

BATTLE OF THE BLOCK

OWING TO HIS tremendous constitution, Doc Savage was normally quick to emerge from any period of unconsciousness or stupor.

But the concoction with which he filled his mercy bullets was an extremely powerful formula, calculated to drop a man as soon as possible by entering his bloodstream and keeping him down for a period of hours.

Doc's golden eyes were strangely dull as he looked about him, and came to rest on Johnny Littlejohn.

The look on Johnny's face told a lot. Doc rotated his head, took in the Mongols, realized that he was in chains, and seemed, if not exactly bewildered, slow to process this situation.

The bronze giant said something that might have sounded foolish under any other circumstance. "Prisoners?"

"Worse," Johnny told him.

Doc Savage must have felt the coldness of the ice through his alloy metal undergarment, because suddenly he was thrashing about, attempting to ascertain the nature of the frigid seat on which he was lying. The golden flakes in his uncanny eyes resumed their illusion of active animation.

That seemed to complete his return to consciousness. The bronze man saw fractured ice, and his melodious trilling came into being, tentative at first, hesitating over its tuneless melody, until it suffused the air with its unusual ventriloquist quality.

This unexpected sound caused the Mongols to stare into the sky. Some produced antique revolvers with which to bring down the rare bird they thought was flying overhead.

But no bird appeared, so they looked to one another, shrugged, visibly suspecting one or the other of authoring the eerie cadence.

Eventually, Doc got control of his senses, and the trilling trailed off into a vague nothingness.

Johnny told him urgently, "They are using the warmth of our bodies to melt the ice."

Doc nodded. "That should take considerable time," he stated matter-of-factly.

This casual comment produced a short laugh of surprise from the bony geologist. He had, in his time, seen the bronze man face everything from a small army to a charging Tyrannosaurus rex, without a change of expression. But this was something new.

"We might," said Doc without emotion, "hasten the process."

"Hasten? I'll be superamalgamated!"

Johnny had no idea what the bronze man meant until Doc abruptly flexed his mighty musculature, grasping the imprisoning chains with metallic fingers where he could. By this leverage, he began rocking the cake of ice beneath them.

SEEING this, Johnny understood the bronze man's intentions. He commenced rocking, too. He timed his rocking to the bronze man's muscular rhythms.

The boxy ice slab was quite substantial, but Doc Savage was powerfully muscled. Visible tendons sprang out like the metallic cables of some mighty machine. It had already commenced a slow process of melting in the sun, so the icy foot now stood in a modest puddle of melted water.

Impelled by the bronze man's exertions, the block started horsing around in place.

Chinua immediately became agitated. He barked out gruff orders.

"Stop him! Stop him from tipping the ice tomb over!"

For that was the bronze man's clear intentions—to tip over the great chunk of ice, and shatter it.

Mongol minions rushed in, took hold of the chipped edges, attempted to stabilize the shifting hunk of frozen matter.

Although chained, Doc Savage had some freedom of movement. A hard elbow smashed into one stupefied face, while questing bronze digits sought the throat of another.

Punishing fingers made that Mongol squawk, and he pulled himself away, stumbling off, hacking and choking and trying to get his windpipe clear.

Johnny lashed out with a foot, which impacted someone's ribs with enough force to send that person stumbling off, clutching his sides.

Other Mongols charged up, but Doc Savage focused on his strenuous exertions.

The ice block lurched, teetering. It doubtless helped that the ground was uneven, although not considerably so.

What truly aided Doc's plan was that he had been chained in such a way that the upper and lower portions of his body spilled over the edges of the top of the ice cake. This gave him considerable leverage.

Too, the heavy links holding him were insufficient for the job, since they appeared to have been welded for some lesser person than confining a modern Samson such as Doc Savage.

Taking a set of links in one hand, Doc exerted pressure. The linkage creaked, began to part. Narrowed Mongolian eyes grew comically round. Some began chewing their lips uneasily.

Normally, the bronze man, when working to free himself from similar chains, employed more science, selecting a weak link and applying slow, steady pressure.

But the dire situation afforded him no such luxury. So Doc simply grasped and exerted sudden yanking force. Possibly the urgency of the situation imparted to the mighty bronze man more muscular power than usual.

Whatever the case, the groaning chain snapped, one end swung free, and Doc used it to lay about any approaching Mongols.

He was not gentle about it. Blunt steel collided with equally blunt skulls, creating havoc and sending bodies and weapons flying.

One attacker drew a blade, and Doc lashed out, snapping the loose chain around the man's wrist.

Screaming, the Mongol dropped his blade, seized his own wrist, and tried to free himself from the snapping python of steel.

This only added to the leverage Doc needed. He exerted a powerful tug.

Suddenly, the great ice block toppled, Doc Savage and Johnny Littlejohn coming down with it.

The noise it made was a little like the sharp sounds small icebergs emit when seasonal changes cause them to fracture. Arctic trees, bursting from the intense cold, also produce a similar report.

In any event, the ice cracked in several places. And when it fell, the frozen extrusion landed in three large chunks.

"Kill them!" roared Chinua, enraged such as he had never been in his entire lawless life.

Chapter XVII

ALIVE, ALIVE, OH

CADWILLER OLDEN HAD been an eyewitness to all of this, of course.

The minute man watched the torment of Johnny Littlejohn and Doc Savage with approval written all over his diminutive features.

But when Doc Savage commenced his Herculean exertions, that expression changed demonstrably.

Seeing the great ice block start cracking, Cadwiller Olden rushed forward, this time screaming, "Stop! Hold on! Stop!"

Chinua and his Mongols had no ear for this. They were intent on punishing the foreign bronze devil and his skeletal assistant for the desecration they had wrought upon their revered ancestor.

With the flat of his blade, Chinua swept backward, and slammed the midget away as if he were nothing more significant than a camp dog.

Stamping around to where Doc Savage struggled free of his chains, Chinua brandished his curved Mongol *kilij* sabre, and was looking for an opening through which to remove the bronze man's head.

Kneeling, Chinua grasped Doc's bronze hair, in an effort to yank his head back and expose the vulnerable throat. To his everlasting astonishment, the entire scalp came free, and then a bronze fist snapped out, rocking his head backward.

Chinua stumbled back, seeing stars.

Other Mongols stepped in, but by this time Doc Savage was climbing to his feet. The chains, which had been driven into the ice with spikes, were no longer holding him to that now-shattered block.

Swinging a length of chain over his head, Doc Savage produced a sound similar to a bull-roarer, and the eerie noise, as well as a threat of the whirling blade of loose chain, caused the Mongols to keep back.

Johnny, too, found his ropes loose, although he had to struggle to pull free. One leg was still looped in a coil of rawhide, and that piece was still affixed to a fang of ice.

No one gave any thought to the figure that now lay half exposed by the fractured ice. They were too busy trying to survive.

A squat Mongol with an antique revolver stepped up and attempted to shoot Doc Savage in the back.

The revolver was a .38-caliber, and so when the bullet smashed into the bronze man's broad back, he staggered only slightly, turned and swung the whirling chain at his attacker.

The blurred links found the revolver, smacked the gunman's hand with such force that he lost his trigger finger as well. The Mongol went running off, maimed hand pumping crimson.

The combination of this bulletproof giant and his Samson-like manipulation of the chain cooled the Mongols' heated desire for vengeance.

Just to make sure, Doc brought the chain around and behind him, where it bisected a rifle clutched in another Mongol's white-knuckled hands.

The rifle was a fine one, but it snapped in two as if it were a dry twig.

This last feat impressed the Mongol band that this foreign man of metal was something more than an ordinary human being.

Then the metallic giant reached down to reclaim his scalp, which he replaced on his bronze skull. Everyone saw that the foreign devil dropped one layer of hair atop the other as if it were a perfectly normal thing to do.

The secret behind that was easy explained. Doc's ingenious skullcap that was cunningly designed to mimic his own bronze hair. The protective shell of sheet steel had come loose when Chinua had violently taken hold of it.

In this lull, eyes shifted around from man to man, as if asking, what do we do next?

Chinua the Mongol chieftain lay sprawled in the dirt, out cold with nothing to offer.

That was when shifting eyes went to the fractured cake of ice over which Doc Savage stood guard. Through the rifts and crevices of the damaged slab, portions of cracked red leather clothing and beaten-iron armor plates could be seen.

Entranced, the Mongols drew close, as if the mighty bronze man was no longer there. Pointing, gesticulating, they fell to murmuring and muttering among themselves.

One word passed from lip to lip. "Timur."

Then, unexpectedly, a long, rusty-sounding groan issued from within the broken ice.

A chorus of gasps rolled around the circle of Mongols, and they reflexively shrank from the shattered chunks of ice.

Doc Savage's trilling sprang forth like a feral cry, containing a startlement that reflected his inner agitation.

Only one person had the presence of mind to speak coherent words. That was Johnny Littlejohn.

"I'll be superamalgamated!" the gangly archaeologist bleated. "He's alive! He's really, truly alive!"

Chapter XVIII

THE OGRE SPEAKS

ANOTHER GROAN ISSUED forth from the broken block of ice that had for centuries encapsulated the body of Timur *il-Lenk,* known as Timur the Lame, Scourge of Humanity.

This ugly utterance was somewhat more pronounced, as the form within gathered strength. It shook, wobbled, as if the trapped being were attempting to free himself.

This was impossible, of course. Both legs were still fixed in one unit of ice. The left arm was likewise trapped in another.

The head, which could not be seen clearly, stood between two separate pieces, the breaking of the ice having fortunately occurred around his head.

Johnny turned to Doc Savage and husked, "We must do something."

The look in Doc Savage's eyes then was strange and stark. The gold flakes that often whirled continuously were now eerily still, as if paralyzed. Doc Savage may have been as shocked as he had been in his entire life.

Wrenching himself out of his momentary paralysis, Doc Savage lowered the chain, and approached the broken figure sprawled in slushy ice.

Shifting around so he could discern the face, Doc saw that the warrior wore an ornate conical helmet that covered much of his crown and the sides of the head. The face itself was shielded by an iron mask, forged in a likeness of an Asiatic warrior, replete with metallic mustaches. It was a face of a ferric ogre. Through ornate holes, the eyes were open and visible. They were an awful hue—a pale, canine yellow.

They locked with the bronze man's golden gaze as if perceiving it clearly. Beneath the mask, through open mouth and quivering nostrils, the man struggled to breathe the first fresh air to reach his laboring lungs in untold years.

Carefully, Doc Savage examined the iron countenance with its brutish features. It appeared to be an Asiatic battle mask, the surface weathered to an unbelievable degree. The bronze man recognized that it had been forged of meteoric iron.

Cadwiller Olden was saying, "You have to save him. You can't let him die. He's too important."

Doc Savage ignored the little man, and instead scrutinized the figure in the fractured ice as if calculating all the possibilities that lay before him.

Here was one of history's worst despots. A cruel conqueror who had put to the sword untold millions of innocent persons. Death claimed him five centuries ago. His fate had been sealed. Yet now he breathed. Tamerlane lived!

Doc Savage watched the awful eyes burning into his own, and suddenly the man fixed in the ice broke into a violent shuddering while his exposed flesh at hands and throat commenced turning a cyanotic blue. He was soon gasping like a beached fish.

"He's dying!" cried Olden in a tortured voice. "You can't just let him die. You're a doctor! Where is your humanity?"

Whether Doc Savage was moved by the tiny man's pleas, or by his own strong sense of right and wrong, the bronze man stepped into the shattered ice, extracting from his equipment vest the same syringe charged with stimulant that he had prepared to use on Cadwiller Olden.

Tearing at the leather-and-iron armor, seeking exposed flesh and a visible vein, Doc Savage grasped the old man's arm, and drove the plunger home.

This had an almost immediate effect. The gasping man ceased gasping. His breathing returned to normal rhythm. The horrible blue cast of his exposed skin soon became the normal coppery hue of the East.

Doc Savage stood up, watching this process with eyes like diamond points.

Then, to the astonishment of everyone, the man from the frozen tomb abruptly started flinging aside odd chunks of ice from his upper body.

He was not entirely successful at this. His right arm did not seem to work properly. So Doc Savage brought down a length of chain, cracking apart the section that transfixed his left arm.

The man sat up, peered around, blinked twice, and asked in a croaking voice, "Where am I?"

Doc Savage responded in the man's own language. "First, who are you?"

Hearing this, the hideous man looked startled, then fell to laughing uproariously in a deep register.

"Do you not know me, gold eyes?" he croaked.

Doc said calmly, "I have heard of you. I am merely trying to ascertain your correct identity."

In a tone that sounded the way rust looks, the other intoned, "I am he of whom it has been rightly written, 'If I still lived, mankind would tremble.'"

AT those words, a great roar of approval came from the throats of the assembled Mongols. Those who had swords thrust them in the air. A few fired revolver shots skyward.

One approached and handed his curved blade to the seated man, saying, "Here, sire. Take my unworthy sabre as your own."

The revived warrior accepted the *kilij* sabre, and used it to attack the ice imprisoning his legs. He showed remarkable strength in doing so. The ice came apart under the flashing steel.

Johnny Littlejohn looked at Doc Savage and made gulping sounds like a fish.

"He—he—"

"Yes," Doc told him in English. "This individual, to all evidence, appears to be Tamerlane."

Johnny Littlejohn didn't seem to know whether to cheer or faint. A wave of conflicting emotions took hold of his gaunt features. His hollow eyes seemed to want to cry, but his mouth appeared to wish to laugh.

It was clear to Doc Savage what was going on in Johnny's mind. Here was a man five hundred years dead, resurrected and able to tell his story of days long gone by. This, in itself, was a triumph of science. Or at least of survival. History could be rewritten by this man's testimony.

Yet here, too, was one of history's worst criminals. A monster who richly deserved his demise, but not this subsequent resurrection.

No doubt the bony archeologist was torn by those very same conflicting thoughts.

Johnny looked to Doc Savage and gulped, "What will history think of us now?"

It was an excellent question. Although Doc Savage had been pledged to preserve and safeguard life wherever he found it, his actions had restored to the world a person entirely undeserving of that rescue.

It was impossible to say whether the bronze man had done right or wrong.

Chapter XIX
THE MASK DROPS

A S TAMERLANE—ASSUMING THAT the man in
the metal mask was the genuine article—hacked himself
free of his icy cage, Cadwiller Olden rushed a canteen of water
over to Chinua the Mongol bandit, dashing it in his face.

This produced the desired results. Shaking his head like a
wet dog, Chinua jumped to his feet. He was without weapons,
but charged into the clutch of Mongols surrounding the resurrection in progress.

Chinua barked out gruff orders, but when his eyes fell upon
the tall Mongol emerging from the shattered and melting ice,
his tongue froze in his mouth.

"Lord Timur!" he breathed. Then he fell to his knees in fealty.

"What are you called?" croaked the armored man.

"I am Chinua, chieftain of this clan."

"No," returned Timur. "You are *Tarkhan* Chinua, chief among
my generals."

Tears streaming down his face, Chinua bowed even lower.
He bumped his forehead to the dirt, kept it there.

"In that case, what would you have me do with these foreign
devils?" asked Chinua.

Timur looked to Doc Savage and Johnny Littlejohn, and
apparently did not like what he beheld. For his citrine eyes
narrowed malevolently.

"Slay them," he said sternly.

Every Mongol heard these words, and took them to heart.

122

They rushed the bronze man, who immediately reached for his discarded length of chain and begin whirling it about his head, producing a low, ominous moan.

One Mongol attempted to slip up on Doc from behind. The bronze man dipped the whirling arc of chain slightly and laid him low with a glancing blow to the attacker's skull that spun the unfortunate man around three times before he fell.

Chinua lifted an arm, and yelled, "No, they are mine. It is my privilege to slay them."

A warrior's blade jumped into the air, and Chinua caught it in his right fist.

The Mongol band stepped back, forming a circle around Doc and Johnny to prevent their leaving camp.

Johnny put up his dukes, which resembled little mallets consisting more of bony skin-encased linkage than padded flesh.

"We don't stand much of a chance!" he undertoned to Doc.

By this time, Timur had clambered painfully to his feet, stamping about in a circle because he could not feel anything below his waist. The overlapping plates of his lamellar iron armor clinked and jingled, and it could be seen that his limbs shivered as if palsied. Evidently, his body still reverberated from his long, icy imprisonment.

The eyes of the Mongols flicked back and forth between him and the impending fight, as if not certain which was of greater importance.

Doc said to Johnny, "Hold your breath."

Johnny did so. He knew what was coming.

Reaching into his clothes, Doc removed a flat silver case, which he flipped open. It resembled a cigarette case, although larger. Nestled within were tiny glass globes, like liquid-filled marbles. The liquid was the color of water.

Doc began pegging these in all directions.

The Mongols flinched, not knowing what to expect. But when the glass capsules shattered, nothing much seemed to happen. Then they relaxed momentarily.

Unbeknownst to them, the oily liquid instantly vaporized, producing a colorless and odorless gas that soon overpowered them.

Mongols simply started falling asleep on their feet. Chinua was the first to drop, landing on his broad sword.

Others were collapsing, too, and before a full minute had elapsed virtually everyone was in the dirt, breathing heavily, even snoring here and there.

The man who had been in a bygone era the feared Tamerlane was not immune to the anesthetic gas. Behind the battle mask of meteoric iron, yellow orbs closed. He fell back into the broken and melting ice, as heavy as a sack of concrete covered in leather-and-iron armor. His spasmodic shivering increased in its intensity.

Other than Doc and Johnny, only one individual failed to succumb to the strange slumber. That was Cadwiller Olden. He had encountered the gas in the past, was familiar with it. When the marble-like bombs had shattered, he knew enough to hold his breath, running away as he did so. The little man disappeared into a colorful tent.

After about a minute, the gas dissipated and became harmless. It was safe to breathe again. Doc and Johnny resumed normal respiration.

The bronze giant went among the fallen, checking that no one had injured themselves, lastly examining the figure of Tamerlane, whose chest was rising and falling with his shuddery breathing.

Bending, Doc Savage removed his mask and helmet. The massive head thus revealed made Johnny Littlejohn gasp audibly.

There was an Oriental temple down near Mott Street in New York's Chinatown. And in it a squat idol which was not Asiatic of feature, nor any other race either, but simply as fiercely ugly as human lineaments could conceivably be made. It was said that an Oriental artisan had spent years making it—a statue of an Asiatic ruler who had caused his legs to be cut off for some crime.

Tamerlane made Johnny think of the Celestial image down near Mott Street. The fellow's face did not wrinkle, but bulged out in pencil-sized rolls; in repose, he showed his teeth in a fierce smile, and it could be seen that the teeth were like large yellow-white kernels of corn.

If the ornate mask had resembled a metallic ogre, the features they formerly concealed were those of a gargoyle, hideous and inhuman.

"Ugly as a burnt boot," breathed Johnny. "What disposition do we make of him?"

Doc Savage seemed to be at a temporary loss for words. The sight of the gargoyle face fascinated him. His hypnotic eyes searched the unlovely features.

"If we leave him behind, his story will be lost to posterity," reminded Johnny.

"But what would we do with him?" asked Doc.

"In his day," expounded Johnny, "he was a murderous tyrant. If he committed crimes in the present day, you would consign him to our College. Let us take Tamerlane to America for safekeeping."

Doc Savage eyed Johnny skeptically. "If we do that, we will have to erase his memory, in which case his story will be lost to history."

Johnny cleared his throat noisily. "We won't have to perform the brain operation right away. We can learn many things from him, then erase his memory."

Doc nodded. "It is a reasonable solution to the conundrum which Tamerlane's survival presents."

The bronze giant reached into a pocket, and pulled out another flat case. This one was studded with dials and knobs, surrounding a loudspeaker grill. It was a wonderfully small radio microwave transmitter-receiver with a range of several miles.

Doc switched it on. The device was already tuned to the frequency used by his men for communication. He spoke into the loudspeaker, which doubled as a microphone.

"Doc Savage to Monk Mayfair. Come in, Monk."

A squeaky voice answered excitedly, *"Doc! We found a salt water lake to alight on. Did you find that Monzingo Baldwin?"*

"Unfortunately, yes," replied Doc. "Take the plane into the air and land as close to the camp as practical. We are getting out of here."

"How did everything work out?" Monk wanted to know.

Doc Savage told him, "That remains to be seen. Hurry."

THE PLANE'S throaty engines disturbed the distance a half hour later, while Doc was occupied scouring the camp for Cadwiller Olden. He found tiny footprints, but they led to an assemblage of ponies, where they disappeared. The ground was sandy in spots, hard and tough in others. Evidently, the midget had taken great care to walk where he would leave no spoor. The bronze man lost the trail in hard turf that retained no impressions short of horse's hooves.

"Baldwin is nowhere to be found," Doc told Johnny Little-john, sounding slightly puzzled.

Johnny looked a little sheepish.

"What is it?" Doc prompted, noticing his expression.

"In all the uproar, I forgot to tell you. He appears to have suffered several blows to his head after he landed. He remembers that he's Cadwiller Olden, not Monzingo Baldwin."

Again, Doc Savage's trilling piped up, weirdly startled. He stifled it at once.

"This compounds our complications," he admitted.

Johnny looked around uneasily, saying, "The gas should have knocked him out, too."

Doc said slowly, "If his memory has returned, so would his recollections of how we operate. He would have had the presence of mind to hold his breath."

"Then the rapscallion could be anywhere," said Johnny morosely.

Doc nodded. "It is urgent we find him."

BUT the search produced nothing, and soon the mighty roar of the flying boat reached their ears. It began descending, silencers turned off.

Monk put the plane down hard, but it was a serviceable landing. No damage was done.

Doc Savage tied the iron-bound body of Tamerlane to an appaloosa packhorse, and used it to convey him out of the camp.

Chinua and his Mongols were still sleeping. By the time they returned to consciousness, it would all be over. And there was nothing any of them could do about it, being merely wild horse nomads and not aviators.

Everything seemed to go well. As Doc and Johnny approached the plane, they saw that Monk kept the motors turning, so that they could take off instantly.

What spoiled everything was a simple rifle shot.

The passing of the bullet made a noise that was distinctive and is known to all men in war. It sounded unpleasantly like a glass rod breaking very close to their startled ears.

Knowing that noise and what it meant, Doc and Johnny naturally ducked their heads, then turned, eyes sharp.

They scanned the surrounding hills.

Another bullet snapped past, even closer.

Johnny had yanked out his recovered superfirer, but it was empty. The gesture was pointless.

Doc Savage's gaze went to the top of a low sand hill, where he spied, thanks to a telltale puff of smoke, a tiny figure cradling a rifle much too large for it.

The bronze man directed Johnny's attention to the gunsmoke with a pointing finger.

"Olden!" hissed Johnny.

There came another puff of smoke, and the packhorse gave a jump, having been stung in the rump.

Doc Savage reached out for the reins, but the appaloosa would have none of it. Whinnying wildly, it charged off, Tamerlane still tied to its saddle.

"He's getting away!" Johnny bleated.

More bullets began arriving. They were coming dangerously close.

To chase after the horse would be a fool's errand. And they had no way to return fire without reaching the waiting plane and obtaining rifles.

There was nothing to do except seek the shelter of the flying boat. They did so with alacrity.

Bullets stormed all around, but Cadwiller Olden appeared to be a poor shot. Nevertheless, the snarling bullets came close enough that they respected the deadly slugs.

At their approach, Monk flung open the door, and they piled in.

"Who's shootin'?" demanded Monk.

"Cadwiller Olden," Doc told him grimly.

"You mean Monzingo?" said Long Tom.

"Not anymore," snapped Johnny. "He has shed that identity. He knows who he is now."

"Holy cow!" thundered Renny. "What more could go wrong?"

"You haven't heard the worst of it," said Johnny, slapping at his dusty tweeds.

Doc Savage went forward to kill the engines.

"Ain't we takin' off?" demanded Monk.

"We must capture that appaloosa," the bronze man called back.

Muttered Monk, "I noticed that there was a man tied to that nag. Who is it?"

"The worst person imaginable," said Johnny glumly.

"You mean Chinua?"

"Tamerlane makes Chinua look like a piker," Johnny retorted. He was pushing a fresh drum into the receiver of his superfirer. The expression on his hollow face was one of great determination. If he had to do it single-handedly, the spindle-limbed archaeologist was going to run down the pony and its unconscious rider.

"Who's Tamerlane?" asked Monk.

"Do you recall the story of Rip Van Winkle?" countered Johnny.

"The old graybeard who went to sleep in the Catskills and woke up twenty years later? Sure, I do."

"Tamerlane is like that," snapped Johnny. "And we must recapture him with alacrity."

It seemed like a simple plan. But Cadwiller Olden continued to stymie it. He must have dragged a great store of ammunition up onto his hill, because he kept peppering the plane with whining slugs.

True, most of them missed and none of them did any harm. But every time Monk or Renny flung open the hatch door, a fresh fusillade came their way, causing them to bang it shut with haste.

"Anyone have any bright ideas?" grumbled Renny in a frustrated tone.

Starting the engines, Doc urged the plane forward, and threw it around in a half circle, shielding the hatch from any and all sniping fire.

This maneuver did not solve the problem of how to leave the shelter of the big plane without being sniped at. But it was a start.

The problem was that precious minutes were flying by, and the plane's diminishing store of gasoline, which had been seriously depleted over the course of the last day, was assuming alarming proportions.

Then, to further complicate matters, a cloud of dust appeared in the midst of the hills encompassing the bandit encampment.

Johnny was the first to notice this. He had exited the plane and was hunkered down by the tail, attempting to slip out from the shelter. He was having no luck. Every time he poked out his mop of a head, a bullet snapped in his direction.

Once, a long lock of hair was clipped off, showing that the diminutive sniper was learning to adjust for windage. Foolishly, Johnny grabbed for the falling lock, but another snarling slug discouraged that aimless action.

The cloud of dust soon turned into a group of horsemen, and that was when Johnny experienced true despair.

Rushing back into the plane, he yelled, "It's Chinua and his bandits! They came to. What do we do now?"

Renny rumbled, "I vote we mow them down with our superfirers."

"I'm for that, too," seconded Long Tom.

Doc Savage hesitated.

Suddenly, wordlessly, he advanced the throttles, throwing the great air leviathan into a take-off run. Johnny scrambled to close the door. He got it shut.

The bony geologist charged for the cockpit demanding, "Are we leaving?"

"What does it look like?" Monk growled. "We're takin' off, ain't we?"

Johnny fell to sputtering inarticulately. To Doc Savage, he demanded once he got his tongue organized, "What is your plan?"

"I have no plan," admitted Doc, with a trace of frustration tinging his normally well-modulated voice.

Chapter XX

AIR ATTACK

AS DOC SAVAGE sent the great four-engined aircraft hurtling into the startlingly blue Mongolian sky, the others called out reports from their stations around the cabin.

Renny thumped, "That runaway pony is still carrying off Tamerlane."

To which Long Tom added, "And the Mongols are riding hard after it."

Monk suggested, "Doc, what say we shove open some windows and start whittlin' down these heathens with our superfirers?"

But Doc Savage was too engrossed in getting the plane into the air to respond. It was clear that the big bronze man was thinking hard. His metallic features were grave and unyielding.

Hovering behind the cockpit, Johnny insisted, "We cannot allow such a rare specimen to get away from us."

Doc said nothing.

"Nor can we permit him to run free, otherwise there is no telling what deviltry he might cause," added the long-worded archeologist.

Doc Savage leveled off the plane, and began sweeping the steppe below in broad circles.

"This is the Twentieth Century," he told Johnny. "It is unlikely that Timur could accomplish much mischief. Remember that he was a warlord, now without much of an army to lead."

"You cannot mean that you are going to leave him behind!" Johnny exploded.

The bronze man's prolonged silence made it clear that Doc Savage was torn between unpleasant alternatives. Finally, he called back into the cabin, "Endeavor to discourage the Mongols from pursuing the pack pony."

Johnny was grinning.

Noticing this, Doc Savage told him somberly, "I am still considering this matter."

Johnny's smile collapsed into a pucker. He began to look worried.

As the bronze man banked the great plane lower to the ground, Monk, Ham, Renny and Long Tom threw open windows, out of which they jabbed the spike-snouted muzzles of their superfirers.

When the stoic bronze man jockeyed the plane into position, they opened up.

Resulting din was deafening. The intricate weapons were not designed to be operated in close quarters multiplied by four. The horrific moan assaulted the ears of everyone in the plane, leaving a ringing sensation deep in their eardrums.

Down on the steppe, the enraged Mongols were charging in a cloud of dust that trailed them, hanging in the air like a dun genie. Dressed in their coat-like native costumes, waving old rifles and longswords, they might have been a remnant of the Golden Horde of Genghis Khan from ages before.

The combined fusillade of the churning supermachine pistols commenced taking a noticeable toll. Horses stumbled, as if encountering gopher holes. Unprepared riders were thrown. Some were trampled. Others broke.

Seeing this, Doc called back, "Cease fire!"

He was not heard over the hammering racket at first. The frightening commotion continued uninterrupted. Finally, his crashing voice penetrated a pause in which there was a hasty reloading of ammunition drums.

Monk called up, "What's wrong? We're just thinnin' out the herd."

"Men are being trampled by their panicked horses. This is a scientific expedition. We did not come all this way to inflict unnecessary casualties."

Reluctantly, Monk latched his weapon on single-shot operation. The others did the same. They fell to sharpshooting. The weapons made distinct snapping sounds, but target shooting from a fast-traveling aircraft was a far different matter than hosing almost three hundred rounds a minute into a tumbling mass of horsemen.

So constrained, Doc's men had considerably less success in bringing down additional bandits.

Then the plane went hurtling past the melée below. Wrestling the control wheel, Doc Savage banked around to give his men another crack at the bandit horde.

Long Tom complained, "At this rate, we could be at this all day."

Renny rumbled, "Maybe we should drop some gas bombs on them, too."

"A good idea," squeaked Monk. "Let me rustle up a bunch of them."

It *was* a good idea. Doc Savage did not object to it. He leveled off the plane, and so got closer to the ground, overflying the gathering Mongols who were getting themselves organized after having been thoroughly dispersed by gunfire.

Coming back from the aft portion of the aircraft, Monk Mayfair lugged an unnumbered case in both furry fists. Dropping it to the cabin floor, he flung it open, revealing racks of very large metallic eggs nested in excelsior packing.

Ham peered down at the cluster of objects and asked, "What are those?"

"Knockout gas," grinned Monk. "It'll put Chinua and his bully boys to sleep like a ton of bricks fell on 'em."

This hairy chemist began distributing the devices.

Doc Savage jockeyed the plane around, this time coming in from the west to give Monk and the others an opportunity to push the cumbersome gas bombs out the windows.

As Doc lined up the aircraft, sinking it even further, the wings started jumping alarmingly and metallic sounds could be heard throughout the cabin. The plane bucked like a stung bronco.

"They are shooting at us!" warned Johnny. "We'd better hurry it up."

By this time, everyone had a gas bomb balanced on his lap. Monk called forward, "Say when."

The powerful engines carried them toward the target, then Doc rapped out a resounding, "Now!"

They fell to dropping their bombs.

The devices were very simple. The shells were not thick, and made of a soft metal resembling pewter. Dropped from a height, they would crack open like metallic eggs, disgorging their volatile liquid contents. Once this potent brew vaporized, it would produce large clouds of anesthetic gas.

The eggs landed in a random fashion, fracturing as expected.

By the time this occurred, the roaring flying boat had flung on past, so it was impossible to tell how successful they had been.

Once again, Doc Savage threw the great plane into a banking turn, and the roar of motors with their accompanying blade scream made the entire aircraft shake and shudder.

Due to the stress on the aircraft, and the drumming sound as motor vibration transmitted itself throughout the great aircraft's bulkheads, Doc Savage and his men failed to detect a new phenomenon.

IT was while they were sweeping around, attempting to line up on the Mongol band, that Monk muttered, "Those engines don't sound right."

Renny cocked an ear, and said, "Those aren't the engines!"

"No!" Ham wailed. "Then what are—"

Suddenly, Doc Savage threw the great plane into a steep dive. He executed a frightening acrobatic wingover, and the men were tossed about the cabin as if they were baggage.

They landed in the aisle, in awkward positions among the seats, while Monk found himself back in the tail section, with cases of equipment falling out of cargo netting onto his barrel chest. He flung them off.

Renny's "Holy cow!" was a thunderous crash.

As they struggled to find their footing, suddenly the flying boat was pointing its broad nose at the incredibly blue sky, and they were once again scrambling to keep from being flung about the cabin.

The drumming that had sounded so alarming, abruptly ceased.

"What's goin' on?" howled Monk.

Doc Savage was too busy fighting the controls, so Johnny offered an explanation.

"Aerial ambuscade," he said, uncorking his long-worded vocabulary.

"Speak English," snapped Long Tom peevishly.

Johnny clarified his remark. "We are being attacked by fighter planes."

Chapter XXI

RETREAT

DOC SAVAGE CLIMBED the great aircraft as if he were pushing it up into the blue by main strength.

When he reached an altitude of six thousand feet, the bronze giant leveled off. He was not gentle about it. But the situation called for extreme measures, inconsiderate of the comfort of all aboard.

Back in the cabin, his men scrambled to windows on either side of the plane. They looked down. A flight of five slivery aircraft were buzzing about far below. At this distance, they resembled loose scales off a mackerel.

Monk wrinkled his beetling brows. "Whose ships are they?" he wondered.

Frowning, Ham remarked, "I do not recognize that type of aircraft, nor did I see markings on any of them."

Renny Renwick, who possibly knew aircraft better than anyone aboard save Doc Savage, muttered gloomily, "If I didn't know better, I would say those are Japanese warplanes. They look like the new Zero-*sen* model."

"What would they be doing up here?" grumbled Long Tom.

Doc Savage answered that. "We are not terribly far from the Manchurian border. There have been border incidents, and even a brief war between Japanese-dominated Manchuria and Soviet-controlled Mongolia two years back."

"So why are they shootin' at us?" Monk wanted to know. "We're not at war with anybody."

The question went unanswered when the five warbirds suddenly spiraled upward, climbing. Winking red eyes appeared on their ruler-straight wings. They undertook to strafe the underside of the air giant like ravenous sharks dogging a great whale.

All of Doc's planes were well armored and could withstand a great deal of punishment. But they were not military machines, nor were they designed to continue operating under sustained fire from a large number of modern warplanes.

Too, they were not armed. They carried no fixed guns in their wings, nor other external armament.

Considering that harsh reality, Doc Savage made a bold maneuver. Necessity demanded it. As the snarling fighter planes charged up, Doc banked his larger aircraft, then threw it into a stomach-churning sideslip, followed by a hair-raising dive.

Unexpectedly, the opposing pilots found a four-engine air behemoth dropping down into their midst.

Releasing the trips of their hammering wing machine guns, they naturally scattered to get out of the way. Whatever their motivations, the opposing pilots were not eager to end up in a tangle of duralumin metal at six thousand feet above hard, cold ground.

Once Doc hurtled past them, he pulled back on the control yoke and leveled out the plane. The way the tendons on his rigid column of a neck stood out, it was clear that the bronze man was putting all of his might into jockeying the plane about the sky.

The air leviathan had not been designed for this type of maneuvering. Everyone knew that. The risk of tearing off a wing—if not both of them—was very great under such extreme acrobatics.

At the same time, Doc Savage had put all of his aeronautical knowledge into the construction of the flying boat. He had hardened the wing roots, and reinforced other stress points, so that the streamlined fuselage could take more than the usual punishment. But there was a limit on what aircraft of this size could do. It was no fighter. Nor was it very nimble in the air. This ultra-modern craft was designed for long-haul flights.

So it was when Doc Savage climbed again that the fighter planes regrouped, buzzing back like silver-scaled hornets. It could be seen that neither the sides or wings of the swarming aircraft were emblazoned with the *Hinomaru*—the red-ball-in-a-white circle representing the national flag of the Land of the Rising Sun.

"Unmarked," muttered Long Tom.

"That's a bad sign," echoed Monk.

Doc Savage got on the radio, and fished around until he found the frequency on which there was excited babbling.

Hearing this chatter, Johnny piped up, "Japanese for sure!"

Picking up the microphone, Doc Savage then replied himself. "This is Doc Savage. Why are you shooting at us?"

The pilot's reply was not what was expected. A harsh voice simply snapped in Japanese, "You will land. Immediately. Or be shot down."

"We are engaged in a scientific expedition," Doc responded firmly.

The harsh voice spat back, "Do not lie! You were conducting military operations near our border. You will land, and subject yourself to interrogation."

In the back, Monk growled, "I'm subjectin' myself to nothing. Those monkeys can go whistle for answers."

Renny pointed out, "They must have seen us shooting at those Mongols. Their suspicions are aroused."

"I don't trust them Japs," Monk insisted. "I say we fight 'em."

"I have a better idea," said Doc Savage.

"Yeah?" said Monk.

"We will lead them into an ambush of our own."

Monk brightened, "I getcha. I'll set it up right away."

"Set up what?" demanded Ham Brooks, face puzzled.

Monk ambled to the rear, moved some dislodged cases to one side and exposed a number of pressurized tanks that had been mounted in the tail section. These were equipped with simple aluminum petcocks. Grinning, the apish chemist turned them. A slow hissing was produced.

Ham asked, "Is that the stuff you use to clog airplane engines?"

Monk's grin made his tiny ears retreat. "It's a new formula. Watch and see what happens."

DOC SAVAGE booted the big aircraft around, as if he were running away from the Japanese warplanes. The fighter pilots naturally lined up in a simple V formation and pursued the four-engined wonder, confident that their smaller aircraft with their supercharged motors would soon overhaul the comparatively slower air giant.

They were very much mistaken in that expectation. For no sooner had the Japanese fighters fallen behind Doc's big bus than they began experiencing difficulties.

Droplets resembling black rain suddenly speckled their windscreens. Every pilot in the world understands what that means—an oil leak from the engine, which could quickly become very serious.

Monitoring their radio frequency, Doc Savage listened intently.

The pilots were chattering among themselves, complaining that their engines were leaking oil. They did not understand this. As far as they were aware, the Doc Savage plane had not returned fire.

Yet with each passing minute, their windshields became smeared with greasy black tendrils of oil.

One Japanese pilot, perhaps brighter than the others, insisted, "It is a trick! Do not land. Do not turn back."

Hearing this, Doc Savage called back to Monk Mayfair, "Add the neutralizer chemical."

Grinning broadly, Monk turned another petcock on a different tank, and a fresh protracted hissing filled the cabin.

From concealed nozzles fitted into the rear empennage of the amphibian, a chemical vapor started shooting out under pressure. This was specially formulated to be drawn into the intakes of a modern airplane motor. It was heavy, greasy stuff, so it would not take long to gum up the main parts of the pursuing engines.

The pilots discovered this unpleasant fact when their motors started sputtering, spark plugs missing fire. That alarming cacophony convinced even the most suspicious of them that somehow, miraculously, their engines suffered from simultaneous oil leaks.

When one three-bladed propeller stopped spinning, followed by another, the pursuit pilots hastily sought safe landing spots.

Johnny called back to Monk, "Can you tell if your 'discourager' is working?"

Monk stood up, turned. "Not unless Doc turns this bus around to give us a look-see."

The bronze man showed little interest in that. Owing to the prodigious size of the flying boat, there had limited visibility in the rear. Doc flew on for a time, until he was certain that no machine gun fire would pepper his craft, handling the plane carefully so as not to put any more stress on its complicated airframe.

Overflying the steppe, the bronze man saw the five Japanese planes dropping in for emergency landings. Only four made it. One had an accident. It stumbled in a rut, caught fire. The pilot could be seen fleeing the wreck.

Over the radio, excited Japanese pilots were communicating with their airbase somewhere to the south in Manchuria.

Listening to this, Johnny muttered, "Calling for reinforcements."

Blocking his mighty fists, Renny rumbled, "This could get bad."

Doc Savage nodded. "We cannot remain in this vicinity for very long."

Eyes stricken, Johnny asked, "What about Timur?"

Again, Doc Savage declined reply. But he sent his plane circling back in the direction of the hill-banked Mongol encampment.

THEY were not long reaching the spot. As they flew over the camp, they saw a scattering of Mongols and horsemen on the hard, barren turf, unmoving.

Of the runaway equine with its unconscious rider, there was no sign.

Doc Savage flew back and forth several times without success. Steppeland in many spots was dry and dusty, but in other places was tufted with hard soil and drying grass. Try as he might, the bronze man could not locate the tracks of the appaloosa pony that had carried off Tamerlane in a wild direction.

The bronze man stayed with it, circling several times, as his men scoured the hills with binoculars, seeking any sign of Cadwiller Olden. But the wily midget had also vanished from view. There was no sign of him on any surrounding hill.

A sudden exchange of words over the radio disclosed that Japanese reinforcements were on the way.

Finally, reluctantly, the bronze man said, "We have no choice but to flee."

Johnny started to protest, but Renny cut him off. "Simmer down, old Cyclops. If we land, we'll be sitting ducks."

That quelled Johnny's expostulations. He took to polishing his monocle magnifier to cover his inner turmoil.

Climbing for altitude, Doc Savage pointed the monster aircraft north, slamming the throttles as far forward as he could. It might have been interpreted as a sign of the big fellow's frustration with the escalating situation, but no one noticed the abrupt gesture.

The large plane responded like a thoroughbred horse, hammering along, eating up the empty air miles over the flat desolation below.

In the cabin, Doc's men were silent. They were not psychologically adapted to retreat. Nor were they accustomed to being thwarted. It was a bitter pill they were swallowing. And if there was any remedy for the trouble lately encountered in Mongolia, the antidote seemed very remote in their minds.

Chapter XXII

COMMON CAUSE

CADWILLER OLDEN WATCHED the Doc Savage plane retreat to the north.

Grinning tightly, he clambered down the dun-colored hill in the direction of the ground. He had laid out on his back and covered his compact body with dirt and his face with scrub so that he could see upward without being spotted from the air.

Now, he shook off his makeshift camouflage, and sat up to observe events.

One by one, the unmarked Japanese planes commenced descending upon the steppe. Their wheeled undercarriages withstood the ruts and clumps of tough grass over which they rolled as the pilots attempted to put down safely.

Only one aircraft failed to make it. It was a Nakajima Ki-43 *Hayabusa*, and it struck a rabbit hole at high speed, pitching about, causing it to ground loop and fold one wing as it crumpled, spinning prop dashing itself into pieces.

The plane quickly caught fire, and after a moment there came a grunting detonation, followed by a larger explosion that cracked the cockpit open.

The pilot managed to scramble out of his seat safely, but he was trailing a comet of flame, apparently unaware of the fact. He ran and ran and finally collapsed, whereupon he rolled in the dirt and the grass, attempting to put out the bundle of flames that had enveloped him.

It was for nothing. After a while, the unfortunate pilot stopped rolling. The flames continued to eat him until it was clear that he had lost the battle for survival.

Cadwiller Olden observed very little of this, for he was trying to flee in the direction of the runaway appaloosa atop which the icy individual in iron armor had been strapped.

The equine, as the breed is wont to do, did not run away in a straight line but broke in zigzagging lines, so that it was soon circling the scrubby hills that sheltered the Mongol camp.

In this fashion, the pony packed the jittering body back toward camp.

Reaching the ground, the midget man rushed to meet the animal, small arms and legs pumping madly. His frantic breath whistled through clenched teeth.

There was considerable racing about, and some desperate grabbing for loose harness, but finally tiny fingers clutched the trailing rawhide reins.

The frantic operation did not go well at first. The horse was no longer galloping quite so swiftly as before, having tired, but it was still moving at a gait far more brisk than the diminutive man who was attempting to arrest it.

Cadwiller Olden found himself being dragged some distance, until he was forced to let go.

Then the crafty rascal rediscovered his innate cunning, and attempted to follow the horse until it reached a spot where it decided to simply stop. There was water at the spot, which explained the pony's behavior.

While the appaloosa drank his fill, the little man crept up on it, then produced a short knife from somewhere on his person, which he had earlier pilfered from a Mongol tent.

Apparently, the midget was no lover of horses. For he simply stole up upon the twitching tail of the drinking pony and, without hesitation, severed its hind tendons, crippling the animal.

The appaloosa fell, screaming and kicking, and almost crushed its tied-down burden.

Racing around to one side, Olden seized the screaming pony by the reins, attempted to jerk the animal off his burden. In that, he succeeded only because the horse was frightened and confused.

Leaping over the horse, Olden reached the insensate Mongol and dragged him free of the rolling and pitching animal.

The man was out cold. And his body was wracked by rolling waves of shivers. Apparently, he had been so long encased in the ice that even unconscious, his muscles and nerves continued reacting to its long, frigid hibernation.

Olden fetched water in his cupped palms, poured it down the man's throat.

This produced no alteration in either consciousness or spasmodic shivering. But the insensate one did swallow the water. At least a little of it.

By this time, the horse had settled down. Or it might be fairer to say that it had given up. It lay down on its side, head pillowed on the dirt, and a single tear rolled down its visible eye.

From time to time, snufflings and a weak series of snortings emerged from the appaloosa's pulsing throat.

"Cut that out," snarled the little man. "Or I'll come over there and cut your throat."

This dire threat appeared to have no effect on the horse's pitiful cries, for it continued making them.

After a time, the Japanese pilots started filtering into the camp, lean-barreled pistols carried before them.

Noticing this, Cadwiller Olden did the only thing that made sense. He threw up his puny arms, bleating, "I surrender!"

He was immediately surrounded, and a half-dozen cold steel muzzles were pointing down at his quivering skull. The airmen wore leather jackets and matching helmets.

The Japanese pilots appeared to speak no English. Wooden-faced, they simply trained their weapons on their prisoner, without indicating their intentions.

One man went over to the prone individual who continued to shiver in the sun. He examined the shivering one for some time. Others joined him. Their excited exchanges seemed to concentrate on the unusual clothing and all that adorned the quaking form.

Another man went over to the horse, took immediate stock of the situation and without asking permission, shot the equine in the right eye, silencing its pitiful complaints. The horse gave a convulsive jerk and collapsed into silence.

Cadwiller Olden squeezed his eyes shut, for he firmly believed that he was next.

Instead, the nervous midget was made to sit on the ground, with his tiny hands clasped over the top of his skull, while one pilot guarded him.

A search of the camp produced very little of interest, according to the frozen features of the returning Japanese pilots.

They ranged outside of the camp, and soon enough came upon the sleeping Mongols who had been overcome by Doc Savage's anesthetic gas bombs.

Olden was dragged toward the profusion of Mongol horsemen and felled steeds, and made to sit down again with his shaking hands held high over his head.

NOTHING much transpired for several hours as the Mongols and their horses continued to sleep. The Japanese aviators stood guard over the captives and their own planes. From time to time, their leader went to his plane and apparently communicated with someone by radio.

It was nearing sunset when a large transport plane circled the area once and then put down rather roughly. Due to its size, the aircraft managed a respectable landing and came to a stop, apparently undamaged.

Big props ceased their mad spinning as the door was thrown open, and an officer stepped out.

This man had a very hard sandstone-colored face, and looked to be about forty years of age. A squad of Japanese marines trailed in his wake.

When the hard-faced officer strode up to the Mongol pile, all the other Japanese pilots saluted him crisply. The salute was returned sharply and a conversation ensued.

Cadwiller Olden could follow none of it. He started feeling very cold inside.

After some twenty minutes of incomprehensible conversation, the Japanese *Kaigun Daisa*, or *Navy Captain*—for that was what his uniform insignia indicated his rank to be—stormed over to Cadwiller Olden and began interrogating him in one language after the other.

"*O namaye wa nan' to moshi-masu?*"

Olden cleared his throat a few times, uncertain whether or not to volunteer his American identity.

The Japanese captain grew frustrated and kicked once. That was enough.

"I speak English," squeaked Olden. "Only English. Savvy?"

A strange gleam came into the Japanese officer's narrowed eyes.

"Are you British, or American?" demanded the hard-faced captain in a harder tone of voice.

Olden hesitated, unsure what the safest answer was. So the Japanese kicked him again.

"American! I'm American!" bleated the rattled midget.

Hearing that, the officer kicked Cadwiller Olden for the third time, but that seemed to satisfy him, for his hard boot withdrew.

"Name?"

"Monzingo Baldwin," Olden told him.

"What is an American doing in Mongolia?"

"I came with the Doc Savage expedition," Olden returned quickly.

The strange glint in the Japanese captain's dark eyes became even stranger.

"Doc Savage is here?"

Olden nodded vigorously. "His transport plane flew north about three hours ago."

"Bound for what destination?"

"Honest, I don't know. He abandoned me."

"Why would he do this?" asked the officer sharply.

To the end of his days, Cadwiller Olden did not understand why he volunteered the next morsel of information. But he did.

"Because we are enemies," he said simply.

"I see," hissed the Japanese. "What was Savage-*san* doing in Mongolia in the first place?"

Olden hesitated only briefly. He looked up into the man's dark eyes and stated, "Doc Savage dug a man out of an ice cave nearby. This man is very important. He had been entombed for hundreds of years, and now he lives again."

This appeared to bewilder the Japanese officer. He seemed to be reviewing the little man's words as if trying to make sense of them.

At last, he demanded, "Who is this important individual?"

Cadwiller Olden gulped, "History knows him as Timur *il-Lenk,* Timur the Lame, but the West calls him Tamerlane."

This seem to take a long time to sink in. There was a great silence.

"Where is this disinterred man?" barked the Captain.

Olden pointed back toward the Mongol camp and said, "Back there. Out cold."

The Japanese blinked. "Still frozen?"

Olden shook his small head rapidly. "No. Out cold, as in unconscious."

"He lives?"

"Absolutely."

The Captain turned to his aide and barked out quick orders, which he transmitted to the pilots. Two men were sent back into the Mongol camp.

Then, the Japanese officer turned his attention to the sleeping Mongols. It was clear they could not be roused from their weird slumber. A great effort by kicking boots and pounding rifle stocks had been expended to demonstrate this fact.

Olden volunteered, "Doc Savage bombed them. Used gas. The gas makes a man sleep for a very long time."

The Japanese officer nodded wordlessly. He studied the Mongols and their horses, then went to the camp and scrutinized the armored man who had been excavated from the ice cave. This individual remained unconscious.

Upon his return, Cadwiller Olden was interrogated about the ice cave, and then the Japanese captain went to investigate that. He saddled up a horse and took two men with him. The group was gone several hours.

When he reappeared, the officer seemed rather grim, or rather, more grim than before, for he wore a very severe visage throughout.

BY evening, the Mongols were coming out of their heavy slumber. Pistols and rifles were trained on their heads as the Captain addressed them in their own language.

There followed considerable shouted insults and excited exchanges. The Mongols were clearly unhappy to see Japanese marines in their home pasture. For a while, it looked as if a battle was about to break out. But as the hot exchanges progressed, tempers cooled, and attitudes simmered down to mere tension and distrust.

After some more of this, the Japanese officer returned to Cadwiller Olden and said to him, "The story these bandits tell matches the story you told, far-fetched as it is."

"It is the truth," assured Olden.

"You say that you are the enemy of Doc Savage?"

"He is the poison in my milk, the thorn in my side, and the burr under my saddle."

"Then you and I may be destined to be friends," said the Japanese officer. "For I have encountered this bronze devil before. My name is Captain Kensa Kan."

Hearing those welcome words, Cadwiller Olden brightened. Suddenly, he felt as if his prospects had vastly improved, much like a man facing the gallows might feel if he was told he was simply going to be in prison for the rest of his life. It may not have been good news, but it was better news—far better a fate than swinging by a rough rope.

So the little man spoke the only words he could think to say. "How may I help you?"

"Help me seize the bronze devil, and I will see that your life is spared, and insure that you have the gratitude of my Emperor."

When he spoke the word Emperor, Captain Kensa Kan snapped his spine into rigidity, as if someone had stabbed him from behind. A worshipful light came into his dark eyes. It was a strange sight to see.

Chapter XXIII

CORPSE CONFUSION

THE CABIN OF Doc Savage's large transport plane was unusually quiet as it hammered north in the direction of the Mongolian capital of Ulan Bator.

The cabin was soundproofed, and the four mighty motors operated with remarkable silence for such leviathan engines. So the lack of conversation was noticeable.

Doc and his men were lost in their thoughts. Even Monk and Ham, perpetually at each other's throats—at least verbally—seemed to have little appetite for exchanging insults. Habeas Corpus had crawled back into the case in which the apish chemist had smuggled him on board. Doc Savage took note of the pig's presence, but failed to react.

Little caught the bronze man by surprise, and his perpetual poker face retained its metallic cast.

Speaking perfect Mongolian, the bronze man radioed ahead to the capital. A great deal of hi-test aviation gasoline had been expended during their hectic expedition, and they would need to refuel.

Officials in Ulan Bator were hesitant.

"Petrol is at a premium," Doc was told. "It is wartime. You know this."

"We understand," the bronze man told the official respectfully. "But I bring news of grave interest to all Mongolia."

"What manner of news?"

"A tremendous discovery has been made in an ice cave on your steppeland. Your government will want to know about it."

"We have more serious matters to deal with. Japanese warplanes have been reported crossing our southern border, in violation of treaty."

Doc Savage told them, "I have seen these warplanes with my own eyes. I disabled a number of them. You can find them at these coordinates." He then recited the longitude and latitude of the Mongol camp from memory. It was a remarkable mental feat, but then again Doc Savage had been known to give the correct hour without consulting a timepiece. In fact, the bronze man rarely wore a wristwatch for that very reason.

Doc Savage added, "This is also the approximate location of the great discovery."

A crackling silence came over the radio loudspeaker.

After a tense wait, the Mongolian official said, "You may land. We will see about fuel. But we will hear your story first."

THEY were not surprised to be met by a contingent of Soviet officers and armed infantrymen when they arrived. Mongolia was under Russian control, and the U.S.S.R. was at war with Germany.

A commissar with a broad Mongolian face strode up and demanded, "Let us hear your report."

He was that brusque about it. No ceremony, nor any invitation to sit down and discuss matters.

Continuing to speak in the man's language, Doc Savage related the account of how he came to Inner Mongolia and what was discovered there.

The bronze man minced no words, but found that he had to embroider the story with extra detail, lest he not be believed. The resurrection of the Mongol warlord who had spent the last few hundred years encased in ice was not a believable one, under any circumstances.

When Doc Savage concluded his account, the Mongol commissar regarded him cryptically.

"Lies!" he spat.

Doc Savage was taken aback. This fact did not show on his metallic features, for he was schooled not to reveal his inner emotions. But the pent silence that followed this accusation told his men that the bronze man was unprepared for this response.

"It is the truth," insisted Doc.

The Mongolian commissar, who was on the squat side, lifted himself up to his full height, perhaps in a vain effort to tower over the Herculean metallic giant.

"Not many months ago," he said gruffly, "a Soviet anthropologist opened up the tomb of Tamerlane, and has been examining the remains. The bones that were found in the Samarkand crypt show severe injuries to the right arm and leg—injuries consistent with historical accounts of the wounds suffered by the Mongol warlord."

Doc Savage's trilling piped out, low and vague, slowly rising to a curious wandering of sound. It ebbed away into silence.

Doc stated firmly, "The inscription on the block of ice encasing this man clearly said, 'If I still lived, mankind would tremble.'"

"The identical inscription is to be found on the tomb in Samarkand," retorted the other.

Of all of Doc Savage's men, only archaeologist Johnny Littlejohn spoke the Mongol tongue. He had heard and understood every word.

The skeletal archaeologist came striding up, and inserted himself into the discussion. "What is the name of this anthropologist?" he demanded of the Commissar.

The name was given.

Johnny made a whistling mouth, but no sound emerged. He turned to Doc Savage and said in English, "The man in question has an excellent reputation."

Doc nodded, for the anthropologist's name was well known in the west.

Frowning, Johnny asked, "If the man who has been disinterred from Tamerlane's tomb is, in fact, the historical warlord, then who on earth did we dig up?"

"That," returned Doc, "is the question of the hour."

Round features impatient, the Mongol commissar demanded that they speak the local language.

Doc Savage explained, "My assistant is wondering which of the two disinterred men is the actual Tamerlane."

A rough laugh emerged from the Mongol's open mouth.

"The one who was buried in his tomb. Who else?"

The others fell to laughing, as if the bronze man's question was somehow idiotic.

Then, the squat Commissar added, "The ice cave you mentioned is a thousand miles from the Otrar, in the Kazakh S.S.R., where history tells us that Tamerlane succumbed to the cold of winter back in the early Fifteenth Century."

Doc Savage admitted that this was true. The two spots were very far distant. And history did record the body of Tamerlane was carried south to the city of Samarkand where it was entombed under a block of black jade in a great domed edifice.

There was no explaining away, or accounting for, the discrepancy. It did tend to cast doubt on the bronze man's rather bold assertions.

Doc Savage changed the subject slightly. "The discovery of a man who has been in suspended animation is tremendous scientific import," he pointed out. "No matter who this individual is, his story should be heard. If the Japanese come into possession of him, that knowledge will be lost to Mongolia, and to modern science."

The Commissar said shortly, "We are not worried about the loss of this iceman you claim to have found. We are at war with the Germans, and that is what must not be lost. This war."

No arguing that point. So Doc took a different tack.

"We will leave it to your government to address these issues. We may have made this discovery, but it is in your country. And therefore it is your business more than it is ours."

Johnny started to object, but a sharp glance from Doc Savage's golden eyes quelled him.

Doc said, "There is a dangerous man with the Mongol bandits who have the iceman. His name is Cadwiller Olden, and he is less than four feet tall—"

The Mongolian commissar popped his eyes and showed huge discolored teeth as he roared out another peal of laughter.

"A dangerous man, you say—standing almost four feet in height?"

Doc suppressed any urge to argue the point. "He was our prisoner, but managed to slip away. Olden is a wanted criminal in America, and we would like to take possession of him."

The Commissar nodded, regaining control of his mirth.

"If we capture him, and he survives, we may mail him back to you in America. Provided we can find the proper postage."

And the Commissar shook his great belly with fresh laughter.

DOC SAVAGE made bronze blocks with his metallic fists, and seemed on the point of losing his normally tranquil temper. The golden flakes of his uncanny eyes swirled more briskly, as if an aureate snowstorm was brewing therein.

Instead of responding as he felt, Doc reminded, "We are stuck here. We cannot refuel."

"You carry money with which to buy gasoline?"

"We do."

"American dollars?"

Doc nodded.

"Good! American dollars are worth a great deal. If you have sufficient dollars, we will fill all your tanks."

It seemed that the bargain was as simple as that. Doc Savage produced his greenbacks, and hoses were brought forth to fill his fuel tanks. They were commodious. This took about an hour.

This time the bronze man and his aides conferred in the security of their plane cabin, which had been thoroughly searched in their absence. Some items were missing. Nothing important, however. Knowing of the suspicious inquisitiveness of the Russian authorities, Monk and Renny had taken pains to lock up all weapons before landing.

Monk wanted to know, "Now that we got gas, do we fly back to the Mongol camp, or do we head home?"

Doc Savage replied, "Our hands are evidently tied. With this new information, there is sufficient doubt cast upon the identity of the man pulled from the ice cave. We may have to let the Mongolian authorities sort the matter out."

Johnny looked crestfallen, but said nothing.

"What about Olden?" asked Ham.

"As much as it may rankle us," replied Doc, "we are at the mercy of Soviet authorities. If they capture Olden, we will press for his return."

Long Tom muttered, "We can't just let that sawed-off rascal get away from us."

"This is a nation at war," counseled Doc. "We do not want to overplay our hand."

Monk pounded a furry fist into a meaty opposite palm. "So we just take off and go home with our tails between our legs? We hardly got to do any fightin'."

Doc remonstrated, "We did not come here to fight. This is a scientific expedition, you will recall."

There was not a great deal of emotion in the bronze man's admonition, but Monk immediately subsided as if there had been.

It was Johnny Littlejohn who raised the next objection.

"Doc, hear me out. What if the man in the ice is the real Tamerlane? Suppose he falls into the hands of the Japanese?"

The bronze man was slow in replying. He was evidently calculating possibilities.

"Tamerlane was marching on his way to conquer China. Japan has done a fair job of seizing portions of it in our time. It is difficult to see, or even predict, which way events might flow. In any event, the United States is not at war with any nation in this part of Asia. We cannot become embroiled in events which might spiral out of control."

Johnny Littlejohn's coat-hanger shoulders sagged. He looked as if he wanted to weep. Instead, he took out his monocle magnifier and began polishing it in a grim silence.

There was no arguing with Doc Savage. But it was plain that the gangling geologist was unhappy with the present course and future trend of events.

Noticing that Johnny was over-polishing his magnifier, Renny clapped him on his knobby spine and boomed, "Cheer up! Maybe you'll find another ice cave somewhere with something better preserved inside."

Renny's well-meaning gesture all but knocked the wordy archeologist off his booted feet. The big-fisted engineer, who for a pastime liked to haul off and bust in stout doors just to show that it could be done, often forgot his own strength.

The casual clap nearly disjointed Johnny's loose skeleton. His magnifier jumped out of his lean fingers and he was forced to go hunting for it.

It was during this operation that Johnny started swearing. He rarely resorted to conventional profanity, and it would have taken an erudite man equipped with an unabridged dictionary to verify that the withering stream of invective dripping from the rail-thin geologist's parted lips could be so classified, but the vehemence with which Johnny erupted in curse words convinced the others that it was so.

Long Tom muttered to no one in particular, "I've never seen the gawky string-bean so worked up before."

Ham clucked, "I have."

"Yeah, when?" Renny wondered.

"Last month, when I told him that he missed out on exploring those weird ruins down in the Caribbean. The ones the Navy blew to pieces when they shelled that dead volcanic cay. Johnny sounded exactly like that, except he turned around and kicked a chair first.*

After a while, Monk asked, "When do we take off?"

Doc Savage told him, "There is no hurry about that. I am sure we will be permitted to remain for a while. It may be possible to monitor events as they move toward a conclusion."

This seemed to brighten the faces of his assembled aides. Having come all this way, they were in no hurry to depart. They also understood that if danger threatened, action might result.

When they emerged from the conference to step out onto the tarmac, the Mongolian commissar rushed up to meet them.

"We have reports of a Japanese aircraft, a transport plane, searching the skies in the vicinity you described. It is escorted by a number of unmarked warplanes. They appear to be searching for something."

"Yes?"

"Our wireless operators have been listening in on their radio communications. We have a good idea what they are looking for."

"Go on."

"They are looking for you, Comrade Savage," advised the Commissar.

---

* *Phantom Lagoon*

Chapter XXIV
COUNTERATTACK

THE REACTIONS OF Doc Savage and his five men would have been predictable to anyone who knew them.

Renny Renwick spoke first. "Holy cow!" he roared, causing the Mongolian commissar to visibly flinch. The latter placed blunt fingers in each ear, lest the verbal thunder repeat.

Monk muttered, "For the love of mud!"

Long Tom Roberts narrowed pale eyes and looked as if he wanted to haul off and sock someone.

Johnny Littlejohn was still in the aircraft, searching for his missing monocle. But the Commissar's words reached his ears, and he stuck his startled head out the door, blurting, "I'll be superamalgamated!"

"Damnable turn of events," murmured Ham Brooks, giving his sword cane a wringing.

For his part, Doc Savage said nothing. If his trilling escaped him, it was brief and lost in the commotion made by his excited men. The bronze giant was taken aback by this news, as was evidenced by a brisker whirling of his golden orbs.

Addressing the Mongolian functionary, Doc asked in a steady voice, "Are you certain of your facts?"

"Indeed, my information is unimpeachable," replied the Red officer, nodding.

Doc Savage told him, "There is no reason that the Japanese air forces would be looking for me, other than the fact that I discouraged their warplanes while they were flying into your territory."

"This may be," admitted the Commissar. "But they continue to swarm over Mongolian soil. Unless they are planning an incursion such as they attempted along the Khalkha River two years ago," he added, "these Japanese pilots appear determined to hunt you down."

Doc said simply, "I have no explanation other than the one I have offered."

The Commissar studied Doc Savage intently for a time.

"There is a way to flush out the truth," he murmured at last, "as my ancestors flushed out the wolves of the steppes during the winter hunts."

Doc returned the Mongol's steady gaze.

"And that is?"

"For you to return to the zone of their operations, and see what happens when they locate you."

A subtle silence followed this pronouncement. The bronze giant remained impassive, as was his habit, but the faces of his men lit up with a curious anticipation. The Mongol official's challenge to Doc Savage promised action. That this action was laced with danger, if not sudden death, mattered not one whit. The five adventurers had flown a great deal of distance, and had not yet had their fill of violent amusement.

Going back to the days when they first met, this was the glue that held them together. Adventure in its rawest form. It was like meat and drink to them.

They were wise enough to hold their tongues while Doc Savage considered the proposition.

At length, the bronze man stated, "I accept your challenge."

The Commissar bestowed upon Doc Savage a broad smile.

"I've heard tales of your bravery," he said warmly. "It is good to see with my own eyes that none of it was exaggerated. I will obtain permission for you to embark upon your foolhardy mission, along with my wishes that you discover the truth behind these strange maneuvers or, if you should die, that your deaths will be swift and glorious."

"Thank you," said Doc.

Then, the Commissar bustled off to the nearest telephone to obtain the necessary official permissions.

DOC SAVAGE turned to his men and said, "As I informed that official, the reason for the Japanese interest in our activities baffles me."

Renny slammed his two blocky fists together, producing a sound that was amazingly like concrete being struck by a sledgehammer. "Holy cow!" he boomed out. "Let's get to the bottom of this crazy stew!"

To which Monk Mayfair added, "Renny's right. Somethin's up. We should dig into it."

There were no dissenters. Doc had not expected any objection. He knew how his men felt about the situation, and its unfinished complexion.

"We have three objectives," he told them. "The first is to smoke out the Japanese raiders. The second is to recover Cadwiller Olden, if that is possible."

Johnny piped up, new life in his scholastic voice. "And the third?"

"Unraveling the enigma of the man from the ice."

The big-worded geologist threw his hat into the air and grinned alarmingly like a pleased skeleton.

Piling into the aircraft, they made preparations for a hasty take-off.

Doc Savage had already warmed up the engines when the Mongolian commissar came rushing up once more, waving his arms excitedly.

"The leadership gives its blessing for allowing the Japanese warplanes to find you."

"What does your leadership expect me to do once this happens?" returned Doc.

The short-framed Commissar produced his biggest grin.

"The leadership," he told Doc Savage, "sincerely hopes that you destroy every plane and pilot that has the misfortune to encounter you."

Doc nodded. "What will your Air Force be doing about this matter in the meantime?"

The Commissar was unusually frank. "In a time of war, with the enemy approaching our capital of Moscow, we cannot afford to lose any planes in any action that is not a declared war. Nor can we violate the neutrality pact the Kremlin signed with Tokyo only last spring. Our pilots have therefore been instructed to stand down. In the hope that you will do our dirty work for us, you see."

"Understood," said Doc, clapping the plane door shut.

The Commissar hastily withdrew.

Props began ticking over, exhaust bayonets coughing malodorous smoke. Soon, they were roaring. As the big plane trundled about, Doc Savage pointed the nose and four yowling motors into the Mongolian wind, which was blowing from the south, the direction they were bound.

Doc Savage sent the plane racing down the tarmac, and into the air with less than half the runway normally needed for such a take-off. It was evident from the bronze man's flying that he was in a great hurry to meet up with the searching Japanese fighter planes.

Chapter XXV
TALE OF TIMUR

IT HAD TAKEN some hours of hard work to scrub out the carburetors of the stranded Japanese pursuit aircraft, but the pilots were diligent in their duty, and they understood their peril. The longer the planes sat immobile and unprotected in the vast Mongolian scrubland, the more likely that a Mongolian Air Force patrol would happen upon them.

On the ground, they would be sitting ducks for an aerial attack. But finally, the work was completed.

Captain Kensa Kan watched his warplanes take off, one by one, and wing north. They spread out, putting great distance between their wings in another effort to avoid detection.

Their orders were to seek and locate the Doc Savage plane.

Captain Kan did not tell his pilots what to do should that happen, other than to radio back its location.

That matter momentarily settled, the Captain returned to the Mongol camp where the diminutive man who called himself Monzingo Baldwin sat under guard, along with Chinua's Mongol horde and the mysterious man who had been excavated from the ice cave.

The latter had fully returned to consciousness and was complaining in a wheezy, croaking voice.

Captain Kan strode up to him, looked down upon his hideously ugly countenance, and listened to the bullfrog voice as it manufactured angry words.

The croaking made the warrior's precise words difficult to follow, for the Mongol tongue was not the natural one for Kensa Kan. But after following it for a time with his ears, the Japanese made out the gist of the old man's ravings.

"This ugly old toad is threatening to cut off my head," the Captain told Cadwiller Olden.

Olden responded, "If he is who he is supposed to be, his threat is no joke. By reputation, Tamerlane is supposed to have piled the heads of his victims as high as houses. I studied his life once. He was—is—a remarkable general of men. History records that when Tamerlane laid siege to a certain town in Turkey, he promised no bloodshed if its citizens surrendered without resistance. After they did, he had three thousand prisoners buried alive. When the conquered survivors complained, the Great Sultan pointed out that he had kept his oath to the letter. No more."

Kensa Kan made a bitter face. "It remains to be seen if his identity is what you all believe it to be."

Chinua spoke up then. Somehow he had divined the trend of the exchange, although it was not spoken in his native language. "This is truly Timur, a great warlord of an earlier day. Let no tongue speak otherwise."

The sincerity of the bandit chief's words impressed the Japanese officer. He was almost prepared to believe that the miserable shaking creature was in actuality the terrible scourge of the ancient world.

In the croaking man's own language, the Captain told the ugly one, "I am Captain Kensa Kan of Japanese intelligence. I am told that once, long ago, you sought to conquer China."

"Only my imminent death prevented this from coming to pass," croaked out the shivering specter.

"Yet you are not dead," retorted Kan. "Explain this to me."

A hideous smile crawled along the grotesque features of the icy individual.

"I fell ill on the march," he barked out. The memory seemed to cause a terrible shudder to rack his rangy frame. "I was taken to a palace in Otrar, where doctors tended to me for many weeks. But to no avail. Seeing that my demise was inevitable, I bade my officers to pack me in ice in the hopes of breaking my fever. This failed to work as I wished. Sensing that death was near, I told them to complete the packing of my body in ice, in the hope that death could be staved off forever. It came to me in a dream to do this. I saw my great ancestor, Genghis Khan, in this vision. He told me to do as he bid. So I commanded my men to obey this vision of the Great Khan. It was done, and so I closed my eyes and slept."

"Until this day," murmured Captain Kensa Kan.

"You see me here, vital and breathing. Now bring me hot tea!"

The officer reflected on the tales he had read of the terrible scourge that was Tamerlane. Wounded at a young age, he was said to have limped all through adulthood, hence his famous name, Timur *il-Lenk*—Timur the Lame.

"Stand up," commanded the Captain. "Let me see how you walk about."

With some difficulty due to the long period in which his muscles were confined to a single position, the old Mongol clambered to his feet, and commenced stamping about in a slow, halting circle.

The icy one walked with a hitching limp so pronounced that it was clear that one leg was permanently maimed.

Observing this, the Japanese captain wore a stiff expression of dawning belief. He reflected upon the histories that insisted that Timur had claimed to be descended by blood from Genghis Khan, in order to cement his legitimacy as a leader of the Mongol people. History called that a calculated lie, one concocted for political reasons, for Timur was neither Mongol, nor of the same faith as the Mongolian people, then or now. He had been a Moslem.

Thus, his fanciful vision was probably a further fabrication. Oddly, this added to the Captain's reluctant willingness to believe the old man's representations.

"I believe you, great Khan of the past," he said at last.

Timur came to a shaky stop, and regarded the Captain with his canine yellow eyes.

"I was not a khan, but an emir," he husked.

The assertion served to cement the Captain's growing acceptance of the other man's identity. In life, Timur *il-Lenk* was not called Khan, but Emir. A prince, not a king of the Mongol horde.

His body still shaking, Timur asked of the Captain, "How many years have passed since my entombment?"

Kan said directly, "Not years. Centuries. Five in number."

The unwinking yellow eyes began fluttering, as if unwilling to believe the report.

Finally, Timur found his voice. "What of my empire?"

"Broken and sundered into pieces. Scattered to the winds."

Now the old man's eyes ceased fluttering. They grew cold and steady, the way a viper's orbs do when regarding prey.

"What befell my capital, Samarkand?" croaked the other.

"Samarkand still stands. There is a tomb there, in which your body is said to reside."

This challenge was greeted with no animosity. Instead, Timur explained, "With my dying breath, I gave instructions that a false Timur be buried in a great tomb, so no one would seek my true body until the time came for me to awaken, to pick up my war sword where I left off."

The Captain looked back and said, "In your long absence, China has never been conquered. But my illustrious Emperor has begun the task you failed to achieve." His back stiffened rigidly when he spoke the last sentence and a fanatic light flamed in his dark eyes.

A creepy smile crawled across the ugly face of Timur. "Then perhaps I will conquer your empire, so that I may rule China at last."

The casual nerve with which these words were spoken deeply impressed Captain Kensa Kan. He almost believed that this shivering, crippled old man possessed the steely will and inner strength to attack and overthrow the Empire of Japan, which had been spreading throughout Asia for a decade.

"I will admit to you that China has not yet been completely subjugated."

Timur demanded, "Do you seek now my assistance and counsel in this matter?"

Nonplussed, the Captain was momentarily speechless. He was anticipating no such thing. But the idea of obtaining advice on the further conquest of Asia from a man who virtually conquered the eastern world and had been making inroads on the west before his death was intriguing to him.

"It would interest me to hear your thoughts on the matter," allowed the Captain.

"Fetch me a map. And hot tea! My marrow feels like ice."

Captain Kensa Kan instructed his aide to do that very thing.

PRESENTLY, a great military map of all of Asia was brought from the transport plane. This was spread out upon the ground, and Timur, with great effort and some creaking of old bones, squatted down to examine the map. He drank his hot tea greedily, as if attempting to warm his long-frozen bones.

He could not read Japanese, of course. And the names of the countries with their unfamiliar borders had to be explained to him.

After studying this awhile, and asking certain questions, Timur locked eyes with the Captain.

"Permit me to gather together an army of warriors, and I will subjugate any nation you point to on this map."

It was an intriguing thought. But privately Captain Kensa Kan doubted his military leaders in Tokyo would permit any such undertaking.

For that matter, he had been wondering what instructions they might give him had they known of his present predicament. Having captured no less than the most successful conqueror in human history, during a secret mission to ambush Doc Savage in Mongolia, might not fall so easily upon their ears.

The Captain decided not to forward this information to Tokyo lest it complicate his mission. Not just yet.

The mission of Captain Kensa Kan was a simple one. Spies in Mongolia had radioed word that an agent of Doc Savage was conducting an archaeological dig. Monitoring radio traffic, the Captain had learned of the urgent summons for the assistance of Doc Savage, and patiently waited for the bronze American to arrive in Mongolia.

Orders from Tokyo were to capture or kill Doc Savage at all costs. These were strange orders, and the Captain could not divine the ulterior motivations behind them. While it was true that tensions between the United States and the Empire of Japan had been simmering for months, and there was talk of war, at present there was no war.

To attack and capture Doc Savage would be not only risky in and of itself, but could lead to dramatic international complications. But the Captain's orders were clear. He was content not to question those orders. He was loyal to his Emperor.

If it was his task to capture and even kill the famous American, Doc Savage, then he would execute his solemn duty, removing the head of the bronze man with his officer's sword if necessary.

As these thoughts wracked the brain of Captain Kan, the wily old Mongol warlord suddenly made a move for the selfsame sword hanging in its scabbard.

It was an unexpected move. It caught the Captain entirely by surprise. A gnarled old hand lashed out, found the unguarded hilt sword and extracted the weapon.

The shining blade was suddenly in the Captain's own sandstone face.

Yellowish eyes grew hot and dark with anger. Timur laid the keen edge against the Japanese officer's pulsing jugular vein.

Snapping his pistol from its holster, Kan pointed the muzzle at Timur's snarling features.

A sword against a pistol was no contest, not even at close quarters.

The Captain fully expected the old man to drop the sword without an argument. He was shocked when the blade point abruptly shifted to his Adam's apple with deadly intent.

Kan quickly realized that Timur did not know what a pistol was. Failed to comprehend that he was one trigger squeeze away from oblivion.

This standoff occupied mere seconds of time. Several audible ticks of the Captain's wristwatch.

While the Japanese officer was attempting to phrase the proper words that would allow him to gracefully not have to shoot the old man in the face, and thereby preserve his own life, Chinua and his bandits suddenly reared up, roaring and leaping upon every Japanese in sight, Captain Kensa Kan included.

A general war broke out.

Even though their weapons were at the ready, the Japanese contingent got the worst of it from the start.

True, a few Mongol bandits were shot dead in the early campaign. But there were many more Mongols than there were Japanese Marines. The Captain had come with a mere squad of men in his transport plane.

In less than five minutes of strenuous activity, during which the flat of his own blade knocked his service pistol from his fist, and then switched back to collide with his opposite temple, Captain Kensa Kan and his detachment of Japanese Marines were overcome.

During this meleé, Cadwiller Olden, otherwise Monzingo Baldwin, once again ducked from sight.

Very little lead flew during the brief exchange of blows, but the knife work was something to behold. The Mongols had managed to stab several Japanese critically. The grunting of the Marines as their bodies were pierced spoke of their abject astonishment.

After it was all over, Cadwiller Olden crawled out from a nearby tent, and took stock of the situation.

Tamerlane and Chinua the bandit chief were conferring. Clearly, they had the situation well in hand.

The problem for Cadwiller Olden was that he spoke no Mongol. There was no way for him to plead his case. Recognizing this harsh reality, he withdrew back into the tent to await developments.

In his dark heart, Olden began scheming for a way to exploit the shifting situation. But for the present moment, he did not know what disposition Tamerlane and his new army of Mongols might make of him, should he show his tiny, pale face. It was a tongue-drying proposition, and for the first time, he began questioning the wisdom of stowing away on Doc Savage's plane.

Chapter XXVI
DEATH ORDER

DOC SAVAGE PILOTED his impressively large amphibian plane in the direction of the Mongol encampment, where he expected the downed Japanese warplanes to be stuck.

The chemical that Monk Mayfair had introduced into their engines during the earlier pursuit was one that deposited a gummy substance into the carburetors of the aircraft, effectively rendering them inoperative.

The bronze man knew that the motors could be restored to working order only after a vigorous scrubbing with detergent and water. These were luxuries that would be impossible to find in the vast wasteland of southern Mongolia.

So it was that the bronze man proved to be somewhat over-confident.

For as he flew south, Doc picked up the occasional radio communication in Japanese. Listening with him was Johnny Littlejohn, who remarked, "It sounds as if they have gotten those planes back into the air already."

From the rear, Monk Mayfair insisted, "I'll eat my hat if they did. That gummy junk is tough to get out of an aircraft motor carburetor."

Ham Brooks drawled, "If Monk does have to eat his hat, I will happily slice it into tasty segments with my cane."

"If I have to eat my hat," growled the hairy chemist, "I may make you eat that dang cane, so that we can share a meal."

The dapper lawyer frowned, momentarily at a loss for words. He was no sword swallower. Monk had once attempted to bet Ham that he, Monk, could swallow that very blade. Monk had employed a bit of sleight-of-hand to fake such a circus stunt. Not to be outclassed, Ham had attempted a similar feat—with the result that Doc Savage had to stitch up his injured tongue.

Doc listened intently, and said, "At least one warplane is aloft. It is difficult to tell about the other communications."

Renny rumbled, "That gives us something to shoot for, right?"

"It does," interposed Long Tom. "What I do not understand is why we are the bait in a double trap."

"Double trap?" wondered Monk, grimacing like a gorilla.

"Sure," the puny electrical wizard remarked. "The Japanese air forces are looking for us, and we don't know why. The Mongolian Air Force wants to see what the Japanese will do if they find us. It's a double snare. We just don't know why we ended up as the cheese in this particular rat-trap."

Ham Brooks mused, "Official relations between Washington and Tokyo have been approaching a boiling point for some months now. There has been a great deal of war talk."

"Talk, sure—but no war," insisted Monk.

To which Ham added, "Tough talk always precedes war."

"But it don't necessarily lead to war," insisted Monk Mayfair. "Leastwise, not always."

Doc Savage offered no opinion on this discussion. He was busy searching the skies with his seemingly all-observing golden eyes.

In the radio cubicle, Long Tom Roberts had a pair of headphones clamped to his oversized ears. He was employing a device, a kind of electronic listener, which could detect at a very great range the sound of airplane motors, even operating from a plane with four mighty engines running in tandem.

The difficulty with this acoustical locator was that it could not be pointed in the direction of the engines—which was naturally the direction in which the aircraft flew. The listening horns were mounted in the rear of the plane, pointing away from the engine drone.

This required Doc Savage to periodically turn the plane full circle so that Long Tom could attempt to discern the sound of distant motors at different points of the compass.

It was a good principle, but in operation was proving to be disappointing.

"Anything coming in through them cans?" demanded Monk at one point.

Long Tom shushed him and pressed the earphones tightly to his head. The device was very sensitive, but at great range it was difficult to pick up the droning of engines over the normal hissing of the device in operation.

Before long, the puny electrical genius lifted his voice. "I may have something!" He sounded excited.

Doc Savage steadied the plane on its current heading, and awaited further reports.

"Try turning south-southeast," Long Tom directed.

Doc Savage wrestled the control yoke and altered the plane's course to the southeast.

"That's it! I hear something!"

"Could it be a Mongolian Air Force warplane?" suggested Ham.

"Stop being such an optimist," grumbled Long Tom sourly. "I detect an airplane motor. Let's investigate it."

Doc Savage sent the big plane shuddering around in the sky and attempted to rendezvous with the plane that Long Tom had detected. Below, the desolate steppeland gave way to the upper edge of the great Gobi Desert, which was a patchwork of terrain that ranged from arid scrubland and shining salt pans to sandy desert plateau.

IF there was a prowling plane, they failed to find it. Not terribly surprising. They were moving too fast, and any fighter plane would be difficult to make out beyond the range of a few short miles. Owing to the vast distances involved, they might pass a warbird and fail to perceive it.

Long Tom went back to his headphones, and his sour face grew intent.

Another forty minutes of flying, and dusk began to show, along with the first lonely stars of the approaching night.

Monk muttered, "Gonna get harder to spot anything in another hour."

That pronouncement prompted Doc Savage to do a bold thing. Triggering his microphone, he began broadcasting on the same wavelength as the Japanese warplanes.

"This is Doc Savage calling. Doc Savage to unidentified aircraft. Identify yourself."

Doc repeated this call several times, in a normal voice. But his men knew what he was doing. The bronze giant was attempting to lure any Japanese aircraft operating within radio range into seeking out their flying boat.

It was not long before the bait was taken. Not one, but two Japanese warplanes came charging at them from different directions.

Doc spoke up. "This is Doc Savage to unidentified warplanes. Doc Savage to unidentified warplanes. State your intentions. Repeat. State your intentions."

The intentions of the Japanese pursuit pilots were not offered directly. Instead, the pilots radioed to someone in command, reporting that they had found the Doc Savage plane, and excitedly requested immediate instructions.

Johnny followed these reports perfectly, translating for the others.

After a while, a thin voice came screeching back over the ether.

"This is Captain Kan. You have your instructions. Shoot down the Doc Savage plane. Repeat. Shoot down the Doc Savage plane at once!"

"Zounds!" bleated Johnny. "They mean to do us in!"

Doc Savage threw the big aircraft into a wild spin just ahead of the first strings of phosphorescent tracers lancing through the dusky sky.

"What's happening?" howled Ham in a wild voice.

Johnny translated for him.

"A Japanese officer has ordered us to be shot out of the sky!"

"Is he crazy? That would provoke an international outrage!"

"Crazy or not," yelled Monk, "them Japs are serious. I spy tracers all around us."

Doc flung the plane about, and the expression on his metallic features was nearly molten.

Once again, pursuit planes proved far more agile than Doc Savage's big amphibious flying boat. No matter how the bronze man ruddered the aircraft, climbed, or stalled, slipping off a wing, there was a limit to the wild maneuvering the ponderous ship could take.

On the other hand, the nimble warplanes danced about the sky, performing pirouettes and chandelles, coming at the big aircraft from every conceivable direction to empty the belts of their wing-mounted 7.7-mm machine guns.

Shoving open windows, Monk and the others cut loose.

They had replaced their superfirer drums with ordinary lead. So the directed streams of slugs were capable of doing real damage to the opposing fighters. The caliber of the tiny weapons was not formidable, but their velocity was considerable. Furthermore, it was very difficult to aim while Doc Savage put the great aircraft through its paces.

Renny got lucky, and managed to snip off pieces of one warplane stabilizer, but failed to do any more damage than to imbue the startled pilot with a sudden dose of caution.

Warplanes roared on and on, hammering at the flashing leviathan, striking in its belly, its sides and its wings and empennage.

176 / A DOC SAVAGE ADVENTURE

Once again, the bulletproof properties of the plane could only stand so much. Glass began knocking out of windows, showering the interior cabin with chunks of crystal-like shards.

One plane motor was smoking, and seized up. Then another emitted a grunting cough, followed by a belch of evil-looking smoke from its exhaust blades.

The only thing that saved them was that both pilots ran out of machine gun ammunition before they could down the silver aircraft. For some reason, they refrained from using their cannon, perhaps due to a lack of shells. This was not a Chinese war theater.

But sufficient damage was done. Doc Savage announced, "This plane will have to be put on the ground."

"We'll be sittin' ducks down there!" moaned Monk.

"Only if the Japanese commander sends additional warplanes," stated Doc. "Our present foes have exhausted their bite."

Then Doc Savage, face grave as metal, slanted the big plane down and snapped on the wing floodlights, seeking a safe stretch of scrub on which to plant the descending air wheels.

Chapter XXVII
SKY SKIRMISH

O NCE THEY WERE out of ammunition, the two Japanese fighter planes loitered for a few minutes in the air. From his radio cubicle, Long Tom reported that it sounded as if they were reporting to their commander. He cut in the transmission through the cabin loudspeaker.

Doc Savage listened intently, then said, "They are providing precise directions to our whereabouts for another wave of planes."

After that, the two fighters disappeared in the direction of the Manchurian border.

Doc Savage said, "Renny and I will investigate the damage to the engines. Johnny and Long Tom will prepare to fend off the attack. Monk, excavate cases marked 47-MET from our stores."

"Gotcha, Doc," said Monk.

Every man leaped to his responsibilities without another thought. Their prior wartime training served them well even in their peacetime pursuits.

Exiting the flying boat, Doc Savage fell to an examination of the most damaged of the four motors. Renny took the other, which was the outer starboard engine.

After only a few minutes of examination, the big-fisted engineer reported to Doc Savage, "We can fix this one. How about yours?"

Doc shook his head slowly. "Beyond repair."

Renny grunted, "We can fly on three motors, can't we?"

"Once the disabled engine is repaired."

Doc investigated that engine, and saw that it would be a three-hour job, using spare parts from the emergency stores.

"Three hours?" blared Renny. "Those Jap warbirds will be back in less than one."

Doc Savage said gravely, "We will leave the repairs until after the battle."

By now dusk was shading into early evening, and once again a Mongolian moon was rising in the night sky. It shed an effulgence that was like a massive silver floodlight, creating long, lean, spectral shadows.

The great emptiness of the Gobi was an impressive thing. It possessed a queer spiritual quality of indescribable loneliness. They shook off the eerie sensation and got down to work.

Long Tom and Johnny had charged every supermachine pistol in their stores with solid slugs. There were plenty of spares.

The pale electrical wizard remarked sourly, "These won't do us much good unless they try to strafe us from a low altitude."

"A presentiment of portentous ominosity," said Johnny, seeming to remember his habit of using long words.

Doc Savage told him, "We will try something else first."

Monk emerged from the aircraft, dragging a very large case, larger than a typical steamer trunk. Its mate was already lying on the ground. Both were locked.

As Monk laid his burden on the ground, Doc Savage went to the first case and began throwing latches, after which he lifted the lid.

The others crowded around. Inside were nestled flat, rubbery bladders as pale as sunfish.

Long Tom muttered, "They look kinda like weather balloons."

"They are," said Doc. "But on a much smaller scale."

Monk flung open his container, and the exposed contents were similar, but in this case the weather balloons, instead of being the regulation white, were a mixture, half white and the rest extremely black.

Renny muttered, "I don't get this."

Monk grinned. "You watch. We're gonna lay a trap for them babies."

Still grinning, the hairy chemist disappeared into the ship, coming back with an industrial-sized helium tank balanced over one sloping shoulder.

Setting it on the ground lengthwise, Monk plunged into filling the black and white balloons. Doc Savage joined in, and the two took turns inflating the rubbery envelopes.

These were equipped with trailing lines which ended in what looked like loose netting, anchored by small black balls that were composed of solid rubber.

Renny the engineer looked these devices over, and a knowing gleam came into his eyes.

"I take back what I said earlier," he grunted. "These are kind of like barrage balloons, aren't they?"

Doc admitted, "That is a fair description. In a manner of speaking, they are."

Monk occupied the better part of forty minutes filling the balloons, and anchoring them to any shrub or rock they could locate.

Before long, they had cultivated a fantastic garden of strange round flowers. The balloons fluttered about their anchorage, propelled by vagrant, ever-shifting winds.

When they were done, Doc instructed Long Tom to kill all the lights on the aircraft. Then they waited.

The rising moon encountered parading banks of dark clouds, so the lunar light turned fitful and intermittent.

Doc studied the heavens, and saw that the ominous thunderheads were coming in their direction.

Seeing this, Ham Brooks said, "We are getting a break."

Doc told him, "We cannot count on the cloud cover for very long. And moonlight will make the skin of our aircraft shine against the ground."

THE DRONE of airplanes came close to the top of the hour by Ham Brooks' watch.

"Release the white balloons first," directed Doc.

Everyone scrambled to take hold of the lines and unhook a balloon. Soon, the bobbing rubberized spheres were rising into the sky in the general direction of the droning, for that was whither the wind happened to blow.

"Another break," murmured Ham.

As he watched the balloons lift off, spaced well apart, Long Tom remarked to no one in particular, "Odds are they'll spot these things."

The Zeros seemed to do exactly that. They roared up in a V formation, six of them. Evidently, the original two had been reinforced.

As they approached, blundering into the aerial field of white globes, the goggled pilots executed frantic maneuvers, breaking off from one another and attempting to evade the balloons, whose purpose they did not understand but did not desire to discover firsthand.

One pilot was not as quick as the others and chanced to fly smack into one of the bobbing balloons. With the result that the aircraft sliced the thing apart with its port wing.

"So far, not so good," muttered Monk, tiny eyes glowing with anticipation.

"Prepare to release the black balloons," directed Doc Savage.

There was a general scramble to take hold of the remaining anchored balloons. These might have been oblate mushrooms growing from the turf.

The Japanese pilots demonstrated their discipline in that, after they had circled around, they lined up in a fresh formation and thundered on toward the stricken amphibian lying on the ground.

"Now!" clipped Doc.

A flotilla of black balloons lifted into the night sky, all but invisible. Doc held the last two in his hands, pacing the ground, watching the oncoming planes, his gaze going frequently to the marching thunderclouds and their unreliable sky cover.

Then he released the last two balloons.

The timing of the maneuver was not perfect. Nor could it be certain the black balloons were entirely invisible against the night sky.

They all watched and waited, barely breathing.

It became obvious that the fighter planes were dropping when the key and pitch of the oncoming motors changed from an approaching buzz to a kind of a whining howl.

Ham exclaimed, "They're diving!"

"Into the plane," rapped Doc.

They piled into the aircraft, slammed shut the hatch, and lay down on the floor of the cabin, below the line of the windows. They knew that the surviving glass would not hold for very long under the hateful hammering of machine gun fire.

The warplane whine lifted into a scream. They listened intently, no one less than Doc Savage, whose hearing was acute beyond belief.

"Here they come!" Renny boomed. "Holy cow!"

Doc silenced him with the squeeze of one arm. He was listening hard. The sound of the engines began to change to a hesitant sputtering, followed by the choking of engines.

They waited for the first strafing run to commence.

It was not exactly an unqualified success. The sound of the machine guns did not reach their ears first, but the drumming and kicking of bullets around the aircraft did.

That it was no simple matter to successfully strafe a large aircraft in the dark became evident when the first wave zoomed overhead, pulled out of their dives, and the big flying boat barely rocked on its wheels.

"Missed!" howled Monk.

Again, Doc signaled for silence.

There were auditory symptoms not consistent with six warplanes pulling out of power dives.

As the sound of the retreating planes diminished in volume, other sounds could be heard. These were indications of airplane motors in distress.

Then came a distinct jar—an aircraft struck the earth with a distinct bump.

The sound came from the west, and Doc popped his head up to peer out a window. He was greeted by a brief flare, indicating a fire, followed by a rather dull explosion, as the gas tanks of a downed Japanese plane ignited.

That brought everybody looking to the windows.

A second fighter was jockeying around in the sky, evidently struggling, and attempting to land in distress.

They could not see it clearly, except to note that it seemed to be dragging one of the black balloons, which jittered madly about.

Monk shouted, "We got two of them!"

Another sound, telling of a hard landing, caused Ham to correct the hairy chemist.

"I count three."

That brought everyone rushing out of the plane to take stock of the situation.

The third Zero was hammering along, trying to find level ground, and more or less succeeded.

It came down hard, its fixed wheels rattled along, duralumin alloy wings shuddering with every bump and rut encountered. Everyone noted that no engine sound was audible.

The fighter plane rolled to a rather difficult stop, after which the pilot threw black his greenhouse canopy and hopped out.

Monk unlatched the safety of his supermachine pistol, and took careful aim.

"Monk!" Doc reminded him. "That weapon is charged with solid lead."

Monk hesitated. Doc Savage had a fixed attitude toward the taking of life. He forbade it in his men. More than once in the past, Monk had managed to bend this rule, but only when the bronze man was not looking. Reluctantly, the apish chemist lowered his weapon.

Then, he shoved into the cabin door and returned with a drum of mercy bullets. Climbing onto a wing, Monk sighted on the Japanese pilot who was attempting to hide behind his aircraft.

The pilot's high-booted legs were visible, so the hairy chemist aimed for those.

The powerful little machine pistol snarled, and the area was lit up with brief flashes of light remindful of firecrackers going off. Powder percussion made their eardrums ring.

Monk hosed the weapon this way and that, ensuring that a spray of mercy bullets riddled the pilot's exposed legs.

Sure enough, he collapsed a few moments later.

Johnny had a flashlight out and pointed the beam at the plane. The propeller was a mangled tangle interspersed with the steel netting that had hung from the balloon lines.

"Supermalagorgeous!" he remarked with satisfaction.

Monk said, "Those balloons are designed to trick a pilot into avoidin' the white ones, but runnin' smack into the black ones, if the wind and altitude are right. Once the props gnash into the hangin' mesh, they get fouled in the metal lines, makin' it impossible to fly."

"Slick!" said Long Tom approvingly. "We cut our problem in half."

As if to emphasize that point, the three surviving Zeros returned, slanting down out of the sky.

There had not been much moonlight before, but now cracks appeared in the cloud cover like veins of silver in a gigantic aerial mine.

There were enough shafts of moonlight to paint the planes in a lunar effulgence.

"That ain't good," grumbled Monk.

Ham contradicted him at once, saying waspishly, "Moonlight makes them better targets too, you dope." He climbed onto the wing with his superfirer in hand.

Monk, possibly showing off, gripped one in each hairy hand. Seeing this, and not to be outdone, Renny Renwick also pulled out a spare weapon and filled his large fist with it. Of them all, Renny was probably the best machine gunner in the group, having distinguished himself in the Great War with his proficiency with large-caliber rapidfirers.

The Japanese warplanes swept in, the familiar and unnerving scream of their engines on approach filling the eerie desolation.

From the fists of Doc Savage's men, compact supermachine pistols started erupting. It looked as if batteries of anti-aircraft fire were opening up.

Despite the small caliber of the weapons, the rate of fire was terrific and the blazing of a high-performance smokeless gunpowder was something to behold, especially at night.

Even Doc Savage wielded a supermachine pistol, something he rarely did.

A concentrated barrage, indeed a storm of lead rose up to greet the oncoming attackers.

Of course, the battle birds had the advantage, shooting down from above, as well as having greater range.

At the same time, they did not expect what appeared to be a prodigious amount of defensive fire to greet them.

This threw the Zero pilots for a loop, figuratively speaking. They riddled the ground around the plane, clipped duralumin shreds off the wings, and then broke in different directions, fearful of being caught in the explosive return fire.

Corkscrewing for altitude, they prepared to make another pass.

All of the supermachine pistols were designed to expend over three hundred rounds per minute; their firepower was prodigious. Consequently, every drum soon ran empty. There was a mad scramble to reload.

Monk complained, "I only got one drum left."

Renny tossed him a spare, saying, "Take this."

Johnny was perhaps the most nervous of them all and had emptied both his first drum as well as his spare. His gaunt face stricken, he plunged into the plane to get another.

The bony geologist came out, clipping a fresh canister into the receiver, and prepared for the next wave of attackers.

They were not long in coming.

THIS time the trim Zeros drove in from different angles, in order to foil concentrated fire from below.

Aiming their weapons at different compass points, Doc Savage's men set their supermachine pistols to hooting and the combined reverberation that was so remindful of the bass string of a titanic bullfiddle commenced assaulting their ears.

Suddenly, one fighter exploded into a ball of fire, passed over their heads like a flaming arrow, so low they could smell the stink of burning engine fuel.

"What the heck just happened?" Monk demanded, open-mouthed.

"Someone fired explosive shells," Doc Savage said sternly.

The bronze man's flake-gold eyes fixed Monk Mayfair with a vaguely accusing gaze.

Shrugging his shoulders, Monk brought his weapons up so that the drums could be seen. To distinguish the contents of individual ammunition canisters, the bronze man painted distinguishing colors on each drum itself. Monk showed that his drums were painted green, indicating mortal lead.

"It wasn't me!" squeaked the homely chemist.

"A likely story!" retorted Ham. "It would be just like you to doctor the drums."

Angrily, Monk protested, "Don't listen to that shyster! I'm tellin' the truth. Honest!"

From nearby, Johnny Littlejohn gave out a stricken groan. It was the longest sound ever to come out of the gangling geologist that was not composed of words.

Johnny was looking at his superfirer, whose muzzle continued to smoke. His eyes were upon the drum, which was painted red.

"I have committed a catastrophic atrocity!" he said to no one in particular.

Doc went to him, saw that the drum was marked for explosive shells.

Johnny looked at Doc Savage and said in a croaky voice, "In my haste, I must have grabbed the wrong drum."

Doc nodded wordlessly. It appeared to be an honest mistake. Nothing could be done about it now. The downed Japanese warplane was a blazing ball of fire, cackling ghoulishly not far from them.

The sight of the destroyed aircraft duly impressed the two surviving Japanese pilots. They circled for a time, as if torn between duty and their sense of self-preservation.

Finally, they made a last pass and emptied their machine guns into the hard-packed desert floor. It was a half-hearted effort at best. The pilots were not trying very hard. It appeared as if they were eager to empty their weapons, and go home with a certain amount of dignity intact.

As they flew off, Ham remarked, "Well, Johnny did us a favor anyway."

The bronze man said nothing. Loss of life under any circumstances was something he preferred to avoid. But he understood how, in the heat of battle, the error had been made. So he did not comment further.

They made a search for any surviving pilots. They found only the man felled by Monk's machine pistol. He could not be awakened even with a stimulant that Doc Savage tried on him.

Rising from the man's form, Doc said, "He will not awaken until morning, for his system is filled with anesthetic chemical."

"I wanted to make sure he went down," Monk grumbled.

"Probably nothing we could get out of him anyway," reminded Renny.

Long Tom said as they walked away from the insensate pilot, "It would be worth knowing why they're all fired up to get us."

The answer to that conundrum would have to wait. They retreated to the plane and set about repairing the salvageable engine. This operation took until morning, and by the time dawn was breaking over the east, making the cool air seem warm when it really was not, Doc Savage announced, "We should be able to fly."

"Fly to where?" Long Tom asked.

Doc Savage said, "We appear to have defeated the Japanese warplanes operating in this area. It may be safe to return to the Mongol camp and discover what we can there."

All eyes went to Johnny Littlejohn, for they knew that his interest in locating the man who had been excavated from ice and restored to life was very keen.

But Johnny appeared to be in somewhat of a daze. He offered no remark, nor did he show any signs of eagerness.

Taking Doc Savage aside, Renny remarked in an undertone that could be heard almost a mile away, "Johnny just isn't himself. He's hardly used any of his jawbreaker words since we got here. That's not like him, not at all."

Doc Savage did not respond to that except to say, "We will take off now."

Chapter XXVIII
DEAD ENDS

THE MOOD IN the cabin of the great flying leviathan was grimly silent as Doc Savage approached the ring of scrubby hills where the Mongol felt tents had once sprawled.

Had, being the operative word.

Renny was the first to exclaim, "Holy cow! The blamed Mongols decamped."

Doc overflew the flat cup amid the hills and saw the camp was no longer there.

Johnny commented in a dispirited voice, "Mongolia yurts, or *gers*, as they are known locally, are constructed so they can be taken down and packed away by cart and horseback."

Doc flew about for a while, looking for signs of the missing bandit band. There were none. Turning back to the camp, he set the big plane down, and then left to investigate on foot.

The truth became apparent to Doc Savage as he examined the signs in the sandy terrain.

"The Mongols did not ride off," he told his men. "They were taken aboard the Japanese transport plane."

"Blazes!" Monk yowled. "Does that mean that Olden and the ogre from the ice, too?"

Doc nodded grimly. "All indications are that they left together. Chinua, his Mongols, and apparently their tents as well."

"What about their horses?" Renny demanded. "They didn't pack those on a transport plane!"

Nor had they. The horses were discovered to be running loose. Having scattered in all directions, they had not been visible from the air.

"What does it all mean?" Ham complained.

No one had an answer for him. Nor did the urgency with which the Japanese wanted to strike the bronze man dead become apparent.

Long Tom said, "They probably lit off for Manchuria. Do we follow them?"

Doc Savage shook his head slowly. "To do so would constitute a provocation we can neither afford, nor likely win."

"That's it?" demanded Renny. "We slammed into another consarned dead end?"

"We have no choice in the matter," replied Doc Savage.

There being no better course of action available to them, they boarded the plane and flew north to the capital of Mongolia, no wiser than before.

THERE was a surprise waiting for them at the Ulan Bator airport.

The short Mongolian Commissar once again came rushing up while Doc Savage braked the plane and Renny flung open the hatch door.

The functionary was not alone. Accompanying him was a Russian, not in uniform. This man was tall and lean and very excitable.

The Commissar made introductions.

"Comrade Savage," he began, "may I present Comrade Gerasimov. Comrade, this is the famous Doc Savage, who claims to have discovered the preserved body of Tamerlane in an ice cave many miles from here."

This conversation took place in Russian, and before the Commissar finished his formal introduction, Comrade Gerasimov was waving his arms and putting up a fuss.

The bronze man listened to a good deal of this, then cut the man off.

"We have not as yet ascertained the exact identity of the individual excavated from the ice cavern," he said simply.

This did not calm the Russian one whit. He continued his harangue.

Calmly, Doc Savage let the man talk himself out. It became clear that the Russian was no less than the Soviet anthropologist who had been given permission to exhume the body of Tamerlane in the great domed temple in faraway Samarkand.

The Russian was insisting that his body was that of the true Tamerlane.

"His hip was badly damaged, and there were other injuries to the right leg that produced lameness in life," he proclaimed. "Also, he was missing the bones of the small finger of his right hand and the one beside it, which matches historical knowledge of the man."

When the Russian finally ran out of breath, Doc stated, "I would like to see this body."

"Impossible!" the Russian spat back. "Corpse was reinterred last month. Would be impossible to obtain permission to exhume it for second time."

Johnny was an avid listener to these excited expostulations. He asked, "Have you any X-rays or photographs of this curious cadaver?"

This request was apparently anticipated, for the Russian opened up a satchel, extracting sheets of papers and glossy black X-ray negatives for inspection.

Doc Savage and Johnny climbed back into the cabin of the flying boat and pored over documents, the excitable Russian and the Mongolian commissar hovering around them. Doc's other men had gone off in search of hot food.

Doc and Johnny examined every negative and photograph and sketch presented to them, conferring quietly.

At length, Johnny spoke up. "All evidence is consistent with the man history remembers as Tamerlane."

Doc Savage nodded somberly. "Of course, many Mongol warriors suffered similar injuries. History does not record Tamerlane's injuries with exactitude."

Johnny blinked. "Are you suggesting that the body in Tamerlane's tomb might be a plant, designed to cover his true resting place?"

"Only that it is a possibility, nothing more. The evidence is merely suggestive, at best circumstantial."

The long-worded archaeologist did not know what to say to that. He seemed torn between alternative theories.

Finally, Johnny cleared his throat and in his best professorial tone expounded, "I would wager one million dollars that the man cut from ice is the actual Tamerlane."

Doc Savage said, "Do you have one million?"

Johnny swallowed guiltily. He seemed unusually rattled.

Doc Savage said, "Be careful that your emotions are not clouding your thinking. The man in the ice may be an impostor."

"If so, he is an impostor from centuries ago."

This exchange took place in English, of which the Russian anthropologist understood little. Turning to him, Doc switched to speaking Russian.

"We admit that the body in the tomb of Tamerlane may very well be that of the notorious conqueror."

Comrade Gerasimov grew excited and insisted, "Who else would it be?"

"But as yet I remain unconvinced that the man from the ice might not be Timur. Possibly a close associate, or even a relative."

The Russian seemed to take the bronze man's even-handed alternative as a slap to his face. He was all but knocked off his feet.

At that point, the Mongolian commissar interjected, "This appears to be an unsolvable riddle, but one which interests me greatly. Where is this ice man now?"

Doc replied, "In Japanese hands."

The Commissar grunted so hard his belly shook. "This is not good. This is very much not good."

"Agreed," said Doc.

The Russian anthropologist recounted, "On the coffin of Timur the Lame I discovered ominous words inscribed. They said this: 'Whoever opens my tomb will unleash an invader more terrible than I.' At first, I did not take this warning seriously, but two days after, the Nazis invaded Belarus and Ukraine. These words now give me chills."

THERE was a long silence while everyone digested the apparent prophecy.

"As Renny might say," barked Johnny, "sacrosanct bovine!"

Then the Mongol commissar remembered the hunt for Doc Savage's plane.

"Why are the Japanese seeking you, Comrade Savage?"

Doc said, "Their stated intent was to murder my men and myself."

"For what reason?"

"We do not know, but in the past we have interfered with Japanese espionage. Perhaps someone in their leadership has a long memory—and a longer reach."

The Commissar nodded slowly, his thoughts racing.

Johnny Littlejohn was going through the papers and came upon a sketch showing a Mongol leader with a high collar, pronounced cheekbones, long rat-tail mustaches and conical cap. He wore an imperious expression.

"Who is this?" he inquired of the Russian anthropologist.

"Who is this? Who is that?" sputtered the Russian. "Who do you *think* that is?"

Johnny looked blank.

Doc Savage studied the sketch and asked, "Is this your conception of Timur *il-Lenk?*"

"Conception, no!" He lifted a decisive finger in the air. "It *is* Timur! I have reconstructed exact features from skull of man buried in tomb of Timur *il-Lenk*. The likeness is ninety-nine percent true to life."

Johnny took another look at the sketch, and remarked, "This man does not resemble the one who came out of the ice. The ice man is exceedingly ugly."

"Additional proof!" insisted Gerasimov. "Timur was not ugly. He was not particularly handsome, for he was old man when he died. But he was not as ugly as horned toad."

Doc Savage interrupted, "We will leave this discussion to another time. Nothing can be done about the man from the ice, now that he has been taken to Manchuria by the Japanese."

Johnny looked stricken. "Are you saying that we are helpless to resolve this vexing problem?"

Doc Savage imparted, "Under present circumstances, it appears so."

Johnny's long face fell. But that seemed to settle the issue.

Half satisfied, the Russian anthropologist gathered up his papers, and everyone disembarked the plane with the intention of seeking out a decent meal.

It was while they were walking toward the airport commissary that Doc Savage's men came running, indeed charging toward them, looking angry and excited at the same time.

They wrenched to a halt and attempted to shout all at once.

Doc Savage calmed them down with his steady voice, instructing, "One at a time, please."

The only result of that was another attempt by Monk and the others to communicate something of great importance.

Doc cut them off. "Ham, what is the problem?"

"A bulletin just came over the radio, Doc!" the dapper lawyer shouted excitedly. He struggled to catch his breath. He was not easily winded and Doc Savage perceived that the short sprint was not what had taken his breath away. It was something else. The news he was attempting to communicate, no doubt.

Then, Ham Brooks dropped the bomb on their shocked ears.

"The Japanese Navy attacked our naval base at Pearl Harbor, Hawaii. It happened only a few hours ago." His cultured voice grew hoarse. "Doc, they sank almost every ship of the Pacific Fleet!"

In the silence that followed, Doc Savage's eerie trilling seeped out and seemed to drift in every direction at once, while failing to achieve much volume or power. It was a rather thin and forlorn sound in the cool afternoon air.

Chapter XXIX

WAR PLANS

THERE WAS A steady wind blowing through the airport at Ulan Bator, and for a long time it made the only sound that reached their ears.

The Mongolian commissar, not understanding what was going on, asked a question in his native tongue.

"What motivates this unseemly excitement?" he demanded.

Doc Savage told him in a brittle voice.

The Mongol's narrow eyes popped wide, and his blocky jaw sagged to reveal metal fillings. It took a few moments to get his jaw back into place and he swallowed twice. He grinned sheepishly.

"This means we are allies, *nyet?*"

Doc and his men stood stunned, trading glances, making motions with their hands and feet like those of men not sure what to do with themselves.

Finally, Doc Savage spoke clearly.

"It is imperative that we communicate with Washington and discover what they want us to do."

"Does this mean we're going back into uniform?" asked Long Tom.

"Very likely," clipped Doc, turning on his heel and rushing back to the big plane.

The next several hours were hectic and unproductive. Employing a secret radio frequency, Doc Savage reached out to the War Department, and other high military authorities. He had trouble getting through. There was chaos in Washington. All radio channels were jammed as casualty reports filtered in from Hawaii.

Doc took a break from his attempts at reaching the nation's capital, and concentrated on radio news flashes.

It was very bad. A sneak attack had taken place at dawn, with waves of Japanese Zeros descending upon the Pearl Harbor Naval Air Station, dropping bombs and machine gunning the ground at will.

The destruction to the Pacific Fleet was utter and all but complete. Casualties were extremely high. The attacking squadrons, having wrought their destruction, returned to waiting aircraft carriers.

Listening in, Monk Mayfair fell to growling deep in his throat. He never spoke a word. Just growled and growled, his tiny eyes fierce.

Ham Brooks unsheathed his sword cane and rammed it home again several times, handsome features red with fury.

Renny looked around for a door to smash, and decided against it. He rarely cracked his knobby knuckles, but he cracked them now. It produced a sound like firecrackers popping off.

Remarkably, Johnny was cursing in a manner that was virtually Shakespearean. No one understood a word he uttered, which prompted Monk to remark, "At least that old bag of bones is starting to sound like his normal cantankerous self."

"Shut up!" raged Johnny, who resumed his fulminations. "Those Hell-hated Visigoths!" was the most understandable of his imprecations.

Hours passed in this manner, and then came the declaration of war from the President of the United States over the radio.

" 'A day that will live in infamy,' kinda understates it," rumbled Renny.

Ham Brooks ruminated, "The Japanese attacked the Philippines, Malaya, Singapore, and Hong Kong at the same time they hit Pearl Harbor. It was all coordinated. Thailand has already fallen."

Long Tom muttered, "We're in the Army now, brothers."

Ham, a brigadier general in the last war, wondered, "I wonder if they'll reinstate us in our old ranks?"

"Me," said Monk, tapping his barrel chest with a blunt thumb, "I ain't settlin' for anything less than full colonel this time around."

Long hours later, Doc Savage finally reached the War Department. An Admiral Grayson came on the air.

Doc told him, "My scrambler is engaged."

"Good, Savage. Now listen carefully. We want you to return to the States as quickly as possible."

Doc immediately objected. "My men and I are presently in Mongolia. We can take the fight to the Japanese through Manchuria without delay."

"No. Any counterattack must be coordinated through the War Department. It is too soon. Get back here at once."

Doc stated, "We are prepared to reenlist upon arrival."

"Reenlist?" blurted the Admiral. "In another day or two, we'll have more enlistees than we need. You would be wasted in uniform. We have bigger plans for you. Return at once, and we'll sort out the details."

A rare ire touched the bronze man's even tones. "My men and I are prepared to fight for our country."

"And fight you shall. But not in uniform. We need you at the upper end of the war effort."

"It will take several days to return safely," cautioned Doc.

"Don't dawdle, Savage," the Admiral said wearily. "We are still picking up the pieces over here."

With that, the radio went dead.

DOC SAVAGE snapped off the sending switch, and turned in his seat to his waiting men.

"You all heard. They do not want us back in uniform."

"That's not fair!" exploded Ham.

"Fair or not, those are our orders."

The faces of Doc Savage's men grew long and disappointed at the news.

Monk suggested, "If we take our sweet time flyin' back, who's to say we might wander off course and take a crack at a few Japs along the way?"

"This ape has half of an idea," Ham seconded.

The others were all for reopening hostilities.

Doc Savage did not dissuade his men from such thinking. It was clear that he, too, was disappointed by the official orders from Washington.

Renny popped one monster fist into the other and grumbled, "Well, now we know why the Japs were hot to knock us out of the sky. They knew this was coming. The Emperor must have thought that slaughtering us was as important as knocking out the entire U.S. Fleet in the Pacific."

Doc Savage nodded grimly. "In the past, we have foiled operations of their espionage apparatus. Evidently, they have not forgotten this."

Johnny Littlejohn had been studiously polishing his monocle. Now he spoke up.

"The Mongol warrior of whom Japanese have charge," he said slowly, "if he is in truth Tamerlane, signifies that the Emperor has control of conceivably the most fearsome general in the history of world conquest."

The lean archaeologist said no more. He made no plea, offered no argument, nor did he draw any other conclusion than that simple declaration of fact.

Doc Savage did it for him.

"You are suggesting that the Japanese now have a secret weapon in the Ice Genius?"

"Genius?"

"As in the spirit of a place, not in the sense of a super-intelligent individual," explained Doc. "Tamerlane has taken on all the qualities of the frozen tomb from which he has been redeemed."

Johnny gulped until his Adam's apple disappeared from view. "I am so suggesting," he admitted.

The bronze man was quiet a very long time.

At last, he offered this: "It may be possible to do something about that problem before we leave Mongolia."

The eyes of Doc Savage's men lit up in the way that they did when a battle was impending.

Quietly and deliberately, Johnny Littlejohn ceased his nervous monocle polishing and solemnly placed the lens back into its customary jacket pocket. Of all of them, the fires of combat did not burn in his studious orbs. Instead, a passion for new knowledge quietly stirred his ashen features. He was exceedingly eager to get his hands on the Ice Genius again.

Chapter XXX
TWO SCHEMERS

CADWILLER OLDEN WAS thrown into a military prison cell in a border town in Manchuria—the Japanese had renamed it Manchukuo—and left to rot there for three days, receiving only plain water, cold rice and bits of cool white flesh which he hoped were fish but tasted like earthworm, also not warm.

Three days of uncertainty, then a turnkey came and unlocked the iron cell door.

"Oide-nassai masu ka!" commanded the jailer. "Speedo!"

The miniature man hesitated. He did not know what to expect, and was not eager to discover his fate.

Seeing this hesitation, the turnkey reached in and used the point of his rifle bayonet to prod the midget out of his plank bunk, barking, *"Hayakusiro!"*

Tumbling off, Olden landed on his feet and made a concerted run for it. The results were comical. The Japanese gave chase, blew on a whistle as he ran, making a poor showing at both procedures.

Olden slammed into a door, caromed off, and ran back between the soldier's churning legs.

The Japanese got tangled up in turning around and lost his rifle momentarily. Olden made a move for it, and managed to yank the bayonet off its mounting.

This he used to open up a long wound in the soldier's puttee-sheathed legs.

The turnkey let out a screech of shock, and dived for his tiny tormentor. This brought his pulsing throat close to his opponent, exactly as Cadwiller Olden hoped.

The midget evinced no hesitation. He plunged the cold steel tip upward and transfixed the man's throat. A grisly series of gurglings commenced, and a crimson flood spewed from the dying man's yawning mouth.

The Japanese fell on his rifle. Olden dived for the stock. It took fully two minutes for the midget to pull the longarm free.

By the time he had the weapon in hand, additional Japanese soldiers came charging through the door.

Olden had already maneuvered his rifle so he could unloose lead. The first bullet struck the lead man squarely in the forehead. The helmet happened to cover that forehead so the resultant ringing was sharp and metallic. The soldier was blown backward by the leaden blow.

So was Olden, for the weapon was too long for him to hold it properly. He had to set the butt of the stock on the ground, grip it in both hands, and squeeze the trigger.

The second soldier drew out his military sword and, screeching imprecations, charged his miniature foe.

Olden shot him square in the belly. The floundering man landed on his flat face and commenced sliding.

The top of his helmet struck the little man, knocking him down. And another rifle bullet jumped from the muzzle, to crack the plaster ceiling.

Recoil of the rifle tore the weapon from tiny fingers and Cadwiller Olden lay there, momentarily stunned. He groaned like an old hound dog.

"This—is—the—end," he moaned.

Strangely enough, it was not.

FOR Captain Kensa Kan soon appeared, flush-faced and sputtering loudly in his native language. Seizing the midget in both hands, Kan lifted him as he would a sandbag and carried him down dank corridors to a cold office, where he slammed Olden into a hard wooden chair.

The Captain took his own chair behind the desk and began speaking.

"I have conducted a thorough investigation of you," Kan said coldly. "There is no such person as Monzingo Baldwin. You are in fact a mysterious individual, Cadwiller Olden, believed to be deceased. You lied to me."

"Prove it," retorted Cadwiller Olden in his hound-dog voice.

"I have a complete dossier on you, Olden-*kun*. You come from an illustrious family of Royalists going back to before the American Revolution. There is a school named after your ancestor, Governor Cadwallader Colden, in New York City. You changed your last name for reasons undiscoverable by our agents."

Cadwiller Olden knew the jig was up. "Guilty," he admitted.

Captain Kan tossed the dossier aside. "Please understand that you are considered an enemy combatant."

Cadwiller Olden's tiny eyes popped. "I—me—" he sputtered. "Since when?"

"Since the air forces of my Heaven-born Emperor descended upon Hawaii and decimated the U.S. Seventh Fleet."

Olden fluttered his eyelids stupidly. "When did *that* happen?"

"Three days ago. The United States and the Empire of Japan are embroiled in war."

Cadwilller Olden did not know what to say to that. He swallowed hard.

"I thought we were friends," Olden said miserably.

The Captain shook his head. "No more. For what you have just done, a firing squad may be convened," he added.

"May?"

"There is a complication. You are an enemy of Doc Savage. We attempted to eliminate the bronze devil."

"And failed?" suggested Olden, catching the officer's drift.

"Temporarily set back," barked Captain Kan.

"I can get him for you," Olden said without hesitation.

"You would say that to preserve your chicken neck," sneered the officer.

"I would. But I can get the bronze man into a position where you can take him."

"Details, Olden-*kun*," snapped Kan.

Cadwiller Olden's tiny eyes narrowed. "I want something for my troubles."

"I offer you your life," said the Captain, lighting a cigarette. He extended one to the midget. Olden, who had been seated, now stood up in his chair, the better to meet his interrogator eye-to-eye.

"That goes without saying," he said.

Olden caught a pewter cigarette lighter, frowned at the cheap military-issue product. Striking the flint wheel, he produced a pale yellow flame and applied it to the cigarette end.

Soon, he was puffing away. The coarse tobacco seemed to imbue the little man with inner fire.

"I want a province of China for my troubles," he said through a spreading plume of cigarette smoke.

Captain Kensa Kan's sandstone features froze. "You—what?"

"You heard me. A province of my own."

"I am not empowered to promise such a concession, Olden-*kun*."

"In that case," shrugged the minute man, "you might as well stand me before the next firing squad."

The Captain's dark eyes became heavy of lid, like a serpent regarding an interesting ground hole that might or might not harbor a rabbit.

"But you won't," added Olden swiftly.

"And why not?"

"Because if you were going to shoot me, you would have done it by now. More to the point, you would be doing it right now, after I butchered your guards. You haven't. Therefore you can't. You need me. Admit it."

Angrily, the Captain slammed a calloused palm against the polished desk top and hissed, "I will personally put a bullet between your eyes for such insolence!"

Nonchalantly, Cadwiller Olden blew out a long stream of bluish smoke.

"How is our boy, Tamerlane, getting along?"

"Why do you ask?" said Kan suspiciously.

Olden shrugged negligently. "Idle curiosity."

"You have more on your mind than curiosity," Kan said pointedly.

"True. That chattering human icicle is the key to luring Doc Savage into a trap."

Leaning back in his chair, the Captain invited, "Continue, Olden-*kun.*"

Cadwiller Olden leaned forward, a crafty gleam coming into his small orbs. He smiled thinly.

"Tamerlane is the reason Doc Savage charged off to Mongolia the way he did. The big bronze guy is a scientist, you know. Unusual things interest him. The more unusual, the better. Tamerlane is one of the most novel items Doc Savage has encountered since that time a few years back when a South Seas volcano coughed up a chunk of rock with peculiar properties. He and I had a battle royal over it. I came out on the short end." A flicker of distaste crossed the tiny face. "Pardon the expression." He frowned resolutely. "But not this time." *

The Japanese captain eyed the cool, nervy midget in subdued silence.

"Tamerlane," said Cadwiller Olden, "is the bait for the trap to snare Doc Savage and his men."

This time it was the crafty captain's turn to act cool and unconcerned.

---

* *Repel*

"By now," he said carefully, "the bronze American and his assistants have flown back to America, to confer with high officials in Washington, D.C. The bronze devil is a very important man in the U.S. He will want to be in on any war planning."

"Which is why you tried to put him on ice before the attack. Am I right?"

"Correct."

Cadwiller Olden gathered up his features into a tiny knot. "If I know Doc Savage, he won't just wing back to Washington for a round of stuffy meetings. He will want to get into the action. Now. And if you give him an excuse, he will come charging in your direction like a maddened bull at a red cape."

Captain Kensa Kan considered this speech for several minutes. His eyes went to the ceiling and he exhaled three long jets of cigarette smoke which rose and banked against the plaster above his head.

"Your thinking appears to be sound—on both scores," he allowed. "But how do you propose to lure the bronze devil into a trap, Olden-*kun?*"

"By offering him the three things he most desires. Tamerlane, and a chance to strike back at Japan."

Captain Kan waited for the amazing midget to voice the third item, and when he did not, demanded, "What is this third thing?"

Cadwiller Olden jerked a miniature thumb, stabbing his own chest.

"Me. Doc Savage wants me. He wants me very badly."

And the cool little man offered a chilly smile that was like a baby shark showing its new, white teeth.

Only then did Captain Kensa Kan understand that he would have to keep this irritating little man alive until he had accomplished his objectives. He made his sand-colored features stiff to conceal his inward distaste. There was something about Cadwiller Olden he did not like.

"Have we a deal?" demanded Olden.

"We have an understanding," returned Kan. "Subject to the approval of my superiors."

The midget smiled. "Just so I get mine."

Chapter XXXI
THE BAIT

DOC SAVAGE SPENT the three days following the news of the surprise attack on Pearl Harbor attempting to repair the crippled third engine of his flying boat.

The bronze man appeared to be taking his time doing so. Of course, replacement parts were not available in Inner Mongolia, so the bronze man prevailed upon the Commissar to permit him to use a local machine shop to fabricate his own replacements. This naturally took considerable time.

Renny assisted in this toil, while Monk and Ham monitored the aircraft's all-wave transceiver.

Thus did Doc Savage receive timely reports of every incident that followed the attack.

Ham Brooks carried the news that the Congress had officially declared war on Japan. This was followed shortly by notification that Italy and Germany—Japan's closest allies—had in turn declared war on the United States.

"We're at war with half of Europe!" he concluded.

The bronze man heard all of this in a grim, contained silence. He maintained that attitude over the following days. It was difficult to discover if the bronze man's silence was due to shock, or if he was calculating future moves.

ON the third day, Doc fitted the last replacement part in the crippled motor, closing an inspection port in the cowling.

Renny grunted, "Let's fire her up and see if she'll turn."

Monk Mayfair did the honors. Clambering into the pilot seat, he snapped switches, and got the engine going. It belched a great deal of evil smoke, but the propeller spun until it was a gleaming transparent disc in the blustery Mongolian air.

Saying their farewells to Commissar Ganzorig—for the Red official had revealed to them his name now that they were allies—Doc and his men buttoned up the big flying boat and took their customary seats preparatory to taking off.

Everyone regarded Doc Savage as he revved all four motors to bellowing life.

Monk asked the question on everyone's mind. "Where to?"

Doc Savage was a long time in replying. "We are obliged to return home."

There was a reluctance in the bronze man's tone as he spoke these words.

"We could take the long way around," Monk suggested hopefully.

"Long way around!" barked Ham. "Why, what do you mean?"

Renny grunted, "I think he means the Pacific skyway. It will take us over the Japanese islands."

Doc Savage asked, "What would we do over Japan? We have no bombs or weapons sufficient to take on the Japanese Imperial Air Force."

No one had an answer to that, but the suggestion was not a serious one. Frustrated by the wait for repairs, they itched to lash out at someone. Everyone understood that they were neither equipped for, nor prepared to launch a counterattack.

Without another word, Doc Savage advanced the throttles and the big bird began gathering momentum, its wheels rumbling along the uneven tarmac until it gained airspeed. The tail lifted.

The leviathan plane lumbered skyward, found a comfortable altitude and leveled off.

Doc Savage pointed the bawling motors west, trimmed the ship, and flew on steadily.

A pent silence seized the cockpit. Each man understood that they were flying home, yet every one in the soundproof cabin ached to swing into action against anyone or anything connected with the Empire of Japan.

"This fracas has been comin' on a while," Monk muttered, apparently addressing Habeas Corpus, who had climbed onto his lap and was looking out the cockpit window, ears extended as if imagining himself to be flying under his own power.

"Those Sons of Nippon may have started it," rumbled Renny, "but we'll finish it!"

"I'll tell a man!" added Monk.

LESS than an hour later, Long Tom at the radio broke into excited speech.

"Doc! Listen to this!" the puny electrical wizard cut the radio transmission into the cockpit loudspeaker so everyone could hear it.

"Emergency! Calling Doc Savage or any of his men within radio range. This is an emergency. Attention, Doc Savage. Calling Doc Savage."

Doc Savage keyed his throat microphone and spoke.

"This is Doc Savage speaking."

"You know who I am," came the familiar hound-dog baying of Cadwiller Olden.

"I do," responded the bronze man.

"I just escaped from that Japanese captain who hates you so much."

Doc Savage asked sharply, "Which Japanese captain?"

"Kensa Kan. Do you remember him?"

"As well as I remember you."

From the back, Renny boomed, "Holy cow! Wasn't that the name of the Japanese naval captain we tangled with in the South China Sea that time we got on the trail of the Buddha of Ice?" *

---

* *The Infernal Buddha*

Ham barked, "Jove, I believe it is!"

Doc Savage said, "Those Japanese pilots reported to a Captain Kan. It appears to be the same man."

Monk puckered up his simian face. "This is gettin' kinda interestin'."

The voice of Cadwiller Olden cut in, demanding, *"Are you still there, Savage?"*

"Yes."

"Good. Listen—I know about the attack on Hawaii. It made my blood boil when I found out. I wriggled myself out of a military cell and snuck into this radio shack. I don't have a lot of time. The Captain's training Chinua and his bandits to fight under Timur to invade Mongolia and take it over. The first border raid takes place tonight. It's at a place called Mukden. Know where it is?"

Doc Savage said, "It is on the map."

"That's where you have to go. That's where you can find Tamerlane before he conquers the first piece of Mongolia for the Japanese."

"How do we know you are telling the truth and this is not a trap?" demanded Doc.

"You don't," retorted the midget. *"Do you think I'm in cahoots with the Japanese? That's not my style! You know that. Besides, I'm a loyal American. I don't like what those Jap rats did to my country. And since we are at war, I know what side I'm fighting on. And so do you."*

"What about you, Olden?" Doc Savage demanded. "Where do we find you?"

"I'm going to make a break for it and try for Mongolia. But never mind that now. I'll look out for myself. I've been doing it all my life. You run down Tamerlane."

The radio went dead. The carrier hiss was all that remained of the unsettling transmission.

An uneasy silence followed. Ham Brooks shattered it. "I do not trust that little devil," he said testily.

"Betcha boots," growled Monk. "This smells like a trap."

Johnny Littlejohn had been silent throughout. Excitement caused his voice to quiver.

"It is worth considering, and weighing the risks of action versus inaction."

Long Tom said sourly, "You just want to get your hands on that infernal ice genius."

"Censurable as indicted," admitted Johnny.

"Eh?"

"Guilty as charged."

Doc Savage pondered all this, then said firmly, "Trap or not, it is worth the risk to intercept this planned incursion, and seize control of Tamerlane, if that is possible."

"If in fact that ice genius is the actual historical Tamerlane," noted Ham.

Without another word, Doc Savage sent the big plane winging south—south in the direction of Manchuria.

His men fell to checking their supermachine pistols and girding themselves for what they expected to be serious battle. Faces grew grim, but there was in their attitudes an eager anticipation.

Monk put their feelings into words. "Brothers, we first got together during the last world war. Now, it's time to take a hand in this one."

Chapter XXXII
SNARE

OUTSIDE THE DESOLATE town of Mukden, Cadwiller Olden sat astride a small dun pony that was nevertheless too large for him.

The little man looked out over the vast Manchurian plain on which numerous circular tents had been erected. Here and there stood standards comprised of tall willow-tree poles fixed up with horsetails that fluttered in the breeze like pennants.

Captain Kensa Kan, standing next to the pony, tore his eyes away from the flapping horsetails and asked, "Are you certain that Doc Savage will fall into this trap, Olden-*kun*?"

"Positively," said the little man brightly. "Doc Savage is a student of history, as am I. If all these tents don't convince him, the horsetail standards will. These were the flags of the Golden Horde in the days of Genghis Khan. That brass-faced phony will fly over this location and recognize that here is the headquarters camp of Tamerlane. He will land at the closest flat spot, which is the valley on the other side of the hills, and steal up on the place."

The Captain nodded. "No doubt Doc Savage will arrive by night, with his engines silenced. He will infiltrate this area, looking for the lame one."

Gesturing to a nearby hill, Olden added, "And we will watch him from up there. Once Doc Savage and his men have entered the camp, we will detonate the dynamite packed inside every one of these tents. No matter from which direction he comes, that nosy meddler will be pulverized."

"It is a good plan, Olden-*kun*," nodded the Captain.

"With Doc Savage permanently out of our hair, we can proceed with our plans."

The Captain regarded the miniature man on the dun pony and said, "You are a clever little fellow."

Olden smiled, his perfect white teeth gleaming in the dying sun. He inclined his head in the gesture of a polite bow.

Under his breath, the murderous midget said, "Cleverer than you think."

The winds blowing through the camp made the felt tent sides flutter and snap, drowning the muttered utterance.

Frowning, the Captain asked, "What did you say, Olden-*kun*?".

"I said," murmured Cadwiller Olden, "I am as clever as you say. I take pride in my cleverness. It was cleverness that got me through life." The midget's face grew thoughtful. "I imagine cleverness will carry me through to the end of my days. Trickery is my stock in trade."

Nodding curtly, the Captain suggested, "Let us repair to the highest hill so that we are ready when the Doc Savage plane arrives."

"If I know that bronze blunderer," said the midget, "he'll be showing his Indian face by sundown."

THE EXPECTED plane arrived only an hour past the last light, when the diamond-point stars were just emerging to freckle the cobalt sky.

It flew overhead, making a hissing sound that was characteristic of the bronze man's plane engines when they were silenced. Had they not been scouring the skies with field glasses, neither Captain Kan nor Cadwiller Olden would have spotted it. The aircraft showed no lights.

The great ship ghosted on by, causing the faces of the watchers to grow long and disappointed.

"Perhaps the bronze one did not see the yurts in this light," suggested the Japanese officer.

Cadwiller Olden's features became like a wrinkled walnut. "Not a chance, my friend. Savage's planes are equipped with all kinds of clever gadgets for seeing at night. Infra-red projectors and ultra-violet gimmicks. He misses nothing."

"You know this man well, I see," said Kensa Kan.

"I know Doc Savage like I know my big toe."

"Your big toe," returned the Captain coolly, "does not cover much territory."

Olden winced. "You watch. He's just being cautious."

They trained their field glasses on the retreating aircraft. It was soon lost from sight. They waited in the cool of the early evening for it to return. The cobalt sky overhead darkened to black velvet. More stars put in an appearance.

Time passed. Five minutes became ten, and ten turned into twenty.

"It is beginning to look as if the all-seeing American has his blind spots," suggested Kan.

"Keep your shirt on."

Captain Kan looked puzzled.

"Be patient," clarified Olden.

Their patience was rewarded, albeit later than they imagined.

The aircraft came hissing back; this time it flew higher. As they watched, something indistinguishable fell from the passing ship.

They watched eagerly, tracking the tumbling bundle with their lenses.

Soon, a black blossom showed faintly against the stars.

"Parachute," said the Captain, hissing the word with sibilant satisfaction.

"Maybe more than one," warned Olden.

But the midget was mistaken. Only one parachute drifted downward. The pilot, whoever he might be, was very, very good, because the man at the end of the dark parachute bell was falling smack in the middle of the false Mongol encampment.

Straining up on tiptoe, balancing atop his saddle of wood, Cadwiller Olden tried mightily to discern who was dropping from the sky, but the starlight was too poor.

"Only one man," murmured Kensa Kan.

Olden smacked his perfect lips. "Doc Savage. I'll bet my life on it."

"It is a large man," noted the Captain. "It could be the engineer, Renwick."

There were two pieces of apparatus on the ground where they were hunkered. One was an electrical device that led away in the form of an insulated electrical cable. The other was a friction igniter, its black handle jutting up from the electric detonator box.

"Let us see who is our visitor," said the Japanese, flipping a switch.

Floodlights popped into scalding life. They made the parachute canopy stand out against the night sky like an evil flower.

Fixing the figure in his glasses, Cadwiller Olden jumped up and down for joy. "Doc Savage! He's wearing dark goggles, but that's him."

Without another word, Captain Kensa Kan knelt, grasped the black handle in both hands and applied sudden downward pressure.

The results were impressive the way an earthquake is impressive.

The entire cup of the valley jumped up in a flash of flame and a clamor like a thousand thunderclaps. Clouds of dirt detonated with tearing violence and large rocks were hurtled skyward. The noise was thunderous.

The effect on the parachuting form was extreme.

The force of the explosion expelled a rush of air in all directions, flattening tents, knocking over the horsetail standards like saplings in a typhoon. The parachute bell was thrown about. Spilling air, it collapsed.

The catastrophe would not matter to the falling figure. Force of the explosion savagely tore at him, removing limbs in a haphazard fashion. These fell away.

Neither man witnessed this. They were hunkered down in a trench where the force of the massive blast would do them little harm, although clouds of yellow-brown dust and grit and speeding stones peppered them relentlessly.

The dun pony ran away, screaming.

IT was quite some time before they could lift their dust-smeared faces and peer downward. Even so, the air was smotheringly thick and everything below obscured.

The flood-lamps had been demolished in the blast, but one hardy survivor managed to spray uninterrupted illumination. It was now askew, but it gave them something to focus upon.

Sweeping the disturbed terrain below, Captain Kan and Cadwiller Olden searched, desperate for any sign of the large man who had descended by parachute.

"I do not see him," said Kan.

"Blown to bits!" crowed Olden, shaking a tiny fist up at the Doc Savage plane. It was fleeing the scene. "Hah! It was too much for them to stomach!"

"That is not good. We want the other *Amerika-jin*, too," snapped Kan, jumping to his feet and shaking dirt from his black naval uniform.

"Doc Savage is the important one. Without their leader, his men are nothing but a disorganized bunch of clowns."

Suddenly, Cadwiller Olden's voice choked off. He commenced coughing violently.

The Captain reached for his canteen to offer water, but Olden batted the container away.

"Look!" choked the midget.

Captain Kan lifted his field glasses and tried to make out what the little man was pointing at.

In the fringe of the surviving floodlight glow, a head could be seen. It was no longer attached to a body. It rolled along, coming to a rest against a rock. The disordered hair was a metallic bronze and the skin of the face was a lighter hue of the same color.

The eyes could not be clearly seen, for dark goggles masked them. But one lens was missing, evidently having been blown off. It was difficult to say at such a distance and in this stark light, but it appeared that only a gaping hole existed where the eyeball should have been.

"He's dead," whispered Cadwiller Olden. "Doc Savage is dead."

"It appears so," said Kensa Kan. "My Emperor will be deeply pleased."

Again, the spine of the Japanese captain stiffened when he spoke the worshipful word, Emperor. It was his way of snapping to attention.

Cadwiller Olden ignored it, having gotten used to the strange reaction over the last few days. But it bothered him, for it meant that the Captain was a blind worshipper of his ruler and would do anything he was commanded to do.

Inwardly, Olden cringed. He did not like men who did not think for themselves.

"This is a great day in the history of the world," said the midget, his tiny smile almost as wide as his face.

The Captain did not respond.

Olden said, "Better radio your fighter pilots to chase after the Doc Savage plane and shoot it down. Smash any chance they'll turn back, looking for revenge."

Cadwiller Olden's eyes were still resting on the severed bronze head. He was grinning at the sight, licking his thin lips like a cat eyeing an unwary robin.

When Olden failed to receive a reply, he lowered his glasses and gazed upward.

The Captain stood rooted, eyes wide and staring and as rigid as a day-old corpse. The look in his open orbs was stark, terrible. A man looking up at a looming Grim Reaper might possess such a fixed expression.

Thinking that Kan had spotted something awful, the midget asked, "What do you see?"

The Captain continued to stare off into space.

Peering in that direction, Cadwiller Olden attempted to discover what had seemingly terrified the Japanese officer. But he failed to spy anything in the settling haze.

"I don't see any—"

A metallic voice sounded from somewhere close by and Cadwiller Olden's blood ran cold in his minuscule veins.

"That is because there is nothing to see," stated the unmistakable voice of Doc Savage.

Chapter XXXIII
DEVELOPMENT UNEXPECTED

CADWILLER OLDEN STOOD without moving. His mouth went dry and he looked as if he wanted to cry.

Out of the side of his miniature mouth, he growled, "You had better be a ghost."

"No ghost," returned the metallic tones of Doc Savage.

"But you were just blown to bone chips!"

"A dummy, painted bronze and wearing goggles to conceal eyes that are insufficiently lifelike," explained the grim voice.

Reluctantly, the tiny man turned, and beheld Doc Savage standing behind the Captain. The Japanese continued to stare off into space. His eyes jerked about in his head as if that was the only portion of his anatomy that was under the control of his brain.

Olden said, more calmly than he felt, "You did something to him."

Doc Savage said, "There are nerve centers in the spine which, properly manipulated, produce an unnerving paralysis in the subject."

"He can hear us?"

"Clearly. He simply cannot move a muscle."

Cadwiller Olden curled his upper lip and said, "You're in the middle of Japanese-held Manchuria. You'll never get away with this, bronze guy."

"I have not done all that badly so far," Doc pointed out.

Doc Savage calmly gathered up Captain Kan under one gigantic arm as if he were but a department store package.

Olden backed away, throwing up tiny hands timidly. "Wh-what are you going to do with us?" he stammered.

Doc Savage did not reply, but a bronze hand reached out, ensnared Olden by his shirt front. The next he knew, the little man was tucked under Doc Savage's other arm. The moving muscles felt like bands of steel.

Turning, the bronze Hercules descended the hill. Being carried by Doc Savage was like being toted by a warm machine. Olden attempted to kick, bite, and scratch, but nothing seemed to phase the metallic giant.

Soon, they were on level ground, moving through a dusky haze that made breathing difficult. It also concealed the movements of the giant bronze man from any observers.

Because he was otherwise hopeless, Cadwiller Olden started hollering for help. He had picked up a little Japanese during his incarceration and he was trying it out now.

"*Goran nasai!*" the midget bayed out. "*Kochira ye oide nasai!*"

If anyone heard him, they did not respond. In order to lay their trap, Captain Kan had not briefed any of his men, nor assembled them anywhere in the vicinity, lest they be injured in the dynamite blast, which was quite massive.

Doc Savage moved through the growing darkness, and out of the zone of dirty air. He seemed to be bound for a definite spot. He traveled with a kind of gliding stride that ate up the miles. The bronze man appeared to be tireless. He avoided hamlets, and kept away from roads.

It was some considerable time before they came to an open field where the big plane waited, engines still turning.

When the aircraft was in sight, Doc picked up his pace and ran rapidly. The bronze man emitted a strange sound deep in his throat. It might have been the call of hidden night birds suddenly bursting into song. The sound carried remarkably.

A few bars of this, and the hatch door popped open. Out thrust the bullet head of Monk Mayfair. A hairy paw waved him forward.

Doc Savage put on speed, and leapt into the open hatch. The door clanged shut. Doc pressed his two charges into separate seats.

"Take off!" rapped Doc

From the control cockpit, Renny Renwick's voice boomed out, "Taking off!"

The plane began gathering itself for take-off, the brakes released, and it slowly rumbled forward over uneven ground, gaining speed.

The big ship leapt eagerly into the sky, knocking high branches off a stand of willow trees before clearing the last obstruction.

DOC SAVAGE was working on the Japanese captain, who was so stiff he could not be seated properly.

Olden sat across the aisle, wringing his hands, practically beside himself. The sudden reversal of his fortunes had only started to sink in.

"You should be dead," he said petulantly.

Working to manipulate the Japanese officer's spine, the bronze man said, "As a trap, your snare was rather obvious."

"Obvious how?"

"When we flew over the camp, there were no signs of people moving about, nor any horses, and that was suspicious."

"Mongols go to bed early. You know that."

"There was also the fact that the clothes you are wearing were impregnated with a chemical that glows green under ultra-violet light," added Doc. "Spying you lying on that hill gave the snare away."

Cadwiller Olden looked down at his clothes, which were the same togs he had worn when he left Doc Savage's strange institution in upstate New York.

"My duds gave me away?" bleated the little man, aghast.

Doc nodded. "All persons who are kept at the College wear such garb in case of escape. It stood to reason that if you were hiding on high ground, there was danger below."

Captain Kan was coming out of his trance, or whatever it was. He tried to jump out of his seat and tear at the bronze man standing over him.

Showing no great effort, Doc Savage forced the Japanese officer into a seated position and held him there with one irresistible hand.

"We meet again," said Doc Savage. "I see that you still hold the rank of captain."

Captain Kan said nothing. He skinned lips off his teeth, which were clenched, hissing like an annoyed viper.

"Since we are so far from water," stated Doc, "I am forced to conclude that you are now an intelligence officer, perhaps a member of the *Tokkeitai,* the Secret Service Branch of the Imperial Navy. This is a quite a fall in status after being commander of your own Naval vessel."

The hissing ceased abruptly. That was the only outward sign the Japanese officer gave that Doc Savage had guessed correctly.

Finally, the Captain said, "It appears that I am your prisoner, Savage-*san.*"

"It would seem so," agreed Doc. "My chief interest is in the whereabouts of the individual extracted from the ice."

"I will never tell you that!" spat Kan.

Doc Savage called over, "Monk, fetch the truth serum."

The Captain's almond eyes popped into roundness.

Nothing was said until Monk Mayfair returned with a charged syringe, and Doc Savage jabbed the needle into the officer's shoulder, not stripping the uniform sleeve back.

It took about two minutes for the serum to take hold, at which point the Captain started speaking in a noticeably slurred voice. He tried to fight it, but to no avail. Doc held him down with one hand, showing no effort in doing so.

In Japanese, Doc asked, "Where is the man from the ice cave?"

In slow, mushy words, Captain Kan replied, "Tamerlane-*san* is drilling his new army in the valley west of here."

"How many men does he command?"

"Hundreds. More are being recruited every day. There are many Mongols or half-Mongols living in Manchukuo."

"Why did you attempt to kill me and my men?"

Perspiration popped out on the dry, sandstone-hued forehead. "It was a directive from Tokyo. The generals understood that you represented as great a danger to their ambitions as the U.S. Pacific Fleet. I was given the task of liquidating you, in part to atone for my failure to best you during the lamentable affair of the Buddha of Ice, but also because of my experience in fighting you in the South China Sea." *

Doc Savage replied nothing to that. He reached out and did a further manipulation of the Captain's neck. This produced a different effect, rendering the man senseless. His head nodding forward, his chin coming to rest on his uniform blouse buttons, the officer simply fell asleep in his seat.

Witnessing all this, Cadwiller Olden asked weakly, "What about me?"

"We will discuss that later," Doc told him.

Lunging forward to the cockpit, Doc took the empty seat beside Renny.

The aircraft was equipped with dual controls. The bronze man seized the control yoke and expertly maneuvered the plane on a westerly heading.

"I guess we're going after that Mongolian horse army?" asked the big-fisted engineer.

Doc Savage said, "Yes. With any luck, we can be out of Manchuria by midnight."

---

* *The Infernal Buddha*

Chapter XXXIV

BACKFIRE TRAP

DOC SAVAGE PILOTED the leviathan amphibian, navigating by feel as well as through infra-red flood-lamps distributed about wings and embedded in the streamlined boat-shaped hull. In the cockpit, he and Renny wore special goggles in order to perceive the darkened terrain below. The landscape looked like a black-and-white moving picture, with deep shadows and stark, high-contrast lights.

Renny rumbled, "Looks like a valley up ahead. I spy armies of horses picketed, too."

Doc nodded. Wordlessly, he dropped the plane and banked in order to get a better view. What he saw caused his lips to part and his unearthly trilling issued forth, low and vague but distinctly surprised.

Renny boomed, "Holy cow! Look at the army he's already assembled!"

It was true. Although the number of warriors was not great, the collection of horses reached into the hundreds. Not many men were moving about, but what could be seen suggested a significant number of warriors had been assembled.

Monk bustled forward, asked, "What do you suppose they're up to?"

Before anyone could answer, Johnny Littlejohn offered an opinion.

"When Tamerlane expired, he was bent upon conquering China. Perhaps he is still of that mind."

Studying the terrain, which consisted of lowland valleys, Doc Savage commented, "It may be possible to land."

"Possible," grunted Renny. "Sure. But where do we find that iron-featured gargoyle in all that crowd? More importantly, how do we go about it without getting riddled by arrows or hacked to pieces by scimitars?"

Doc Savage seemed not to have an immediate answer to that question.

Finally, he said, "We will land and see what can be accomplished on the ground."

Doc wrestled the plane about, scrutinizing the ground below. It was scrubland. Not a lot of trees. Very few boulders. Landing seemed practical, if risky. Ideally, they would have dragged the field several times to be certain, but these were not ideal conditions. Even on this cloudy night they would be seen soon enough.

Carefully, Doc brought the plane in line, dropped the landing gear.

From the back, a hoarse voice could be heard asking plaintively, "Are we landing?"

"Pipe down," said Monk. "You caterpillar."

Cadwiller Olden would not pipe down. "Are we landing? We're landing out here? Isn't that dangerous?"

No one replied to that anxious question.

Olden had his concerned face pressed to a cabin window and was peering down. He could see very little, owing to the absence of landing lights and the fact that he did not have a pair of infra-red goggles.

There was enough light, however, to make out the sea of felt tents, and the unmistakable backs of shaggy-maned ponies.

Launching himself from his seat, the minute man charged for the cockpit, screaming at the top of his lungs, "Don't land! Don't land!"

"Why not?" thumped Renny.

"It's too dangerous!"

Long Tom shot out of his seat, collared the agitated midget, and forcibly marched him back to his seat, planting him there. "You stay put, you buzzard bait," he growled.

"But we could die!" Olden insisted.

Doc Savage was by this time concentrating on his landing. His flake-gold eyes shot back and forth, ready to pull back on the control yoke if he spotted any obstruction along the natural runway.

There would be little enough time to pull up, but the bronze man trusted in his piloting skills, which verged upon the miraculous.

So intent was Doc on the stretch of natural terrain standing out in stark contrast that he had little time to pay heed to what was transpiring on either side of his sweeping wings.

Renny and the others, of course, were watching from every angle with anxious attentiveness.

It was Ham who spotted the trouble first.

"WHY are oxen lined up out there?"

On the opposite side of the cabin, Monk Mayfair muttered, "I see a bunch of oxen over here, too."

Doc Savage's head shifted to the left and then to the right, and he saw that up ahead numerous oxen loitered in two lines, with their posteriors facing one another, spaced well apart.

By this time the landing gear had been cranked down, and they were hurtling along, only yards away from the strangely-grouped animals.

The positions of the oxen struck the bronze man as suspicious. Instinctively, he hauled back on the control wheel, seeking to regain altitude.

It was a prudent move, but it was too late.

Suddenly, men in Cossak-like Mongolian costumes jumped up from concealment and fell to beating the oxen, causing them to lurch forward.

The oxen charged in opposite directions, revealing long lengths of chain that had been buried in the dirt. These now jumped into view, snapped taut by muscular teams of oxen pulling in opposition. For the chains were yoked at both ends to the moving beasts.

With a mighty heave, Doc tried to pull up, but the landing wheels snagged the chains—with calamitous results.

The nose wheel simply snapped off. The sound of it being twisted off its mounting was nerve-shattering.

It was a mere prelude to what followed. The unfortunate oxen were yanked off their feet, to be dragged screaming in frightened consternation by the surviving wheels as they snagged taut chain and hurtled forward.

The combined weight of the oxen, as well as the smashing of snapping chain against hull, brought the aircraft careening around, shedding its wheels and striking the ground forcefully.

The aircraft was well constructed; it did not fall apart. It made a terrible screaming and screeching as it slid along the ground on its belly. The noise that filled the cabin assaulted the ears and made them think that their remaining lives were measured in seconds.

There was nothing Doc Savage could do. He held onto the control wheel by force of habit. The plane slid along, began to skew and then turn half around until it lurched to a tilting stop.

The shock of landing held them in their seats far longer than would have been normal. Even Doc Savage was a little slow to react. Possibly the bronze man was not certain until the last that they would also survive.

Then, he jumped from his seat and flung down the aisle, checking on his men.

Ham and Long Tom, the lightest members of the group, had been flung about until they were no longer in the seats they originally occupied. Monk and Ham had traded places somehow. Captain Kan had ended up in back, a tangle of limbs, with

Habeas the pig splayed atop him. There was no sign of Cadwiller Olden.

Doc Savage hunted around and found the midget cowering beneath a seat. Doc reached down and pulled him free.

Olden was slightly dazed. But his eyes soon cleared.

"I told you not to land," he complained bitterly.

Doc stated, "You knew about this trap."

A weird wolfish grin crawled upon the midget's countenance. "I figured in case you missed the first trap, it was smart to have this one in reserve."

"Clever," said Doc without emotion.

"I live by my cleverness," declared Cadwiller Olden.

"One day you may become too clever for your own good," warned the bronze man.

"That dark day," retorted the little rascal, lifting his perfect chin defiantly, "will never dawn."

Then, the air was full of excited war cries intermixed with the pounding thunder of horses' hooves.

Cadwiller Olden's weird grin grew foxy. "Here come Tamerlane and his pack. All fired up for the slaughter." His hound voice grew shrill with anticipatory delight. *"Yours, you big brass monkey!"*

Chapter XXXV
THE EMPTY BELLY

DOC SAVAGE RAPPED out urgent orders.
"Arm yourselves. We will make a stand here."

Growling, Monk Mayfair checked his supermachine pistol, knocked out the broken glass from one mangled cabin window-frame. The others took a leaf from his book, and fell to punching clear windows out of which to shoot.

Seeing this, Cadwiller Olden said sneeringly, "You might as well give up right now. You're outnumbered."

Long Tom pointed out, "You're in here with us, shaver."

Olden winked mischievously. "Think again. That's the rescue party. They're coming to save me."

No one said anything to that. They were too busy checking their weapons and preparing to open up on their attackers.

Mongol warriors came charging in the time-honored fashion of men of their breed. They lifted out of their saddles, virtually standing on their stirrups as they fitted arrows and prepared to let fly.

The first wave struck the hull of the crippled bird like the hammering of hailstones. The sound was nerve-jarring.

That was when Monk and the others began cutting loose. Supermachine pistols hooted and blared, stuttering relentlessly. In the dark it was difficult to pick out individual targets, but also unnecessary.

The weapons spit out slugs in swarms, like furious bees. Mongols began dropping into their saddles, then out of their saddles. This did not discourage the survivors in the slightest.

The grimly silent warriors charged them, forming a threatening circle of riders, much in the fashion of Comanches harrying an old pioneer wagon train, but without the bloodcurdling war cries.

Monk ran to the other side of the plane, dashed out window glass, and resumed firing. The others joined in. They did a pretty good job of whittling down their attackers. But there were too many of them.

Seeing the meager results of all the shooting, Doc Savage said, "Conserve ammunition."

Everyone switched to single-shot operation, and commenced picking off what foes they could.

By this time, zipping arrows began finding broken windows, and chugged into the cabin.

Ham almost lost an ear. Monk jumped out of the way of one sharp missile just in time. It traveled clean through one cabin window and out the other, striking a hapless horse, which threw its startled rider.

Doc Savage had gone to the back of the plane and opened an equipment case. This was full of small grenades of various types. He gathered up a number of tubular devices, brought them forward, to distribute them among his men.

"Flash bombs," he said.

Grinning, Monk took two, primed them, and flung them out through different windows. The others followed suit.

The grenades were filled with potent flash powder of the type that newspaper photographers used to employ in the days before disposable flashbulbs were invented. It was pretty eye-hurting stuff, when ignited. The darkness helped.

The flash bombs detonated in all directions, taking the circling Mongols by surprise. Hardly a warrior did not have his eyes on their intended victims. Consequently every one of the attackers found himself temporarily blinded by the shocking effect of the sudden flashes of light on their optic nerves.

This created enormous confusion among the horsemen and their mounts, which were also blinded. Frightened horses collided, tumbled, and there was a great deal of shouting and screaming by man and horse alike.

In this tremendous confusion, Doc Savage picked up Captain Kan and Cadwiller Olden, and led his men out of the plane and into the dark of the night.

Monk lugged Habeas Corpus under one burly arm, and toted his chemical laboratory under the other.

WHEN the Mongol horsemen settled down, and could see again, they first turned their attention to their frightened horses. When they finally got the ponies gentled down, they saw that the airplane door stood open.

Some of the bravest of the Mongols approached, and slipped inside. Foremost of these was Chinua, the bandit chief who was second only to Tamerlane.

He came out swearing. "The belly of the *namdu* is empty. Search them out!"

Enraged, the Mongols charged off in all directions, seeking their missing quarry.

By this time, an imposing man on a black stallion rode up, wearing an iron mask that matched his armor.

"Hold!" he commanded.

At the sound of the croaking voice, every Mongol suddenly wheeled his mount and looked in the direction of the iron-clad individual who commanded them.

"Do not ride in all directions like foolish children, or cranes who have been scattered by an eagle. Instead, follow me."

The Mongol leader threw his helmeted head back and seemed to sniff the air like a dog. Behind the iron-rimmed holes of his battle mask, canine yellow eyes burned savagely.

Finally, he said, "Follow me."

Without a word, every warrior followed the shivering horseman in the fanciful iron mask.

Chapter XXXVI
SUBTERFUGE

THE TERRAIN AROUND the Mongol encampment
was varied. There were low hills, the odd willow tree, even
a meandering river. Doc Savage had spied all this from the air
and committed the contours to memory.

Carrying Cadwiller Olden and Captain Kan under each
mighty arm, the bronze giant led his men in the direction of
the brook.

They reached its banks. They all plunged in, then laid low
while the Mongol horsemen charged past.

Doc had Cadwiller Olden's nose and mouth firmly clamped
in one metal hand. The Japanese officer was still in a state of
slurred intoxication from the truth serum and barely reacted to
being immersed in water.

The Mongols thundered by. Doc waited until the inevitable
stragglers came into view.

Handing off the prisoners to Monk and Renny, Doc Savage
flashed out of the water, and began hurling small glass globules
in the direction of the stragglers.

The galloping horses suddenly went to sleep on their feet.

It was a comical sight, the horses succumbing first and pitching forward. The men in the saddles floundered about, then lost
consciousness, still in their saddles, or half in them, as their
staggering mounts collapsed onto the ground.

Rushing up, Doc Savage swiftly stripped the men of their
native costumes, waving his men to do likewise.

Very quickly, everyone was swathed in a padded, long-skirt-ed Mongolian *del*, and was drawing on fur caps with pendulous ear flaps to help disguise their Caucasian features.

Monk asked, "What are we gonna do with these guys?"

"Drag them to cover," directed Doc.

This was quickly done, and everyone assembled around the sleeping horses. Charging a syringe plucked from his equipment vest, Doc Savage supplied every horse with an antidote to the sleeping anesthetic. The animals came around in a matter of minutes and, although dazed, allowed themselves to be helped back on their nervous feet.

"Mount up," Doc ordered.

Everyone climbed aboard a mount of his chosing, Monk gathering up Habeas the pig and Renny taking the Japanese captain and laying him across his own saddle.

Seizing Cadwiller Olden, Doc prepared to do likewise. The midget started yodeling, until Doc Savage pinched shut his mouth and nose, warning, "If you would prefer, I can manipu-late your spinal nerves until you cannot move at all."

The midget subsided.

VAULTING into his own saddle, Doc Savage led his men in the opposite direction of the searching Mongolian warriors, whose pounding hoof thunder was receding in the night.

Johnny trotted up beside Doc Savage and started a conver-sation.

"The man in the iron mask was Tamerlane. What are we going to do about him?"

Doc Savage said, "We are going to capture him, if at all possible."

Johnny cracked a grin of approval and asked, "How are we going to do that?"

"By laying a trap."

Perplexity crawled across the gangling archeologist's hollow face. "What manner of trap are you contemplating?"

But Doc Savage failed to reply. Characteristically, he did not wish his men to know his plans, should any of them fall into the hands of their enemies and be tortured to reveal them. But, in his innermost heart, Johnny the archaeologist wondered if Doc Savage in fact had any plan, given how far awry the evening's undertakings had careened.

They rode back to the plane, and dismounted. Moving swiftly, they armed themselves with as many spare drums of ammunition and other weapons as possible. The plane was, of course, beyond repair. Not far away came the sounds of the maimed and injured oxen who had been dragged along after being pulled apart by the chains that had snared the big bird.

Hearing this, Renny took a shotgun from the stores and walked down to where the dumb beasts were crying out in agony. Methodically, he put them out of their misery, one by one, and came back, stony of countenance.

"That's done," he said somberly.

They reclaimed their mounts and rode off into the midnight of Japanese-occupied Manchuria.

Chapter XXXVII
HEADS IN A PILE

SEVERAL HOURS SHORT of midnight Doc Savage and his men came upon the Chinese village. It was a pitiful place of mud homes sitting amid an arid landscape in which red soil blew about in tiny dust devils that seemed somehow like imps cavorting.

It was late enough that the villagers would have turned in for the night, as this was a part of the world where electric lights were in short supply.

Upon approach, Doc Savage noticed two things. Strange silence, and even stranger scent on the wind. The smell was somehow metallic, and it made the tongue feel thick in the mouth whenever one inhaled.

Monk put it into words. "Smells like blood."

Ham added, "Maybe someone butchered a bullock for a feast."

Somehow no one believed that to be the case.

They dismounted cautiously, and picketed their horses. Then, they continued on foot. The unpleasant tang in the air grew stronger and more pungent.

The village was not much of anything—a few dozen scattered hovels built around a well and surrounded by rice patties. The rice patties had frozen over in the cold, and nothing was growing.

Seeing that the village appeared to be either asleep or deserted, they crept forward as silently as possibly.

They found the first head a dozen yards outside of the outskirts of the village.

It belonged to a man who looked to be about age forty or fifty—it was difficult to tell—and had been swept off the body with one clean stroke of a very sharp sword.

The beheading had not taken place many hours earlier. That much was clear. The expression on the dead man's features was horrible to behold, depicting manifest terror.

They discovered the decapitated body not very far away. The unfortunate wore the common Chinese costume that resembled a cotton nightshirt and sandals. The dead man appeared to have been a rice farmer.

Moving on, they found more headless bodies. These were scattered as if the dead had been cut down while fleeing. There were women and children among the slain.

"Holy cow," moaned Renny, aghast. "No one was spared."

"Where are their heads?" wondered Long Tom.

Creeping forward, they discovered the missing heads. They were stacked in a pyramid, as neatly as it was possible for human heads to be piled atop one another and not come toppling down.

Many eyes were open and staring. An evening breeze was stirring the hair on many of the piled craniums. That was the only sign of life in the macabre construction.

"No need to guess who did this foul deed," murmured Ham, eyes sick.

Monk growled, "That Tamerlane is up to his old tricks. Right, Johnny?"

When the gangling geologist failed to reply, all heads turned.

JOHNNY LITTLEJOHN stood rigid in his boots, his expression aghast, his skeletal face turning green. His elongated frame was trembling, like a scarecrow in a steady wind.

Doc Savage went to him. "What is wrong?"

"I—I wish I had never gone into that accursed cave," bleated Johnny.

"Get a grip on your nerve," said Renny. "You couldn't know what this would turn into."

Johnny got control of himself and they entered the village.

It was the same everywhere. Heads without bodies, bodies scattered about with raw stumps where their heads should be. Some were young, others old. Most were adults of assorted ages.

Renny grunted hoarsely, "He makes Genghis Khan look like a piker."

"There appear to be no survivors," said Ham, nodding somberly.

But that was wrong.

Hunting in the huts, Monk Mayfair discovered a pigtailed man cowering in a corner. He hauled the trembling individual out into the night. The latter wore one of the native costumes that resemble an old-style cotton nightshirt.

Doc Savage spoke to him in two different dialects before he received a response. They conversed for several minutes, then the bronze man turned to the others and said, "This man says that a group of Mongol horsemen led by a man in an iron mask did this. They rode in, demanded that every villager surrender without resistance, promised that no one would be harmed, then simply slaughtered everyone with their swords."

Johnny looked around. "Curious. They did not employ their arrows at any time. I wonder why?"

"The answer is simple," said Doc.

All eyes went to the bronze man.

"This village is practice for something greater."

Ham snapped his fingers abruptly. "The Japanese do not yet control all of China. It is too vast. By terrorizing countryside villages, they may be able to bring the entire nation under thrall."

They went back to the horses, where Captain Kensa Kan had been left, tied to a saddle.

Doc undid his bindings and set the man down forcefully. He was still under the influence of the intoxicating truth serum.

"Why did Tamerlane attack this village?" demanded Doc.

"To train his growing army in the arts of war," said Kan slowly.

"All of this slaughter, for practice?"

"They were only Chinese peasants," murmured the Captain.

"There you have it," stated Ham grimly.

Doc Savage addressed his men. "We have to stop this army of terror before it grows any larger."

"How do we do that?" grunted Renny. "There's only six of us against hundreds, and they're probably growing every day."

"Which is why we have to crush it here and now," said Doc Savage grimly.

A strange laughter broke the silence that followed. It was the tittering of Cadwiller Olden.

"What are you laughing about, you wormling?" Long Tom accused.

"Stop Tamerlane? The greatest, cruelest conqueror in human history? How are you going to do *that*?"

The laughter rolled out of the little man's mouth in nervous peals.

Abruptly, it stopped, and Cadwiller Olden gave out a wild yelp.

From behind them came an odd sound. A *thunk*. Another came. Then another.

Looking about, they could see nothing. But the unpleasant sounds continued.

Doc Savage and his men looked up.

The night sky was alive with moving things. Thin, reedy projectiles. Some of them whistled like banshees unleashed.

"Blazes!" squawled Monk hoarsely.

It started raining arrows!

Chapter XXXVIII

RED BLADE

"TAKE COVER!" RAPPED Doc Savage.

It was not so easy as that, however. There was little immediate cover to be had, and the first wave of arrows sprouted all around them. They struck the ground like fast-growing weeds. Not every shaft missed.

Monk let out a yipping howl. *"Ye-o-ww!"*

Struck in the chest, he fell backward, attempted to scramble to his feet and ended up taking another arrow in the right shoulder, which turned him half around.

Going on all fours, monkey-like, the hairy chemist bounded for the shelter of a grisly cairn of human heads. He was forced to drop his portable chemical laboratory, which he had carried from the wreck of their airplane.

Doc Savage raced to retrieve Cadwiller Olden from the saddle. This was not the humanitarian gesture it first seemed, however. The bronze man understood that Olden might become a bargaining chip.

But the distance was too great and the flood of barbed shafts forced the bronze giant to seek immediate shelter. He was too large a target to long evade the close-packed fusillade.

Calling to Johnny Littlejohn, Doc directed, "Get Olden to safety."

Johnny hesitated, then leaped in, presenting a tall target to falling arrows. A bit of humor said at the bone-thin archeologist's expense was that he was so thin he could take a bath in a shotgun barrel. Conceivably, his elongated thinness had something to do with his reaching the pack pony safely and hastily undoing the lashings holding the midget in place.

Cadwiller Olden was screaming, "We are all going to die!"

Johnny yelled, "Shut up!" and pulled him from the saddle.

By that time the second wave of arrows had quilled the hard earth.

"Is anyone hurt?" asked Ham from concealment.

"I took two," grunted Monk.

Renny thumped, "I caught one, too."

"Injured?" asked Doc.

"Naw. Bulletproof vest turned it."

"Same here," said Renny.

THEY waited. The night was too dark to see much. But, given the direction the arrows had been launched, it seemed that the Mongol force must be hiding to the southeast.

This was a good guess, but it had its shortcomings.

For a second wave of warriors suddenly erupted from the east. They could hear the relentlessly unnerving twanging of powerful recurved bows. Soon, a splintery cloud of missiles could be seen.

They struck all about. This time no one was harmed, although there were some close shaves.

"A detachment of archers has shifted into a different position," Doc called out.

"A typical Mongol battle tactic," added Johnny.

"Then why didn't you tell us before now?" demanded Renny.

The wordy geologist offered no reply. He was severely rattled.

Everyone commenced checking their superfirers, readying for what they assumed would be a full-on assault.

Johnny declared, "The armies of Tamerlane invariably called for surrender before charging in. That will give us time to strategize a counterattack."

They waited. No such call came. Instead, the ground commenced shaking and the thunder of horses' hooves split the Manchurian night.

"Guess Tamerlane forgot his old tactics," grunted Renny.

The horsemen came from two different directions—the east and the southwest.

Doc and his men took positions to defend both approaches. They knew it was hopeless. Between them, they had a plentiful supply of mercy bullets, but in order to beat back the armies of the Mongol conqueror they would have to make every shot count—an impossibility in the dark. Nor did they dare bring to bear their powerful spring-generator flashlights, for the brilliant beams would make of them perfect targets.

"How do we handle them?" asked Renny.

The question was directed at the bronze man, who suddenly said, "Let me try something."

The bronze giant streaked for the nearest horse and mounted it. He wheeled his startled steed about and raced off to meet the horde coming from the east.

Whether Doc Savage was lucky or had some inkling of the truth was never revealed. But at the head of the eastern horde stood the iron-masked warrior who might or might not be the Mongol conqueror, Tamerlane. He sat astride a magnificent black stallion, whose ornate wooden saddle was so filigreed with gold and silver it resembled an equestrian throne. Atop his pointed helmet, a horsetail danced with macabre half-life in the breeze.

On either side and behind him rode the main force of his horde, burly men stuffed into the long padded coats favored by Mongol horsemen. They brandished swords, pistols, pikes, lances, the odd battle axe, colorful lacquered shields and other accoutrements of ancient war.

At an imperative gesture from their leader, the archers lowered their bows, and held nocked arrows at the ready.

Doc rode up to meet him and brought his horse to a halt. Placing one hand over his heart, the bronze man shot out an open palm in the universal gesture for friendship and peace.

At first, this had no effect on the hard-charging Mongols. But Doc Savage stood tall in his saddle—taller than any Mongol who ever lived. The unflinching way in which he awaited the oncoming charge impressed the Mongol chieftain.

Abruptly, Timur called for his Mongols to slow their charge. This was instantly obeyed. The hard-riding horsemen slowed to a trot, but continued closing in.

Doc Savage did not flinch. Flake-gold eyes met sulfurous yellow orbs, and locked, unafraid.

Lifting a mailed hand, the chieftain brought his men to a halt. He stood in his saddle regarding the bronze giant with canine yellow eyes peering through the iron mask of an Asiatic ruler. He showed the teeth, fang fashion. Cold hate rode his feral eyes. And all the time he laughed, softly and unmusically. The awful sound had a creaky edge.

Without a word, the Mongol commander dismounted and came ahead on foot, striding with a halting, jack-legged gait and favoring one armored arm.

Doc Savage swung out of the saddle and advanced to meet him.

In Mongolian, Doc Savage called out, "I am Doc Savage."

The other croaked back, "I am Emir Timur Beg Gurkhani, destined ruler of all humanity. You know of me?"

"I do," admitted Doc.

They halted only a few paces apart, two imposing men of metal.

Tamerlane grunted, "And I have heard of you. A mercenary who fights for no pay. They call you the Man of Bronze. My name means Iron. Now I ask you, which is superior? A sword of bronze, or a blade of iron?"

Doc Savage replied, "That might depend upon the man wielding the blade, not the metal from which it was forged."

The self-proclaimed Tamerlane shook a mailed fist in Doc's impassive face. "I say iron is stronger!"

Doc did not reply to that.

The iron-faced one looked the bronze man up and down. "Where is your sword, brazen one?"

Doc Savage tapped his right temple. "Here. My brain is my sword."

This seemed to impress the Mongol leader. He grew quiet.

During this pause, Doc said, "We hold the Japanese officer as captive."

Tamerlane grunted. "What of it?"

"I offer him in exchange for safe passage for myself and my men."

Pale yellow orbs narrowed. "I will consider this."

Doc nodded. Folding formidable arms he waited, impassive of countenance.

The consideration did not take long.

"What of the small man?" asked Tamerlane.

"I have him, too," said Doc, concealing his surprise. "Why do you ask?"

"Why do you ask that I ask?" countered Tamerlane—if it was indeed he. "He amused me."

Doc looked momentarily puzzled.

Banging his mailed fist against his armored breast, the other barked, "He has a heart like mine."

Then, Doc Savage understood. The Mongol chieftain had recognized in Cadwiller Olden a rogue as black-hearted as himself.

"Throw him into the bargain," said Tamerlane, his voice vaguely rusty.

Doc hesitated. The thought of one of the worst Mongol conquerors falling in league with the modern scoundrel, Cadwiller Olden, made his blood run cold.

"Bring them both," snapped Tamerlane, turning on his heel and striding clumsily back to his stiff-faced horde.

That settled the matter. Doc Savage returned to his horse and rode back to his waiting men.

"Tamerlane has agreed to give us safe passage in return for Captain Kan and Olden."

"Me?" bleated the midget. "What does he want with me?"

"That is unknown at present."

"So you're just going to give me up? Some gold-plated hero you are!"

Doc informed him, "It is our only way out of this predicament."

Johnny asked tensely, "What about capturing Tamerlane?"

"I did not give any guarantee against further action on our part."

DOC SAVAGE went to Captain Kensa Kan and administered a stimulant by syringe, which brought the officer's mind into sharper consciousness despite the lingering effects of the truth serum.

"Tamerlane is willing to ransom you in exchange for our liberty," said Doc.

The Captain looked baffled. "Liberty? You are in Manchukuo. Where will you go?"

Doc Savage did not answer that. Instead, he instructed, "Come with us."

Everyone got on their horse. Johnny kept charge of Cadwiller Olden, who was fighting to get out of the former's saddle, but to no avail. Johnny cuffed him into subsidence, looking like he almost enjoyed it.

They rode up quietly. The cloud cover parted about this time and all around there filtered down shreds of thin moonlight, resembling lunar cobwebs.

This made what followed easier to track.

246 / A DOC SAVAGE ADVENTURE

Again, Doc Savage dismounted. He brought Captain Kan forward, presenting him to the masked Mongol.

"He is yours."

Johnny lifted Cadwiller Olden by the scruff of his neck and dropped him unceremoniously into the scrubby turf, saying, "You have earned your fate."

The midget scrambled to his feet and looked all about. There was no safe place to run, nor nook in which to hide. Reluctantly, he went toward the waiting horsemen.

As Olden walked by, Doc Savage said in English, very low, "We can locate you if you keep those clothes on at all times."

"Thanks for nothing," said Olden out of the side of his mouth.

Tamerlane climbed out of his saddle and approached the Japanese officer.

In the thready moonlight, Captain Kan looked relieved.

When the two drew near, the Mongol warlord quickly put his fist inside his coat, took it out, and the Captain gave out a hiss of surprise. He turned to run.

Tamerlane hit the Japanese in the back as hard as he could.

There was a long knife in the fist. The point stuck out two inches in front of Kan's heart.

"Iron beats bronze!" yelled Tamerlane, laughing.

"Double-cross!" howled Olden.

Leaping back into his saddle, Tamerlane vented a sharp command.

Chinua charged up, and speared Cadwiller Olden in one shoulder, lifted him high on his sword like a living joint of mutton. Tiny arms jerking, the midget began squawling horribly.

A phalanx of bowmen fitted fresh arrows to bowstrings and pointed them in the direction of Doc Savage and his men.

From his saddle, Tamerlane croaked, "We have what we want. Do not follow, swordless ones. Otherwise, I will take your heads."

With that, the Mongol chieftain whirled and, as one unit, his magnificent army turned with him. They parted to permit their leader to ride on ahead, taking the lead.

Together, they rode off into the cold Manchurian night, leaving Doc Savage and his men entirely unharmed.

Chapter XXXIX

RETREAT

DOC SAVAGE WENT immediately to the stricken Captain Kensa Kan.

The Japanese officer lay in the dirt, a wet crimson serpent creeping out from under him. His narrow eyes were wide and staring up at the stars. Out of his pale mouth came a cherry-colored froth.

With his dying breath the man kept repeating, "Do not understand. Do not understand."

"What don't you understand?" asked Doc urgently.

"The cursed Mongol," the officer choked out, "swore fealty—to the—Emperor."

With that last word, Captain Kan's spine stiffened reflexively, and all life departed from him. His rigid body collapsed like a deflated balloon.

Doc Savage stood up. Turning to his men, he said, "It is obvious what just happened here. The Japanese thought they could bend Tamerlane to their will, making him an arm of the Imperial Army. They underestimated his ambition."

Johnny nodded somberly. "The Captain was blind to the reality of Tamerlane's thinking. The warlord sees himself as fated to rule over all mankind. The Japanese are nothing to him."

Ham Books offered, "I believe I understand. Now that he has assembled an army, Tamerlane intends to conquer China, not for the Empire of Japan, but for himself."

Monk brightened. "Heck, that shiverin' specter oughta give the Japanese a run for their money. Maybe we should let 'em sort it out."

Doc Savage shook his head slowly. "Whether under Japanese control or not, Tamerlane has become one of the most dangerous menaces in Asia. Now that he has Cadwiller Olden, that makes him doubly dangerous."

Long Tom commented grimly, "From the way they took Olden away, I don't think he has very long to live."

"Long or not," Doc said grimly, "Tamerlane can pick his brain for many devilish schemes."

Renny rumbled, "Either way you slice it, we're stuck in the middle of nowhere without a plane and only enough horses to reach the next town. What do we do now?"

Doc Savage said, "There is a Japanese airbase within a day's ride of this spot. Where there are Japanese planes, there may be the opportunity to do some damage and acquire the means by which we can return to the sky."

The prospect of infiltrating a Nipponese airbase in the heart of Manchuria should have made the thoughts of each man somber and uneasy. Quite the contrary. Their faces lit up again, and they looked eager to be on their way.

There remained the matter of the disposal of Kensa Kan's remains.

"We should bury him," Doc suggested. "It is the humanitarian thing to do."

Monk objected straightaway. "If we bury him on humanitarian grounds, don't it mean we have to bury all those villagers back there, too?"

It was a fair statement. Doc Savage gave the matter some thought.

In the end, the bronze man walked away from the corpse of the dead officer and mounted up. The others followed suit. They followed their leader in the direction of the Japanese airbase, looking like the strangest group of Mongols who ever rode ponies, Monk resembling a costumed circus gorilla while skeletal Johnny towered so high in his saddle that he looked like the living embodiment of the Biblical horseman of the Apocalypse chillingly named Famine.

THEY reached the airbase two hours before dawn, and saw that it was not very large.

There were only thirty warplanes sitting in the open, and a large transport plane. It was the transport to which they turned their attention. The ship was a twin-engine Kawasaki Ki-56, modeled after the Lockheed Super Electra.

Still clutching the compact container holding his portable chemical laboratory, Monk muttered, "That Jap bus is big enough to take us wherever we want to go."

"Not back to the states, it won't," thumped Renny.

"We can hike back to Mongolia in it," insisted Monk.

"First," grumbled Long Tom, extracting his superfirer, "we have to take it."

That turned out to be the easiest part of the undertaking.

The airbase did not have much of a fence, and this was easily breached in the darkness. Doc employed a pair of wire cutters tucked into his special vest. They left their ponies behind, of course, giving them their freedom by removing the saddles.

Doc Savage moved first, drifted up behind a Japanese sentry, and dropped him with a single blow to the side of the head. The man went down like a sapling, his rifle ending up in the bronze men's lightning-quick hands.

Doc Savage went to the next sentry and accomplished the same thing. His men noticed that he used his fists liberally, something he preferred to avoid, not wishing to damage his hands since his highest calling was that of a surgeon. No doubt the bronze man's anger over the bombing of the naval base at Pearl Harbor prompted this rough treatment.

Doc reached the transport plane, got the door open, plunged into the cockpit, began snapping switches. He had the radial engines turning before his men even reached the plane.

Batting the throttles, Doc got the plane turning into the wind while his men scrambled aboard the cabin.

Last to board, Johnny pulled the hatch shut, the Kawasaki lifted its trim tail and flung itself eagerly into the night.

On the ground, the rudely awakened Japanese airbase got itself organized. It wasn't long before three nimble-winged Nakajima Ki-27 fighters were in hot pursuit.

As it happened, Doc had taken off in the direction of Russia to the north. With the Nakajimas buzzing after them, it was not practical and moreover very dangerous indeed to try to turn west toward Inner Mongolia.

Running all engines to their maximum, the bronze man sent the transport hauling south.

The Nakajimas soon overtook the Kawasaki and one appeared on either side of the cockpit. The pilots threw back their canopies, waved frantic arms, pointing to the ground, demanding that the transport land immediately.

In the co-pilot seat, Monk Mayfair opened the window, aimed carefully, and put one Japanese pilot to sleep in his seat.

Slumping forward, the pilot rode his careening warplane into the ground.

"One down!" Monk shouted gleefully.

Doc Savage said nothing. Normally he would upbraid the hairy chemist against inflicting unnecessary loss of life. But the bronze giant seemed in no mood for such admonitions tonight.

Another Nakajima popped up and Monk fired once. This time he missed, clipping the cockpit combing. That Nipponese pilot hastily closed his canopy and drove away, wings flashing.

The third Nakajima stole up from behind and attempted to fire what might have been a warning shot.

Red tracers made fiery webs in the night. No sound of lead striking the fuselage came, however.

Doc sent the transport into a sudden sideslip, and the enemy pilot who pulled alongside suddenly was staring at a winged monster seemingly about to ram him.

Japanese pilots are well-disciplined by reputation. This one was not. He panicked. Bringing himself out of his seat, he seemed poised to bail out.

His aircraft immediately lost control, and went into a screaming dive, to smash itself to bits against the side of a low mountain.

They never saw what became of the pilot. The last sight of him was a khaki dot disappearing from view, for he had been thrown out of the open cockpit.

"I do not see a parachute," commented Ham.

Renny replied casually, "Japanese don't believe in giving their pilots parachutes."

Doc simply righted the plane and kept going south.

Johnny bustled up and demanded, "Are we not returning to Mongolia?"

"No," returned the bronze man.

"Why not?"

"Have a listen."

Doc handed over his radio headset and Johnny pressed one earphone to an ear. He quickly became excited.

"The Japanese airbase commander is issuing phony orders to fly into Mongolia to create a provocation!"

Doc said, "He wants to trick the Mongolian Air Force into shooting us down if we cross the frontier."

Monk grunted, "So that means we can't enter Mongolian skies, right?"

"Correct," Doc Savage told him. "And if we fly south into Nationalist-held China, we will surely be attacked by the Free Chinese air forces."

From the back, Renny grumbled, "Holy cow! So what do we do now?"

Doc Savage said, "It will be difficult if not impossible to refuel. We will fly as far as we can manage, and then abandon this ship and attempt to find refuge somewhere."

They flew along until they passed over the meandering stone snake that was the Great Wall of China. It stretched out in an east-to-west line, climbing rolling green hills and dipping into verdant valleys.

Johnny remarked, "This fortification was constructed to hold at bay foreign invaders such as the Manchu and the Mongol armies. The current version dates back to the Ming Dynasty."

Ham observed, "Perhaps it will be enough to keep Tamerlane's forces from burrowing too deeply into the Chinese interior."

"Don't bet on it," scoffed Long Tom.

Looking down at the inhospitable terrain below, Monk wondered aloud, "How the heck did we wind up in the middle of China?"

It was an excellent question, for which no one had any sensible answer. Fast-moving events had seized them by their throats and carried them all into present circumstances, which would have been unimaginable mere days before.

THE REPUBLIC OF CHINA, which constituted the vast interior of the sprawling Asiatic nation, was under the control of a certain Generalissimo, who had as his provisional capital the city of Chungking, on the winding Yangtze River.

Knowing that Nationalist air forces were concentrated around that city, Doc Savage avoided it. He did not desire an air clash with friendly forces, especially as their stolen Japanese transport was unarmed. In aerial combat, they would be virtually defenseless.

The American Volunteer Group had, early in the conflict with Japan, established a spidernet of aircraft spotters and ground communications. Doc Savage had a good—but not perfect—understanding of this network. Doc employed this knowledge to avoid being spotted.

When they ran low on fuel, their future began to look grim.

Turning the controls over to Monk, Doc Savage and Johnny consulted Japanese military maps they discovered. They were very complete.

"It would be possible to land here, or here," suggested the gangling geologist.

"Here would be best," said Doc, folding the map.

Johnny looked puzzled, but did not question his bronze chief. Doc Savage always had a sound reason for his decisions, even if they sometimes baffled his men.

They landed at dusk in a wide valley. Doc immediately exited the plane and started foraging for tall cane plants that only Johnny recognized.

"Sorghum?" commented the perplexed archeologist. He was helping with the gathering, as were some of the others.

A pile was created. Monk came out of the plane, carrying his portable chemical laboratory, which he had managed to lug all this way. Setting this down in the dirt, he examined the long green stalks, and pronounced them satisfactory.

"Satisfactory for what?" complained Ham.

"For brewin' up moonshine."

This only caused the dapper lawyer's perplexed brow to darken.

Long Tom explained it to him. "They're going to try to distill something that will pass for aviation fuel."

"Can this be done?" Ham questioned.

No one replied. Doc and Monk were too busy rigging up a crude still from the cargo of the Japanese transport plane, which was crammed with handy odds and ends, that could be transformed into the appropriate apparatus.

It took more than a day before they had decanted sufficient ethanol to fill the tanks. This was combined with the unused fuel in the hope that the unorthodox mixture would work.

Doc fired up the engines, which caught with noisy explosions. When both radial motors ceased vomiting malodorous smoke, the bronze man released the brakes and engaged the throttles.

Everyone held their breaths as the air wheels bumped along. When the bumping stopped, they released relaxed breaths.

Climbing into a clear blue sky, Doc Savage said, "We should be able to make it to Burma."

As a prophet, Doc Savage was no Cassandra. They encountered a patrol of Republic of China fighters, a gang of outdated Curtiss Hawk biplanes and Boeing P-26 Peashooters, painted brown with blue-and-white stripes on their tails. They were easy to evade and Doc quickly left them behind, but at a price.

Inexorably, they were forced to fly south, farther away from their intended destination. The mood in the cabin became grimmer. South of China lay French Indo-China, which had fallen into Japanese hands. They would receive no welcome there....

Chapter XL
THE DOODLEBUG

H E HAD A kind of streamlined masculinity, and he was
in a hurry. He had walked from his hotel, although it was
raining, briskly waving aside a jinrickshaw because it was not
far, and already he was late; furthermore he was anxious—keen,
on edge—to come to grips with the trouble that had intruded
itself into his confident, two-handed life, like a piece of bitter
wormwood falling into a good tangy wine.

He had arrived in Hanoi less than an hour ago. His first
discovery was that the telephones were not working. So he sent
his valet with a message to Anne. He was proud of his dignified
Filipino valet. He had a valet because—well—once in every
man's life, he buys a cane, too.

Striding across the lobby toward the tiny tan bar, he looked
like an oilfield roughneck, dressed up for Saturday night—well,
not completely like an oilfield roughneck—just enough like
one that anybody could tell that was where he got started in
life, a little less than thirty years ago. The rain outside had put
a fine dew on his rough, expensive tweeds. A few drops as small
as mustard seed had fallen on the solid brown face when he
looked up, with utter carelessness, at the Japanese searchlights
that were suspiciously fingering the Indo-China sky.

The Japanese had changed Hanoi, all right. The city had gone
grim. Not that this worried him. It didn't. From his plane, he
had looked down at slate bulldog shapes of river gunboats at
leash in midstream, and naval seaplanes on the rusty water of

the River Song-koi, like dried insects mounted there with pins. The Japanese. The arrogant little uniforms with the sandstone faces that had been coming down from the north for a long time now. They didn't worry him. He had an attitude for them. He paid no more attention to them than to the coyotes chasing jackrabbits over the Oklahoma flats. He was Bill Saxon and he had another million dollars to make. Another million, maybe twenty. He had climbed out of an Oklahoma pipeline ditch the hard way, with his two fists. It had taken a long time to make himself a gold skyrocket, but now there was no top.

There was no rotary mud under his fingernails tonight. No photographic chemical stains from the recording truck on his square, strong hands. Head up, jaw angular. He was not thinking of geophone jugs, contrasting velocities, elastic earth waves, velocity of sound—6890 feet per second in Cretaceous lime—and the propagating sensitiveness of dynamite, sprung holes, salt domes, Napierian logarithms, computing. He wasn't concerned with these, or any of the other thousand things you have to know about to doodlebug for oil. He could doodlebug for oil, too. His bank balance proved that.

Saxon strode confidently into the bar. He remembered the pocket bar with the golden mirrors often during the past weeks when he was buried in the Mindoro jungle, doodlebugging. It had a Vandyke brown carpet, and saffron candleflame against the backbar, and a little door with a picture of Mickey Mouse, and another door for Minnie, and a round barman who did magic tricks with matches, and mixed American cocktails that would take hair off a dog.

His eyes swept the place. A rack that normally held newspapers from home—*The New York Times, The Kansas City Star, The Tulsa World*—was empty. But he took little notice. Immediately, he began to have a cold bath, for he was tall enough to look over the heads of everyone. His eyes were not finding Anne.

The barman who did magic tricks saw him, and hailed, "Good evening, Mr. Saxon. Very glad to have you back."

"Hello, Joe," he answered. "Seen any sign of Anne?"

"No, sir."

Frowning deeply, Saxon turned away. He took out and lighted his pipe. Then, he moved toward the hotel lobby, feeling vaguely disturbed.

He checked with the front desk, was told Anne had checked out several days ago. This further disturbed him.

"I received a message to come see her here."

"We have not seen the lady," said the Annamese man. His eyes shifted in a look that might have been guilty.

Saxon went back out. It stopped raining.

A object lay in the street, dry in spite of the recent rain. Its striking familiarity caused him to stoop and snatch it up. A matchbook. Green. He closed his horny fist over the thing.

He rode through the rain-washed night in a jinrickshaw. It was a two-man jinrickshaw, and the pair of Tong-king boys between the shafts had rounded backs and the bare sturdy legs of draft horses.

There were no civilian automobiles on the streets, only Japanese military ones. No gasoline was to be spared these days for civilian machines, because the United States had put an export restriction on gasoline to Japan, and the Japanese had found themselves frighteningly short of it. So you became old-fashioned and took a jinrickshaw.

The big flat feet of the two human steeds splattered through drying puddles left from the rain. The moon came out, and the dark shoulder of the Pagoda of the Great Buddha was limned against its silver fog. The moonlight pooled its deepest blue in Saxon's eyes.

He thought of Anne Coffelt.

Thanks to what the Japanese were doing to foreign businesses—the New Order in Asia—the Coffelt purse had shrunk from twenty to less than ten. Millions, of course. Bill knew that the Coffelts were taking a beating. Her father was in Manila, the Philippines. Anne had remained behind in Hanoi, only because a guy named Bill Saxon was coming back there. Anne was her father's business aide.

He opened his fist, looked at the little green matchbook from Sandakan. It advertised the New York Store, in Sandakan, North Borneo—a long way from here. A simple matchbook, like the ones they hand over the counter with a pack of cigarettes.

Out of his pocket, he extracted the one that had been waiting at his hotel when he had returned from the jungle.

They were identical. But one said, "Meet me at my hotel when you get this."

It was not signed, but he had assumed it was from Anne. She liked to slip him notes in matchbooks such as this one.

Opening the new-found matchbook, he found another note. It read:

AC-TAY ATURAL-NAY

It was not signed, but the printing was identical to the other note. Suddenly, Bill began to doubt that Anne had written either. So who had?

Someone who knew American English well enough to write "Act Natural" in pig-Latin, obviously.

STEPPING off the jinrickshaw, he walked through the rain, eastward along the street in which the sidewalks are very narrow, hardly enough width for his striding form.

Drab Japanese army trucks moved past him in the somber, streaming darkness. The trucks rumbled unendingly one behind another, headed ominously northwestward toward the jungle jugular vein that was the Burma Road. In the bleak east, half a dozen anti-aircraft searchlights thrust stiff white fingers upward and begin to feel suspiciously of the flanks of the clouds. Saxon looked at the trucks, then stared up at the searchlights. Enough hard amber light came from a shop window to reveal the grim expression on his face.

Saxon returned to his hotel. He had taken the most expensive room in the place, and the decorations were as Oriental as a New York chop-suey joint. He stared at the place with grim disgust. His valet had put out his red silk pajamas. He threw these into a corner. Then, he lay on the bed with a lit cigarette and a glass of gin and tonic water.

His body felt stiff and sore. He was suddenly very, very tired. To reach Hanoi, he traveled hard for three days—donkey, dugout canoe, plane—almost without sleep. His eyes ached. Standing open, the window let in the coldly muddy night wind. Big raindrops dripping down on the sill made kissing sounds. The anti-aircraft searchlight beams were still waving stiffly in the night. He stared at them. He cursed the searchlights in a low voice. The light in the room hurt his eyes and finally he turned it out. He did not seem to be able to think....

His valet was shaking him. When he opened his eyes, grimy daylight streamed into them. The Filipino said, "A gentleman to see you, sir. A Japanese gentleman."

He sat up disconsolately. "What time is it?"

"Nine o'clock, sir. The morning."

He had slept, or been unconscious, almost ten hours. But he did not feel refreshed. "What did you say was wrong?" he asked stupidly.

"A Japanese gentleman. A General Miyagi. To see you, sir."

"Oh." He arose and shaved, showered, toweled himself. The valet tried helping him dress. He scowled irritably. "Get out of here, dammit," he snarled. "Go fetch that Jap."

GENERAL MIYAGI was quite bald. His eyes were somber, yet as vital as crouching black rabbits. His skin was well-worn buckskin; his medals waved when he bowed. Bill noticed that he carried a dark leather dispatch case which he immediately opened, taking out the folded bulk of the document which was ornamented with official seals.

Miyagi said, "The contract. I have brought it for you to sign. You will notice that it reads as between yourself and the Dutch company. A new Dutch company. That is for—shall we say—international harmony. But you, naturally, must understand that you will find oil for the Japanese government."

He said this all in a rush, the way he probably—the Japanese were imitators—imagined that Yankees do business. Bill Saxon felt somewhat contemptuous.

"Got a pen?" Saxon asked shortly.

General Miyagi held out a fountain pen.

Bill Saxon took the pen, and the moment it was in his fingers, his brain missed a beat. He stared at the pen. It seemed to sting his fingers. Once he used it, and signed on the dotted line, he would be putting a lock on a gate.

Suddenly, he shoved the pen back. Lamely, he said, "Maybe I better read this over. Might save a misunderstanding later. Tell you what," he added, "see me tomorrow morning, and we'll settle the whole thing."

General Miyagi looked disappointed, then suspicious. His eyes glittered with angry feeling. "The terms here are exactly those we discussed and agreed upon," he said flatly.

Saxon studied him thoughtfully.

"You need me a lot, don't you?" he said.

"You have a verbal agreement with us," General Miyagi warned. "The Japanese government expects you to live up to it." He did not add that there would be dire consequences otherwise, but his tone conveyed the idea.

"Don't worry," Bill said wearily. "It's just that I always read the fine print in these things."

Uneasily, he watched General Miyagi, now resigned and carefully polite, bow and say, "Until tomorrow, then. *Mata aimasho. Sayonara.*" And, as his eyes followed Miyagi out the room, he got a concretely harsh feeling that the man could be very ruthless.

Bill Saxon jammed his hands into his coat pockets, paced around the room, and finally went to the window and stared out. An armored car stood in front of the hotel, an olive-colored fortress with two Japanese flags on the radiator grille. General Miyagi came out of the hotel and got in the vehicle. Bill Saxon watched the machine go out of sight.

Now his strongest thoughts went to this predicament he was in. Nothing else had much importance. Turning his mind back to the past few weeks, Bill felt ashamed. Ashamed of being such a dupe. In the beginning, he did not know that the contract was with the Japanese. The simple fact was: he had been caught off guard. He did not like to admit it, but his pride, his fool pride, kept him from recognizing the truth. He could remember the way he got into this mess, like a prize jackass.

The offer had come to him after he had proved the efficiency of his new method of doodlebugging for oil. He had just located three oil fields with sensational success. Offers showered on him, and naturally he picked the one that offered the most money. The company with the proposition had a Dutch name, and Dutch—he thought—officials. It never occurred to him that the Dutchmen were Germans, and a false face for the Japanese. He found that out later, when it was too late. But by then he had given his promise. And anyone who did business with Bill Saxon could file his word with their Liberty Bonds. He kept his promises.

Well, he hoped it wasn't too late to tell Anne all that.

After his valet had gone out to resupply the pantry, an insistent knocking disturbed his thoughts.

"Who is it?" he demanded.

"Friend of Monk's," came an unfamiliar voice.

"Monk who?"

"Monk from Tulsa."

"Monk from—"

Saxon threw open the door and stared at his visitor standing in the hallway. He appeared to be an undersized Annamese man of indeterminate age.

"Who are you?"

"Monk wants to see you," stated the man, ignoring the question.

For the first time, Bill Saxon put two and two together. The Annamese man was not speaking his own language, or Pidgin English. His English wasn't the stilted speech that passed for formal English among the Annamese populace. He sounded American.

"That greasepaint on your puss?" he asked.

"Monk needs your help."

"Tell him to come on up."

"Monk can't do that. Now are you coming or not?" asked the pseudo Oriental with irritation.

"Hold onto your shirt while I get my coat," returned Bill Saxon with equal impatience.

Chapter XLI

HUNTED MEN

BILL SAXON HAD never been inside the Pagoda of the Great Buddha in the heart of Hanoi. But that was where the slender man who was not an Annamese gentleman took him. They did not go directly, but took a circuitous route, with the tight-lipped man looking about making sure they were not shadowed.

He did it so often that Bill started looking around, too.

Eventually, they came to the glorious grounds of the pagoda, and slipped in through the side gate, where they were met by a saffron-robed priest. Appropriate bows were exchanged. The abbot followed silently and waved them inside. There they passed through chambers that grew increasingly smaller until they came to one where Monk Mayfair was waiting.

A sitting Buddha-like image cast in black bronze brooded over the chamber, flanked by subordinate statues of a serpent and a turtle. The Buddha weighed four tons.

Monk was hardly recognizable, inasmuch as he was encased in a tent-like Mongolian caftan.

"Monk!" exploded Bill. "You old hound dog. It's been ages since I've laid eyes on your ugly mug."

The apish chemist's grin was lopsided and sincere, but worry rode his homely features.

"Great to see you too, you horny-knuckled walkin' derrick," laughed Monk.

Bill got down to brass tacks. "What are you doing here? Who are you hiding from?"

"Who do you think?" barked Monk. "The dang Japs are tryin' to hunt us down."

Saxon looked perplexed. "What for?"

Now it was Monk's turn to look puzzled.

Before either man could question the other, a slim figure came from the other room, wearing something dark, caught at the throat with the frozen fire of a diamond clip. A vision of loveliness with honey hair and dancing gray eyes. They were not dancing now. They were grave.

"Bill...."

Bill's face froze. "Anne! What are you doing here with my old pal, Monk?"

"Knowing that we were friends, Monk came to me and I hid him here. You know I have connections to this temple."

"What's this all about?" Bill demanded. "Why all the subterfuge? Did somebody murder somebody?"

Anne looked at him steadily and asked, "Don't you know what happened?"

"I've been in the jungle the last few weeks, remember?"

Monk asked, "Ain't you seen a blasted newspaper since you got back?"

Bill shook his head firmly. "Too busy. Mostly I've been sleeping. Will somebody give with some facts?"

Monk and the Annamese man—who proved to be Long Tom Roberts in disguise—exchanged glances. Anne said, "The Japanese attacked an American naval base in Hawaii. We are at war with Japan."

Bill Saxon blew out a long slow breath that, if it had turned into a whistle, would have been one of astonishment.

"That puts me in a spot," he said in a low voice.

Monk said, "Not like the spot I'm in. We just escaped the Japs and ditched one of their planes out in the Gulf of Tong-king. We need to get out of here. But we can't get near the airfield. They're looking for us somethin' fierce."

"And I have a Japanese general on my back who wants me to sign a contract to help them drill for oil," returned Bill miserably.

"Oh, Bill!" gasped Anne.

"You can't do that!" Monk said sharply. "Them Japs are our enemies now."

"I gave General Miyagi my word," Bill growled stubbornly. "You know my word always sticks."

No one said anything for a very long time.

FINALLY, Monk pointed out an indisputable fact. "Drillin' oil for the enemy will make you a traitor."

Anne cried out, "Why would you do such a thing, Bill? Why?"

"Because they bamboozled me," snapped Bill hotly. And he told them the tale, concluding, "Don't get me wrong. I didn't know at the time—"

Anne seized his words. "You didn't know!" she accused with bitter force. "There was Manchuria—you knew about that. And Shanghai. Do you remember Shanghai? I do. I saw it. It was—not nice. Horror to turn your tears to dry dust. Then the Japanese army coming down the coast of China like a black leech on the map, to suck the life out of everything it touched. South China. Then this part of French Indo-China, like taking a bite out of a corpse."

Strain drew her voice as thin as a silver bell. "Why haven't you mentioned this before, Bill?"

"The deal wasn't closed," he said. "It's been hanging fire several months. They propositioned me right after I made those first three big strikes, and got a name for myself as a doodlebug. I closed a verbal contract then, to take effect when they got leases on a big acreage in the Dutch Indies. They got the leases, and notified me by radio. I go to work right away."

"No, Bill!" How strangely she said it, tone low and silvered, with an edge that cut him deeply. "You don't want to do that, and you mustn't!"

Bitter impulse drove him to say, "The Japanese have shaved about ten million off your family bankroll. That wouldn't have anything to do with it?" Because he was hurt, he spoke angrily. "Are you telling me I should be careful not to find any oil for the Japanese," he said contemptuously, "and do my bit as a missionary?"

"No, Bill. The only one who can tell you to do that is yourself."

"For Heaven's sake!" he ripped out. "Just because the Japs got your money—"

He had not meant to slap her with his words. But this was his way—the only way he knew—this two-fisted method of lashing out with full dynamite at trouble. He had been an oil field tool-dresser in younger days. You had to hit the best licks early to shape the red-hot drill bit before it cooled.

She stared at him, gray eyes dull.

"I got a contract," Bill repeated stiffly.

"With a government whose word is worth nothing." Anne added bitterly, "I should know. My family had contracts, too."

"The point is," he said stubbornly, "that I keep my promises."

"Oh, Bill," she said with a deep hurt in her voice. "You don't understand. This thing is bigger than your promises. You must lift your head, look around you. Responsibility as an American must mean something to you—something powerful, compelling. You must realize you're no longer one dog in a dog-eat-dog world, so you can't continue to center your interest on Number One Dog."

Monk interjected, "I couldn't of said it any better myself."

Distractedly, Bill ran his fingers through his hair and groaned, "We got to get out of this mess."

Monk asked, "You still got that cloud-hopper plane of yours?"

"Yeah, parked at the airfield south of the city."

"We were kinda hopin' that plane would be our ticket out of Hanoi."

Bill looked distracted, but asked, "How many are with you?"

"Counting Doc and Long Tom over there—six."

"That's eight with Anne and me. We'll be overloaded, but we can probably get off the ground if we all eat light and hold our breaths."

Long Tom spoke for the first time in his natural voice. "Swell. When can we start?"

"Let me go back to my hotel and clear up some things."

"What things?" Anne asked worriedly.

"General Miyagi expects me to sign a certain contract. I need to destroy it."

"How do you know you weren't followed here?" asked Monk suspiciously.

Long Tom answered that. "I kept a sharp eye peeled. We weren't followed."

"I did the same," added Bill. With that, he barked, "Give me an hour. I'll be back."

Long Tom blocked his escape, fists tightening. "How do we know you won't give us up to the enemy?"

Making his own fists hard, Bill growled, "I keep my promises, remember? Now step aside or I'll paste you one."

"Let him go, Long Tom," said Monk. "He's on our side."

"Count on it."

With that promise, Bill Saxon slipped outside and mingled with the pedestrian traffic of Hanoi. He walked aimlessly through the narrow streets in the gray morning light. He was disgusted with himself for his folly, his indecision. He wandered along the river waterfront where short, bloated steamers with a draft of no more than six or seven feet of water were disgorging troops like brown ants.

Bill studied their stiff, expressionless faces. The Japanese were mobilizing for something big.

That settled it. He knew what he had to do. Having made his decision, Bill returned to his hotel as fast as his long legs could carry him—and crashed headlong into catastrophe.

Chapter XLII

FOR BROKE

NO ONE COULD miss the olive-colored armored car which stood in front of Bill Saxon's hotel, two Rising Sun flags affixed to the radiator. *Click!* went Bill Saxon's brain, and he stopped dead. This was Miyagi's car. A military chauffeur sat stiffly behind the wheel. General Miyagi had returned!

With shocking certainty, Bill Saxon understood why Miyagi was in his hotel. That damned Filipino valet of his! He was probably a Jap agent. Why else did he fail to hand him a newspaper upon his return, or volunteer the small fact that America had declared war on Japan? With the fanatic zeal of admirers of the current Emperor of Japan, the valet must have appointed himself a one-man Gestapo and ratted on him.

Bad, this was. As Bill's mind slowly explored the ugly probabilities that would result now, he was appalled.

Stunned, he stood in a cold sweat. And now the urge to act was flowing up in him, becoming a hot pressure. He carefully restrained the passionate impulse to blind anger. He could do this well, putting a cool control on his mind in an emergency; it was an ability he had long ago mastered, and had done much to put him where he was now. Rage crawled vainly in his muscles.

Saxon crossed the street in a casual walk and entered his hotel. The telephones were in the lobby. They were—thank Joseph!—now working. He telephoned his valet and used short sentences and profane words, so there would be no doubt in the treacherous valet's mind about the urgency.

270

"Now, get moving!" finished Bill. "And if you fall down on the job, I'm going to beat the hell out of you."

After that, Saxon sat in an empty brown leather chair in the lobby, holding a newspaper someone had left behind. He smoked his pipe. His only nervousness was in his long legs, which he kept crossing and uncrossing. It took a long time.

General Miyagi stepped out of the elevator; he straightaway exited the hotel, a soldier walking briskly behind him. They got into the armored car, Miyagi taking the commodious back seat, the aide turning down an auxiliary seat to sit facing him. He carried the document case.

Bill crossed the sidewalk. He opened the door of the armored car, and swung inside. He growled, "I'm going along." And he turned down the seat beside the soldier for himself.

The hard-faced soldier had drawn a pistol and was holding it tight against his hip, but with the muzzle pointed downward.

AT first, no one spoke. Amazement had spread a flatly blank expression on General Miyagi's face; he was adapting himself slowly to the new situation, and not very agreeably. He did not like this. But then Bill Saxon had not expected him to like it. However, Bill had staked everything on the momentarily important fact that he was a man who could find oil, and therefore to be coddled. The number of that gamble won.

"*Isogu ni wa oyobani,*" General Miyagi ordered the driver. "Drive slowly," he repeated in English, so that Saxon would know everything was still calm.

The car moved ahead, running like a truck, with a solid tone of steel.

"What is the meaning of this?" demanded Miyagi. "I thought we were friends."

"What were you doing back at my hotel so soon?" Saxon asked him.

The General looked uncomfortable. His lips compressed in silence.

So Bill let the cat out of the bag. "I finally heard about the ambush on Pearl Harbor."

General Miyagi shifted his eyes to and fro, said coolly, "What has this to do with our business arrangement?"

"You know that it has everything to do with it!" snapped Bill.

The General said, "You will sign the contract. There is no choice in the matter. Not for you, and neither for me. It must be done."

Bill sat there, saying nothing for the longest time as the armored car trundled through the colorful streets of downtown Hanoi.

Then he made his move. The soldier was easy. Bill Saxon just grabbed the gun and held it fast with his left hand while he half turned to bring his right fist around. After that, his knuckles hurt, but it was a good hurting, and the gun barrel—the soldier's weapon—made a decisive sound on General Miyagi's head, and another sound, equally decisive on the driver's head. The car ran wild against the building, but it was an armored machine so that was not important. Bill Saxon was already climbing behind the wheel. The chauffeur had banged his head against the windshield, and clutched his head as if dazed. Bill cured his headache with a roundhouse right.

As he sent the armored car back into traffic, Bill muttered under his breath. "Think I can pull this off."

Excitement flew with him after that. It beat its hot wings close overhead during the whole tense, fast drive through the noisy city, to the Pagoda of the Great Buddha.

Chapter XLIII
INVASION

B ILL SAXON PULLED up near the ivory-gated Pagoda of the Great Buddha, and slipped out as quietly as he could. He reached the side entrance, eased inside, and was quietly taken to Monk Mayfair by the silent abbot in saffron.

This time Monk was in the company of Doc Savage and the other members of the fugitive group. Anne stood with them, looking somehow radiantly pale. There was also a tired-looking pet pig, who looked as if he had traveled hard.

"No time for introductions," Saxon told him rapidly. "I just commandeered General Miyagi's armored car. It's waiting outside with Miyagi and two of his polite monkeys flat on the floorboards."

"Will it accommodate us all?" asked Doc Savage in his re-markably vibrant voice.

"Not easily. But we have to chance it."

Since he was still disguised as a local Annamese gentleman, Long Tom went out first to investigate. He came back wearing the Japanese chauffeur's crisp military uniform.

That was when they made a break for it. Going in groups of two, they ran down to the waiting armored car and piled in.

Climbing into the back, Doc Savage took the seat next to General Miyagi and propped him up as if he were conscious, holding him in place with one strong fist.

Long Tom took the wheel. His make-up enabled him to pass for a Japanese flunky. The others hunkered down as best they could. Since this was an official car, it was unlikely to be challenged.

They drove straight for the flying field, and got in the line to the gate. Military vehicles hastily got out of their way to make room for the General's car to go on ahead. This helped enormously.

Coming to the guard at the gate, Doc Savage employed ventriloquism to make it sound as if Long Tom was speaking perfect Japanese. Long Tom kept his head down and his cap visor pulled low so the imposture would get by. He moved his lips soundlessly.

They were waved on through, and Bill Saxon provided directions to the hangar where the plane was waiting.

There was another difficult moment where they had to leave the vehicle in order to enter the hangar and take possession of the aircraft.

This went smoothly, however.

They left the General and the unconscious military chauffeur and soldier on the floorboards, where they were not likely to be discovered any time soon.

Doc Savage took the controls, and began familiarizing himself with them. Monk and Renny ran corrugated hangar doors open as the others climbed on board.

Engine howling, the trim high-winged ship pulled itself out onto the runway, lined up and started scooting along, hopping and bouncing until the tail lifted and she went straining up into the open sky.

No one spoke during this maneuver, and more than one passenger held their breath. Anne kept her eyes closed, lips moving silently in prayer.

"We made it!" Bill said cheerfully.

"Good thing, too," breathed Anne beside him.

"You don't have to tell me twice," grinned Bill.

"What she means," inserted Ham, "was that if we were discovered, we would all have been shot as civilian spies."

Bill blinked. "Oh. I hadn't thought about it that way. I guess this being at war with the Japanese is just starting to sink in."

"We're still gettin' used to it ourselves," admitted Monk.

A renewed silence once more overtook the cockpit as Doc Savage banked and pointed the smart-looking ship west.

Ham Brooks broke the silence when he asked, "Where are we headed, Doc?"

"Between the Vichy French and the Japanese, most of Asia is in enemy hands. Hong Kong and the Philippines are out of the question. So is Cambodia. We will make a run for Burma and hope it works out."

"I'll settle for any place the Japs don't have their boots planted," said Bill Saxon.

Anne gave him a comforting hug as Doc Savage turned the plane west in the direction of Burma.

REACHING Rangoon, the capital, was no milk run. They ran out of fuel twice and had to evade a Japanese air patrol once. Since Bill Saxon's plane was a civilian ship, it was not shot down.

But it was challenged.

Doc Savage took the radio microphone and attempted explanations in perfect Japanese. When they questioned him, he gave them an argument.

That, miraculously enough, fooled the pilots, and they were not pursued.

"Those Zeros are operatin' awful close to the Burmese border," said Monk Mayfair.

Anne said crisply, "The Japanese are spreading throughout Asia. They took Shanghai and Thailand, interning British, American and other nationals they considered the enemy. It's the most horrid thing you can imagine."

Renny rumbled, "Them pipsqueaks have gone for broke, taking on practically the whole world."

"Yeah, but they're in for a pastin' now that we're in the fight," promised Monk. "Right, Habeas?"

The pig grunted as if in porcine agreement.

FINALLY, they made it to Rangoon, landing at the Mingaladon airfield, which was maintained by the British Royal Air Force.

Doc Savage had radioed ahead, to arrange a meeting with American military officials who were stationed there, coordinating lend-lease to the Nationalist Chinese.

A Major Dunn met them.

"Washington has been worried about you, Savage." He said it as if it were an accusation of desertion.

Doc said, "My men and I ran into some trouble over Manchukuo, and were downed. We managed to evade capture, and make our way to Hanoi, finally reaching Rangoon, thanks to Bill Saxon."

"Well, you are in luck, Savage. The supply ship *Tulsa* has docked here. I will see about getting you back to the States, where you belong."

"That will not be necessary," said Doc. "During our flight, we discovered an army being massed to attack the free Chinese territories. An army of Mongol horse cavalry, led by a man calling himself Tamerlane, after the historic conqueror. He has mobilized a growing force for the sweep south."

"You don't say! The Generalissimo will be very interested to hear about this."

Doc cut him off. "My men and I want to fly back to quell this army before it gets out of hand."

A frown darkened the officer's weathered features. "I doubt the War Department will go for it, Savage. They want you safe and sound on American soil as soon as possible. Your brains are needed for the war effort."

"If this army is not stopped, China could fall to the Japanese," insisted Doc.

Major Dunn looked troubled. "The only way back is by air. You know that. Even if the generals are agreeable, getting you a flyable aircraft will be tough. Very tough. Practically impossible."

"I prefer a bomber," said Doc, brooking no argument.

Major Dunn whistled sharply. "The brass may tell me to inform you that you are getting too big for your britches."

"Let me know if that is the case," replied Doc.

The meeting adjourned and Doc conferred with his waiting men, who set up temporary headquarters at a Colonial-style teak mansion in the diplomatic quarter, which now served as a hotel.

"I have requested a light bomber," he told them.

Ham exclaimed, "Rather doubt they can spare one at this time."

"I designed the bomber," countered Doc. "They may make an exception."

The answer that came back hours later was a firm, "No."

In the lobby, Major Dunn tried to be conciliatory. "Why don't you turn in for the night and we'll see about getting you on a safe ship bound for the good old U.S.A.?"

Seeing that it was out of his hands, Doc Savage thanked the officer and returned to his hotel suite, where he broke the bad news to his aides.

"Well, I guess we're all going to get seasick," muttered Long Tom.

"Not necessarily," said Doc. "British authorities may be more reasonable. Turn in for the night, and I will work on the proposition."

THE R.A.F. was very interested in Doc Savage's report of a Mongol army of invasion massing in Manchukuo.

"A bomber, you say?"

"I would like to leave in the morning, if at all possible," said Doc.

"I daresay our American friends will look unkindly upon an ally doing you this special service."

"Have you any plane requisitioned for delivery to the Nationalist Chinese which we could ferry to the interior?" prompted Doc.

"Not a bomber. But perhaps something could be worked out."

IN the end, the matter was settled in the most decisive way possible. But not by the R.A.F.

The next day, the Japanese invaded Burma from the south, coming in from Thailand, and overrunning the Tavoy airfield at Victoria Point, south of Rangoon.

Major Dunn rang Doc Savage by telephone and barked, "If you still want to go to China, I can let you have some aircraft. Better get down here before they're blasted apart."

They took a careening taxi through streets milling with confused Burmese men and women, many wearing rakish turbans. The air was filled with shrill whistling sounds that ended in explosive reports. Detonations speckled the sky.

"What are they firin'?" Monk demanded. "Cannon?"

"More to the point, what are they firing at?" countered Ham, craning his head out to look up at the sky.

"Not cannon," Doc Savage informed them. "Those are skyrockets."

"Are they celebrating the invasion?" rumbled Renny.

"Some are," said Doc. "There are many pro-Japanese elements in Burma. But the skyrockets you hear are a form of Buddhist prayer."

"Huh?"

Johnny explained patiently, "The people of Burma insert written prayers into bamboo rockets. The whistling sound combined with detonations of the prayer papers are calculated to appeal to their gods, much the way devout Tibetans employ prayer wheels."

"Strange," murmured Ham.

"This is a land in which many have perished in sanguinary wars over religious relics," added Johnny. "But not as many as during the old Mongol invasions."

"The Mongols got this far, huh?" Long Tom mused.

"There is practically no corner of Asia not touched by past Mongol invasions," Doc Savage advised them.

BILL SAXON met them at the airport, saying, "I would join you lads, but I don't want to be shot for desertion."

"Desertion!" barked Monk.

"Hell," grinned Bill. "I enlisted last night. Regular Army. They told me I was too old, but when I barked back that I knew where Uncle Sam could find oil if we took the right patch of ground, they changed their khaki minds. Now I gotta get Anne on a safe boat headed home."

Monk and Bill solemnly shook hands and went their separate ways.

"This war is sure spreading fast," Renny rumbled. "Let's see what kind of crates they mustered up for us."

The ships were not what they expected. Instead of a bomber or even a transport plane, there was a hangar full of P-40 Curtiss Warhawks, painted tan with ribbons of olive drab camouflage crawling along fuselage and wings. Back of the props, snarled the gory shark-fanged snouts that were fast becoming famous as the trademark of the American Volunteer Group, the U.S. pilots who had taken the Chinese side against Japan months before the Pearl Harbor sneak attack, who had been nicknamed for some reason, "Flying Tigers." The aircraft were pocked with steel-rimmed bullet punctures. But they looked airworthy.

Doc Savage checked the Allison V-1710 engines, Monk and Renny helping. The motors fired up nicely, and appeared sound.

"We won't get all the way to China in these crates," suggested Renny. "Not enough range."

"Better than nothing," said Doc, climbing into his cockpit.

280 / A DOC SAVAGE ADVENTURE

The others hastily did the same. Soon, they went roaring off, one by one, and flying north in formation.

Over the radio, Doc Savage said, *"We will link up with the forces of the Generalissimo and hope that they can spare fuel."*

Long Tom said, *"When that old warhorse hears what's in store for China, he'll probably lend us his entire army."*

"When did you turn optimist?" asked Ham.

"Radio silence," warned Doc, touching his throat mike. *"We do not want to attract patrolling Japanese fighters."*

THEY were over sun-drenched green jungle, following the Irrawaddy River northward, when the tiny squadron encountered a patrol of Zeros which had crossed over from the border of newly conquered Thailand.

The Zeros were flying low, in a chevron formation. As soon as the enemy pilots spotted them, the latter peeled off and gave chase, climbing like silver rockets emblazoned with red balls on wings and sides.

Pressing his throat mike, Doc Savage said, "Engage the enemy. Remember that their aircraft are more maneuverable, but ours are faster and better armored. Good luck."

All of Doc's men were expert pilots and a few had combat flying experience. Furthermore, the bronze man had managed to impart some of his extraordinary piloting skills to his aides. They pressed those skills into service now.

Doc Savage pushed his stick forward and dropped to meet the Zeros. The Warhawk was equipped with twin .50 caliber machine guns mounted in the nose, with a set of .303-caliber guns in each wing. Spitting a devastating barrage of lead, the bronze man slashed through the formation, blasting one enemy fighter so badly the pilot sought level earth, and causing the rest to scatter.

His men pounced on the fleeing flock. Renny cut across one from above, chopping his foe's port wing to silvery splinters. The pilot threw back his cockpit, as if to fling himself free of his corkscrewing bird. Instead, he rode the stricken craft to the jungle canopy below.

The fight was short, bitter and intense. The Zeros got the worst of it. The formidable fighters, despite their 7.7-millimeter machine guns and paired 20-millimeter cannons, were frail in comparison with the well-armored P-40s.

Doc Savage proved this when he continued diving, luring a solitary Zero to follow him. The Japanese pilot, thinking he had the American ship on the run, failed to notice the skin of his wings start to wrinkle. He realized he was in trouble only after his wings were shucked off by the aerodynamic force of his reckless dive.

Pulling out of his own dive, Doc sought altitude. He saw immediately that only two Zeros remained aloft.

One had leaped upon the tail of a frantically maneuvering Warhawk, and winking red sparks told of stuttering machine guns. Doc could not immediately discern whose ship it was.

Then, Johnny's voice crackled through his earphones.

"I'll be superperforated!" he cried out in alarm.

"Johnny is having difficulties," warned Doc.

"I see 'im!" howled Monk. *"Hang on, you long bag of bones. I'm comin'."*

Monk's ship climbed. But he did not engage—dared not engage. The Zero was dogging the Warhawk's gyrating tail, and to fire at one would mean striking the other.

Johnny flew like a champion, breaking and rolling, but failed to shake his fixated foe.

Ham shouted, *"Monk, you hairy goon. Do something!"*

"Watch this!" yelled Monk, rolling his ship hard.

The simian chemist's fighting tactics on the ground had often been described as animalistic. Monk was known to take the occasional bite out of an opponent with his apish teeth. He also liked to roar and howl in the most unearthly fashion when taking on a foe.

Every one of Doc's men heard one of those bloodcurdling war whoops crackle over his cockpit radio.

"Ye-e-o-w! Powder River!"

Monk's Warhawk jumped on the Zero's bright tail. He chased it like a bulldog. The nose propeller came into contact with the Zero's vertical stabilizer, which promptly flew to pieces.

Peeling away, Monk howled, *"The old buzzsaw maneuver! First in aviation history!"*

The Zero pilot lost control of his steed and was flung free of his out-of-control aircraft, with predictably fatal results.

Relief in his precise voice, Johnny called out, *"Benedictions, you audacious anthropoid."*

Doc asked, *"Monk, how is your propeller?"*

"Airworthy," reported Monk.

"Form up on me," instructed Doc, leveling off.

One by one, the Warhawks fell into line with Doc's plane. At Doc's direction, they strung out in a tight V formation so they could examine one another's ships for damage.

Other than the fact that they had collected more bullet holes, and Renny's port wingtip was missing, no significant damage had been acquired. The Warhawks could take considerable punishment and remain airworthy. That, and the psychological effect of the shark-mouthed snouts, had won the day.

Renny rumbled, *"Guess we can limp on to Mandalay."*

"Those Nipponese pilots never knew what hit them," Long Tom offered.

"Demonstrably," chimed in Johnny.

Doc Savage did not reprimand them for the loss of life. Their actions had been ones of self-defense and the deaths had been as a direct result of enemy action in a time of war.

Monk's voice had a grin in it when he exclaimed, *"At the rate we're goin', we'll all be aces by next week."*

A piggy grunt coming from Habeas Corpus seemed to second the hairy chemist's boast.

"Radio silence," reminded Doc grimly.

Chapter XLIV

THE GENERALISSIMO

THE LITTLE SQUADRON flew north, refueling at
Mandalay, then turning northwest, skirting Japanese-held
Thailand and aiming for a secret airbase in China—Kunming,
at the Chinese end of the Burma Road, which was the main
supply route into the beleaguered nation. From time to time,
they spied ancient temples resembling ornate vanilla ice cream
cones poking up from the lush mango tree jungle. Riotous
macaws lifted high, as if eager to join up with them.

Refueling was done along the route in out-of-the-way air-
strips. They were expected and promptly serviced before getting
back into the air.

Finally, the group reached Kunming, where they were wel-
comed by local authorities and allowed to rest and eat. Radio
reports apprised them of the situation in Burma. Japanese forces
were driving hard into the country, and while the British were
pushing back, victory for either side was by no means certain.
Malaya was under severe attack. Japanese bombers had sunk
two Royal Navy warships, the battleship *Prince of Wales* and the
cruiser *Repulse*. Japanese invaders were pouring through Thailand, which had initially resisted pressure, but finally acceded.
The Philippines were also embroiled. The American Asiatic
Fleet stationed there was forced to withdraw to distant Java.

The Empire of Japan appeared to be sweeping unchecked
throughout Southeast Asia.

"The entire civilized world seems to be coming apart," lamented Johnny over a heaping bowl of steamed rice.

"Buck up, you long-worded cuss," rumbled Renny. "Tokyo has bitten off more than it can chew this time. Right, Doc?"

"We had better get back into the air," the bronze man said quietly, laying aside his empty bowl. "There is no telling how much progress Tamerlane has made in our absence."

IT was the morning of the next day when they reached their ultimate destination, the city of Chengdu, in the heart of Western China.

The Generalissimo himself was there to greet them. He was an impressive figure in his bemedaled uniform with his shiny bald pate and military mustache.

Towering over him, Doc Savage briefed the leader of Free China on the situation in Manchuria.

"This is an army intent upon slaughter, nothing else," he concluded. "Tactics we observed are those that go back to the days of Genghis Khan and his Golden Horde."

The Generalissimo's eyes glowed as he soaked up all this. Smooth brow furrowing, he asked impatiently, "Who is this warlord who leads these Mongols?"

Doc Savage said truthfully, "We are not certain. He calls himself Timur. Wears an iron battle mask, which conceals his features. The important part is that he is a seasoned leader of men, and knows what he wants to do."

"You say he is a creature of the Japanese?"

"Was," returned Doc. "At last report, he broke away from Japanese control and was heading south. That was only three days ago."

"What will you need, *Ren-Beh-chingtung?*" asked the Chinese leader, invoking the honorific, Man of Bronze.

"Have you a fast bomber available for our use?"

"Not one I can spare."

"All we need is one bomber and time to fit it for the mission," pressed Doc. "Otherwise, this modern Tamerlane will cut through the heart of China like a hot knife."

The Generalissimo fingered his mustache thoughtfully. "We cannot spare any plane, but neither can we afford to raise an army to meet these invaders. I will loan you a Heinkel He 111 medium bomber, which is scheduled to be converted into a transport plane. It will need some repair, of which you are very capable of performing satisfactorily. What else will you require?"

"Certain chemicals, ordnance that we can alter for our needs."

The Generalissimo said, "If we have it, it is yours. How many fighters to support you?"

"None. Not at this time. Let us try to quash this army of terror alone. If we need further assistance, we will let you know."

"This is highly irregular, you understand," the Generalissimo said tersely.

"This is a new war," countered Doc. "It will not be won by regular tactics."

They clasped hands and Doc Savage went to tell his men that they had their bomber.

The bronze man wasted no time with explanations. "Monk, we're going to need special chemical bombs. Also fresh mercy bullets. Renny, see about finding the appropriate caliber ammunition and we will get right to work."

It took two days working round-the-clock to prepare the bomber. In the meantime, the Japanese were pounding Burma mercilessly.

On the second day, there was a *gingbow*—an air raid. It was brief. Three Japanese bombers dropped their loads, producing the dully monotonous *crump-crump-crump* sound when their payloads detonated.

After Chinese fighters chased them away, resulting damage proved to be insignificant.

"This dang war ain't going so well," Monk grumbled.

Doc reminded, "Wars are settled in the end, not at the beginning of conflict."

The Generalissimo drove out to meet them, bearing news.

"This nomad army crossed the border of Manchuria and has descended upon a small town in the purple frontier. I have reports of wholesale butchery, in which no one was spared."

"We witnessed exactly that in Manchuria," replied Doc.

"I was forced to dispatch troops to deal with these Mongols." The leader hesitated. "They were approaching the main column but were ambushed from behind by a hidden detachment of cavalry. My men were slaughtered. There were no survivors. I dare not squander any more soldiers on these mounted demons. It is up to you to accomplish this."

Doc Savage said nothing. The look in the Chinese leader's sun-squint eyes was troubled.

The Generalissimo said, "You are a man who knows history, Savage. Genghis Khan sacked this very city, massacring some million citizens. We Chinese built the long wall to keep the Mongol scourge at bay. Now that menace has returned, and at the worst possible time, when China is sundered and reeling, her coastal cities in Japanese hands."

Doc Savage promised, "We will not return until the army of Tamerlane is no more."

The Generalissimo nodded curtly, and without another word left them to their work.

OVER the following two days, Doc Savage supervised modifications to the Heinkel, which included souping up its twin engines and making interior alterations to accommodate the type of ordnance Monk and Renny were devising.

Finally, the bomber was ready. As a gesture to Doc Savage, Chinese mechanics had scrounged up some bronze paint and applied it to the olive drab skin, adding a crude U. S. flag to the tail.

Noticing Chinese brushstrokes along the nose, Monk asked, "What do these chicken tracks say?"

Johnny grinned. *"Brazen Devil."*

"Swell. Let's give Tamerlane merry hell."

They squeezed in. Doc crowded into the cockpit, with Monk claiming the navigator's position beside him. There was a flexible machine gun in the blunt nose. Renny took that. Ham folded himself in the dorsal gunner's blister, directly behind them. Below, Long Tom squeezed his slender form into the ventral gunner's position situated in the Plexiglas belly gondola. Lastly, Johnny crawled into the bomb bay, distributing his lathy limbs in a corner of its cramped confines. The bomber permitted a crew of five, so space was tight.

The Heinkel took off at dusk, trailing a dusty serpent behind it. The Wright Cyclone radial engines Doc and Renny had refurbished pulled the ship into the sky with a scream like two howling banshees. High above them, searchlights made pale ghosts that hunted among the clouds.

"Feels good being back in a big plane again, don't it?" asked Renny, from his position in the Plexiglas-nosed forward gun position.

Long Tom remarked, "I kinda liked my Warhawk. The Flying Tigers have been protecting the Burma Road from enemy planes with those scrappy crates."

Doc did the flying. Habeas Corpus, who had been along for all the hectic flying, slept on the floor of the rear bulkhead by himself.

Johnny had been silent, deeply troubled by the hell he had inadvertently awakened. Now he spoke, addressing no one in particular. "I wonder if that devilish Cadwiller Olden is living or dead."

Long Tom groused, "Last we saw him he was on a spit. Maybe that defrosted demon roasted him alive."

"Serves him right, after all the deviltry he stirred up," Monk muttered. "Maybe being cooked alive prepared him for the hot place."

Doc Savage offered no comment. He concentrated on his flying. Any concern as to the fate of the murderous midget did not show in his face or actions. The little man seemed like an insignificant piece of a larger problem now.

All through the night, the Heinkel droned north, on a direct heading with the first Free Chinese town to fall before the Mongol invasion—a spot called Wu Lung on the map. The name of the place, in English, was Five Dragons.

Chapter XLV

CRIMSON CONSEQUENCES

CADWILLER OLDEN AWOKE with his throbbing head feeling three times its normal size. He peered around, winced, and saw that he was inside a round Mongol tent which was sumptuously furnished.

Groaning, the midget attempted to rise, but almost fell off the shelf-like brick bed on which he had been placed.

Scrambling, he seized the coarse bedding with his left hand to keep himself from falling over. For some reason he could not immediately see, his right hand refused to obey him.

Working himself around, he managed to get himself into a seated position.

That was when a fiery agony flared up in his right shoulder like dozens of red-hot needles.

Then, he remembered—remembered being speared like a joint of meat on the sword of the wolfish bandit chief named Chinua. The memory bit and seared.

Feeling for his throbbing shoulder, Cadwiller Olden discovered that it had been bandaged, but the bandages were soaked with blood. His good hand came away sticky with the stuff.

Moaning aloud, Olden attempted to use his right hand. It was completely paralyzed. The entire arm felt numb.

He considered his situation. Calling for help seemed the poorest of choices. So he bit his thin lips, and fought back the urge to cry out in pain. His shoulder ached, but below that everything felt dead and heavy. It was as if his right arm no longer belonged to him, even though it was attached to his body.

Without both arms, the only way off the shelf-like bed would be to throw himself down and then roll and crawl. Cadwiller Olden did not feel up to such strenuous exercise, so he waited, fear and agony twisting his small features.

AFTER an hour, Tamerlane entered, his unmasked face revealed in all its grotesque, toad-like fascination. His windy-featured general, Chinua, accompanied him.

Seeing that the little man was awake and seated upright, they began discussing him, stabbing fingers in his direction.

Olden said bitterly, "There was no need to treat me the way you did. I'm on your side."

The Mongols did not understand English, of course. The pair continued their earnest discussion, and after a bit leaned in and examined the wounded shoulder, after roughly stripping away the bloody bandages.

This ripped a long groan from Cadwiller Olden's throat, and sparked amused laughter from the withered lips of Tamerlane the Great.

After the examination came more discussion. Without warning, Tamerlane bit out instructions to his general.

Abruptly, Chinua yanked his sabre from his scabbard, wheeled, and advanced on Olden, who shrank back, cowering fearfully.

"No, no, no!" pleaded the little man. He threw up one minuscule hand, as if to fend off the lifting sword.

Without hesitation, the blade flashed downward. There came a meaty sound, which ended in a thud, punctuated by a long scream that made it sound as if raw lining was being torn out of the midget's tortured lungs.

After the outcry trailed away, there followed a moment of silence in which the rasping voice of Tamerlane lifted in cruel cackling, to be joined by the hearty laughter of his general.

Somewhere outside, wild dogs could be heard barking. Their yipping sounded weirdly like raucous laughter.

CHAPTER XLVI
FIVE DRAGONS

FROM THE AIR, one Chinese town looks very much like another. It might be nestled amid terraced mountains or stretched out among vast rice paddies. Distinguishing one from another would be difficult, even for a native Chinese flyer.

Doc Savage found the town that had fallen to the new Golden Horde without any difficulty whatsoever. He had its longitude and latitude, good maps, and his navigational skills were excellent—if ultimately superfluous.

For the hapless town was easily discovered without any map coordinates.

A great pall of ebony smoke hung over what remained of the spot. The evil cloud was slowly thinning into a gray haze at its outer edges, but the blot was intensely black where it smothered the habitation.

"What did you say this place was called?" asked Ham Brooks, eyeing the spreading smudge.

"Five Dragons," said Doc, grim-voiced.

Monk grunted, "Looks like all five up and breathed scorchin' fire on the joint."

In the cabin, Johnny Littlejohn was half out of his drop-down seat and scrutinizing the ground with a pair of powerful field glasses. What he beheld through the thick smoke made his long features turn the color of scraped bone.

"It was a massacre," he croaked.

In the transparent gunner's gondola, Long Tom pressed binoculars to his eyes.

"Johnny isn't exaggerating. Looks like no survivors."

"What can you make out?" asked Doc, sweeping around and bringing the plane closer to ground.

"Bodies. Heads. Lots of both. Not many together, though." He sounded sick.

Monk looked to Doc Savage. "Do we land?"

"Finding Tamerlane and his army takes priority," returned the bronze man.

Climbing the Heinkel bomber dubbed *Brazen Devil,* Doc Savage sought the trail of hoofprints leading away from the blighted town. He soon found what he sought, and planted the plane on a heading following the marching army of terror.

The others fell to checking their weapons. Except Johnny Littlejohn. He had his face buried in his thin hands, as if unable to fully comprehend the horror that he had witnessed.

Long Tom whispered to Ham over the intercom. "Looks like Johnny is taking it hard."

"Wouldn't you?" countered the dapper lawyer. "None of this would have happened had he not discovered that damnable ice cave."

"I just hope he doesn't suffer a breakdown, his mind clouded by guilt the way it is."

"When the fighting starts," declared Ham, "Johnny will be in the thick of it, with the rest of us."

In the cockpit, Monk glanced back at the skeletal archeologist, who seemed to be lost in a trance of horror. The expression on his hollowed-eyed face was frosted with shock. He resembled one of the ancient desiccated mummies he had once excavated from the Nile.

A low moan lifted from deep within Johnny Littlejohn's being. It made everyone who heard it squirm uneasily.

Chapter XLVII

THE KHAN OF IRON

RIDING AT THE head of his army, wearing his battle mask forged from meteoric iron, the Mongol warlord who called himself Timur surveyed the rolling landscape of northern China with canine yellow eyes.

Alongside him rode Chinua, his wolfish second-in-command. Strapped to the otherwise unoccupied saddle of a Mongolian pony, was an ornate box of intricately carved teak, resembling a casket in miniature.

Behind them, stretched out in ranks of five, followed his ever-growing army, the new Golden Horde, which Timur had dubbed his Iron Horde, insisting that gold was too soft a metal to describe the hard-bitten warriors at his command.

"It is a great day to be alive!" proclaimed Chinua.

"No," said Timur in a voice that reminded one of a rusty gate hinge creaking in the wind. "All days that one tastes life are great." His feral eyes flamed. "Some days, however, are greater than other days."

Chinua beamed, drawing in a long breath of air. "For me this is the greatest day so far of my existence," he boasted. "I have never dreamt of such a day."

Surveying the Chinese countryside all around, Timur growled, "Far greater days lie ahead. Days of conquest. Nights of satisfaction."

"With such days stretching before us, I do not care if I never sleep again. I do not want to miss any of this earthly glory."

Casting his voice in the direction of the teakwood box bouncing on the empty saddle, Timur demanded, "What say you, my little oracle?"

From the carven casket came a miserable voice. In rough Mongolian, the voice said, "I don't care anymore. I just want to die."

And Timur laughed—an awful, ugly chattering sound, for his peg-like teeth could not stay still.

From the coffin-like container came a low groan, articulate and helpless.

Chinua laughed, "His command of our language is improving."

"With every whack of my sword," Timur grunted, "I fortified his desire to learn."

This brought another groan from the bouncing box. It was very small. A young child might squeeze into it, but he would have very little room. There was so little space in the receptacle box that not even the diminutive Cadwiller Olden would have found room for all of his tiny person. Yet somehow the inhabitant of the casket he had been crowded into its tight confines.

The marching army came at last to a bulwark of mountains and struggled to wend their way up the difficult pass that cut through them.

"What lies beyond this mountain range?" wondered Chinua. "I do not know these peaks."

"I do not know, nor do I care," returned Timur. "There is always something worthwhile beyond every mountain range. Something to seize, or crush, or pillage. Perhaps a city, or possibly only another town. It matters not. Whatever it is, by nightfall, or no later than the dawn, it will belong to us. Nothing can stand before the Scourge of Humanity."

"Nothing under Heaven," praised Chinua.

Timur nodded his iron-shod head. A sweeping horse tail blew from the tip of his pointed helmet.

"In the life that I formerly lived," he ruminated, "I was a powerful emir. But only an emir. Never a khan. In this new life, awake in a new century, I proclaim myself to be a true khan. Timur Khan."

Chinua lifted his voice, and it swelled with pride.

"All hail Timur Khan, the Khan of Iron!"

Behind them hundreds of Mongol swords leapt from their scabbards, and what sounded like a thousand throats lifted in praise.

"The great Khan of Iron!"

Chapter XLVIII
THE BRONZE DESTROYER

THE BRONZE HEINKEL BOMBER volleyed west, Doc Savage gripping the control yoke. He flew low, active golden eyes sweeping the terrain ahead. His metallic features were graven in a way human flesh rarely achieves.

There were times when the comrades of the mighty bronze man doubted that he was entirely human. This was one such time. He might have been a machine of metal parts cunningly wrought and assembled. Tireless, single-minded, indomitable in the manner of Achilles or Atlas, or some comparable hero of ancient times.

Every iota of his being was focused on finding Tamerlane and his horse cavalry before it could commit further depredations. His golden eyes, usually animated, possessed the bleak look of frosted metal.

Night fell. The light died early and rapidly, in accordance with the season.

"We might lose 'em," muttered Monk in the co-pilot seat.

The bronze giant shook his head slightly. "They are making for those mountains yonder. No habitation lies before them. It is my hope that we overtake them before they reach the pass that cuts between the peaks."

Soon, Monk and the others saw what concerned the bronze man.

Even in the dying light, the size of the army of Timur could be discerned.

It was immense. A metallic serpent composed of segmented lines of horses riding five abreast. It bristled with what appeared to be pikes carried high. Many wore round shields strapped to their armored backs. Here and there, specimens of the two-humped camels common in this part of the world, trooped majestically along, laden with booty.

The bronze man dipped the plane and called back, "Ready all bombs."

Ham and Long Tom climbed out of their gunnery perches and raced for the crates containing their armament. They flung open lids while Johnny roused himself from his numbed stupor and pitched in. His eyes were feverishly bright.

Monk pitched out of his seat to assist. Most of the containers housing the bombs were of his formulation, and the apish chemist wanted to wring the most destruction out of them.

As ordnance went, the bombs were simple in construction. Some were filled with anesthetic gas. But others were nastier. There were copious quantities of tear gas of three different types. There were potions that stung the skin, or inflicted uncontrollable itching. Vapors that, once they touched exposed flesh, discolored it, turning their skins a ghost white. This last was for psychological effect, for Doc Savage had reasoned the best way to discourage an army of terror was to terrorize it. White was the Chinese color of death, and men so marked would be seen as wandering ghosts, or at least carriers of death.

Banking slightly, Doc lined up the bomber on the sinuous army of conquest. In the nose, Renny swiveled his machine gun. The weapon had been charged with mercy bullets, but the initial rounds were explosives.

"Now!" shouted Doc.

That was the signal to Renny Renwick to commence firing. He had clamped a belt of explosive rounds into his machine gun to open up the festivities.

"Let 'er rip!" encouraged Monk.

Renny cut loose with his nose machine gun. His purpose was to sow fear and confusion, not inflict casualties. Working the machine gun around, he blasted the terrain on either side of the Mongol cavalry.

The landscape lit up. Small explosions, like strings of firecrackers, detonated on either side.

This produced the desired result. Mongolian ponies began to rear and rebel. Swords came out, and the warriors angrily berated their mounts with the flats of their blades.

What had been a minute before a well-organized cavalry, broke in the center. An equine rout manifested. It could not be controlled.

In this confusion, Monk Mayfair hastily tripped switches. The bomb bay doors heaved downward. Rushing noise filled the interior of the plane, followed by violently cold slipstream.

Long Tom and Johnny pitched their bombs out this aperture. They did this in a methodical manner, knowing that their greatest need was to create blind panic the entire length of the Mongol procession, and disrupt the well-disciplined columns of horsemen riding abreast.

A great many of the bombs were anesthetic in nature. This had the predictable result of dropping men and their mounts in their tracks. Warriors pitched off their saddles, or slipped off to one side. They succumbed barely seconds before their steeds, who staggered and tipped over in the manner of cows being pushed over by pranksters.

"Tear gas next!" howled Monk, flinging open another container. He distributed a number of bombs, and filled his burly arms with more.

They began pitching these out the bomb bay hatch.

The tear gas erupted in yellowish clouds that precipitated a panic greater than that occasioned by the spectacle of Mongol warriors dropping in their saddles.

Along the columns of cavalry below, arrows lifted upward. Some were fire arrows, but others whistled so loudly they could be heard over the roar of the motors.

"What are they doing?" Ham wondered as he pitched out a pair of oversized bombs.

"Signal arrows," explained Doc, as he drove the plane lower. "Watch for incoming shafts!"

No sooner had the bronze man spoke those urgent words of warning than an iron-barbed missile jumped up into the plane, almost clipping Long Tom, who recoiled with alacrity.

"Lucky shot," Long Tom gritted. He pitched down a bomb that hatched a thick cloud of black smoke below. It swallowed part of the column, throwing it into chaos.

In the greenhouse nose, Renny Renwick was mowing down what riders still remained in their saddles with furious storms of mercy bullets. He alternated short and long bursts, where they would inflict the maximum consternation. The nose filled with acrid burnt-powder fumes, causing Renny's eyes to smart.

After one pass, Doc Savage brought the bomber around to make another run at the confusion of warriors below.

"Any sign of Timur?" screamed Johnny over the slipstream howl.

Doc Savage called back, "He is riding in the front."

"Did we get him?" demanded Johnny hotly.

"That is uncertain. We will know after the second pass."

"What are you waiting on?" yelled Johnny. "We need to find him!"

DOC SAVAGE said nothing. The others looked at the lanky archaeologist with wonder. They had never known Johnny to talk back to Doc Savage, but so great was his anguish and concern over the tragedy he had wrought that the skeletal scholar was beside himself in his determination to bring down the resurrected Mongol warlord.

This time, Doc Savage flew across the heads of the Mongol cavalry. Swooping low, he turned on his landing lights, which sprayed white illumination everywhere.

Arrows continued rising, but none were lucky enough to reach the bomber. A very few came close. The power of the Mongolian composite bow was impressive.

There were some number of rifles distributed among the Mongols, and these started snapping in anger.

Long Tom finished pitching the last of the bombs out the hatch, and called for Monk to close it. Bomb bay doors toiled back into place.

"We're fresh out of eggs!" complained Monk. "They went faster than I thought!"

"They did their job," returned Doc Savage.

In the nose, Renny was machine gunning anything that moved. Men, horses, and probably whatever passed for Chinese jackrabbits went hopping away from the calamity unfolding below.

Doc Savage called back, "Renny, we are coming up on the head of the army. Endeavor to bring down the horsemen in the lead."

"Right," roared back the big-fisted engineer.

As the *Brazen Devil* slammed toward the mountain pass, over which the lead horsemen were distributed, Renny Renwick poured out a withering stream of slugs.

"I can't see what I'm shooting at!" he boomed.

Grabbing a signal flare, Johnny ignited it and snapped opened a firing port. Out went the sizzling flare.

"See if that helps!" yelled Johnny, who then stuck his super-firer out a loophole and blazed away indiscriminately.

The others followed suit. There were shielded gun ports distributed throughout the interior. Supermachine pistol snouts pointed earthward, commenced shuttling and yowling like a chorus of riveting guns. Gunsmoke made the cabin air hard to breathe, and brass cartridges jumped everywhere.

Numerous riders were charging up the mountain pass, the less disciplined of which had apparently overtaken those in the lead, and were attempting to flee the destruction of what had formerly been an iron-disciplined cavalry on the march.

Doc Savage flung the Heinkel around, trying to line up on the tip of the procession, but the darkness combined with the panicky confusion of horsemen made it difficult to discern individuals.

For the head of the horse column had gotten itself organized. Mongols hastily unstrapped their war shields, and held them high over their heads. This transformed horsemen into a crawling dragon of gigantic scales.

"Did we get him?" howled Johnny, as they overflew the mountain peaks.

"Impossible to tell," returned Doc Savage.

"Well, don't give up! Come around again!"

It was hardly necessary to make that suggestion but, so great was the bony archaeologist's anguish, he could not help himself.

Doc Savage brought the *Brazen Devil* sweeping around. There was a lull in the firing. Ammunition drums were hastily extracted, and replacements inserted. Johnny found more flares, ignited one, and tossed it out prematurely. This only encouraged him to ignite more. In his frantic pace, he almost set his coat afire, and juggled a little flare with singed hands until he got it out the loophole.

It felt to earth, hissing and producing a hellish glitter.

As soon as Doc's men spotted horsemen charging up the pass, the chorus of superfirer pistols resumed hooting. More smoke filled the cabin. Eardrums rang. But the raised shields defeated the hollow shells drumming against them like a chemical rain.

"We need more bombs!" Johnny complained.

"Well, we're fresh out," retorted Monk.

From the nose, Renny thundered, "If this keeps up, we'll be plumb out of ammunition before you know it!"

Loud enough so everyone could hear him, Doc Savage said, "Timur has amassed an army larger than expected. No doubt

302 / A DOC SAVAGE ADVENTURE

he has acquired recruits along the way, or impressed farmers and coolies into his service against their will."

Johnny snapped, "Never mind the peasants. We have to concentrate on Timur!"

"What do you think we're doing?" Long Tom called back sourly. He had crawled back into the belly gondola, where he worked the flexible machine gun. It soon ran empty. He gave the hot breech a hard spank with the heel of his hand, searing his palm.

Looking about frantically, Johnny demanded, "Is there anything we can throw out the bomb bay?"

"Just the crates," Monk grumbled. "Fat lot of good they'll do us."

"They are better than nothing," Johnny insisted.

"He has a point," said Ham.

Shrugging, Monk muscled an empty crate onto the closed bomb bay doors.

Johnny leapt to the control lever, and reopened the doors. The crate dropped from sight, and was abruptly swept away.

They began pitching the remaining containers out the screaming aperture.

The boxy missiles smashed horsemen off their mounts. But the column refused to break, survivors reforming into a sinuous armored skin.

Once these crates ran out, they searched for other items to drop on the milling horsemen.

They discovered tools—screwdrivers, crowbars, and even a big monkey wrench. Beaming mischievously, Monk tossed the latter out, remarking, "Maybe that'll brain somebody who deserves it. With any luck, Rip Van Terror himself."

While they were scrounging up additional articles with which to torment the breaking Mongol army, Ham Brooks suddenly looked strange. His wide, mobile mouth worked soundlessly. Noticing this, Monk Mayfair eyed him dubiously.

"What's eatin' you?"

Ham made fish-mouth shapes. Finally, he got what he was trying to say out of his paralyzed mouth.

"Where's Johnny?" he gulped.

Everyone looked around, but there was no sign of the gangling geologist.

Long Tom moaned. "Maybe in all the confusion, he got swept out the bomb bay."

Monk muttered, "Was he wearin' a parachute?"

"We all are, monkeywits!" exploded Ham.

Everyone craned their heads downward, searching below.

But it was Doc Savage who enlightened them in the end.

"Look off to starboard."

All attention veered to the starboard side of the bomber.

Below in the darkness, but above the confusion of smoke, gas, and general chaos, the white bell of a parachute blossomed.

Long Tom yelled, "He jumped! Johnny jumped! Is he crazy? Why did he do that?"

From the cockpit, the voice of Doc Savage lifted over the motor drone.

"No doubt Johnny is seeking to bring down Tamerlane with his bare hands."

Chapter XLIX

HOSTAGE

DOC'S WORRIED MEN exhausted the last of their supply of flares attempting to follow the progress of Johnny Littlejohn as the elongated archeologist landed hard, shucked off his parachute harness and plunged into the swirling cyclone of Mongol horsemen.

His supermachine pistol emitted tiny flashes as he fought his way up the mountain pass.

"Lookit!" Monk exploded, leveling a hairy arm downward. "He's tryin' to bust his way through."

"It's suicide!" Ham gritted. "Nothing less."

"Foolhardy for sure," added Long Tom.

Doc Savage made swooping pass after pass, employing the landing lights of the *Brazen Devil* to illuminate the swirling sea of figures.

A Mongol horseman, curved sword raised high, charged the bony beanpole, evidently intent upon separating him from his head. Johnny's long neck no doubt presented a tempting target.

Yet the wild maneuver did not come off as planned.

Johnny dropped the Mongol with a single well-placed shot and, reaching up, hauled him off his stunted pony. Mounting the riderless equine, he leapt into the vacant saddle and, lashing his new-found steed, charged up the mountain pass, fighting his way through the swell of cavalry seeking escape.

Evidently, the maddened geologist wasn't recognized at first, for his scarecrow form managed to disappear into the panic.

Soon, Johnny was lost from sight.

Crisscrossing the pass, Doc Savage failed to pick up any sign of him again.

Dousing the landing lights, the bronze man banked sharply, his flake-gold eyes intent in a brittle way. The bomb bay doors had been raised, but the interior remained bitterly cold.

Monk groaned, "How are we gonna find that wordy old bone bag if we can't see 'im?"

"Wait," cautioned Doc. "Johnny has not exhausted his ammunition."

A jittering series of flashes lit up the mountain pass. It was the unmistakable sign of a supermachine pistol discharging with blinding rapidity.

Booting rudder, Doc arrowed toward those brief detonations. The bomber lurched sickeningly, dropping off one brazen wing.

Heeling, they overflew the spot. Doc tripped the landing lights. They blazed forth, scalding the fantastically rugged terrain below. This time, the bronze man spotted the long-limbed figure he sought.

Johnny was being hauled off his frantic pony by hooked poles designed to unseat enemy riders. Long arms flailing, he was attempting to brain his tormentors with his empty superfirer, knocking one worthy off his booted feet. But there were too many of them. He was surrounded.

Finally, a horseman surged up and laid the flat of his blade against Johnny's angular skull. Longish hair flying, the skeletal archeologist went down, angular limbs folding awkwardly.

As they flew on by, the lights picked up the face of a Mongol looking up and shaking his fist at them. They all recognized his wild, windy countenance.

"Chinua!" yelled Monk. "Chinua got Johnny!"

"But where's Timur?" asked Ham.

No one knew. There was no sign of the metal-masked warlord in the milling sea of horsemen below.

"What the blazes do we do now?" howled Monk.

"We cannot very well land in the mountains," Doc pointed out.

"So we leave Johnny to the wolves!"

Ham offered gallantly, "I, for one, am willing to parachute down after him."

"Count me in, too," rumbled Renny.

To which Long Tom added, "That too-tall drink of water can't last long by his lonesome."

Doc shook his head gravely. "We will lay plans for his rescue."

"What if they lop off his fool head first?" Monk demanded.

"Timur is too wise for that," insisted Doc. "He will value Johnny as a hostage."

"Mebbe," muttered Monk. "But I ain't so sure about that Chinua."

But that was the only consolation the bronze man offered as he lifted the brazen bomber over jagged peaks in search of a suitable landing field.

Chapter L

THE ORACLE

TIMUR KHAN WATCHED the moon-burnished airplane disappear over the mountains. Behind his mask of meteoric iron, his canine yellow eyes blazed with naked hatred.

He did not know what manner of soldiers had descended upon him in the winged wagon of metal, but he had his suspicions.

Those suspicions were confirmed when General Chinua rode up and presented him with the prisoner who had fallen from the sky.

Timur had only a rudimentary understanding of aircraft and parachutes, for these things did not exist in his own time. But he did not doubt this evidence of his senses. He had flown in a Japanese transport plane, and while it was a wondrous if not miraculous experience, the novelty of airplanes had since worn off. Being a man who lived in the saddle, he did not like them.

"My Khan," boomed out Chinua. "I bring you a trophy of battle."

"A trophy of defeat, you mean," chattered Timur.

Undaunted, the wolfish Mongol threw the limp-limbed figure of Johnny Littlejohn from his saddle, sprawling him out at his Khan's booted feet.

The skeleton-thin archeologist rolled on the steep mountain road. Moonlight shone on his exposed face, which was etched with skull-like lunar shadows, hollowing out his sunken cheeks and deep-set eyes.

"I know this long one," snapped Timur. "He rides with the brazen giant."

Chinua said, "The bronze devil is the one who attacked us. Therefore, he is going back on your warning, and his mercenary must pay the penalty."

With those words, Chinua drew his *kilij* sabre. It flashed in the moonlight.

Timur looked down at the unconscious archaeologist, then twisted his armored head around and cocked one ear to listen for the motors of the bronze-winged aircraft. Their moan continued to dwindle in the night.

"The foreign devil is not returning," Timur Khan said stiffly.

"He has exhausted his fight," spat Chinua.

Stepping down from his saddle, Chinua marched over to Johnny Littlejohn, seized his long hair in one hand, and lifted the throat while he knelt in preparation to remove the head.

"No," commanded Timur.

"You would spare him?" Chinua asked in surprise.

"For a time. He will be our hostage. For the bronze barbarian will return."

A twinge of surprise on his face, Chinua released Johnny's head, which fell and struck a flat stone. The bony archaeologist was oblivious to the fresh injury. Chinua stood up, sheathing his sword.

Timur looked around him. The greater portion of his newly raised army had been scattered by the brazen bird that laid eggs so terrible that strong men fell from their saddles, or were driven mad by pestilences which ranged from an uncontrollable itching to crying and wailing.

"Behead those who wail like women," Timur commanded his general.

"They cannot help it," Chinua retorted. "It is a potion that makes them carry on so."

"Then behead only one quarter of them, as a lesson to the others. Timur Khan does not lead crying women into battle."

Turning, Chinua remounted and rode off to do his Khan's bidding.

GUIDING his horse over to the pony on which was balanced a tied-down carven casket, Timur Khan gave the perforated teak container a rap with his curved sword.

"Oracle!" he barked out. "You know the bronze one. What will he do next?"

A miserable voice coughed out, "He will return. He will not abandon his man. He will hunt you down."

Timur laughed creakily. "You would like that, would you not, little worm?"

"I would like to die," said the deep voice from the box.

"If I ever awaken with mercy in my heart, I will grant you that boon. Until then, you are my plaything."

A low groan escaped the box. That was all.

Calling out to a Mongol infantryman who was catching up, Timur barked instructions to place the lanky body of Johnny Littlejohn astride the pony which carried the oracle in the box.

Two Mongols were needed to accomplish this task, owing to the shortness of the average Mongol and the great height and prodigiously long limbs of Johnny Littlejohn. The bony archaeologist was soon tied down. He did not reawaken.

Out of the night, the swish and chunk of keen-edged blades removing heads came with alarming regularity. This went on for some time. There were cries, screams, and abrupt silences that choked off unfinished pleas for mercy. But there was no mercy. Many of those cut down were the unfortunates whose exposed faces and hands had been turned white by chemical action, their ghostly faces marking them for death by the superstitious Mongols.

In time, Chinua returned with the remustered cavalry. Twelve dozen strong.

"My lord, these men are with us to the death," he reported.

"Our numbers have decreased greatly," Timur Khan said in his rusty creaking voice.

Chinua laughed cruelly. "We will replenish them! For there are many Chinese who would rather ride with us, their heads held high, than go to their ancestors without skulls between their shoulders."

Timur Khan nodded, and wheeled around, leading his Iron Horde up the mountain pass in search of what lay beyond it. Moonlight shining on his iron countenance made him resemble a cold-faced, sulfur-eyed demon of destruction.

Chapter LI

THE IRON DRAGON

IT TOOK THE greater portion of the night to cross the winding mountain pass.

Timur Khan rode along in silence, his head swiveling this way and that, his feral eyes looking out from his moon-silvered battle mask.

General Chinua studied him carefully. He had not known his Khan very long, but already he could read the man's moods by his words and his silences.

Although Timur's face was concealed by a cunningly wrought mask of metal, which rendered his features unreadable, General Chinua watched the armored limbs of his Khan as he rode along. They did not tremble so much as before. That meant Timur was angry. The fury burning his heart had spread out to his limbs, stilling them. Chinua had seen this phenomenon before. So he knew the signs.

The bronze American known as Doc Savage had been spared his life by the generosity of Timur Khan. He had gone back on that assurance of safe passage and rained destruction upon the Iron Horde. Chinua knew that this was an unforgivable offense. Timur rode along silently because his cunning brain was seizing upon ways in which to get back at the bronze devil.

There was no doubt in Chinua's mind that Doc Savage and his men faced a cruel and implacable justice should they dare to place themselves at Timur's mercy. Their fate would be terrible. Their heads would be forfeit. Well did General Chinua know the details of Timur's retribution back in the days when he was the most powerful emir ever to storm across Asia.

Truly, the fate of Doc Savage and his warriors would be awful. Memorably so.

The sullen remnants of the Iron Horde were still wending their way through the mountain pass when the red sun started peeping resentfully up in the east, presaged by a deep purple sky. It shed a blazing light that made the flattened tops of mountains—which had been terraced in order to plant rice and other Chinese vegetables—glow like furnaces.

Far in the distance, Timur spied a smoky smudge. It appeared to be moving along the ground. He stared at this for a long time.

Finally, he turned to Chinua riding beside him and demanded, "What makes that smoke?"

From his saddle, the Mongol general took out his antique telescope. Unfolding it, he trained the glass upon the distant blot. He worked the lens around, studying the ground as well.

"It is a locomotive," he told Timur.

"I do not know that word. What is a locomotive?"

Passing the spyglass over to his Khan, Chinua grunted, "It is like a dragon forged of iron which belches fire and smoke as it moves along its tracks."

Lifting the spyglass, Timur studied it intensely. "It walks in its own tracks?"

Chinua shook his head. "Behold the rails of steel that run along the ground."

Timur shifted the telescope, and saw something he failed to comprehend. Bars of steel running parallel along the hard ground, resting atop wooden cross-pieces. They swept along the undulating countryside, having no discernible purpose.

Soon, Timur was able to perceive the locomotive more clearly. It was a monstrous thing, incredible to behold, which raced along the tracks, throwing a broad beam of light ahead of it.

Even in the early dawn, this headlight made the tracks stark against the rugged terrain.

"What manner of war machine is this?" demanded Timur, reaching for the hilt of his sheathed *kilij* sabre.

"It is not a weapon of war," returned Chinua.

Timur grunted. "What does it do?"

"It is like the metal birds that fly, only it does not fly. It runs along the tracks like a caravan of wagons, but cannot travel anywhere but where the tracks guide it to go."

Timur growled, "You told me what it is. I asked you what it does."

"The locomotive is an engine that pulls great wheeled wagons behind it."

Something stirred deep in shadowed yellow orbs. "What is in these wagons?"

"Men, women, children. Mail. And goods for market."

"How does one stop it?" asked Timur, a thread of interest in his rusty tone.

"The one who runs the locomotive can stop it."

"By my words I meant, how can *we* stop it?" returned Timur.

"The locomotive must follow the tracks," explained Chinua. "If we get ahead of the tracks to tear them up and block the way, the locomotive must stop, otherwise it will destroy itself in its headlong charge."

Raising his voice, Timur commanded, "Give the order. Tear up the tracks and stop the smoking dragon of iron and fire, for I wish to defeat it."

"At once, my lord," returned Chinua. Wheeling about on his pony, he gave voice to the order. Mongols carried the directive down the line into the mountain pass through which they were steadily working.

Chinua did not wait for the orders to reach the back of the Iron Horde. He sent his pony galloping forward; the others charged after him.

They made no more sound than they needed to, for they were racing to a point where the tracks were nearest, inasmuch as the locomotive was still far away from this point where the pass cut through the mountains and gave out onto flat yellow-brown land where nothing seemed to grow.

Carefully they rode, with Timur Khan in the lead, General Chinua only a few paces behind, his bright sword in one hand and reins in the other, leading back to the pony on which Johnny Littlejohn and the perforated wooden box bounced along.

Tearing out into the open, they spread out, rolling toward the tracks like army ants over the carcass of a grasshopper.

REACHING the gleaming rails, Timur and his general dismounted in haste. They fell to examining these rails, Chinua with an engineer's eye, for he knew he needed to uproot them, his Khan studying them so as best to understand them.

Soon, it became apparent that nothing they carried—no sword, no knife, no dagger, nor any tool—was stout or sturdy enough to uproot the heavy steel rails.

"We must halt this juggernaut," Timur told Chinua, employing a word he had learned five centuries before during his sack of Delhi.

"It will be done," the other returned. Rapping out orders, he brought scores of Mongols leaping from their saddles to seize rocks and boulders, as well as brush and other debris. This they began piling along this stretch of railroad track until it was choked with untidy debris.

Not satisfied with that, they struck primitive tinder boxes and set the driest of the brush ablaze.

As the sun rose, crackling flames leapt madly and smoke billowed in the wind. Timur, back astride his pony, watched the locomotive's approach with great interest in his burning yellow eyes.

"What makes it run?" he demanded of Chinua.

"Steam."

Timur grunted, as if in understanding. But it was doubtful if the wily old warlord understood at all. Still, the great iron boiler with its belching smokestack and its jutting cowcatcher thundered on. By now there was sufficient dawn light that the locomotive's powerful headlight had been doused.

The engineer had his head stuck out the side in the manner of Casey Jones. His moon face went slack when he spied the bonfire obstructing the way.

Frantically, he blew the whistle while applying the air brakes. The din thus created drew Timur Khan up in his throne-like saddle. He had taken out his recurved composite bow, and nocked a birchwood arrow on the string, using only his thumb.

As the great iron wheels of the engine struggled to bite and grind in a desperate attempt to stop, Timur let fly with the single arrow. The air vibrated to the bowstring's sinewy twang. Eagle-feather fletchings made it fly true.

The iron point struck the face of the boiler, bounced off harmlessly, and, falling, was swallowed by the spidery cow-catcher.

Undaunted, Timur fitted another bolt and let fly once more. This one struck the headlight, smashing it.

A low growl of satisfaction, almost like a dog's bark, came from the immobile mouth of the ogre-masked warlord.

By now the cacophony of the tortured engine was assaulting their ears, and it was all they could do to keep their ponies rooted in place.

Seeing that he could not stop in time, and observing the horsemen on either side of the tracks, the Chinese engineer changed his mind abruptly. He released the brakes, simultaneously advancing the throttle.

Chinua warned Timur, "He is going to try to bully his way through."

"He will fail," Timur predicted.

But General Chinua was not so certain. The rocks they had placed on the tracks were not exactly boulders. They did not possess a great deal of mass.

Whistling shrilly, the train grew in size, and suddenly it went plowing toward them, throwing off sparks and cinders.

There was a terrible sound of rock and dirt and splintering debris being swallowed up by the mighty steel wheels—what debris the cowcatcher did not toss to either side.

The mighty locomotive careened ahead, its stride unbroken, causing the horsetail atop Timur Khan's steel battle helmet to flip about in the slipstream.

To the Khan's stern-eyed amazement, the convulsive engine clicked by, its heavy wheels spitting out brush and flaming debris. Cinders given off by the smokestack stung his eyes.

Angrily, Timur Khan pulled back. His Iron Horde did likewise. They could not halt the juggernaut of a thing. Passenger and other cars hurtled by, Chinese faces staring out in horror.

Very soon, the forlorn red caboose rattled past and the Iron Horde got busy getting their skittish mounts organized.

While this was taking place, sporadic gunfire commenced erupting from the caboose.

ONE bullet struck Timur's ebony stallion in the neck and the horse promptly fell over, spilling his rider.

Timur Khan was no stranger to being thrown from his saddle. He managed to fling himself to one side so the horse did not fall upon his legs. With difficulty, owing to old battle injuries, he struggled to his feet, lifted his curved sabre from the dirt, and cast blazing yellow eyes in the direction of the retreating train.

Around him, Mongols were falling from their saddles under sniping fire.

Seizing one riderless pony, Timur threw himself into the saddle and, lifting his voice, cried out, "*Allah Akbar!*"

To which *Tarkhan* Chinua added a single ripping word, *"Surun!"* Charge!

In very short order, the Iron Horde got itself organized and started after the fleeing train. They made no outcry, for that was the way of the Mongol cavalry charge going back to the era of Genghis Khan.

It was an unlikely race, and even Timur knew that his horse would surely tire before catching up to the snorting metal beast escaping him.

As it happened, some amount of debris—flaming and otherwise—which the locomotive had sucked up in its headlong attempt to escape became entangled with the wheels of the passenger cars.

These lighter cars were not as heavy as the massive locomotive with its driving wheels, so they started to drag. The immediate result was that the rattling train swiftly lost headway. The entire procession of cars slowed and swayed in an alarming fashion.

To General Chinua's eyes, it looked as if a train wreck was imminent.

Abruptly, the caboose broke away and commenced rolling backward.

The Mongol could see that a man had scrambled out to uncouple it. This was a deliberate act.

Emboldened by the sight, Chinua exhorted his horsemen to fall upon the vulnerable caboose.

They pounded in, silent as apparitions out of history, swords and shields held high. Archers hoisted up in their saddles, drawing back on their bowstrings in preparation for raining arrows upon the wood-sided car.

A man stepped out the back of the caboose, and seized the braking wheel. He gave it two strenuous turns, and the caboose jarred to a stop.

This wrung involuntary cries of anticipated victory from the throats of the charging Mongols.

One cry died suddenly. It was the harsh voice of General Chinua. For he got a clear look at the person who stood at the brake wheel.

He was a giant, his brazenness that of a hammered brass gong. From behind him, poured out others—none of them Chinese.

Chinua's jaw dropped open, and his tongue attempted to form words that would give voice to what he had seen.

The Iron Khan beat him to it.

"The bronze devil!"

Redoubling his effort, Timur Khan spurred his pony ahead. He gripped his sabre more tightly, his feral yellow eyes fixed upon the metallic head of Doc Savage. It was a head he fully intended to harvest.

Chapter LII

THE MIGHTIEST SWORD

DOC SAVAGE FINISHED turning the creaky braking wheel and called over his shoulder, "Here they come!"

Out ambled homely Monk, grinning, "Boy, oh, boy, are the breaks with us this time! Ol' Rip Van Terror had better watch out!"

"Do not be overconfident," cautioned Doc.

Renny and Ham shoved out next, and a rain of arrows came slipping through the air. Some of them whistled in a frightening manner.

Monk stared up at the weird sounds, jaw sagging.

Doc lunged, hauled him back ahead of a descending bolt.

"Huh!" grunted the hairy chemist.

"Old Mongol hunting trick," rapped Doc. "Bone arrowheads carved to produce a noise calculated to capture the attention of prey, making it easier to bring them down with a second arrow."

"Doggone! And I almost fell for it!"

Ham snarled, "Not the first time you've needed rescuing from your anthropoid instincts!"

Everyone, including Doc Savage, retreated into the caboose and closed the door while the fleet missiles noisily embedded themselves in the wooden skin of the car.

Side windows were hastily raised, and supermachine pistols aimed out the apertures. Immediately a deafening howling commenced. The distinctive bullfiddle roar of the supermachine pistols drowned out the sound of the whistling signal arrows.

Only Doc Savage did not wield one of the compact rapid-firers. Even in this difficult predicament, he eschewed the use of firearms.

In between riveting-gun bursts, Renny rumbled, "It was sheer luck we happened upon this rattler, and that it was going in the right direction."

Doc Savage admitted, "I did not anticipate Timur and his Mongols attempting to rob the train."

Monk chortled, "Well, he did—and now he's in for it!"

"Do not count your chickens just yet," Long Tom cautioned. He was emptying his drum as rapidly as he could while not wasting precious ammunition.

Charging Mongols began dropping from their saddles; horses, stumbling and shrieking, collided with one another.

In the forefront of this wild charge rode Tamerlane. It was on this forge-faced figure that the greater portion of their firepower concentrated itself.

Unfortunately, Timur was armored from toes to pointed crown. The mercy bullets splashed harmlessly against his complicated lamellar armor, accomplishing absolutely nothing.

Switching tactics, Ham Brooks aimed for the charging pony. Timur's steed was also armored but with leather interspersed with thin plates. There were chinks in this. But hitting one exactly right on a moving target was proving difficult.

In this confusion, suddenly the caboose was surrounded. Mongols rolled around in a perpetual circle, launching arrows, attempting to work close enough to bring their flashing swords into play.

"I feel like an old-time wagon master who ran smack into a war party of Comanches!" howled Monk.

"Yeah!" seconded Long Tom. "Except these birds don't want our scalps, but our whole heads!"

"Well," thumped Renny, reloading, "they're going to have to work mighty hard for the privilege."

Moving fast, Doc Savage was already tossing out grenades of various types. These detonated here and there, creating complications for the Mongol attackers.

There was tear gas, black smoke, as well as a few grenades that erupted in eye-searing flashes.

Between superfirer lead and Doc Savage's pitched pyrotechnics, the Mongols were forced back in spite of their Khan's bitter imprecations.

In an amazing reversal, it became very quiet.

In this early morning silence, smoke and tear gas gradually thinned out and soon shredded to rags as morning winds plucked at and dispersed it.

Doc Savage's men slammed the windows shut to keep out the more noxious stuff.

A great deal of time passed, as sometimes happens in pitched battles when the momentum of attack is broken.

When the worst of the fumes was dispersed, Doc Savage stepped out onto the back platform of the caboose and cupped his hands over his mouth.

"TIMUR IL-LENK!" the bronze man called out in the Mongolian tongue.

"Speak, brazen one!" Timur flung back.

"Your army is broken. I have broken it."

Tamerlane said nothing. It was more true than not true, but not so true that he was willing to admit it. He looked to his general.

Chinua stared back, saying, "Your army is less than before, but it is still your Iron Horde. And will do your bidding to the last man."

"Well spoken," grunted Timur.

"We can surround them, starve them out," suggested Chinua.

Timur shook his iron head ponderously. "No," he said. "There is a superior way." Stepping down off his mount, he advanced on the mobile fort, his curved sabre in one mailed fist.

"Bronze infidel," he called out.

"What is it?" Doc Savage returned.

"My Iron Horde, although diminished, is still greater than your band of mercenaries. For I have bent them to my will, and they remain subject to it."

"My warriors are better equipped than your army."

"Agreed. But let us set our armies aside for the moment. Step out and face me, warlord to warlord."

Doc Savage did not immediately answer.

Timur Khan continued to advance toward the immobile caboose. Its sides were quilled with feathered shafts. Otherwise, it stood intact on steel rails.

Timur appeared unafraid of being cut down by mercy bullets. He had already learned that his plated armor turned them easily.

Inside the caboose, Doc Savage eyed Ham Brooks and said, "Give me your watch."

Ham sputtered, "My watch?"

"And your sword cane," added Doc.

Frowning, the dapper attorney handed over his stick, then removed his watch, which Doc Savage accepted.

Methodically, the bronze man unsheathed the flexible sword, examined the tip, and tucked it under one elbow. Taking the expensive timepiece in both hands, he caused it to pop open, revealing a flat reservoir brimming with a brown sticky substance. This was the fast-acting anesthetic with which Ham often coated the formidable blade.

Doc held the reservoir to the sword tip briefly. A gob resembling molasses adhered to the metal. The bronze man then handed the watch back to Ham, who closed it and replaced it on his wrist.

"Await me here," directed Doc, swinging out onto the platform.

The bronze giant stepped off into the clay of the Chinese countryside, carrying the slim rapier in one metallic fist. He strode confidently toward Tamerlane.

The two men advanced on one another, Timur striding with jack-legged difficulty, while the bronze giant moved with a flowing ease. They stopped only a few paces apart.

Doc Savage towered over the other. Both gleamed in the sun, the Mongol leader in full iron armor, the bronze man resembling a burnished idol.

"I challenge you," said Doc Savage quietly.

The ironclad skull of Timur Khan dipped in acknowledgment, causing the horsetail decorating the helmet's pointed top to twitch.

Timur lifted his curved sabre and asked, "Where is your sword?"

Doc lifted the rapier saying, "Here."

Canine yellow eyes fixed on the slim blade, suddenly the Khan started shaking from head to toe. It looked at first as if the palsy that plagued him since his excavation from the cavern of ice was returning in full force. Not so. From deep in his belly, rumbled a ghastly laughter, as if a long-rusty robot were attempting speech.

"You would fight the Iron Khan of Samarkand with that pitiful blade?" he challenged.

Doc nodded firmly. "I would."

More laughter pealed out, issuing forth from the furnace-like vent in the forged iron mask.

Tamerlane could barely contain himself. Laughter rolled and rolled out of him. Until finally it exhausted itself. The Mongol's eyes had squeezed shut. Now they popped wide in the eyeholes of his grotesque mask.

"Then let us get to it," he said in his rough and rusty voice.

RAISING his sabre high, Timur rushed forward, charging. Due to his bad leg, he hopped every other step.

Behind him stood at parade his Iron Horde. Their almond eyes were fixed on the duel.

Tamerlane attempted a hacking charge, one designed to sever Doc Savage's head at the root.

The bronze man did not bring up his guard, merely awaited the headlong attack, a calm patience written on his metallic features.

A screaming fury ripped forth from Tamerlane's armored mouth. At the last possible second, Doc Savage sidestepped the mad, limping charge and pivoted, and so stood in a twinkling behind the bewildered Mongol warlord.

Tamerlane had to catch himself before he fell flat on his mask. Riveting yellow eyes quested about, lancing hate.

His golden eyes whirling only a little more briskly than normal, Doc Savage stood impassive, awaiting the Iron Khan's next move.

Again, Timur charged, yelling bloody murder. Doc Savage sidestepped once more.

Three times Tamerlane came on, each flailing rush more furious than the one before. Every time the big bronze man stepped aside, not even bothering to parry the heavy blade.

"Why do you not fight me?" demanded Timur hotly. "Are you a coward?"

Doc Savage said without emotion, "I am a young man. You are an old one. Moreover, you have been crippled in many wars. My limbs are sound despite all of my battles."

Hearing this, Tamerlane screamed as if insulted, and charged anew.

This time, Doc Savage lifted his lean blade and used it to spank back the descending sabre.

The lighter rapier of course could not stand up to the heavy war sword, which was designed for a slashing attack. But the straight blade possessed a greater reach, which, combined with the bronze giant's longer arms, gave him a distinct advantage. Doc displayed this by a series of rapid clanging parries, countering each hacking thrust, then disengaging and stepping away so rapidly that Tamerlane stalked about, switching his head around as if his big bronze opponent had evaporated.

The fact that Timur Khan wore a heavy iron mask, which defeated his peripheral vision, added to his confusion. Stepping stealthily, Doc Savage continued moving with a liquid grace that defeated ordinary eyes.

"You are a coward!" croaked Timur.

Doc Savage returned without rancor, "Before, you boasted that iron beat bronze."

"My sword is mightier than yours!" raged the Iron Khan.

Without responding, Doc Savage took three steps forward, flipped his blade once, and sank the point between two loose plates of lamellar armor, piercing the red leather jerkin beneath.

Doc stepped back, mere inches ahead of the sweeping, slashing counter thrust.

The slash was never fully executed. Timur lurched ahead, but seemed to lose his footing. To all observers, it appeared that his bad leg had failed, folding under him.

But the truth soon became apparent. For Tamerlane suddenly pitched forward upon his immobile mask of a face, and the sounds coming from him were the struggles of irregular breathing. Muffled by the battle mask, they sounded strange, until it became clear that some of the noises resembled rude snoring.

Turning to the wide-eyed Mongol horde, Doc Savage scooped up the fallen sabre and lifted it on high, along with his rapier, proclaiming, "Bronze beats iron!"

A stricken wail lifted from the Mongols' anguished throats.

"Lay down your weapons," Doc Savage commanded in their tongue. "Your cause is lost. For I have defeated your Khan."

It took fully a minute for that pronouncement to sink into their bewildered brains. What the assembled Mongols might have done at that point could not be read on their startled faces.

It did not matter. What did matter were the words coming from the open mouth of General Chinua.

"The foreign devil has desecrated the mighty Timur!" he bellowed. "He has defeated him through trickery! For that, he deserves death. Smite him! *Slay the bronze one!*"

Hearing those ringing words, the Iron Horde vaulted into their saddles and, screaming vengeance, charged Doc Savage.

Chapter LIII

BATTLE

IT WAS RARE that Doc Savage miscalculated.

Facing a difficult situation, the bronze man had reasoned that the diminished Iron Horde could be further demoralized by witnessing the certain defeat of their ancestral warlord at the hands of the masterful bronze giant.

Possibly that might have been the ultimate outcome, but for the deep loyalty of the former bandit chief turned general, *Tarkhan* Chinua.

Doc Savage had little time to reflect upon this unexpected change in his fortunes. For the enraged Mongol bowmen were charging, unloosing arrows, waving bright swords over their helmeted skulls, preparatory to shucking his head from his body.

A few fired revolvers, but shooting from the backs of pounding ponies did not promote accuracy.

Behind, Monk Mayfair could be heard bellowing, "Doc! Get back in here!"

But it was too late for an easy retreat. Bolts fletched with crane feathers slipped through the air. Doc handily sidestepped one, then another, but a third one scored the top of his shoulder. Only his alloy mesh undershirt saved him from a serious laceration.

Another feathered shaft flashed in his direction. There was no time to avoid this one. Doc bent forward just in time for the iron tip to strike the top of his skull, dead-center.

The arrow bounced off with a distinctly metallic note. Doc was staggered backward slightly, but quickly recovered. No blood seeped from his close-lying metallic hair.

The iron arrowhead had been defeated by the steel foundation of his protective skullcap. His powerful neck muscles, strengthened by a lifetime of physical training, had also helped absorb the impact.

No sooner had the bronze giant recovered, than the first wave of charging cavalry landed all around him.

Doc employed the mismatched blades in his hands. He banged skulls with Timur's curved sabre in one hand, while pinking horses and riders with Ham's supple rapier.

In this fashion, the bronze giant swiftly defeated the first wave of attackers. Numerous unhorsed Mongols melted before his controlled fury, or reeled away, staggering.

Behind him, Monk, Ham and the rest cut loose with their formidable superfirers. These remarkably efficient weapons quickly whittled down many of the still-active Mongols.

Very quickly, however, Doc Savage was overrun. Not wishing to inflict fatalities, he did an astounding thing under the circumstances. He dropped both blades, made his fists into metallic blocks, and began laying out attackers with powerful blows that staggered man and horse alike.

It might have been a scene out of some Biblical fable—a brawny bronze Samson standing his ground as fierce horsemen wheeled and charged around him. Doc did not even have to pick his targets very carefully. Steel-hard knuckles lashed out, knocking horses off their hooves, and men out of their wood saddles.

Two Mongols bore in, carrying long poles. One ended in a rope noose, the other a steel barb. These tools were used to capture wild horses to be broken or hook an enemy out of his saddle. Closing hard, one attempted to loop his lariat over Doc Savage's imposing form, while the other employed his curved hook to harry his formidable opponent.

Massive bronze hands reached out, seized the hooking rod, and yanked the owner from his saddle, swiftly knocking him out with his own device.

The other was spurring his whinnying horse close, trying to maneuver his noose into position to snare the bronze-haired head. Doc snagged the loop, wrenched, and took possession of the pole. With his other hand, he found his foe's kicking boot, grasped the ankle firmly, and hauled the Mongol off his mount, stunning him.

One wily horseman, driving in from another direction, did succeed in dropping a conventional lariat—called an *uurga*—over the bronze man's shoulders. Doc simply set his feet, turned about several times, winding the rawhide rope around his massive muscular form, inexorably yanking both the stubborn rider and his snorting steed in his direction.

When this worthy was pulled into striking range, Doc Savage reached out with both hands, and seized him. Off from his saddle he came. The bronze giant lifted his flailing foe over his head and flung him bodily into another clutch of milling riders.

Doc was giving an incredible account of himself. Using only his mighty muscles, he winnowed down his immediate attackers. But the sea of cavalry prevented him from seeing much of what else transpired on the battlefield.

OBSERVING how the tide of battle was going, General Chinua led a detachment of archers around the busy knot of combat in which Doc Savage was the active center, sweeping around toward the stalled caboose.

Special shafts were taken from quivers, set ablaze, and fitted into taut horsehide strings. Bowstrings twanged loudly.

Fire arrows riddled the caboose, which promptly began to smoke and smolder at various spots.

By the time Monk and the others transferred their attention to this new menace, the caboose was burning merrily.

"Blazes!" howled Monk. "We gotta get out here!"

"You ain't woofing," bellowed Renny.

Having no choice in the matter, they piled out of the fiery caboose, supermachine pistol muzzles detonating in all directions.

A new array of bolts were produced and set to launch. These were fitted with blunt heads. When they were released, they travelled close to the ground, and whomever they struck, that man was summarily knocked over.

Concentrated supermachine pistol fire accounted for some of the attackers. But waves of arrows kept flying. Many, encountering bursts of slugs, were knocked off course.

Amid this concentrated hell, General Chinua rode up, leading a second pony by its reins. He did not know much English, but the wolfish Mongol had picked up a few words. He used one of them now.

"Surrender!" he ripped out.

To make his point, Chinua roughly prodded Johnny Littlejohn, who was strapped to a saddle. Johnny had been slowly coming around, but had not quite regained full consciousness. When the tip of the sabre pierced him along his reedy arms and legs, the bony archaeologist found his voice and his strength.

He produced howling words of ungodly length and incomprehension.

"A supersanguinary ultra-catastrophe!" was one choice example.

Johnny possessed quite a pair of tonsils, the result of giving long lectures in the classroom during his college professor days. His voice carried. There was no mistaking it.

His bleats of anger diverted all the attention toward him.

"Surrender!" repeated Chinua in a louder voice.

As it happened, Monk, Ham, Renny, and Long Tom were running low on ammunition.

Growling like a grizzly bear, Monk released a last spiteful burst or two. His weapon ran empty.

"I'm out!" he complained.

"Me, too," groused Long Tom.

"That means we're sunk!" Renny said gloomily.

So it appeared. They looked for their bronze chief, but he could hardly be seen amid the cyclone of combat in which he was inextricably embroiled.

Then they saw something utterly amazing.

A PONY—and not a very small one at that—suddenly lifted skyward, his wide-eyed rider struggling to stay in the saddle. The horse appeared to have jumped straight up into the air.

But that was an illusion. All saw the pony being lifted by a pair of muscular bronze arms that appeared to possess more strength than human thews could conceivably contain.

For Doc Savage had ducked under an attacking horseman and, setting himself, lifted equine and rider straight up, toppling them in the direction of a knot of fresh attackers.

Almost everyone witnessed this prodigious feat of prowess. And for a moment it stunned them, making jaws drop and eyes bug out, stilling tongues and dazing brains with disbelief.

Then Doc Savage snatched up a dropped bow and some loose arrows scattered about, ones he selected for their blunt heads, intended to unhorse riders.

He fitted one into the string and prepared to drop the first man who approached. At first, no one dared.

Then a crafty Mongol attempted to slip up from behind. Others, standing in plain sight, shifted about to distract the bronze titan.

Doc Savage was not fooled. A footfall behind him reached keen ears.

Doc whirled and let fly in one liquid motion, as if possessing eyes back of his head.

The blunt head struck the creeping man full in the chest and no tree ever fell more swiftly before a woodman's axe than he.

There followed a momentarily lull in the fight. Such a thing sometimes happens in wartime. It is as if all combatants had been spiritually drained of their energy. For a few heartbeats, there was no will to fight on.

Then, General Chinua raised his red-tipped sword and said, "Steel beats bronze!"

No one was quite sure what this meant. Although the blade in his hand was clearly hammered out of steel.

Doc Savage eyed the scattering of warriors and milling mounts, swiftly sizing up the situation. His men were all but surrounded, their backs to the blazing caboose.

Johnny was obviously utterly hopeless and stuck in his saddle.

There was no sign of Tamerlane, but he would be at least an hour regaining consciousness. So the frosty fiend was out of the picture for the time being.

The next move appeared to belong to Doc Savage or General Chinua. But if either man had anything in mind, it was not brought into play.

For out of the early morning skies of China came a concerted moan.

Everyone looked up and about, seeking the source of the unnerving sound.

The sun had not climbed far, but the sky was already a brazen bowl of light. This made it difficult to see.

Suddenly, vaulting over the mountain peaks buzzed a squadron of fighter planes. They could not be immediately identified. Identification suddenly became unimportant when they rolled out of the sky and commenced strafing the battlefield.

Everywhere dirt and dust began to jump up and stark-faced men scrambled for shelter, seeking to preserve their lives, all thought of further combat evaporating like so much steam.

Chapter LIV

STRAFING RUN

WITH MACHINE GUN bullets raining down from the sky, Doc Savage vaulted into the saddle of the handiest Mongol pony. Seizing the reins, he heeled the horse in the direction of General Chinua and the pony across which Johnny Littlejohn was strapped. The archeologist hung in his ropes like a careless daddy longlegs spider caught in his own web.

The bronze man's thinking was simple. His fighting men could fend for themselves. But Johnny was utterly helpless.

Seeing Doc Savage riding hard in his direction, General Chinua had other ideas. Lashing his own pony, he led the other steed in galloping away.

Doc Savage gave chase. He had a disadvantage in that he weighed much more than the average Mongol horsemen. His pony struggled to carry him.

Chinua, however, did not realize this. Hearing the bronze man hard on his heels, he switched tactics.

Dropping the other pony's reins, he drew his vicious sabre, and, windy features fierce, wheeled to meet the bronze giant.

Coming on, Doc leaned half out of his saddle, reached down and scooped up a fallen sabre lying in his path. He lifted the dusty blade high.

When the two combatants collided, steel rang and sparked. Chinua attempted to hack away, seeking to sever the wrist back of his opponent's sword hilt.

But this was no easy feat. Doc Savage's muscular strength was not only greater, his swordsmanship was considerably more adept.

With two swift strokes, Doc disarmed the general, and unceremoniously banged him out of the saddle, employing the flat of his blade. Chinua tumbled off his mount, landing in the yellowish dirt.

A low-flying fighter plane swooped in at that moment and began peppering the ground. Dun-colored spikes of dust erupted everywhere. Mongols caught between them screamed and fell, writhing. Blood flowed liberally.

Doc Savage was forced to retreat.

BY now, it became clear that the attackers were Nationalist Chinese fighters. They were doing a credible job of scattering the combatants in all directions.

They were perhaps not the greatest marksmen, because they missed more targets than they hit. But they sowed a considerable quantity of death when they did place their rounds accurately.

Doc Savage knew that the warplanes had been summoned by the remarkable radio relay network that gave Chinese towns and villages early warning of Japanese air attacks. The ambush of the train had no doubt helped raise the alarm.

Unfortunately, the Chinese pilots were making it all but impossible for Doc to regroup his men and fight their way out of the bloody mess.

Time after time, the Chinese warplanes barreled around, emptying their guns. Eventually, ammunition belts ran dry. And with no place to land, nor any other means by which to inflict further damage, they turned around and buzzed away in the direction of their distant airbase.

By the time they had departed, the moan of their motors still lingering in the morning air, most of the combatants had fled into the foothills and mountains that ringed this particular valley.

Doc Savage ranged the terrain, but could find no trace of his men. Nor could he locate the pony on which Johnny Littlejohn had been lashed. The animal had last been observed racing away, Johnny's loose-limbed figure bouncing in the saddle, along with the strange carven box, the purpose of which Doc Savage failed to fathom.

The train which had been stalled on the tracks had managed to work itself loose from the burning rubble and was huffing away, hurling dirty smoke and cinders into the sky.

Cupping hands before his mouth, Doc Savage called out, "Monk! Ham! Answer me!"

But there were no answering calls.

This told Doc Savage, more than anything else, that his men were either prisoners or incapacitated, possibly both. The maddening confusion of hoof and foot prints, combined with the enormous amount of obscuring dust kicked up by the many strafing passes, further hindered his ability to locate his associates.

When a second wave of Chinese planes appeared to resume the strafing run, the bronze man was forced to slip into the foothills and seek shelter until this latest aerial attack had passed.

He lay hunkered down amid some boulders and brush for some fifteen minutes before a familiar snuffling grunt sounded behind him.

Out of the brush came a porcine apparition—dog-legged, long-snouted, scrawny-spined Habeas Corpus the pig. The ungainly shoat had been forgotten in the general excitement. It was clear that he had managed to escape the burning caboose, but had failed to rendezvous with his master, Monk Mayfair.

"Here, Habeas," said Doc Savage.

The beady-eyed pig commenced to squeal disconsolately. He brushed up against Doc Savage before lying down to await developments.

Chapter LV

GONER

WHEN THE SLASHING storm of lead initially commenced, General Chinua's first thought was for his lord, Timur Khan.

Racing to the field among the wounded, he located his fallen warlord, jumped from his panting, wild-eyed steed, and roughly laid the unconscious Timur across his own gaudy saddle. Mounting another pony, Chinua picked a direction and lashed this animal madly, dragging his own horse by its rawhide reins.

Shouting at the top of his lungs, he cried for all who could to follow him. Many tried, but only a few succeeded. Steel-jacketed lead lancing from the skies tore many Mongols to bloody scraps of flesh and bone, strewing the ground with fractured teeth.

In this wild confusion, the fighting men of Doc Savage also sought escape.

So it was that General Chinua and his surviving Mongols found themselves racing the Doc Savage mercenaries toward safety.

Safety, of course, lay among the foothills of the mountains over which they had just traversed. All else was flat or gently rolling terrain, parts of it yellowish loess—a sediment comprised of wind-blown salt, sand and clay that created pockets where nothing grew.

With the buzzing aircraft diving, swooping and ripping the ground asunder with each noisy pass, there was no opportunity to trade words or blows. They spurred their horses and, as it happened, both sets of foes found themselves choking into a deep cleft in the foothills.

This was an altogether different cut than the pass over which they initially traversed. It had a strange quality, as if it had been excavated. When the horsemen charged in, they soon realized why.

Monk exploded, "Bless my boots! It's a dang *tunnel.*"

That it was. Evidently, in times past there had been an effort to dynamite a railway tunnel through one low mountain. This had been abandoned before completion. The tunnel was very wide at this, the western entrance, but as they slowed their ponies in the cleft where the climbing sun did not reach, the way narrowed until they were forced into going single file.

It was then, with the yammering of machine guns still hanging in the air, that General Chinua growled a low command. Monk, Ham, Renny and Long Tom found themselves ringed by glittering steel.

They still toted their supermachine pistols, but had holstered them, for the still-smoking weapons were completely devoid of shells.

Monk began growling deep in his throat. The simian chemist looked ready to spring out of his saddle and brave the viciously curved *kilij* sabres prodding his barrel-chested upper body.

Ham spoke up sharply, warning, "Monk, you hairy mistake! They have us dead to rights."

"Blast me!" snarled the apish Monk. "I hate lettin' any of these horse-happy heathens get the better of me."

Renny rumbled, "Unless you want to be skewered where you sit, I'd lift my mitts." By example, the big-fisted engineer erected his monster hands.

Reluctantly, pain etched upon their faces, Ham Brooks and Long Tom Roberts did likewise.

Monk looked around, cavernous jaw sagging.

"What's the matter with you? Where's your moxie?"

Long Tom spoke for the others when he said, "We know when we are outnumbered."

"Well, I ain't outnumbered," said Monk, and then he did a foolhardy thing.

ONE hirsute paw swiped out and slapped the sabre out of the hand of the closest Mongol warrior. Monk snatched for the spilling blade, but it was no good. He missed. Probably that is what saved his fingers. For, had he clutched the wicked cutlass, no doubt Monk would have cut himself severely. But so great was the hairy chemist's rage that he no longer cared.

Two more sabres leapt in and embedded their points in his chest, their steel grating against the links of Monk's alloy undervest.

Monk growled more deeply. "Try anything funny and I'll shove my hand down your gullet and pick apart your spine from the inside," he warned them. It would have been humorous, had the situation not been so perilous.

Turning his mount, General Chinua suddenly wheeled and drove the heavy hilt of his sword against the back of Monk's bullet skull. The gorilla-like chemist pitched out of the saddle, knocked entirely out.

Ham let out a sharp yell as if the blow had struck him, too. A keen-edged blade swept in to tickle his throat, and the dapper barrister subsided. His fingers twitched, as if aching for his absent sword cane.

Grinning fiercely, Chinua instructed his men to heave Monk back onto his saddle and tie him down. This was done, although four men were needed to accomplish the task. Monk weighed approximately two hundred and fifty pounds.

The Mongols got themselves reorganized, and climbed back in their saddles, and so it was that Ham and the others found themselves once again surrounded. Now they were being prodded deeper into the cleft in the mountain that represented the abandoned tunnel.

When the party passed over to the other side and into bright sunlight, they became aware of a pony being led by one warrior. Draped across the saddle was the ungainly form of Johnny Littlejohn. He resembled a scarecrow liberated from a cornfield. A fresh bruise on his forehead explained how the unfortunate archeologist had once more been rendered insensate.

Ahead of him, lashed to the pommel of the ornate wooden saddle, was a small casket carved from teak. It was perforated with numerous holes, as if containing an animal that needed to breathe.

They could not help but notice this intricate receptacle, which caused Long Tom to remark to the others, "I wonder what's so important about that box?"

To his surprise, a hollow voice seemed to come from the perforated container.

It said, "Mind your damn business."

Everyone's eyes became very strange, for they recognized the basso hound-dog voice. Measuring the small box with their eyes, they could not imagine how Cadwiller Olden had managed to squeeze inside.

Nor did they discover how. For every effort they made to entice the miniature man into conversation was pointedly ignored.

Except one time.

That was when Renny remarked to the others, "I thought for sure the little runt was a goner."

"I *am* a goner," moaned Cadwiller Olden.

Chapter LVI

TRAIL

W HEN THE LAST sortie of Free Chinese Air Force warplanes broke off to return to their base, Doc Savage emerged from concealment, the long-eared pig, Habeas Corpus, walking in his wake like a deformed version of Dumbo the elephant.

The porker appeared reluctant to venture out into what had been a blood-soaked battlefield.

Doc Savage halted, turned.

"Wait for me," the bronze man said. Habeas promptly sat down. He had been trained by Monk to obey simple commands. In that respect, he was as intelligent as any superior breed of dog.

Doc managed to get only a few rods before the drone of aircraft engines again filled the spacious valley. He looked up over the mountains. A lone B-10 bomber bearing Chinese markings flashed into view.

The bomber banked sharply, and seemed intent to overfly the battlefield.

Reversing course, the big bronze man plunged back into the underbrush, scooping up Habeas on the fly. With the pig secured under one arm, Doc hunkered down in the shelter of the largest boulders he could handily locate.

The B-10 dropped only one bomb. It was a large one. It came whistling down, smack in the center of the field, detonating with terrific force. Doc simultaneously cupped his hands over

340

his ears, and squeezed Habeas' long head between his knees, blocking the pig's winglike ears.

Had he not done so, it was conceivable that the loss of hearing would have been more severe than it eventually was.

Dirt, rocks, debris, mixed with parts of bodies, both human and equine, were flung in all directions, and there followed a brief rain that was composed of sanguinary matter.

Deadly cargo deployed, the bomber turned around and disappeared over the jagged mountains, its mission completed.

Doc emerged once again from shelter, and made his way out into the open. It was now a very changed landscape. There was a great upflung crater, and an extremely dry dust, yellowish-brown in color, hung in the afternoon air.

Doc Savage moved among the dead and wounded, and the sights and sounds and smells that greeted his senses were horrific.

The Chinese bomb had landed with devastating results. Where before, there had been many wounded, now there were only a few. Doc Savage went to those unfortunates first, and discovered that none of them would live very long.

Out of an abundance of mercy, the bronze man manipulated the spinal centers on the necks of the dying, causing them to fall into the oblivion of sleep, in this way shortening their suffering. Nothing more could be done for them.

Doc ranged the battlefield, seeking any sign of his men, but found none. Nor was there any trace of Tamerlane, who had been entirely helpless when the attack commenced.

The only item of interest the bronze man found was Ham Brooks' half-buried sword cane. He harvested this and carried it back to where Habeas patiently waited.

CASTING his gaze to the north, Doc saw that the Chinese train had disappeared into the undulating north. It was now too far away to overhaul, had the bronze man contemplated any such action.

The Mongol horde of Tamerlane had melted into the surrounding foothills, and of them there was no sign. Upflung clods of yellow loess had eradicated all tracks and traces, much to the bronze man's frustration. It was as if the horses and men had melted into the rocks in some uncanny way.

Even his acute sense of smell provided no direction, for the air was rank with noisome smells ranging from gunpowder to freshly spilled blood.

Normally, there was no spoor Doc Savage could not trace, but he had no way of knowing of the abandoned railroad tunnel cutting through one mountain.

Nor did he suspect that the detonation had sealed it with rocky debris at this near terminus.

Habeas at his side, the bronze giant scanned the surroundings in all directions, picking through his phenomenal memory in an effort to ascertain his exact location. The nearest town lay to the southwest. He considered whether to make his way in that direction, or return and reclaim his plane.

With the big plane, Doc could cover more territory but he would be hamstrung by the need to put the aircraft down should he discover anything of interest.

On the other hand, the surrounding valleys stretched out in rolling waves. To cover them all on foot constituted a colossal task.

What ultimately decided the bronze man was the unexpected sight of the twin-motored transport plane coming down from the north.

Doc took out his monocular, unfolded it, and scrutinized the aircraft through the slim but powerful tube.

The ship was unmarked, but the aeronautical lines were unmistakable. It was a product of a factory in Yokohama, Japan. A Mitsubishi Ki-57—the civilian version of a Japanese Army heavy bomber.

As the bronze giant watched, the aircraft rolled into a rapid descent. Doc saw that it was heading in the direction of the nearest town, over in the next valley beyond the mountains.

Picking up Habeas Corpus, the bronze man began walking in that direction. He did not know whether this new arrival would lead him to his quarry, but the mere fact that a Japanese transport plane dared to land this deep into the interior of Free China was a matter that greatly intrigued him.

For Doc Savage did not think it any coincidence.

Chapter LVII

HORROR IN A TEAK BOX

JOHNNY LITTLEJOHN AWOKE with a start.

His dazed eyes snapped open, falling into focus. The skeleton-thin archaeologist looked about him, watery gaze lancing in all directions.

A favorite word escaped his bloody lips.

"Supermalagorgeous!"

This meant that Johnny was immensely pleased to find himself among the living. He had not expected to last long once he fell under the power of Tamerlane the Terrible.

Johnny attempted to stand up, but failed immediately. His wrists and ankles were lashed by rawhide, which had been soaked in brine or something like it. This caused them to shrink, cutting off circulation. Johnny looked at his hands. He could see the thready pulsing of the veins on his wrists, and beyond the constricting hide, the long, thin fingers were turning purple from congested blood.

Johnny attempted to bring his wrists up to his mouth so his strong teeth could get at the rawhide.

That was when he discovered to his horror that the rawhide bindings at his broomstick wrists and ankles were connected by another strip of soaked hide. This, too, was shrinking. Try as he might, the elongated archaeologist could not bring his wrists to his face.

Undaunted, Johnny next squirmed about, trying to bend his body double so that his teeth could find the wrist lashings.

No sooner had he attempted it, than Johnny began choking. That was when he realized that a loop of rawhide had been wound around his scrawny throat and tied to the back of his belt, where he could not reach the knot.

Johnny attempted to swallow, but he found the action difficult. This suggested that the drying rawhide wrapped about his throat was essentially a constricting noose.

The long-worded archeologist rarely swore. He did so now.

"Well, Hell's bells!" he gritted out. "A fine fix this is!"

An agonizing death lay in the offing, Johnny knew. Thrashing about, he slowly became aware that he was lying on an earthen floor.

THERE was not much light, but in the unknown structure where the hogtied archeologist had been consigned, there were breaks in the walls and roof and these chinks let in threads of sunlight, rather like illuminated spider webs.

Johnny's urgent contortions produced an unexpected result.

"Who's there?" demanded an agony-filled voice.

"Who are you?" retorted Johnny, eyes questing about the dim confines.

"I asked you first," hissed the other.

The voice sounded vaguely familiar, and Johnny finally realized that it was coming from a wooden container that sat on a taboret of Chinese workmanship. He could not tell what it was, but the box had the look of a reliquary—a casket designed to protect a religious relic, such as a Buddha's tooth, or some such arcane thing.

Struggling mightily, creeping as a serpent moves along the ground, the skeletal archaeologist inch-wormed his way to the taboret.

It was possible to sit up, although this took some effort and Johnny asked again, "Who is it?"

"Who do you *think* it is?" snapped the voice that was coming from the small box. It was muffled, but its qualities brought to mind a morose hound.

"Olden?" husked Johnny.

The deep voice in the box released a resigned sigh. "What is left of him," admitted Cadwiller Olden.

"What happened to you?" Johnny wanted to know. He studied the box, remembered that it had been tied to the saddle before him, and was amazed at how small it was, given that a human voice was emanating from it.

Johnny suspected a ruse. Perhaps there was a radio apparatus concealed within the box, and Cadwiller Olden was communicating with him at a distance, in an effort to engineer some duplicitous trick.

"One way to find out," Johnny murmured to himself.

"What is that?" asked the muffled voice.

By getting up on his knees, Johnny was able to maneuver himself so that he could lift the lid of the box. He used the sharp tip of his nose to do so.

The heavy lid came up easily, and Johnny, by twisting his head around, managed to peer inside with a single expectant eye.

That orb went very wide. Johnny's fleshless features were well tanned by recent weeks working out of doors. Now they paled as if all the blood rushed from his head to his extremities.

"I'll be superamalgamated!" he bleated out in horror.

Unwilling to accept what his eyes transmitted to his brain, Johnny recoiled. The lid fell back into place with a woody clap.

"Now you know..." moaned the miserable voice of Cadwiller Olden, muffled once more. "Aren't I a sight?"

Chapter LVIII

PRINCE SATSU

THE JAPANESE TRANSPORT plane circled the Chinese town three times before daring to descend.

When it was not fired upon, the pilot selected a serviceable stretch of hard ground, overshot it once due to nervousness, and came around, making a perfect three-point landing.

The fuselage hatch door opened. Out spilled a contingent of Japanese Marines. They ranged the area around the Mitsubishi transport and, encountering no challenge or resistance, returned to the hatch, where they formed an honor guard of two rigid green lines.

The object of their concern emerged into the dying afternoon light.

Readers of international newspapers would have recognized him at once. In the Western press he had been dubbed Prince Satsu. He was a member of the Royal Japanese family, several steps down in succession to the Imperial throne.

One would not know that from the way he comported himself. Head held high, one white-gloved hand on the ceremonial *katana* sword swinging in a scabbard at his side, the Prince emerged wearing a formal swallowtail coat and striped trousers set off by a gray silk tie in which a pearl stickpin gleamed, as if arriving for an ambassadorial dinner and not stepping forth upon enemy territory.

His retinue filing behind him in a formal entourage, Prince Satsu walked along the wheel-rutted cart road as if he was the viceroy of this section of China. It could not be said that he lacked nerve. For had Satsu encountered any Chinese troopers, he would have been summarily shot as a spy.

The dignitary did not see himself as a spy. Instead, he considered himself the future military ruler of this province. Just because the territory had not yet fallen before his revered Emperor, did not mean that Satsu could not make an advance inspection of his future protectorate.

So Prince Satsu marched boldly into the town known as Fragrant Flower. He went hatless, so that his pinched ears stood out and his huge shock of coarse black hair stood up stiff and straight as a wire. His skin resembled parchment drawn taut over projecting facial bones.

The town was girded by a low adobe wall—a holdover from the days when successive waves of Mongol, Manchu and other conquerors came down from the north to pillage at will. No guards stood at the open gate. There was an unpleasant odor, but this was common in these rural hamlets where sanitation was rudimentary.

When no resistance was encountered, Prince Satsu and his green-helmeted Marines ranged about the town, seeking someone in authority. But the place showed every sign of having been hastily evacuated.

The reason became clear when they came to the town square, an unlovely spot overrun with pigs and chickens. Wild dogs slunk along the deserted streets, their ribs showing through mangy coats. Dogs were sometimes roasted for food in China, but these specimens had managed to evade that cruel fate, possibly because they were not worth the trouble.

There, General Chinua and the remnants of his ragtag Mongols were setting up makeshift headquarters. Ponies stood hobbled. Houses were being ransacked and piles of clothing and other goods had accumulated in the square.

Someone had roasted a sheep on a makeshift spit and all that remained of the animal were some raw bones the dogs were fighting over, a pile of soiled-looking gray wool, and a big bamboo bowl of cold, greasy mutton.

At sight of these Mongols, Prince Satsu wrenched to a halt. Purposefully, he lifted his voice. His command of the Mongolian tongue was adequate, but not exceptional.

"Who is in charge of this army?" he asked in the hissing inflections of his island race.

General Chinua turned at the sound of the arrogant inquiry. Wishing to protect his Khan, who had been laid in a house to sleep off the spell that had robbed him of his consciousness, the former Mongol bandit barked back, "I am *Tarkhan* Chinua. General, to you."

"And I am Prince Satsu Hiroyasu, of the Royal House of Japan. I demand an audience with you."

General Chinua was tempted to produce his sabre and rush over to skewer the demanding man, but the Japanese prince's unflinching fearlessness stayed his eager hand.

Striding over, General Chinua said coldly, "Speak your mind."

"I will come to the point. I understand that you ride under a new Khan."

"You understand perfectly."

"You have done very well up to this point—in vanquishing the small towns in this province. But you have yet to sack a city."

Chinua said nothing.

"Furthermore," continued the Prince, "you would have cut through the heart of rural China had you not encountered unfortunate resistance in the person of the American known as Doc Savage."

"You must have many spies."

Prince Satsu smile thinly. "Many, many spies."

"What do you want?"

"What I wish, is what my Emperor desires," he hissed. "The conquest of China. You were brought to Manchukuo to ensure that. Yet you broke away from Imperial control. Why?"

"No one controls the Iron Horde of Timur Khan, except the great Khan of Iron himself," professed Chinua.

"Where is he then?"

"Marshaling his strength for the next campaign."

The Prince looked around, eyes growing thin. "With what army? You have been decimated."

With restrained anger, General Chinua asked, "Did you fly all the way from Tokyo to recite the obvious?"

"No," returned the Prince. "I am here to convey respects of my illustrious Emperor, and to offer you reinforcements and additional arms, with which you may prosecute your conquest of the Chinese interior."

Suspicion darkened Chinua's windy features. "And what do you expect in return?"

"Even if you subjugate all of China," the Prince returned smoothly, "you cannot undo your present lamentable circumstances. You could not hope to administer its provinces with uneducated nomads you pick up along the way. We will do that for you. With you. My Emperor proposes an alliance of equals."

General Chinua considered these words at length. He looked the insolent little Japanese up and down, taking his measure. At last, he spoke.

"I do not speak for my lord, Timur the Terrible. You will have to await his pleasure."

The Japanese dignitary inclined his head in a slight bow, murmuring, "I will accept your hospitality until your honorable Khan is ready to treat with me."

General Chinua had to resist the overpowering urge to withdraw his sword and beat some of the arrogance out of the presumptive Japanese prince. He refrained from doing so with an effort.

"Come. I will show you Mongolian hospitality."

Turning to his protective guard, Prince Satsu clipped out a brisk order to follow. His Marines fell in behind him.

"Lead the way, then," he told Chinua.

AS the Mongol general escorted the new arrivals to a nearby house, the honor guard dutifully followed their prince.

General Chinua conveyed the Japanese dignitary to a respectable looking house, and invited him in. The Prince stepped inside, looking about warily.

Chinua raised his sword to block the protective guard, saying, "You are not permitted in this house of honor. You will be quartered elsewhere."

Wishing to respect Mongolian hospitality, the Japanese soldiers did as they were instructed.

Prince Satsu smiled thinly, and told General Chinua, "I appreciate sensitivity to protocols of Imperial hospitality."

Chinua smiled back with wolfish cunning, and said, "Await my lord within." He closed the door behind the Prince.

Stepping back, Chinua escorted the green-clad guard to a lesser house, which might best be described as a benign hovel.

The Japanese Marines turned up their noses at the sight and smell of it, but etiquette forbade them from making complaint. They were well disciplined. So they entered the hall, and gave no resistance when waiting Mongols leapt up from the corners of the main room and relieved them of their heads with quick, expert swipes of their broad blades.

The dull thuds of their decapitated bodies falling to the floor sounded no more alarming than chairs being moved about. For the floor was covered by a thick carpet, which absorbed the clanging of liberated helmets bouncing off the floor.

Thus Prince Satsu sat patiently in his house of honor, awaiting the pleasure of Tamerlane, entirely unsuspecting of what lay in store for him.

Chapter LIX

THE AWAKENING

TIMUR THE LAME shivered in his sleep.

He lay stretched out in a bed that had belonged to a merchant who had fled the town. The sheets were silk, pillows stuffed with goose down. But the Khan knew nothing of this luxury.

His armor had been removed and his bizarre battle mask set on the taboret beside his misshapen head. His awful visage was exposed for anyone to see. The hideous pleats and rolls quivered and twitched. It was as if, after so many centuries of having been transfixed in ice, every nerve and muscle quivered with revived life.

General Chinua strode into the bedroom and observed his Khan's convulsions. He drew a deep breath, and waited patiently.

An hour passed before the pale yellow eyes pried open. Timur sat up with difficulty. He favored his left arm, which had been crippled in battle generations ago. Maneuvering his quivering frame around, he set his good leg upon the hardwood floor to steady himself.

Eyes resting on his general, Timur's age-rusted voice croaked out.

"What news?"

Chinua handed him a thermos jug of scalding hot tea, which Timur quaffed greedily. He drank the beverage constantly to fight off his ever-present chills.

"The Iron Horde has been broken and shattered," reported Chinua. "Chinese warplanes tore it to shreds. Our arrows were nothing against them."

"How many survive?"

"Less than fifty," replied Chinua.

"With fifty Mongols, I can conquer any city in China. What of the bronze barbarian?"

"Doc Savage has vanished. But we have captured his men."

Timur finished his tea in one greedy gulp. "All of them?"

"Yes, my lord."

"As before, the bronze one will seek his men. Let us lay a trap for him."

"What manner of trap?"

"One that will ensure victory over the brazen devil."

Timur struggled to stand up. All of his limbs were still stiff from his long hibernation. He began buckling on his armor, which he did with difficulty, owing to his withered arm with its maimed fingers. It was then that General Chinua could see clearly that the Great Khan was but an old man who had seen many battles, and suffered many war injuries.

Finally, Timur placed the heavy iron mask over his terrible countenance, and donned the helmet with its leather side skirts and high horsetail plume.

"Great Khan," said Chinua, "a Japanese prince has come, seeking audience with you."

"What did you do with this Japanese prince?"

"I placed him in a house where he awaits you. After I separated him from his honor guard."

"How large a guard?"

"Six heads strong."

Behind the iron battle mask, canine yellow eyes narrowed.

"I cleaved in twain the honor guard at their necks," explained Chinua.

"You saved me the trouble," murmured Timur.

Chinua smiled like an eager wolf.

Together, they stepped out into the afternoon sun and Timur Khan plunged into an explanation of what disposition he wanted made of Doc Savage's warriors. The aged warrior walked stiffly, favoring his limping right leg. His bad arm dangled aimlessly, as if broken. An armored glove concealed his missing digits.

As he listened, General Chinua's eyes grew bright and his wolfish smile increased noticeably.

"It will be done at once, my lord," he promised.

Chapter LX

ESCAPE

JOHNNY LITTLEJOHN LAY supine on the earthen floor for a very long time, his eyes squeezed shut. Grimly, he attempted to shut them even more tightly, but nothing he could do could erase the image burned into his brain: the sight of Cadwiller Olden squeezed into a narrow casket far too small for even his diminutive body.

After a while, the midget's deep hound-dog voice came again. "Are you still there?"

"Yes," croaked out Johnny.

"Listen, we have to get out of here. They'll kill us for sure."

"Why do you say that?"

"They are Mongols. That is what they do. They're only holding you until that damn Doc Savage shows up, so they can lop off his head. They got his other men stashed somewhere. The only reason you're not with them is that you were unconscious."

"I fail to comprehend."

"The others are probably being tortured, and it would spoil all their fun if you weren't awake. These demons love their sport."

Johnny blinked. "Does Doc know that we are here?"

"How would I know?" retorted Olden in a petulant tone.

"Precisely where is our present location?"

"I don't know the name. It's a town Tamerlane's army happened upon. When he rolled in, it was practically deserted. The peasants saw that he was coming and took to the hills."

"Doc will find us," said the wordy geologist firmly.

"That's easy for you to say," Olden complained. "You are in shape to be rescued. But not me. Oh, how I wish I had never laid eyes on this wretched corner of the globe. I had such ambitions."

"Ambitions for evil," Johnny flung back.

"I could have ruled the world, if I got enough breaks." Olden's voice choked back a sob. "My mother is going to be so disappointed."

Johnny opened his eyes, blinked twice. "Mother?"

"She encouraged me to make my first million in oil."

Johnny remembered the rumors that Cadwiller Olden got his start in the Oklahoma oil fields. He had never particularly believed them.

"You should have stayed in that business," he remarked.

"Never mind."

The room fell silent once more. Johnny resumed struggling with his bindings. The rawhide continue to shrink. Despite outward appearances, the bony human skeleton was far stronger than he looked. He attempted to exert pressure on his bindings. But they only dug more cruelly into his flesh. The rawhide noose around his throat continued to constrict. It became difficult to breathe.

"If only I could get my teeth into these lashings," Johnny complained.

"Why can't you?"

Johnny explained his predicament in small words in order to conserve his oxygen.

"My teeth still work," Olden pointed out. "That's about all that's left that does. Maybe I could bite through them."

Johnny hesitated. He was not eager to again lift the lid of the teak box. Or disclose the horror that lay nestled within. But the relentless tightening of the rawhide noose forced him to shove his reservations into the back of his horrified mind.

SITTING up, Johnny worked his way back to the teak coffin, again employing the tip of his nose to lift the lid. This time he gave his shaggy head a quick toss, which caused the lid to fly fully open and bang down.

Averting his gaze, Johnny inserted his lashed hands into the receptacle. Very quickly he could feel strong teeth nibble and gnaw at the rawhide. It felt like a rat going to work.

"This stuff is tough," Olden complained.

"Can you manage it?" pressed Johnny.

"Give me another minute."

The little man in the toy casket chewed and ripped with the ferocity of a ferret. It took many minutes, during which Olden would pause to spit out bits of rawhide he had chewed loose. The windings loosened and, before long, Johnny was able to pop his lashings apart by main strength, completing the job.

Once his hands were free, they began tingling with the pins and needles sensation that accompanies the return of blood flow after a long hiatus. Johnny could not feel his painfully thin fingers.

"What's keeping you?" demanded Cadwiller Olden.

"Sanguinary superstasis," responded Johnny.

"What did you say?"

"Loss of circulation."

The long-worded archaeologist sat helplessly, enduring the anguish of returning sensation. Eventually, he could move his fleshless digits and with these he attacked the noose around his throat, digging in and attempting to free himself. It was not easily accomplished.

Johnny crawled around until he found nail heads sticking out the side of a rude wall. Yanking one free, he methodically scored the rawhide over and over, weakening it until he could part it with finger strength alone.

The ability to breathe freely lent him added strength, and the skeletal archaeologist went to work on the lashings around his ankles.

They came undone much more quickly. Johnny awkwardly levered himself up until he stood standing on his own two legs, although he could barely feel his blood-starved feet. He took two halting steps, then fell over. This helpless feeling forced him to wait until he could navigate safely. It took ten agonizing minutes.

With great care, Johnny advanced on the teakwood coffin and once more his horrified gaze fell upon helpless Cadwiller Olden.

The midget glared back, as if angry with the entire world. Johnny clapped the lid shut and tucked the narrow container under one angular elbow.

"What are you doing?" Olden demanded hotly.

"Escaping," returned Johnny, slipping for a door whose lighted outlines were very indistinct.

"Do me a favor, if you get free?" Cadwiller Olden asked plaintively.

"Never!" Johnny retorted vehemently. Then he caught himself. "What manner of favor?" he asked, puzzled.

"If you come to a lake or pond, just toss me in."

Johnny blinked. "But you would drown for certain!"

Cadwiller Olden murmured without feeling, "I'm looking forward to it."

Chapter LXI

TORTURE CAGES

A S THE SUN set ponderously on the walled village of Fragrant Flower, a pig wandered into town.

Few noticed this pig, who was stringy and not very delectable to look at. There were wild pigs throughout the town, almost all of which were plumper and more desirable for eating than this scrawny specimen.

The pig wandered around aimlessly, rooting through refuse, sniffing here and there at intervals. The porker might have been searching for something to eat. Someone willing to ascribe intelligence and cunning to the meandering shoat might have guessed that it was searching after the fashion of a hunting bloodhound. Whatever the case, it continued its perambulations through the exceedingly narrow streets of town, for Chinese hamlets are constructed along very close-packed plots.

Eventually, the pig's sniffing and snuffling brought him to the center of town. He arrived in time to witness a sight.

Bamboo contrivances resembling enormous square birdcages were being hoisted onto rough scaffolding. Trapped in these wicker-and-bamboo boxes crouched four of Doc Savage's men. Monk, Ham, Renny and Long Tom. They were hunkered down on the floor of each cage. Resting on their bent backs were great lead slabs. These flat weights served as roofs, but were unsupported, only held in place by greased columns that served as tracks, up and down which the suspended roofs could slide. The tracks allowed Monk and the others to shift about under the obdurate roofs. But that was the limit of their ability to move, for the awful weights continually pressed down upon them.

It was a particularly fiendish form of Chinese torture. As long as they squatted in place, keeping their backs arched and the oppressive slabs raised, they would not be crushed. The confining cages prevented them from throwing the weighted roofs off their painfully bent bodies. There was no room to stretch out and lie down. Had they endeavored to do so, pressure would surely suffocate them.

In times past, Chinese coolies were reduced to pitiful cripples by exactly such punishment. Some had been reduced to a state close to that of an animal, because their backbones were permanently bowed.

This surely was the cruel fate that awaited Doc Savage's men, if they were not released from the cages eventually.

Monk was discussing this prospect with his fellow prisoners.

"Last time I was in China," he growled, "I heard talk of a coolie they called the dog-man."

"Dog-man?" wondered Ham.

"Yeah. They put him in a cage exactly like this for five years. When they finally let him out, he went about on all fours like a dog with a broken back. He could never walk upright again."

Long Tom said sourly, "Did you have to share that yarn?"

"It ain't a yarn. The dog-man later went on to become a big-shot pirate down around Macao."

Renny thumped, "How could he do that if they turned him into a human dog?"

Monk grunted, "I guess his bark was as bad as his bite."

No one laughed at this grim jest. They were concerned about the numerous cuts that had been inflicted upon them as they were prodded into the cages. Had they not crawled in, they would have been sliced into ribbons, which was another form of torture with a dishonorable history in this part of China.

The four prisoners were so preoccupied with their predicament that they failed to notice Habeas Corpus peering around the corner of one slovenly hovel with beady eyes.

The porker gave a grunt of recognition, and seemed on the verge of hurling himself forward. But some instinct stayed him.

Backing up carefully, Habeas turned tail and raced away from the town square.

Not long after, Habeas found Doc Savage, who was waiting at the outskirts of town. The bronze man had sent the pig on ahead, knowing that his powerful snout would ferret out Monk and the others, were they present, without attracting suspicion.

Habeas cavorted as excitedly as a dog and pawed the ground with one sharp hoof.

"Did you find Monk?" asked Doc.

The pig grunted three times.

"Lead me to him," Doc directed.

Turning tail, Habeas scampered off.

DOC SAVAGE crept stealthily through the gathering dusk, golden eyes alert. During the long trek beyond the mountains, he had picked up the tracks of what remained of the Iron Horde. They led to this spot, which had been the apparent destination of the mystery plane from Japan.

In entering the walled town, the bronze man had skirted the waiting Mitsubishi transport. But not before loitering long enough to overhear conversation among the plane's armed guards.

The name Prince Satsu had been mentioned exactly three times. That was enough to inform the bronze man that Tokyo had sent an emissary to make terms with Tamerlane. It was a development that was most unwelcome. But Doc Savage had no time to waste upon the Japanese aircraft. Finding his men was of paramount importance to him.

Doc moved along the narrow twisting streets, taking care not to turn any corners without first using his monocular, which had been converted into a periscope. His ears were alert for the sound of voices. His acute sense of smell, normally helpful in navigating unfamiliar environs, was defeated by the malodorous conditions of the place.

Low murmuring in the Mongol tongue told him he neared the place where the Iron Horde remnants had gathered together.

Removing a small folding grappling hook and long silk line from his equipment vest, the bronze man gave it an expert toss, snagging an ornamental roof projection.

Doc climbed this line until he gained a sloping pagoda-style roof. Creeping along it, he moved from roof to roof until he found himself looking down upon the town square, which was not much more than a half-frozen patch of tamped-down earth.

He was just in time to see Tamerlane, arrayed in his full battle armor, step awkwardly out of the house, limping alongside General Chinua.

Tamerlane strode awkwardly up to inspect a quartet of square bamboo cages, through the bars of which Doc could perceive his men struggling to keep hoisted the heavy lead roofs that threatened to crush them.

Doc Savage's trilling filtered out, low and concerned. He stifled it immediately. Crouching, the bronze man took silent inventory of the equipment left in his versatile gadget vest. Through the long series of battles, he had gone through many pockets and used up quite a bit of his store of gimmicks. But certain items remained.

His metallic features were grim as he finished his inventory. For one of the few times in his life, the bronze man almost regretted not packing a pistol in a shoulder holster. But he gave the thought no second consideration. For if he possessed such, Doc would have long before exhausted its ammunition drum, and no doubt revealed his position owing to the riveting-gun racket of the rapid-firers.

Doc still toted Ham Brooks' sword cane. He had tucked the slim blade into his belt. It was not the best weapon under the circumstances, but it was better than nothing.

Retreating to the other roof where he had left his grappling hook, Doc clambered down the line, reaching ground again.

Wild dogs—of which many foraged in the deserted streets— eyed him with hunger on their starved faces. Doc pegged several stones in their direction, scattering them.

Working his way closer to the town square, the bronze man remained wary. It was during this reconnoiter that he discovered the Mongol going through a collection of swords in what appeared to be a blacksmith shop.

The Mongol was a burly fellow, with sloping shoulders, and he seemed to be seeking a particular blade. Each time he selected one, the fellow ran his calloused thumb against the edge. Then he examined the ball of his thumb. Whenever he did this, he frowned heavily. For the edges failed to break the thick skin.

Finally, he found a *tulwar*—a heavy scimitar of a thing which suited him. For when he ran his thumb against it, the blade left a distinct line of crimson. Sucking at it briefly, the Mongol toted the broad weapon out of the shop.

Doc Savage faded into an alley, crowding Habeas behind him. For the bronze man recognized the sword as the proper type with which to behead a prisoner.

The only question in his mind was—whose head was about to be removed?

Chapter LXII

BETRAYAL

THE DOOR WAS fastened from the outside, Johnny Littlejohn discovered.

Setting down the casket which contained the compressed form of the midget, Cadwiller Olden, the bony archaeologist attempted to peer through the chinks in the portal to ascertain what type of fastening held it closed.

It appeared to be a simple hook-and-eyelet arrangement. Johnny scrounged around the interior of his prison until he found a flat piece of metal strapping. Maneuvering this, he slipped it into a crevice, and repeatedly worked the crude blade upward in a jerky motion.

He had no expectation of sawing through the metal fastener, but by maneuvering the strapping, he discovered that it was held firmly in place.

Peering out again with one eager eye, Johnny endeavored to see which way the fastener ran. He studied it for a time in the fading light.

Satisfied, Johnny gave the strapping a sharp, upward slice. The hook jumped out of the eyelet, and the door swung loose on tin hinges.

Repressing a grin of triumph, Johnny again tucked the box under his arm, and slipped out into the street.

From the outside, he could plainly see that he had been housed in what the Chinese call a *godown*—a simple storage house for goods and other bric-a-brac. Johnny crept along the rough sides of the *godown,* watching for signs of movement. He could hear voices, people moving about. The voices spoke Mongolian. Not Chinese. That told him that he had to be extraordinarily cautious.

The lanky geologist crept along, creeping between hovels that passed for houses. Wild dogs slunk in and out of alleyways, eyeing him hungrily, but with disappointment etched in their eager eyes. There was not much meat attached to Johnny's bones.

Since he had no idea where he was, nor in which direction safety lay, Johnny made his cautious way in the opposite direction of the Mongolian speakers.

After a time, Johnny found a house whose door stood ajar. He considered entering. The sound of booted feet came stamping in his direction. Johnny hugged the side of the house. Tucked under his elbow, Cadwiller Olden spoke up from his toy coffin.

"What's happening?"

"Mongols approaching," hissed Johnny.

Hearing that, Cadwiller Olden did a wholly unexpected thing. He plunged into a fit of screeching.

The words were in rough Mongolian. He cried, "Here! We're here! Over here!"

"What are you doing!" Johnny blurted out.

"Ensuring your execution," returned the midget blandly. "And mine."

Having no choice in the matter anymore, Johnny blundered through the half open door, and clapped it shut behind him. He found the floor under his feet tacky, and the odor in his pinched nostrils carried a metallic tang. Johnny knew what the odor was. Blood. There was a lot of it. And it made the floor stickily unpleasant to step on.

The light inside was dim, owing to crude shutters being shut. But the humped shadows on the floor were unmistakable. Human bodies. And other things—smaller, rounder objects.

Johnny toed one, and the thing rolled heavily.

Emitting a sharp squawk, the startled archaeologist leapt backward. He knew what the round object was. A bodiless head.

Peering about in the interior gloom, Johnny saw that the detached head formerly belonged to a Japanese Marine. Thanks to tight chin straps, he still wore his green helmet emblazoned with an anchor symbol. Going about the room, he discovered this to be true of every separated cranium.

Johnny did not understand why, but he hunkered down on the floor, hoping the Mongols would rush blindly by.

OUTSIDE, Cadwiller Olden continued his mad screeching. Johnny had dropped him unceremoniously.

A contingent of Mongols blundered across the perforated box and an excited conversation ensued. The gist of it was that the Mongols were demanding to know how Cadwiller Olden had escaped the *godown*. The malevolent midget told them.

"That damn human string-bean broke us free. I can tell you where he is."

"Where?" demanded one ruffian.

"First, promise me one thing," asked Olden.

"What is that, small worm?"

"After you find him, lop off my head. You'd be doing me a big favor."

"Why do you wish your own death?"

"I thought I was so smart," Olden said hoarsely. "But I was too clever for my own good."

Outside, the amused Mongols fell to laughing.

While they were engulfed in cruel hilarity, Johnny decided to make a break for it. He plunged out of the door unexpectedly, and threw himself at the nearest Mongol.

The nomad, taken entirely by surprise, dropped his jaw and attempted to lift his broad sword. He was quicker manipulating the former than the latter.

Johnny's swollen fist—a flesh-covered knob—slammed into the point of the man's loose jaw, dropping him in his tracks.

There were two other Mongols; they sprang to their comrade's defense.

Johnny showed then that he was not purely a creature of the classroom. Looking somewhat like a thing that had been put together out of odd broomsticks and baling wire, he flung himself upon the other two before their steely swords could come into play.

The three combatants formed a knot of furiously flailing arms and legs. Blows were exchanged. Eyes blackened. Bruises earned. Johnny had a well-padded skull, thanks to his long, scholarly hair, and used this to butt his opponents at every opportunity.

One Mongol staggered back stunned, while the other stood stupefied before hammering blows that felt and sounded like a jackhammer at work.

It looked for several minutes as if the bony geologist was going to best his burly opponents.

Unfortunately for Johnny, reinforcements arrived and someone swung a flat blade, with the result that the back of Johnny's head received a staggering blow.

Johnny fell, sprawling in the dirt, his ludicrously long limbs splayed this way and that like a spindly puppet whose strings had been severed.

Off to one side, Cadwiller Olden spoke up from his confining casket.

"I'll take that beheading now, please."

Pulling themselves together, the Mongols threw back their heads and roared out laughter. It was a cruel and mocking sound, which offered no hope for mercy of any kind.

Chapter LXIII

PREPARATION

CROUCHING IN A filthy alley, Doc Savage heard the nearby commotion, and watched as the Mongol swordsmith suddenly reversed himself, exchanging his formidable scimitar for a smaller *kilij* sabre. With that in hand, he went tearing out to join whatever fracas had ensued.

Other Mongols came pounding past, waving their wicked blades. One, Doc Savage saw, was wearing an expensive platinum watch. Recognizing this ornament, the bronze man slipped out of concealment and rushed after the straggler, overhauling him.

This worthy was running so rapidly he failed to see or hear the giant bronze man slip up behind and seize him by the neck. Doc slammed the man to the ground and, employing both hands, seized his throat, choking off all outcry.

The Mongol was a fighter, and he struggled to tear loose of Doc Savage, who had overpowered him easily.

Squeezing off all ability to cry out with one irresistible hand, Doc employed the other to locate sensitive spinal nerves at the base of the man's skull. Metallic fingers expertly manipulated this nerve center until the Mongol subsided. His eyes remained open, and from the stark light deep within, it appeared that he could still see. Yet his entire body and limbs had stiffened into a kind of rigor normally associated with that of a cold corpse.

Doc dragged the helpless man into an alley, stripping his wrist of the platinum watch. This he carried back to the blacksmith shop, where he located the great scimitar-like headsman's sword.

Popping open the watch, Doc disclosed the reservoir of brown compound that was the anesthetic Ham Brooks employed to coat his sword cane. There was a plentiful supply.

Removing Ham's sword from his belt, Doc maneuvered the tip until it was sticky with the substance resembling brown molasses.

Then, using his thumb, he applied very carefully the rest of the reservoir onto the great *tulwar* blade, coating it thoroughly, but so thinly that it would not attract notice, looking now like dried brown gore.

Once that was accomplished, the bronze giant left the blade where he found it, and disappeared from the vicinity. His going was ghostly.

Chapter LXIV

GENIE UNEXPECTED

PRINCE SATSU COULD hear a great commotion as he paced the guest house to which he had been consigned. It was the kind of vocal tumult he associated with an angry mob.

Pressing an ear to the front door, Satsu listened carefully. While his command of Mongolian was adequate enough to understand one person speaking, this was a cacophony of many voices raised in anger. The Prince could make out very little of it.

In time, the hubbub settled down. Shortly after that, General Chinua approached and entered the domicile.

"His Highness, Timur Khan, will speak with you now," he announced.

Satsu bristled. It sounded like a summons or, worse, a dictate. Prince Satsu was not used to being ordered around.

Stepping out into the dying afternoon light, he told Chinua blandly, "Please to summon Imperial Marines."

Chinua said without expression, "They are resting."

Satsu's purring voice stiffened. "Kindly inform them that they are needed at my side. A prince of the Imperial House cannot treat with a foreign dignitary without his honor guard being present. It is unacceptable to do otherwise."

Prince Satsu stood stubbornly on the brick step of the guest house, refusing to budge. In his own mind, he was an emissary of the Emperor of Japan, which all civilized persons understood to be a literal God on earth.

A dark gleam deep in his wolfish eyes, General Chinua barked orders to his retinue. They swiftly trooped away, returning a few minutes later, bearing on litters the fallen honor guard.

Each of the six parties were laid out on an individual litter, while a number of green steel helmets were piled in a seventh container. Most were affixed to human heads, which glared and goggled in glassy-eyed horror.

The Mongol warriors who did this arrived very poker faced.

"Your honor guard," declared General Chinua blandly. "They will follow us without shirking."

Prince Satsu began sputtering inarticulately, his tea-colored face darkening with rage. The frustrated fists he made were fattish, without distinct knuckles.

"Do you not understand that I serve the Emperor, who is God for the whole world?" he demanded, in his righteous rage lapsing back into his native language.

General Chinua ignored this display, blandly wondering how long before mortal fear would overtake the Japanese's angry countenance.

But Chinua could not wait for that. His Khan awaited him.

"Follow," he directed, as if speaking to a dog.

Having no other recourse, Prince Satsu walked stiffly along behind General Chinua, surrounded by the Mongols bearing his defeated honor guard. The Japanese dignitary kept his eyes averted from the severed heads and bodies, and one hand on the scabbard of his sword, steadying it, but also in the likely event he required its keen edge.

Turning a corner, the procession came to the town square where the prisoners from America hung helpless in great bamboo cages.

But that was not what drew Prince Satsu's smoldering gaze.

In the dusty center, Tamerlane was seated on an ornate iron chair resembling a throne, one evidently scavenged from some local temple. He wore his lamellar armor, as well as his ogre mask and battle helmet. The Iron Khan's grotesque face was concealed from the sight of his troops, none of whom had belonged to the bandit clan that he had first recruited to his bloody cause on the Mongolian steppe. For all of Chinua's original followers had perished in service to Tamerlane.

Placed before him stood a great block of bloodstained wood, and beside it stood a broad-faced Mongol holding a great *tulwar* at the ready. Juxtaposition of the sword and the sanguinary block of wood meant only one thing to Prince Satsu.

Someone was about to be beheaded.

The Japanese prince felt his mouth drying. He swallowed twice as he approached the throne of the Iron Khan.

Seeing the approaching Japanese, Timur's feral eyes lit up in his immobile countenance, and his cruel mouth opened in a kind of a chortle. Peg-like teeth were disclosed, as yellow as old kernels of corn.

The Mongols frog-marched him up to the throne, and Prince Satsu offered the glaring Khan a stiffly formal bow.

This brought more chortling from the hard gash of a mouth.

"What is it you want, Prince of Japan?" demanded Timur.

"I am the Royal Highness Prince Satsu, fourth in line to the throne of Japan."

"So I am told," spat Timur. "You have not answered my question. Out with it!"

Satsu flinched at the vulgar words. He made an effort to compose himself and said, "I must protest in the strongest terms the treatment of my honor guard."

"Treatment! You mean execution! I am sure that, wherever their souls now reside, they agree with you," sneered Timur in a contemptuous tone. "I will ask you one final time. What is it you want?"

Prince Satsu's fists tightened as he performed his duty. "I am empowered by my Emperor to make the following offer. We applaud your success in cutting swordlike through the heart of China. But your army is small, and not mechanized. My esteemed Emperor is prepared to offer you support in the way of tanks, modern weapons, fighter planes to support your military advances, and anything else you need in order to vanquish this nation."

"This is most generous of your Emperor," purred Chinua.

"In return," continued Prince Satsu, "we are prepared to give you a province of China. Any province you wish, so long as it resides in the interior and not along the coast."

Timur Khan fell to laughing. His entire body shook in a different way than usual.

"Generous! Most generous!" he roared.

His aide, General Chinua, joined in the merriment. Other Mongols chimed in, their laughter coarse as their slovenly surroundings.

"I am pleased that you see it this way," said Prince Satsu formally. For he did not know what to make of all this rude barking.

When the unpleasant mirth had died down, the canine yellow eyes of Timur focused again on the Japanese emissary, and out of his slit metal mouth came growling words.

"Most generous to offer me any province of my choosing after I have already undertaken the conquest of all of China!"

Prince Satsu flinched. His eyes veered toward the impassive headsman and his wooden block. He became apprehensive that he was about to join his retinue—and his honored ancestors— at any moment.

Just then, however, fate took a hand.

Around a corner came a group of Mongols dragging a starved-looking white man. This collection of skin and bones was dragged forward and laid unceremoniously at Timur's boots. He did not move. He might have been dead.

A Mongol warrior said, "Sire, we found him attempting to escape, along with the oracle in the box."

Another Mongol stepped forward, offering the closed teak-wood casket to Timur.

The Khan took up this container and demanded of it, "Why did you seek to escape, slave?"

"I didn't have any choice," returned the deep voice of Cadwiller Olden. "He picked me up and carried me off."

The Mongol who had offered the box said, "The worm requested that his head be removed at the earliest opportunity."

Timur demanded, "Oracle, is this so?"

"Yes," admitted the midget.

"Do I not feed you? Do I not treat you like the prince of all princes?"

"By consigning me to live in my own coffin? I just want to end it all...."

"I refuse to grant you that boon," said Timur, laughing rustily.

"What good is keeping me around?"

"You amuse me," croaked Timur. "You dared to offer yourself as an equal and co-ruler of China with me. Such audaciousness is admirable. I will keep you around until I am bored with you."

"Thanks for nothing," spat the midget.

"You are very welcome for nothing," grunted the Khan, without humor.

TURNING his attention back to the Japanese dignitary, Timur announced, "You are just in time to witness the execution of these prisoners."

"Who are they?" asked Prince Satsu, more out of the desire to turn the conversation away from his uncertain future, than out of true curiosity.

"These are the war-dogs who follow the brazen devil who is called Doc Savage."

"He is a very, very dangerous man," admitted Prince Satsu. "My Emperor would be most pleased if you rendered Doc Savage harmless. But know that they are worth more alive than dead."

The Iron Khan nodded somberly, and flicked his gaze to the unmoving form of the waiting executioner.

The latter broke his imperious pose, strode over, and roughly seized Johnny by his long hair. Dragging him over to the wooden block, the Mongol executioner laid his bony neck on the chopping block, like a hapless chicken about to be decapitated.

As he lay unconscious, the painfully thin archeologist bore some startling resemblance to a medical skeleton enclosed in a gray skin and some loose, disheveled clothing. A newspaper journalist had once described Johnny as resembling an advance agent for a famine. Now, he looked like the proverbial death warmed over.

From the cages suspended on scaffolding not far away, Doc Savage's men, Monk Mayfair, Ham Brooks and the others called down their vituperative complaints.

"You let him go," bellowed Renny, "or so help me, I'll break every Mongol neck I catch!"

"That goes double!" howled Monk.

But their threats meant nothing to the assemblage, who spoke no English.

Prince Satsu regarded them coldly, then turned his dark gaze back to the chopping block.

After arranging Johnny's head in the proper position, the Mongol headsman used one hand to expose the back of Johnny's long neck, then he stood off and raised his great curved sword.

All eyes were upon the elongated figure who lay supine, oblivious to his imminent execution. Thus no one noticed a figure creeping along nearby rooftops, who pitched something small and round out into the town square.

The object landed with a modest sound, but almost immediately erupted into a black cloud of vapor.

It was as if a dragon's egg had arrived from some celestial welkin, and began hatching.

Astonished gazes were torn from Johnny Littlejohn's thin frame, to take in the unexpected spectacle.

The smoke was intensely black. It billowed up and out in great coils, as if angry serpents were being born.

Even in the Twentieth Century, the Oriental mind is filled superstition. Belief in ancestors, demons, and dragons coiled high up in the sky have yet to fully die out. The Mongols, who are not the product of cities, but of portable villages and open steppe watched the smoke expanding, and the thought uppermost in their minds was that a sky dragon had come to earth.

The hissing that accompanied the eruption of this imagined dragon added to that impression.

Yet, although many cowered and retreated from the convulsing pall, no one fled. For Timur stood up from his iron throne and commanded all to remain by his side.

As fearful as the Mongols were of erupting dragons, they feared their Iron Khan even more. Every warrior remained rooted in their sheepskin boots, watching as the "dragon" expanded boisterously until its outer edges began to thin.

Out of this great pall of darkness, stepped a tall, imposing figure who was stripped to the waist, displaying tremendous muscles which stood out in startling relief.

He stood taller than any. He was as bronze as an idol. His face was as hard as the forged mask that sat upon the true countenance of Tamerlane. Eyes as gold as a lion's raked the faces of all who beheld him.

"*Seidohito!*" Prince Satsu breathed in wonderment. "The bronze man!"

Tamerlane barked, "You were a fool to come here!"

But Doc Savage ignored them both. His eyes locked with those of the burly Mongol headsman.

The bronze giant lifted a commanding finger and directed it. "Should you raise your sword against that man, you will be struck down before you can deliver the fatal blow."

The Iron Khan saw this as an immediate challenge to his authority. Pointing his own mailed finger at the executioner, he roared, "Behead him at once!"

His wide face firm, the headsman made an elaborate show of displaying his great curved *tulwar*, and as a gesture to theatricality, he ran a forefinger along the edge of the blade and lifted it to show how sharp it was.

A thin line of scarlet was visible for all to see.

Grinning evilly, he gripped the sword in both hands and swung it up above his head.

Inarticulate yells came from the big cages in which Doc Savage's men were suspended. As the downward stroke commenced, they averted their eyes.

Ham Brooks pleaded, "Doc, do something!"

The bronze man merely folded his bare arms and stood as resolute as a statue. He might have been some brazen genie who had emerged from the spreading smoke.

All participants stiffened in expectation of the downward stroke. But it never came.

At the apex of the upward swing, the headsman rolled up his eyes. His gripping fingers loosened. Overbalanced, the heavy scimitar tumbled back over his broad shoulder.

Sprawling, he fell backward upon his own blade, covering it, lying utterly still.

Chapter LXV

NEMESIS IN BRONZE

DOC SAVAGE, MIGHTY MAN OF BRONZE, stood in the center of the town square with the coiling black smoke slowly turning gray around him, the evident master of the situation.

His face working with fury, Timur Khan commenced hectoring his Mongols to pick up the headsman's fallen *tulwar* and finish the task which the brawny executioner had failed to accomplish.

One warrior leapt in, and dug his hands under the fallen executioner, seeking the smothered sword. He had no sooner touched the edge than he let out a sigh, and collapsed beside the headsman.

This brought blood into the Iron Khan's feral eyes. He screamed further orders.

Another Mongol leapt in, and attempted to excavate the *tulwar.* But it had fallen so that the sword hilt was entirely covered by the original wielder. In his fumbling, this new entrant also managed to cut himself on the blade's keen edge, and so succumbed to the sticky anesthetic which Doc Savage had foresightedly smeared there.

"No one may touch that accursed blade and survive," intoned Doc Savage in a portentous tone of voice.

It was an exaggeration, of course, because the fallen Mongols actually succumbed to sleep, not death. But no one yet suspected that.

Striding forward, powerful torso muscles rolling, Doc Savage approached the throne of the Iron Khan.

His compelling golden eyes flicked in the direction of Prince Satsu. He recognized the Japanese, for he had encountered him years ago in Tokyo.

The Prince drew back at the bronze man's approach. Doc ignored him.

General Chinua threw himself between the bronze Hercules and the iron warlord he served.

"You must go through me before you may touch my sovereign," warned Chinua.

Doc Savage stopped, and suddenly flung out his mighty arms. No one noticed a tiny object escape his fingers, and go sailing away.

The gesture was dramatic, yet also deceptive. It was a bit of magician's misdirection, pure and simple. For with his right hand, Doc had swept the rapier from his belt.

All eyes flew to the thin, supple blade, with which the bronze giant had previously felled Timur Khan in such a miraculous manner.

Thus, no one noticed the tiny vial escape his left hand to sail between two bars of Monk Mayfair's cage and land between his bandy knees.

The simian chemist's gimlet eyes fell upon the vial, and recognized it for what it was. His hairy hand scooped up the clear glass container.

In perfect Mongolian, Doc Savage proclaimed, "The army of Timur Khan is no more. It is only a ragtag remnant, composed of brigands and ruffians."

General Chinua said sharply, "It will rise again."

Only a few paces away, Timur Khan lifted his quaking voice and said, "Will you fight me to the death, brazen devil?"

The surrounding Mongols began to murmur in anticipation.

Their interest darkened when Doc Savage said, "I have already bested you once. Besides, you are an old man—aged and crippled. I am young and strong. It would not be a fair fight."

The Iron Khan scoffed at that, and his horde started laughing derisively.

With his free hand, the bronze man palmed the tiny grappling hook he habitually carried. It was still attached to its thin silk cord. He cast the thing in the direction of the Iron Khan, and it snagged the ferric battle mask at the edge beneath the concealed jaw.

Doc gave a quick tug, and off popped the iron countenance, revealing the hideously wrinkled visage, dominated by the yellow eyes of a cur.

"Is this the true face of Timur?" demanded Doc of his audience in the Mongolian tongue. "Is this the mighty champion who left his glorious mark upon Asian history?"

CRIES of shock and surprise rippled from tongue to tongue. Although these horse Mongols were ill-educated, many never learning to read, some had seen picture books in which the stern but wise features of Timur the Great Emir were depicted.

This hideous gargoyle wore no such lineaments. This was instead the awful countenance of a demon. All could see this with their own dumbstruck eyes.

Doubt as to the true identity of the unmasked Khan took hold of their shocked brains—just as Doc Savage had intended. With his rolls of blubbery facial fat, Timur looked like some grotesque, incredibly ugly Oriental demon come to life.

The imposing bronze giant drove the point home. "Is this the Iron Emir of Samarkand returned from Heaven to lead his people into war—or a ghoul who lures them into fruitless destruction? Look around you. Your vast numbers are no more. How many have died following this wretch? How many more will perish because of this foul pretender?"

At this insult, Timur the Lame lurched forward. But his jackleg buckled beneath him. He stumbled, fell, clanking as his segmented armor struck ground.

Features darkening, General Chinua barked, "You lie, bronze devil. You will fight me instead!"

Doc lifted his rapier in response.

"No," proclaimed Chinua, lifting his sabre. "We will fight as equals, with matched swords."

So saying, Chinua threw his sabre in Doc Savage's direction.

Doc caught it easily, while Chinua accepted another blade from a subordinate.

The second the hilt slapped into Chinua's coppery fist, he charged.

What followed was an example of swordsmanship mixed with brute force that would long be remembered by those who witnessed the duel and survived to tell of it.

Chinua came slashing in. Doc Savage flung his lean rapier away.

Again, no one noticed the cunning way in which the bronze giant accomplished his aim. For the blade went flying in the direction of Ham Brooks' cage, impaling itself on the floor between two bars.

Hastily, the dapper lawyer reclaimed his weapon.

With the broad Mongol sabre, Doc parried Chinua's first attack, and the two blades banged, sparked, clashed again. General Chinua was accustomed to hacking and slashing his opponents, wearing them down with his ferocious might.

Doc Savage was larger, and more skilled. The blade in his hand might have weighed no more than a dagger, for the effortless way he wielded it.

Artfully, the bronze giant beat back every attack. To show his superior skill, he began cutting and chipping away at Chinua's armor until it became undone in spots. He speared the man's scabbard, sending it into the dirt.

Soon, the furious Mongol general became a ludicrous sight as more and more of his protective raiment was slashed off and carelessly flung aside.

As a gesture of contempt, the bronze giant knocked Chinua's ornate helmet off his skull, plunged in and booted it away from the Mongol's grasping fingers.

Tiring of that play, Doc switched tactics.

Instead of counterattacking, he faded back, shifting around to show his bewildered opponent that his flashing blade could not come near his bronze tormentor, no matter how hard he hacked.

Chinua became furious. He charged, lunged and failed to make contact. The big bronze American might have been so much metallic smoke. Nothing he could do could bring his blade tip in contact with his lightning-fast foe.

Finally, Doc swept in and disarmed his opponent with a deft maneuver that slapped the other blade aside and knocked it to the ground in two blinding strokes whose sharp clangs blended into one ringing sound. Stopping, the Mongol lunged for his weapon. Doc kicked the sabre out of reach.

Panting like a frustrated dog, General Chinua fell to his knees, utterly exhausted.

A thin sheen of perspiration showed on the bronze man's tremendous muscular physique. Otherwise Doc Savage was not even winded.

The bronze giant lifted his voice, proclaiming, "Bronze bests steel!" He stepped back, and his animated orbs swept the field.

The surviving army of Timur Khan stared like an assemblage of brown owls. They gaped, unblinking. They looked to their general in the dirt, and their Khan struggling to stand up in his heavy armor.

They made no move. For a moment, it seemed as if the bronze giant had the upper hand.

That was when a new element entered the picture.

Up the street marched a squad of hard-eyed Japanese Marines. Evidently, they had become concerned over the long absence of their prince, and the resulting din of combat had summoned them to investigate.

The squad marched up, rifles pointed ahead of them, bayonets fixed.

Seeing rescue at hand, Prince Satsu raised his voice and cried, "Kill the bronze devil! Slay all the American enemies of the Emperor!"

Chapter LXVI

SLAIN LEADER

JAPANESE RIFLES SNAPPED up to epauletted shoulders, and pointed in the direction of the bronze man. Eyes under green helmets were without mercy.

Doc Savage wore nothing above the waist, so he was not in a position to stand up to a volley of slugs.

Worse, one of the riflemen aimed for the kneeling form of Johnny Littlejohn. The bony archaeologist was helpless, and about to be riddled with slugs.

Doc pitched in his direction, ahead of the first whistling leaden missiles. Scooping up the long, dangling form, the bronze flash slammed into a nearby building, taking the heavy door off its hinges with one brawny shoulder.

Bullets snarled all about, peppering the façade.

One Mongol—a huge fellow nearly the size of Doc Savage—happened to stand closest to the building. Encouraged perhaps by his great size, he made a bold move.

The giant drew his sword, leaped inside, and struck. The blade disappeared into Doc Savage, who could be glimpsed by some. He staggered back, out of sight. Several witnessed this through the open doorway.

An audible groan, such as might be emitted by a man who had been impaled by cold steel, rang out. All heard this ugly sound.

The big Mongol disappeared from view, bent upon finishing off his victim.

High up in his cage, straining to keep the ponderous lead roof balanced on his broad back, Monk Mayfair let out a blood-curdling howl.

"Doc! That big bruiser got Doc!"

Ham said weakly, "Maybe it was Johnny instead."

To which Long Tom added gruffly, "Don't kid yourself. That sounded like Doc Savage."

Whoever had been felled, the knowledge impelled the men of Doc Savage into furious action.

Monk uncapped the captured vial that Doc had sent his way, carefully tracing the lines around himself, along the edge of the cage bottom. Very quickly, the liquid began smoking.

"What are you doing?" demanded Ham.

"Acid," Monk retorted. "I'm bustin' outta this overgrown canary cage."

Ham took up his rapier, and struggled to cut through the rattan lashings that held his own cage together. The blade was not designed for this kind of work, but Ham put all his wiry might behind it. Soon, bamboo bars were popping free.

Below, arriving Japanese Marines were firing indiscriminately into the Mongol crowd, very few of whom possessed pistols of any sort. Those who gripped such weapons ducked for cover, returning spiteful fire.

High above them, the men of Doc Savage were momentarily out of the fray.

That is, until Monk Mayfair felt the floor of his cage separating. The combined weight of his two hundred and fifty pounds, along with the flat roof weighing on his broad back, produced the desired result.

The hairy chemist knew that when he landed, the detached roof would break his spine. So he rocked his gorilla-like body, swinging his cage back and forth.

When the floor fell out from beneath him, Monk was ready. He hooked the bamboo bars with both hands, and swung outward, rapidly switching his grip from the inside to the outside of the cage.

Floor and roof fell free, landing with an unpleasant thud that threw up yellow dust.

Emitting a great victory whoop, Monk commenced swinging on his perch, until he let go, landing atop Long Tom's cage.

The simian chemist was howling now. He grasped the bamboo bars, and set about shattering them in his strong fingers. Very quickly, Monk excavated a hole and hauled out the slender electrical wizard. The released roof smacked the floor, tore loose its moorings, and both made a dusty commotion on the ground. That left Monk and Long Tom hanging precariously to the empty cage in full view of the combatants.

In his own confines, Renny Renwick placed his monster knuckles against the floor, set himself for maximum leverage, and attempted to straighten up. He did this in one violent motion, with the result that the cage twisted on its rope, and somehow unhooked itself. The woven contraption landed on its side, splintering open. Finding himself free of the backbreaking weight, Renny wrenched and tore at the bars with his gigantic fists.

By this time, Ham Brooks had cut a sufficient aperture that he could climb out and cling to the outside of his own cage, although he lost a shoe in the process. He held onto his slim sword, however. The descending roof slammed flat on the flooring, which miraculously held in place.

Ham dropped to the ground, rapier at the ready.

Below, Prince Satsu drew his ceremonial sword out of its scabbard. Stone-faced, he marched over to General Chinua, who had sought shelter behind a makeshift corral of frightened ponies.

General Chinua was still exhausted from his sword fight with Doc Savage, and so when the Prince strode up to him, blade gleaming, Chinua was unprepared. The *katana* sword lifted in both hands.

Giving vent to a high shriek of rage, the Prince managed to sever the Mongol's spinal column at the neck, although he failed to completely decapitate the man.

It did not matter. General Chinua crumpled without further resistance.

Despite the confusion, this did not go unnoticed. Having at last struggled to his feet, Tamerlane picked up a curved sabre in order to avenge the death of his right-hand officer.

The sword fight that followed was no spectacle. Tamerlane was handicapped by age and shaking limbs, while Prince Satsu, while soft in appearance, wielded a sword that was superior to the Mongol *kilij*.

They hacked and slashed and parried against one another, grunting with muscular exertion, without inflicting any particular damage.

MEANWHILE, Monk and the others picked up heavy stones, fallen blades, and anything else they could lay their eager hands upon. They ignored the milling Mongols. Instead, they jumped the Japanese Marines who had spread out and were attempting to pick off any and every Mongol they could fix in their gun sights. The squad had made good progress in whittling down the opposition, when flung rocks started bouncing off their helmeted skulls. Unexpected Mongol sabres chopped away at their unprotected limbs.

Renny popped one Japanese with his gargantuan fist, with the result that the man's head flew out from under his helmet, and his rifle suddenly smacked into the severe-faced engineer's oversized paws.

Renny used the rifle's hard stock to bang the unprotected skull of the Japanese Marine. "That settles you," Renny rumbled, seeking a fresh victim.

Monk had found another Marine, and lifted him up bodily, spinning him overhead until his rifle went flying. Then the hairy chemist threw the unfortunate man to the ground and commenced jumping up and down on his spine. The Japanese made little lamb bleats every few seconds until he ceased to move or make sounds.

Ham Brooks was moving among the Mongols, slipping the tip of his sticky blade into unwary ribs. Every time he pinked one, the victim released a leaky sigh and collapsed into a disorderly pile.

One Japanese Marine got the drop on Long Tom Roberts. The pallid electrical wizard had become entangled with a pair of Mongols, and was relentlessly hammering their faces into rawness. Despite looking so feeble as to belong in a sanitarium for invalids, Long Tom was extraordinarily violent in a bare-knuckled brawl.

Seeing this affront to Japanese military dignity, the Marine rushed over. Screaming *"Banzai!"* he shot down one struggling Mongol, then bayoneted the other twice. Withdrawing the bloody blade, he then pointed the rifle muzzle at Long Tom.

Long Tom understood very little Japanese, but he got the idea when the man hissed, *"Jishu! Jishu!"*

Having no choice in the matter, Long Tom lifted his hands in surrender.

Renny was the first to notice this. "Holy cow!" he bellowed. "A Jap captured Long Tom."

Monk and Ham turned their attention that way. And saw that Long Tom was on the verge of being shot in cold blood.

Renny attempted to lay his gunsight on the Japanese Marine when he felt something cold and sharp digging into his back.

"Please to drop rifle, Renwick-*san*," purred Prince Satsu.

Renny's long face grew longer. Reluctantly, he lay down the rifle. He then did an unusual thing. He smiled. That meant the big-fisted engineer was close to tears.

Prince Satsu had managed to overcome Timur. The Iron Khan staggered back and was sitting on his throne, breathing heavily. It could not be seen whether he was wounded. There was no evidence of blood.

Seeing the grimness of the situation, Monk and Ham hesitated. They wanted to fight. They did not wish Long Tom or Renny to be killed. The latter impulse dominated their thoughts.

At that moment, the big Mongol who had chased Doc Savage into the building emerged, dragging Johnny Littlejohn by the hair. In his other hand was his sabre. It dripped copious amounts of gore.

When they saw this, Monk Mayfair let out a roaring groan and Ham Brooks joined in with a sharp exclamation.

"The bronze devil is dead," boomed out the big Mongol, "for I have slain him with my own blade."

"Americans, you will surrender now," purred Prince Satsu in a smugly self-satisfied tone.

Chapter LXVII

EVIL ALLIANCE

MONK, HAM AND LONG TOM were marched over to the spot where the big Mongol had deposited bedraggled, insensate Johnny Littlejohn.

Someone fetched a bucket of dirty waste water, and hurled its contents at the wordy archaeologist's tangled frame.

After a few buckets of this watery abuse, Johnny shook his shaggy head and looked up and about. His battered features lacked all expression. One half-closed eye was purple.

He finally saw his comrades and asked a croaky question. "Where is Doc?"

Prince Satsu answered that. "The bronze American is dead. He will trouble us no more."

Johnny looked to his friends for signs the Japanese was lying. The downcast expressions on the faces of the others told a far different story.

Johnny buried his head in his hands and said, "It is my fault. All of it. Every drop of blood is on my hands." His long linkages of finger-bone shook.

No one offered any words of comfort. For there were none.

Prince Satsu then marched over to Timur Khan, who sat heavily in his chair, winded and seemingly helpless.

"My offer to you," he said stiffly, "still stands. What is your answer?"

Tamerlane got control of his breathing, and glared feral hate in the direction of the Japanese. But he recognized the reality of the situation.

"If you give me an army," Timur croaked, "I will conquer all of China."

"An appropriate force will be raised and placed at your disposal," promised the Prince.

"This army must be composed of Mongols," barked Timur gruffly. "No warriors are more fierce than those in whose veins run the blood of my ancestors."

Satsu said, "You will get your Mongols, but you will accept others as well. Men who can drive tanks, wield modern military rifles, and fly warplanes."

"Then it is done," intoned Timur Khan.

Pointing a trembling finger in the direction of the great Mongol warrior who had defeated the mighty Doc Savage, Tamerlane demanded, "What is your name?"

"Arslan," said the hulking worthy.

"Your mother named you after a lion," said Timur, "but she should have named you after a mountain. For I have never before beheld a warrior so large as you."

Inclining his head in a gesture of respect, Arslan said formally, "It is my honor to serve the Khan of Iron."

Then, turning his attention to Doc Savage's men, Timur grunted, "Your chief is no more, so it is no longer necessary to keep you alive as a club to hold over him. You will now be killed."

To this, Prince Satsu made a sudden objection.

"My Emperor is at war with the country from which Doc Savage hails," he said quickly. "Now that Doc Savage is no more, his men must be taken to Tokyo as prisoners of war."

Timur spat contemptuously. "Prisoners? The Iron Horde does not take prisoners."

Prince Satsu added, "A handsome ransom will be paid for them at the conclusion of the war, no matter who is victorious."

"Such a ransom must belong to me!" thundered Timur.

"Consider it a gift from my Emperor. But I must take charge of them, to ensure their survival against that glorious day of victory."

Timur grunted, "So be it. They are yours. I expect gold in return."

The surviving Japanese Marines surrounded Doc Savage's beaten men at bayonet point.

"Things are looking grim, brothers," rumbled Renny.

"You said it," muttered Monk.

"Looks like our luck has finally run out," agreed Long Tom sourly.

They were marched to the decrepit *godown* where Johnny Littlejohn had originally been imprisoned. Johnny was prodded along with them. He looked as miserable as a cat that had been caught in a long rainstorm. His head hung low, his eyes were squeezed shut in pain, and his skeletal shoulders sagged like broken rafters.

When the door was slammed shut and locked tight, they were left alone in the darkness. In that gloom, no one spoke a solitary word.

They were prisoners of war, with no hope of rescue.

OUT in the town square, Prince Satsu was conferring with Timur Khan.

The Japanese was saying, "Our aircraft cannot long remain in this province. If it is spotted by Chinese warplanes, they will bomb and strafe us. We will convey you and what remains of your army into Japanese territory. It is there that we will work to raise for you a new army, a new Golden Horde."

"I will not lead men made of soft gold, but hard iron," Timur retorted rustily.

The Iron Khan surveyed what remained of his Mongols, and the look in his shaded eyes was unpleasant to see. He did not speak for a long time.

"I do not like you, Japanese prince," he said at last. "However, I live to fight, to wage war, and since my destiny is to conquer, I will go with you so that I may once again scourge the Chinese nation with my new Iron Horde."

Prince Satsu nodded gravely. "It is settled then."

As they made preparations to evacuate the Chinese town, Timur Khan ranged about the town square, carrying his battle mask and helmet under one arm. He was clearly looking for something.

Finally, he found it. The sought object was a small casket, cunningly carven, its lid closed tight.

Seeing this, he gave it a kick. The box went flying, and out of it emerged a howl of surprise and fear. For the toy coffin contained a tiny man.

"I see you have survived this latest skirmish, Oracle."

"Go to hell," said the miserable voice from the box.

Turning to the big Mongol named Arslan, Timur ordered, "Pick him up and take him with us."

Without a word, the imposing warrior padded over and picked up the box. He studied it with curious eyes for several moments, and apparently seeing no harm in it, lifted the lid.

The Mongol had something of a poker face, but it collapsed when he saw what lay within the container. His intensely dark eyes went a little wide, and his lips parted. From those lips escaped the beginnings of what might have been a whistle, but the sound went unheard, for the man sealed his mouth instantly.

"What are you staring at?" growled the voice from the box.

The monster Mongol said nothing. The sight of the figure in the box might have frozen his tongue.

The remnants of the Iron Horde were sullenly picking up their scattered sabres and other personal items, when out of the building in which Doc Savage had been slain emerged a tattered figure.

It was no less than the giant Mongol who had called himself Arslan. He staggered into the presence of Timur Khan, gasping, "I fought with the bronze devil. He tore away from me and escaped."

This manifestation struck all tongues momentarily dumb. In all the turmoil, no one had seized the opportunity or possessed the presence of mind to investigate the body of the slain Doc Savage that supposedly lay within.

Timur Khan shivered where he stood, and his teeth chattered when he demanded, "If you stand here, then who is—?"

All eyes went to the spot where the other giant Mongol stood holding the teakwood box containing Cadwiller Olden.

But that worthy had evaporated.

Chapter LXVIII

BODYGUARD

FURIOUSLY, TIMUR KHAN ordered his Mongols to seek out the mysterious giant who had stolen off with the teak box containing his personal oracle. They hastened to comply.

The Iron Khan walked jerkily up to the big Mongol, who stood in what amounted to his underwear.

"What is your true name?" he demanded gruffly.

"Ondor, Oh Khan of Iron."

"You say you fought with the brazen devil?" Timur croaked out.

"Yes, sire. And I would have bested him, too. But he seized me by the neck and performed sorcery on me, for I was immediately robbed of my senses, recovering only now."

Timur glowered fiercely. "Normally, I would behead any soldier in my army who failed in his duty. But a man who is a physical match for Doc Savage harbors the promise of becoming a great warrior."

"I thank you," said the Mongol, bowing reverentially.

"You will remain at my side, Ondor. From now on, you are my bodyguard. And if you prove your prowess in battle, you may become my next general."

The Mongol bowed more deeply, murmuring, "I will serve you to my dying breath."

"If not beyond that hour," croaked Timur.

Prince Satsu bustled up and spoke nervously. "We must retreat to the airplane without delay, great Khan."

The cold iron countenance swiveled, and burning yellow orbs fell on the Japanese dignitary. For Timur had restored the fanciful battle mask of meteoric iron to his face. He was no less ugly for that gesture.

"I will not depart this place until the bronze barbarian's head is laid at my feet and his cold brains scooped out of his skull," intoned Timur. "Which I will do with my bare hands."

"Is not his bodiless head sufficient?"

"No," spat Timur. "For the bronze infidel boasted that his brain was his sword. I will crush those brains under my boot heels, as I intend to reduce China to helplessness. We will depart when my will has been done. Not before."

Nervously, Prince Satsu cast his gaze into the Chinese skies, a pained expression on his normally inscrutable tea-colored features.

Chapter LXIX

SURPRISE VISITOR

IN THE *GODOWN* where Monk Mayfair and the others sat in abject darkness, consumed by bitter defeat, the rattling of the door snapped them out of their profound funk.

"Company," growled Monk.

Renny was the first to jump to his feet. He bounded to the portal, making mammoth fists. He peered through a crack in the door, returned to the others in haste.

"It's that big bruiser who did for Doc Savage," he thumped.

"My lucky day!" grunted Monk in a low voice. "I want a crack at him."

Hastily, he and Renny stationed themselves on either side of the door and awaited events.

The door came open and the big Mongol stepped in like a shadowy mountain in motion.

Monk and Renny piled on, fists poised to strike.

What happened next, they never fully comprehended. Their fists collided with one another, producing painful results. It was as if they had taken a swing at an Oriental phantom.

Miraculously, the big ghostly Mongol had evaded their attack, and stationed himself off to one side with a gliding ease.

Getting themselves organized, Monk and Renny charged again.

They were stopped as if by a stone wall when the Mongol said quietly, "We have no time for this."

The combative pair skidded to a halt so fast it took a moment for surprise to catch up to their features. The well-modulated tones of their visitor were ones that they recognized immediately.

Monk said it first. "Doc!"

"Yes."

The others scrambled to their feet, their faces lighting up, joy popping up in their eyes.

"But we saw that big Mongol drive his sword into you," blurted Ham.

Doc explained, "You only thought you did. By maneuvering, I allowed his blade to slip between my arm and side, then exerted pressure, clamping the sword tight. Employing that leverage, it was no great feat to pull my attacker toward me, and out of view. We struggled, during which I managed to render him unconscious. While all the fighting was going on outside, I swapped clothes with him, and smeared some of his own blood on his sword to make it appear as if he had been the victor."

The others expressed relief in various ways. All but Johnny Littlejohn. He was still consumed with guilt and self-recrimination.

Then everyone noticed the perforated box in Doc Savage's massive hand.

"What's in that?" wondered Long Tom.

"Cadwiller Olden," replied the bronze man grimly.

"How the heck did they fit him in there?" asked Monk, blinking tiny eyes.

"By removing his arms and legs with a sword," replied Doc.

It took several moments for this news to sink in.

FROM the miniature casket came the familiar hound-dog voice. It croaked out, "Fellows, we've had our differences in the past, but I'm all done fighting. Finished. I would sincerely appreciate it if you would drown me like a kitten."

A trace of horror in his voice, Doc asked, "You wish to die?"

"Wouldn't you?" countered the midget bitterly. "They hacked off my limbs one at a time. I would have bled to death, but they burned the stumps to cauterize them."

No one said anything to that. The question had gotten them thinking.

Finally, Doc Savage said, "We will endeavor to do everything we can for you."

Olden made an ugly sound. "That's a laugh. Are you going to sew my arms and legs back on? They fed them to a pack of wild dogs. Showed me the raw bones afterward and laughed in my face."

"I think I am going to be sick," moaned Johnny. "None of this would have happened if not for my meddling."

"Guilt," said Cadwiller Olden, "fits you like your suit. Badly. I did this to myself. I spent my whole life scheming, and look what it got me. A rag doll has more going for it than me. Finished, that's me."

Sounds of booted feet moving up the street brought a halt to the discussion.

Doc Savage said, "This does not sound good."

"What have we left for weapons?" wondered Ham.

Everyone looked to Doc Savage. He drove bronze hands into his pockets, and extracted an assortment of items. They looked at it.

"That's just theatrical make-up stuff," muttered Renny. "What's left of what you used to make yourself look like that big Mongol."

"This is a fine situation we find ourselves in," complained Ham. "We are completely outnumbered and have no weapons whatsoever."

Monk dug a thumb into his own barrel chest and said, "I ain't outnumbered. It takes ten guys to outnumber me. And there's six of us here. That means it would take sixty guys to a outnumber us all. There ain't that many Mongols left."

400 / A DOC SAVAGE ADVENTURE

Making no noise, Doc Savage moved about the gloomy confines of the *godown*.

He came back with a dusty crate which contained strings of firecrackers. They looked so old and faded it was doubtful that the gunpowder would ignite.

"Not enough to go around," murmured Long Tom.

"And not so effective, even if they still work," added Ham.

"They will sound like gunshots, if placed properly," said Doc, as he filled the pockets of his Mongol *del*.

In the gloomy space, they listened as the Mongol search party ranged around the town, seeking the vanished Doc Savage.

As one detachment pounded close, Johnny Littlejohn slipped up to the casket in which Cadwiller Olden lay and lifted the teak lid.

"What are you doing?" asked Long Tom suspiciously.

"He likes to attract attention when he thinks he can get away with it."

Johnny had a bit of handkerchief on him and he stuffed this wad into Cadwiller Olden's mouth. The muffled sounds that followed were disturbing.

Finally, the Mongol patrol trooped on past, apparently not thinking to investigate the place where Doc Savage's men had been consigned, evidently fooled by the closed door.

Doc went to the door, used his transformable monocular, and was able to ascertain that they were drifting down the street.

"If we split up," he suggested, "we may be able to ambush them in the dark. In that way we can obtain useful weapons."

"I'm all for it," said Renny, flexing his well-skinned fists.

"Monk and Ham will handle that task," Doc directed. "You and Long Tom station yourself at the Japanese transport. Prevent it from taking off, should any attempt be made. Keeping Tamerlane from falling into enemy hands is our top priority."

"What about me?" asked Johnny anxiously.

Doc Savage addressed the much-battered archeologist.

"You have suffered worse than anyone. Remain here and guard Cadwiller Olden from harm."

"But—"

"If we fail to accomplish our goals," added Doc, "it will be up to you to finish the task we started."

All understood the import of the bronze man's words. He was giving the bony archeologist the job of carrying on if they fell in battle. This quelled Johnny's excited protestations.

Doc eased the door open, and one by one they slipped out and drifted off in separate directions.

Doc Savage took to the rooftops, bounding along from building to building. He was seeking the Khan of Iron, Tamerlane. So great was his haste that he did not divest himself of the make-up and skirted costume of the giant Mongol who had been promoted to personal bodyguard for Tamerlane the Terrible.

Whether this made him more or less of a target for violence and sudden death was debatable.

Chapter LXX

THE HEADSTRONG ONE

EACH OF DOC SAVAGE'S men was a specialist in his own field. Every one of them was also unique in other ways. They were not ordinary men. Far from it.

Probably no man alive possessed fists the equal of Renny Renwick, the engineer. Monk Mayfair certainly had no double outside of a zoo, or even the jungles of Africa. If there was a man more quick-witted and well-dressed than Ham Brooks, he would have been difficult to discover.

In addition to being a renowned archaeologist and geologist, Johnny Littlejohn possessed the string-and-bone physique of a marathon runner. His endurance was phenomenal.

Johnny showed his wiry capabilities now.

He raced through the narrow and crooked streets of the deserted town, making better time than some Olympic sprinters. Over the last several days, Johnny had been beaten several times, knocked unconscious at least twice, and otherwise abused. Crimson seeped from various lacerations. One empurpled eye was fully shut.

Yet despite these injuries, which certainly would have crippled a less hardy individual, the fleet-footed archaeologist charged in the direction of the town square.

Tucked under one arm, he carried the small casket containing Cadwiller Olden. His bronze chief had charged him with guarding the helpless little man. That instruction Johnny fully intended to honor. But that one alone.

Determination rode Johnny's gaunt features. He was bound and determined to settle accounts with the man he had helped restore to animation, the scourge of humanity known to history as Tamerlane. For this intensely personal reason, he was disobeying the direct orders of Doc Savage—something otherwise unthinkable.

First, the stubborn archeologist would have to run the gauntlet of Mongol swordsmen.

Two popped up after Johnny turned a sharp corner, and nearly tangled his long legs over a clutch of chickens. The chickens set up a squawking. This commotion naturally attracted attention. That was when the Mongols showed their blandly interested faces.

They wielded the wicked curved swords of their breed. Johnny had only his fists. Balling them, he lifted the bony members high. He squared off. The knuckles were scarred and bloody. Several had split open, revealing gleaming bone.

Screaming imprecations, the Mongols came at the reedy archaeologist from two directions.

The intestinal fortitude of the gangling former university professor was unquestioned. Johnny Littlejohn would march through Hades, Purgatory and even worse places if it furthered the pursuit of justice.

The sight of the two Mongols and their exceedingly sharp swords caused him to rethink his battle plan.

Stooping painfully, Johnny found a couple of stones, commenced applying them to the situation. He had played a little baseball as a youth, and the skill he had acquired then had not departed.

The lank geologist beaned one Mongol—the one who loomed closest to him. This worthy was driven backward, and landed flat on his back. Breath was expelled forcibly from the ruffian's lungs. His sword escaped his fingers.

Seeing his opportunity, Johnny pounced for the skittering blade, took it up in both hands, and proceeded to beat back the second Mongol.

His long arms swinging, Johnny smashed, ducked and parried his way to victory.

The burly Mongol must have assumed that an easy victory lay at hand. He all but laughed at the sight of the wasted-looking American coming at him, appearing so frail and emaciated that he needed both hands to lift his sword.

In actuality, Johnny made short work of his opponent. Relentlessly, he drove him backward until the grunting swordsman lay sprawled on the ground, knocked flat and senseless by a driving blade that could not be withstood.

"Take that, you flagitious, widdiful knave," Johnny puffed.

Lungs laboring, he charged on, a sword in each hand. These slowed him down not at all. He had left behind the coffin containing Cadwiller Olden, safely hidden in a house.

PREDICTABLY, Monk and Ham teamed up. Over the long years of their association, they acted like mortal enemies. But in reality, they were the closest of friends. They just had peculiar ways of showing it.

Monk led the way, with Ham guarding his back. The hairy chemist picked up loose cobbles along the way, holding one in each hairy paw, creeping forward with his small ears alert.

Hearing footsteps pounding in their direction, Monk pushed Ham into a malodorous alley, and crouched impatiently.

The tip of a Mongol sabre showed first, gleaming in the afternoon sun, followed by the man wielding it.

Leaping out of the alley, Monk brought the two stones together with a resounding thud that caused the bright blade to drop from numbed fingers.

For the unfortunate Mongol happened to be caught, not by accident, between the colliding cobbles.

Sweeping up the *kilij*, Monk tossed it to Ham. The elegant attorney, hardly presentable now, tested the blade by flaying empty air with it.

"Watch where you point that thing!" growled Monk.

Ham listened to the hiss and flutter of the blade cutting through air. A satisfied expression lit his patrician features.

"One side, you miserable mistake!" he snapped. "Let a true swordsman lead the way."

Monk gathered up the two stones, which were now very red and sticky.

"You stick them, and I'll brain 'em," he muttered.

They rushed off to carry out their violent intentions.

Chapter LXXI

EVACUATION

SEATED ON HIS throne, Timur Khan, Scourge of Humanity, listened to the sporadic sounds of violence. He sipped piping hot tea from a ceramic cup to fight off the morrow-deep chill that never seemed to leave his quaking limbs.

"My Iron Horde is defeating the bronze barbarian's mercenaries."

Prince Satsu wrung his plump hands nervously, and complained, "How can you tell who is winning?"

"Mongols fight to the death. If fighting persists, that means some live."

The confident assertion sounded dubious, so Satsu turned to his Japanese Marines.

"Be prepared to depart on a moment's notice."

The stiff-featured soldiers dipped their helmeted heads obediently.

It was a nervous time. The Japanese dignitary wanted more than anything to evacuate this Chinese pesthole. It was only the stubbornness of Tamerlane that prevented this.

Listening hard, the ancient warrior cackled with each ringing report of combat. Prince Satsu started to wonder if Timur was not unsound of mind. He had been told by his advisors that the man had been excavated from ice after five centuries. This appeared to have affected his brain, as well as cold-plagued, perpetually shivering body.

Pacing, clutching his scabbard so it did not bang against his striped dress trousers, the Prince fretted silently. He could almost feel a gritty brick wall at his back, and remorseless Chinese bullets slamming into his unprotected chest. This would be his lamentable fate if he were to fall into enemy hands.

Came a long lull in the fighting.

Timur the Lame stood up, metallic head rotating about. He seem to sniff the air like a canny old dog.

"They are victorious," he croaked out. "My Mongols have conquered the brazen devil. They will soon drag his corpse before me. Then we will depart."

Prince Satsu raked the narrow streets with anxious eyes, peering into the town square. Minutes crawled past. Sweat started to creep from the large pores of his tea-hued face. But there was no sign of returning Mongols, or their prisoners.

The waiting became tense. Standing in his fur-trimmed felt boots, Tamerlane commenced shaking as if it were suddenly cold. This was a return of the palsy that had plagued him since he was brought forth from his icy tomb.

Behind his ogreish mask, yellowish teeth chattered like castanets.

Muttering half under his breath, Timur complained, "Where are my loyal Mongols?"

No reply in any form resulted.

The nervous moments dragged on, and all eyes remained fixed on every approach path.

Unexpectedly, a high-pitched voice sounded almost above their heads.

"You misshapen abnormality!" the voice called out in under-standable Mongolian. "You low cur! You cold cadaver that should have remained interred!"

They looked up and about, seeking the source of the hector-ing.

Prince Satsu was the first to discover that tormentor.

It was the famous archaeologist, William Harper Littlejohn, more familiarly known as Johnny. The stork-like American stood on a roof, a Mongolian sabre held in each lean hand.

Without warning, he leapt from his perch and, with both curved blades, lunged for Tamerlane.

"You wish to defeat me, Long-bones," Timur barked. "Have at it!"

The Iron Khan swept out his sword, and there commenced a strange battle.

Timur fought one-handed, while the American drove in with his matched sabres.

Anger is a powerful thing, and the bony archaeologist was evidently consumed with it. His battered face was red. He flailed about like a maddened scarecrow that had been brought to life by some witch's frustrated fury.

Ondor, Tamerlane's giant man-mountain of a bodyguard, stepped in to intercept the gawky attacker.

Johnny shifted slightly, hardly breaking stride, and beat back the man's questing sword.

By all rights, the thin geologist should have been chopped up into so much human kindling. Instead, he pivoted, and spinning about in place, became a whirling dervish of flashing steel.

The big Mongol never got a chance to fight back. Johnny employed the flat of one blade and the dull back of another to beat Ondor about the head, until the stunned giant staggered back, reeling out of sight.

After that, all attention focused upon the main battle.

Tamerlane stood his ground, confident in his lamellar armor of iron plates over red leather.

Johnny flashed at him, and Timur, employing his good arm, smashed away the first blow. It was in that moment that the raw power of the ancient warlord became evident for all to see.

The spindly archaeologist had a firm grip on his blades. Yet for all that, one went flying out of his fist.

Momentarily stunned, Johnny switched the other blade into his right hand. Then, the duel proceeded in earnest.

It was as much a battle of wills as it was of steel. Johnny was driven by human passions, and these impelled him now. He rained curses on the masked Mongolian.

"You superannuated blot on humanity! You knotty-pated xanthodotous toad! Foul, loathsome, limping litch—prepare to die again!"

Laughing behind his battle mask, Tamerlane beat back every blow, searching for the tall man's vitals. The tip of his blade, and sometimes the edge, sliced in and drew blood. This forced Johnny to fight a defensive battle. For he wore no armor.

Back and forth they battled, stepping forward, retreating, lunging again, Timur's blade licking out like a steely fang, forcing the skeletal archeologist to fight two-handed. It did not seem to make much difference. Sparks flew. But neither man gave any ground.

Johnny had one distinct advantage: he presented not much of a target. A jest often made at his expense was that encountered full on, he was often mistaken for a man standing sideways. Several times, Tamerlane's blade nicked his pipestem limbs when they should have driven through meat, of which the rail-thin scholar possessed little.

Perspiration coated Johnny's narrow skull, getting in his eyes, blinding him. Perhaps this, more than anything else, turned the fierce tide of combat.

For while he was swiping the sweat from his brow, Tamerlane let out a vicious scream, and lunged suddenly, virtually hopping on his good leg. The blade pierced the unprepared archaeologist's abdomen.

Johnny's eyes went wide; he emitted a queer sound that was part grunt and half gasp.

When Tamerlane withdrew the sabre tip, he displayed it. The blade was slickly red.

"Now you die!" the icy individual proclaimed.

He brought his bloody blade up and around his head, swishing it several times, preparing to remove the head of his tottering foe.

Only seconds loomed before that awful decapitation occurred.

A RESOUNDING voice broke the moment, shattering it.

The giant Mongol whom they knew as Ondor suddenly commanded their attention.

He stood stationed in the mouth of an alley, where he had evidently crawled or staggered back after Johnny had defeated him. His colorful clothing was disheveled.

"The Chinese! They come. And Doc Savage is leading them! We are overwhelmingly outnumbered!"

A sound very much like rapid gunshots commenced, not far away. The smell of gunpowder soon soured the air.

Prince Satsu screeched, "We have no time for this! We must flee if we are to survive to fight another time."

Tamerlane hesitated, poised on the verge of finishing his grisly task.

The towering Mongol rushed up, took him by the wrist, and said gently, "If we go now, Great Khan, we can finish this later."

Grunting with disappointment, Tamerlane acquiesced.

Forming two groups, they charged from the square, leaving their ponies behind.

The big brawny Mongol gathered up the limp archaeologist, as if to bear him along for later execution. But when he examined the abdominal wound with his deeply dark eyes, he evidently decided that the American would not live long enough to be decapitated alive. He flung him away into a pile of clothing that had been pilfered from the adjoining houses.

Together, the ragtag survivors of the Iron Horde, along with Prince Satsu's decimated retinue, rushed in the direction of the Mitsubishi transport plane.

Manifest shock rode their faces, for they knew that if they were caught, they would not live to see the sun set over this desolate region of China.

Chapter LXXII

GRIM DISCOVERY

MONK AND HAM, by working around the abandoned town of Fragrant Flower in a rough circle, managed to defeat in various ways five marauding Mongol warriors.

Ham accounted for three of them, employing a dazzling display of swordsmanship that caused the hairy chemist to look at him with new eyes.

"I didn't know you could handle anything bigger than that infernal pig sticker of yours," Monk muttered.

"If I still had my Damascus blade," Ham retorted snappily, "I wouldn't need you to handle the stragglers."

It took some doing to make it this far, but when Monk and Ham finally burst into the dusty town square, and surveyed the scene—all that was left were the remnants of their former cages and a few scattered ponies, whinnying nervously.

The Khan's throne sat where it had been, but it was empty.

The bitter stink of gunpowder was everywhere. A gray fume hung in the air over one ornate roof.

Going to investigate, Ham discovered a blackened string of red firecrackers that had exploded. Further along, he found others.

His agile mind assembled the evidence into a clear picture. Doc Savage had set them alight for some certain purpose.

Ranging about, Monk found Johnny Littlejohn deposited upon a pile of clothing. Crimson was leaking from a wound in his abdomen. The lean archeologist never looked more pale. His face had a bloodless cast that was not reassuring to the eye.

"For the love of little laughing Buddhas!" Monk blurted. Lifting his squeaky voice, he called, "Ham! I found Johnny!"

The lawyer trotted back, winced at the damage, and plunged into tearing up Chinese shirts in a frantic attempt to staunch the wound.

"He hurt bad?" Monk demanded.

Ham frowned. "Difficult to say. But the puncture does not look mortal, for the blade merely penetrated his side."

The homely chemist examined the wound with worried eyes, saw that this was the case. It appeared as if the blade had entered close to the skin and not pierced any organs.

"Looks like bein' so dang skinny saved his hide," muttered Monk.

"No doubt," seconded Ham.

"Where did everybody go?" wondered Monk, peering about belligerently.

"Why don't you find out?" Ham suggested waspishly.

Monk went hunting. He popped his bullet skull in and out of buildings, until he found something of interest.

"Here's the big Mongol that fought with Doc earlier," he called over. "Out cold, too. Must've been a big fight here not long ago."

Finishing up his bandaging, Ham Brooks rushed over, and got a good look at the unconscious Mongol bodyguard. The big fellow looked very much the worse for wear. His padded *del* was in rags.

"It appears that Doc Savage has been here," murmured Ham. "I found exploded firecrackers he evidently used to create a diversion. He may have driven Timur and his band off."

"Sure," said Monk. "Doc chased 'em off, and is hot on their trail."

Then, Ham began making concerned faces. "Something is wrong here," he murmured. "But I cannot put my finger on it."

Monk made a monkey-like face expressing his puzzlement.

The elegant attorney snapped two fingers. "This man is wearing the wrong clothes," he blurted out.

"Whatcha mean? Those are the same duds he had on before."

"No," returned Ham. "These are the clothes Doc appropriated earlier. That is the costume Doc was wearing when we last saw him. This isn't a Mongol. This is Doc Savage! And he's been knocked out cold!"

"Blazes!" Monk moaned. "We gotta bring him around!"

Not far away, the sound of airplane motors banging into life reached their ears. With a sinking feeling, they realized that their quarry was getting away.

Abandoning the fallen man, they pounded off.

RENNY and Long Tom, having been directed to do so by Doc Savage, had worked their way to the outskirts of town and crouched low in a miserable vegetable patch watching the big Japanese transport wait to take off.

Idly, Renny sampled some red radishes.

Long Tom said peevishly, "What a time to think of your stomach!"

"When was the last time you ate anything?" rumbled Renny.

Long Tom did not have to think about that very long. He, too, partook of a fresh radish, for their job was to prevent the Mitsubishi transport from taking off with Timur Khan and his Mongols. It showed no such signs, for the props stood still in the cool air.

Exactly how they would accomplish that feat without weapons had not been explained to them. But there did not seem to be many Japanese placed around the aircraft. One Marine stood stiffly at attention with a rifle, and another on hand was evidently the pilot. The pilot wore a brown leather jacket and matching helmet, similar to attire modern aviators were wearing around the world.

The pilot was smoking furiously. His nervousness was apparent. For the transport plane was deep in unconquered China, which was for them enemy territory. Summary execution would be their fate were they to be discovered by Chinese authorities.

Behind them, in the near distance, came rackety sounds. Steel meeting steel, suggesting sporadic clashes.

This did not contribute to the peace of mind of the waiting aviator and guard. Their heads came up, faces twisting.

Renny husked to Long Tom, "Sounds like Doc and the others are making progress."

"Pipe down, you bullhorn," Long Tom cautioned. "Do you want them to hear us?"

The warning was timely, for the guard suddenly started. Both Japanese peered about, seeking the source of the sound they thought they heard.

Crackle of gunfire in the distance interrupted, drawing their attention away from the vegetable patch where Renny and Long Tom crouched.

After another few seconds, noises suggesting a pitched battle commenced volleying through the walled Chinese town.

"Getting to be a blamed war," Renny mouthed to Long Tom.

"M-a-y-b-e w-e s-h-o-u-l-d p-i-t-c-h i-n?" the slender electrical wizard signed back using his fingers.

Renny employed the same deaf-and-dumb system in replying, "D-o-c-'-s o-r-d-e-r-s a-r-e t-o h-o-l-d t-h-i-s p-o-s-i-t-i-o-n."

Several minutes raced by, in which additional clamor of combat was heard.

More rattle of rifle fire. Rings of blade steel. Loud shouts. Blows.

Then a group of men rushed into view.

Clutching his thigh-banging sword scabbard, Prince Satsu ran at the head of the group, accompanied by a contingent of his Marines.

Behind him trailed what remained of Tamerlane's Iron Horde. They had surrounded the Iron Khan, who ran with difficulty, owing to his gimpy leg.

Bringing up the rear, throwing fearful glances beyond him, was the nameless Mongol giant who had been appointed his personal bodyguard.

"Holy cow!" breathed Renny. "Looks like Doc has them on the run!"

They watched from concealment as the fleeing group rushed for the Mitsubishi, whose pilot had leapt into the cockpit to fire up the engines.

Eyes scouring the dusty road from the town, Renny and Long Tom watched for any sign of pursuit.

As the twin motors coughed into life, they saw none.

"W-h-e-r-e-'-s D-o-c?" wondered Long Tom with his fingers.

Renny shook his horsey head. "W-h-a-t d-o w-e d-o n-o-w?" signed back the big-fisted engineer.

"L-o-o-k-s l-i-k-e i-t-'-s u-p t-o u-s."

Together, they heaved out of the vegetable patch and charged for the shimmying plane.

Chapter LXXIII

HOLOCAUST

SEEING THEIR ENEMIES on the verge of escaping, Renny Renwick and Long Tom Roberts charged for the Japanese aircraft with one thought in mind.

"We got to stop them from taking off!" bellowed Renny.

"You said it!" agreed Long Tom.

They were without serviceable weapons, but that did not stop the two intrepid adventurers. They came charging out of the vegetable patch and attempted to intercept the racing groups who were making for the snorting Japanese transport plane.

The cabin door of the plane hung open. Everyone made for that as if their lives depended on it, for conceivably they did.

For all his elephantine bulk, Renny made better time than Long Tom. He veered in toward the man running at the back of the pack.

It was the big bodyguard of a Mongol, whose name they did not know.

Lunging low, Renny attempted to tackle the giant.

But the Mongol was both watchful and wily. He had been casting sharp glances behind him all the time. He spotted the big-fisted engineer charging in like an enraged mastodon. The mountainous Mongol pivoted, and set himself in the fashion of wrestlers the world over, feet planted wide apart.

A titanic collision appeared unavoidable. Renny had every expectation of grappling with the giant. Instead, something miraculous happened. Reaching in with his massive hands, Renny endeavored to capture the man in a massive bear hug.

In some strange fashion, the big-fisted engineer came off his feet and went flying away, to land in thick brush that cushioned his humiliating fall. It was as if an invisible rug had been yanked out from under him.

Long Tom Roberts fared no better. Complaining under his breath, he dived for the Mongol's left leg, thinking to take hold and bring him down to the ground, there to pummel him with his hard fists.

Manfully, he clutched at the thick limb, got hold all right, but the Mongol did something powerful with his big body that caused the undersized electrical genius to be shaken off without any effort.

Long Tom also ended up in the brush. He took hold of his head, and sat up, making eye contact with Renny Renwick, who looked similarly dazed.

"What hit me?" Renny thumped.

"That man-mountain," Long Tom told him.

"He was too much for you, too?"

"Let's try him again," Long Tom gritted.

They picked themselves up, and resumed chase.

LEADING the main group, Prince Satsu was the first to plunge into the safety of the Mitsubishi transport. His much-thinned contingent of Marines piled in after him. Next came the Mongols, who formed a protective human shield so that their armored leader could enter.

Bringing up the rear, the mountainous Mongol abruptly reached out and took hold of Tamerlane.

Taken by surprise, the Iron Khan was lifted bodily. His hitching jackleg way of running had slowed him down. The bodyguard appeared to be attempting to rush him into the waiting plane. He halted, turning.

The giant barked out something to the Mongol horde who, after a moment of confusion, scrambled aboard ahead of their leader.

It seemed the bodyguard had berated the Khan's followers for dallying.

They disappeared inside, leaving only the hulking bodyguard and his armored charge.

Renny and Long Tom rushed up, knowing that only seconds stood between them and the transport plane taking off.

The giant Mongol strode up to the cabin door and, employing one booted foot, slammed it shut.

Ahead in the cockpit, the Japanese pilot took this abrupt noise for the signal to take off. He released the brakes, and howling propellers dragged the bouncing ship along the dusty runway.

Renny bellowed, "They're taking off without Tamerlane!"

"Why the heck did the big guy kick the door shut?"

The individual in question was backpedaling madly as the aircraft took off in haste. In his burly arms, Tamerlane kicked and struggled, but he was helpless against the giant's overpowering brawn.

Evidently, the pilot became aware that he had taken off without his prized passenger. Prince Satsu no doubt noticed the omission, for his screaming orders to cut the engines lifted over the motor roar.

Flustered, the pilot applied the brakes, with the result that the lumbering transport plane careened out of control and executed a disastrous ground loop.

Somehow, it managed to land upside down. One wing burst into flames. The aircraft ruptured along its fuselage and the hatch sprung open, leaving a clear opening for the disoriented passengers to escape.

The first person out of the plane was, predictably, Prince Satsu, clutching at his scabbard, and beating at his swallowtail coat whose long tails had caught fire.

He was forced to shuck the garment as he ran away. Another explosion took hold as the other wing gas tank burst into vaporous flames.

After that, the Mitsubishi commenced melting. No one else emerged, nor was it possible to rescue anyone. The conflagration was too great.

Not that the big Mongol did not try. One arm thrown across his face to shield it from the blistering heat and dense black smoke, he circled the fast-melting aircraft, looking somehow gigantic and helpless at the same time.

Renny and Long Tom came up from behind and attempted to jump him again.

The results were no more productive than before.

The monster Mongol did not pause to lay down his burden, but employed booted feet to trip first Renny, and then Long Tom, off balance. They landed flat on their backs, the wind expelled from their lungs.

"This big bozo is no pushover," Renny rumbled.

"He's almost a match for Doc Savage!" Long Tom concurred.

Monk and Ham arrived about that time. And when they saw their comrades sprawled prostate at the feet of the hulking Mongol, they came charging in to administer appropriate punishment.

They, too, found themselves in over their heads.

Transferring Tamerlane to one hand, the mighty Mongol put out a beam of an arm. Ham ran smack into it, and rebounded as if he had unexpectedly collided with a war tank.

Growling, Monk Mayfair took a running leap, and attempted to slam both feet against the Mongol's great chest.

The results were remarkable. Long arms flailing, Monk bounced away while the giant Mongol staggered back barely a pace.

The hairy chemist found his feet and, bellowing, came in for more.

What stopped him dead in his tracks was not physical. It was a voice. The voice said, "That's enough, Monk."

It was the unmistakable voice of Doc Savage.

"JOVE!" Ham said excitedly. "So that was not you back there dressed as the Mongol bodyguard?"

Doc Savage shook his head. "I swapped clothes with him a second time, after Johnny had banged him loose of his senses. In all the violent commotion, no one noticed."

"Bless me!" grunted Monk. "So you pulled a double switcheroo?"

Doc nodded. "It was necessary to force the combatants toward the plane, so I could separate Timur from the others. Regrettably, the results were not what I desired."

Doc unscrewed a vial, and splashed it on his face, which served the purpose of eradicating the last of the Mongoloid cast of his bronze features. Wiping them with a bit of waste rag he carried, he was left looking like Doc Savage once more.

They turned to watch the plane blaze up one more time before settling down into a slowly diminishing holocaust.

Among the observers was Prince Satsu, trembling in his dress shoes.

Doc Savage had set Tamerlane on his feet, and now removed his helmet and mask of meteoric iron. The fat-seamed face revealed was hideous, eyes glaring with hatred.

"Hold him," Doc instructed the others.

Monk and Renny took a firm grip on either of Tamerlane's arms, fixing him in place. The Iron Khan attempted to resist, but his strength was not sufficient for the task. While ferocious of face, he was weakened of limb. He trembled from head to toe.

Face purposeful, Doc Savage strode over to Prince Satsu and said, "I will accept your surrender now."

Prince Satsu began spitting vituperatively. The words coming out of his mouth were not understandable, so great was his rage and frustration.

Without regard to formalities, Doc Savage reached out and withdrew the man's ceremonial sword from its scabbard.

Prince Satsu swiped a fattish hand out for his blade, which was an ancestral heirloom. He missed.

Doc Savage took the blade and broke it over one knee, tossing the two segments in opposite directions.

At sight of the magnificent sword coming apart, Prince Satsu did the same. His tea-colored face broke with shock; tears streaming down his eyes. He sank to his knees, writhing in anguish.

"Consider yourself a prisoner of war," Doc Savage told him.

The aircraft soon burned down to a heap of blackened slag, after which Doc and the others poked at it with sticks. But it was evident that no one could have survived its destruction. The last of the Iron Horde was no more.

Suddenly, Doc Savage surged in the direction of town. He moved like metallic lightning.

"What's that racket?" Long Tom wondered aloud.

"Wild dogs," grunted Renny.

"Sounds like they got hold of something, too," snapped Long Tom.

"Johnny!" declared Ham.

Homely features scowling, Monk Mayfair yelled, "Habeas!"

There was a concerted rush for the awful clamor, with Renny remaining behind to watch over Tamerlane and Prince Satsu.

But it was neither Johnny nor Habeas Corpus who thrashed at the center of the pack of starved-looking canines. It was Cadwiller Olden.

The midget had been left behind in all the ruction, and had been discovered by a roving pack of dogs. The teakwood casket in which he had been kept had been knocked over and the limbless little man had spilled out.

He resembled a big-headed baby wrapped in swaddling silk clothes. Snarling yellow dogs had clamped on his torso and were pulling in different directions.

422 / A DOC SAVAGE ADVENTURE

Cadwiller Olden was screaming at the top of his tiny lungs. "Save me! Save me! Oh, I don't want to die after all!"

Doc Savage swept in, booting the canines this way and that. Snapping and snarling, they gave ground, slinking way.

The bronze man reached down, and took hold of the blood-soaked windings that concealed the midget's truncated limbs. Olden looked up into Doc Savage's face and his lips writhed. He appeared to be trying to speak, but his voice was not up to the task.

"What is it?" asked Doc, bending an ear.

Without warning, Olden snapped up his head and attempted to clamp ratlike white teeth onto the bronze man's ear.

Doc flinched, evaded the snapping incisors in the nick of time.

"The Devil!" blurted out Ham, his eyes horrified.

Caught off guard, Doc Savage lost his hold. Olden fell and the hovering dogs lunged for him anew. One cur was swifter than most, seized the stump of a leg, and managed to carry off the bundle with a wide-eyed head atop it.

"I did so want to die!" screamed Cadwiller Olden. "I just wanted to take a piece of you with me, big boy! When I was Monzingo Baldwin, you tricked me into thinking you were my friend. I loved you then. Now I hate your guts!" And the miniature man started laughing maniacally.

For a fateful moment, Doc Savage stood rooted. They all did. Stark horror rode their astonished faces. It was unbelievable what had transpired.

Doc Savage shook off the spell first. He started after the fleeing dogs. Before he got far, the others of the pack turned on him, and the bronze giant had his hands full fending them off.

The bronze giant seized canine necks from behind, and squeezed hard, rendering two curs insensate. Others yipped at him, snapping at his ankles.

Doc still retained a last string of firecrackers on his person. Pulling it out, he got the fuse lit and dropped the sizzling package into their snarling midst.

The popping detonations and resulting smoke scattered the remaining pack in all directions.

By the time Doc and his men got organized, there was no sign of Cadwiller Olden, or the ravenous cur that had carried him off.

Chapter LXXIV

DOKU

ONCE THE FRUITLESS search for Cadwiller Olden had been exhausted, Doc Savage and his men sought out Johnny Littlejohn, who still reposed on a litter of looted clothing. He was stirring. At the sound of their approach, he sat up.

The bony archaeologist looked confused, but at the sound of voices, his working eye fluttered rapidly.

Doc Savage knelt, looked to the dressings that Ham Brooks had applied, and appeared satisfied with what he found.

Johnny was murmuring incoherently.

Doc Savage listened, seemed to understand what the dazed geologist was attempting to ask, and said, "The battle is over."

"Tamerlane?" Johnny breathed, good eye snapping wide.

"Our prisoner—along with Prince Satsu," Doc Savage informed him.

Johnny attempted to smile, but his gore-smeared lips writhed into a gruesome grimace.

"I disobeyed your orders again," he gasped out.

"We can discuss that later," the bronze man said.

Johnny shook his shaggy head. "All my fault. Everything that has happened hangs over my excerebrose, morosophic head."

Doc Savage said nothing. Everyone knew there was more truth to that confession than otherwise.

While the bronze man was tending to Johnny Littlejohn's injuries, Monk Mayfair stumbled over to the mountainous Mongol whom Doc Savage had twice impersonated.

There was something about the way the man lay sprawled in the dark that caused the apish chemist to kneel down and examine him.

Monk came back muttering, "That big goliath up and died on us," he revealed.

"I must have struck him harder than I intended to," Johnny murmured, the long lineaments of his face etched with horror.

No one spoke. It was perhaps a small thing amid all the carnage they had encountered, but it was regrettable nonetheless.

After a bit, the bony archaeologist remembered something. "Doc, I left Olden ensconced in a house nearby. Regrettably, I do not clearly remember which one."

No one said anything for a long moment.

Johnny noticed that no one was in a hurry to fetch the missing midget.

"Is something wrong?"

More bloodthirsty than the others, Monk Mayfair volunteered, "A pack of wild dogs got to him first, and one of them made off with the little runt."

Johnny rolled his eyes up in his head and did not seem to know what to say in response. The crestfallen geologist appeared to be overwhelmed by all that had transpired.

Not long after that, Monk Mayfair called out for Habeas Corpus. He used the type of hog call common among farms throughout the American Middle West.

"*Soooeeee!*"

Grunting excitedly, Habeas trotted up many minutes afterward, his long ears erect.

After a boisterous reunion, homely Monk got an idea. He found a bloody piece of rag that had been torn off Cadwiller Olden's swaddling clothes.

Holding this foul fragment under the porker's snout, he let Habeas sniff it and then said, "Go fetch, boy!"

Eagerly, Habeas put his snuffling anteater snout to the ground and sniffed about. He quickly picked up a scent, then vanished on long, spindly legs.

Doc attempted to follow, but he could not keep up, for the pig wriggled into cracks and crannies too small for a grown man to enter.

Not ten minutes later, Habeas Corpus returned with a larger fragment of bloody garment in his tusks. The shoat dropped this unpleasant rag in the dirt.

Monk stooped, examined this. Stuck inside the cloth with a reddish paste was a sanguinary trophy. A tiny ear, rather well-chewed.

Standing up, Monk concluded, "Guess that's about all that's left of the rascal."

Renny volunteered, "Serves him right. Doc tried to rescue him and he bit at the hand that might have saved him."

That, as much as anything, served as the epitaph for Cadwiller Olden.

Sharp-eyed Ham Brooks discovered his sword cane in the dirt and remarked, "This would appear to settle everything."

Monk added, "I'll go round up some ponies. It's a long hike back to our plane."

AFTER they had gathered together a suitable number of horses, Doc Savage led them out to the smoldering plane wreckage where Renny Renwick had charge of the two prisoners.

"What are you going to do with these two?" Renny wanted to know.

Doc Savage replied immediately. It was obvious that he'd already given the matter some thought.

"Tamerlane is too dangerous to be allowed to remain at large," supplied the bronze man. "We will remove him to our special institute, where the Ice Genius will live out the remainder of his days, which should not be all that long."

All eyes went to Johnny Littlejohn, who had long favored such a plan.

Johnny said nothing, his thin lips bitterly sealed. The cadaverous-featured archaeologist seemed to possess no appetite for prying from the twice-thwarted conqueror of China the secrets of his life in antiquity.

Jerking a hirsute thumb at abashed Prince Satsu, Monk then asked, "What about this overdressed diplomat?"

"The best thing to do," suggested Long Tom Roberts, "is to turn him over to the Chinese authorities."

Ham Brooks pointed out, "If we do that, he will certainly be shot as a spy."

Prince Satsu understood sufficient English to turn very pale of countenance. He cleared his throat and finally said thickly, "Savage-*san*, I much prefer to please remain your prisoner of war."

Doc Savage's animated eyes flickered. "Washington would be very interested in interrogating this man."

Ham offered, "If we try to smuggle him out of the country, and the Chinese authorities catch us, we could be shot for aiding the escape of an enemy spy."

That put the bronze man on the horns of a prickly dilemma. Even in wartime, he was loathe to permit death where more humane outcomes were available.

In the end, they decided to ride out to the plane while they gave the matter further consideration.

Tamerlane, after his strenuous and unsuccessful run, was having difficulty navigating, so Renny had to boost him into the saddle of a waiting pony.

Satsu was allowed to climb onto his own mount, and when everyone was firmly seated in their saddles, they rode off.

Now, it was late afternoon and the reddening sun was hanging low to the horizon.

It was a long trek to the plane, but it was through hills and shallows that were not heavily populated. By riding carefully, single file, they were able to avoid inhabited towns or wandering peasants.

It had now been several weeks since they had departed America on what been a peaceable scientific expedition. A great deal had changed in that time. They had fought many battles, and now that the final victory had been won, fatigue was beginning to set in.

Had they not been so exhausted, what next transpired might have been avoided.

A velvety darkness was settling in when Prince Satsu, who had been forced to ride with his hands tied before him so he could not escape, abruptly spoke up.

"Honorable Savage-*san*," he inquired, "have you made a determination as to my fate?"

Doc Savage did not reply. Those who knew him understood that this was a quirk of his personality. When he did not wish to speak, he pretended not to hear a question.

In this case, the silence indicated that the bronze man still had the matter under consideration.

Prince Satsu did not understand this about the bronze giant. He took Doc's silence as an indication of the worst outcome. Again, he imagined the gritty feel of a Chinese brick wall at his back. His expressionless features grew slack and lifeless.

In the center of the Prince's formal cravat nestled a pearl stickpin. The Prince mumbled vaguely, then he dropped his chin, and managed to squirm his lips around the pearl jutting out.

Whispering what might an been an invocation to his ancestors, Satsu took this object into his mouth and began to chew, demonstrating that it was not actually a cultured pearl. The sound of crunching was momentarily lost in the noises of the horse's unshod hooves on dirt and gravel. It was only when the

Prince fell to coughing and choking and making strange strangling sounds that the attention of the others veered to him.

"What's he saying?" wondered Renny.

"Tenno Heika Banzai," translated Johnny. " 'Long Live the Emperor.' "

Tea-colored features turning chalk white, Prince Satsu reeled from his saddle, then smashed into the ground. His horse stopped, flicking its tail.

Doc Savage bolted from his saddle, and reached the stricken man.

Prince Satsu lay on his back, his mouth open, his body shaking uncontrollably. A single syllable escaped his lips. *"Doku."*

Then, he collapsed like a deflated balloon. All life departed from him.

Monk Mayfair asked, "What's *doku* mean?"

Doc Savage translated the word for everyone. "Poison."

They buried Prince Satsu where he fell, as best they could. The soft yellowish loess turned easily. They made a cairn of heavy stones. By the time they were back in their saddles, night had fully fallen.

Nothing was said for a very long time until Monk Mayfair offered to no one in particular, "Things are kinda sortin' out all by themselves."

This comment brought no reply from the fatigued band.

They rode on. A half-moon showed itself in the sky, giving them a little light. That lunar lamp enabled them to locate their waiting plane, which sat quietly, amazingly unmolested, for they had camouflaged it imperfectly with the buff-colored loess.

Dismounting, they cast aside their saddles, released the horses into the wild and climbed aboard the *Brazen Devil.*

While Renny planted Tamerlane in a folding seat in the bomb bay, Doc Savage took the controls. He knocked the engines into life, and ran them until he was satisfied with their performance.

Releasing the brakes, then advancing the throttle, Doc sent the big bronze bird barreling along until her tail lifted and the roaring engines struggled up into the night sky. Doc had to circle several times, spiraling for altitude, for the aging bomber was showing the strain of recent activity.

They were soon winging their way west.

In the co-pilot's seat, Long Tom was communicating with the Generalissimo, conveying the news that the Iron Horde had been thoroughly smashed, and that Free China could in the near future expect a shipment of up-to-date bombers, courtesy of Doc Savage, in return for the permanent loan of the Heinkel.

"That satisfied him," Monk reported to Doc, after the radio call was terminated. "He didn't ask about Timur."

The bronze man nodded. "The fate of Tamerlane is no one's business but our own."

In back, the subject of the discussion sat stiffly, his limbs occasionally shaking. Timur said nothing, but when anyone looked at him, he glared back with his disquieting yellow canine eyes that had first looked upon the world when their distant ancestors were still living.

Johnny Littlejohn was the one who looked at him least. The deflated archaeologist evidently lost all interest in interrogating the warrior from five centuries past.

Monk asked Doc Savage, "Where are we headin'?"

Doc replied, "We will refuel where we can, but my aim is to fly over the Himalayan Mountains to Calcutta, where there is no active war."

Renny frowned. "Do you reckon this old crate will make it over the hump?"

Doc nodded. "If we nurse her along."

MANY hours later, they were watching thick ice forming on the *Brazen Devil's* brassy wings as great ice-capped mountain fangs sprawled beneath them. Ice forming on the spinners built up, was flung off to bang against the fuselage like buckshot. It was exceedingly cold in the cabin. The electrical heaters were not up to the task, but this was an expected hazard of flying sufficiently high to clear the towering peaks.

This had an unfortunate repercussion.

Seated by himself, Tamerlane had dozed off. The coldness creeping into the cabin found his limbs, and he commenced shaking vigorously.

At first, this was not noticed because the old Mongol had periodically exhibited such nervous reactions. After a time, his teeth began chattering, unlovely features showing signs of extreme agitation.

John Littlejohn noticed this and eyed the hideous face, which was trembling uncontrollably.

Rushing forward, he told Doc Savage, "The cold is getting to Tamerlane. He is in difficulties."

Leaving the controls to Monk, the bronze man rushed back to attend to the aged Khan. He checked the wrist pulse, lifting eyelids and attempting to ascertain exactly what was causing the Mongol to convulse.

Doc Savage immediately saw that Tamerlane was in some sort of respiratory distress. Doc pressed a palm against his gullied forehead, detecting signs of a fever—perhaps a return of the ailment that had brought him to the edge of eternity five hundred long years ago.

In the middle of this examination, the grotesquely wrinkled features slowly shaded to blue. This was not the blue of extreme cold, but another blue. The bronze man recognized it at once.

"He is having a heart attack!" Doc reported.

He rushed to a receptacle where a first aid kit was stored. This he rummaged through, seeking something in particular. His eerie trilling filtered out, indicating his agitation. When it trailed off, rather suddenly, it became clear that the bronze man was not discovering what he sought.

Countenance grim, Doc returned to the stricken man.

He was just in time to watch one of the most famous and feared warlords in human history expire in his seat.

Once final time, Tamerlane spoke, his voice a rusty bullfrog croaking.

"Before Allah," he gasped out. "I am not—a man of—blood…. All my wars—started by—others…."

It was a lie, of course. As death approached, some fragment of a conscience had evidently stirred in his demented mind, but too late to matter.

The canine yellow eyes rolled up in his head, and the hideously seamed features ceased their agitated trembling, then went slack.

Kneeling, Doc checked his vital signs. He found none.

In the end, there was nothing that Doc Savage could do. He had been seeking a vial of the heart stimulant called adrenaline with which to save the man. But the Chinese plane carried distressingly meager first aid equipment. There was no hope of inhibiting cardiac arrest.

Ham Brooks placed what remained of his ragged coat over the dead man's grotesque, slumped-forward cranium.

More than two hours passed before anyone spoke. Doc Savage was too busy wrestling the *Brazen Devil* over the mountains. Winds were fierce and the aircraft dropped alarmingly, rising and falling in the perilous updrafts and downdrafts. Shards of built-up ice continued to fly off the spinners to rattle their strained nerves.

When they at last descended into warmer air, Doc Savage said, "We will find a place to set down and bury him in secret."

It was done exactly as Doc Savage wished. Doc and Renny found the ground too hard to excavate very deeply, but they managed to dig a shallow trench, after which they stacked such stones as they could gather into a rude cairn.

After they had interred the cold corpse, Doc Savage presented Johnny Littlejohn with the Mongol's peaked helmet and battle mask of meteoric iron.

"A souvenir of this undertaking."

"Which I fervently wish I had never embarked upon," Johnny said hoarsely.

"Do not berate yourself so. Events got out of control." The bronze giant pondered a bit. "As the man who discovered the true tomb of Tamerlane, Johnny, it would be fitting if you said something over his grave."

Johnny Littlejohn did not have to think very long about that. He walked over to the freshly turned earth and intoned solemnly, *"Igitur ualeas cum malis obruti."*

"Ain't that Latin?" Monk muttered to Ham.

Ham translated. "Johnny said, 'Good riddance to bad rubbish.'"

"You said it, brother," grunted Renny.

To which Long Tom added, "Amen."

Chapter LXXV

AFTERMATH

BY THE TIME they got back to New York City, the calendar said it was the day before Christmas, 1941.

Patricia Savage was waiting for them when they returned to their headquarters in the heart of Manhattan, bone weary. She was a vision in bronze, Doc's energetic young cousin, and the owner of a successful beauty salon on Fifth Avenue.

Pretty Pat's face was twisted in agony.

"Oh, Doc, it's been perfectly awful while you were gone. I was so worried about you. Where on earth have you been, and what have you been up to?"

"We will relate that story at another time," the bronze man said somberly.

Taken aback, Pat asked, "You *do* know we're at war, don't you?"

Renny grunted, "What do you think we've been doing these past weeks?"

"Yeah," said Monk. "We already started payin' Hirohito back for all the hell he stirred up."

Pat's clear golden eyes sparkled. "Well, count me in for the next secret mission."

Normally, this offer to join in brought a ready argument from the others. For years, Pat had been trying to insinuate herself into Doc's fighting band. Instead, the bronze man quietly went to his enormous desk and placed a long-distance telephone call to official Washington.

434

"Doc ain't wastin' any time, is he?" Monk said to Ham.

"He is anxious to get into the thick of it," declared the decidedly undapper lawyer.

"Where were you boys?" whispered Pat.

Renny rumbled, "In the thick of it."

Pat looked perplexed, but no one enlightened her.

THEY all repaired to the great library to give their bronze chief some privacy. Ham had carried his rather worn sword cane back from China and was examining the blade for nicks and other imperfections. The others roamed about, checking various devices designed to alert them to intrusions or other problems that might have cropped up during their extended absence.

"Tell me all about it," invited Pat eagerly.

Monk grinned widely, boasting, "We practically licked the whole Jap army and air force already."

Pat frowned. "That wasn't in the papers."

Talk of newspapers caused Johnny Littlejohn to move to a long director's table where an assortment of newspapers and magazines were strewn. He began riffling through them, frowning as he realized they were all a month out of date.

Monk asked Pat, "Whatever happened to that Hornetta Hale dame you partnered up with before we left?"

Pat shrugged. "Last I heard of her, she was trying to get machine guns fitted on her private plane, and was talking a wild streak about personally strafing Tokyo."

The door opened and Doc Savage entered. "Every official in Washington appears to be too busy with urgent war planning to speak with me at this time."

Ham offered, "They may be upset with us for taking such a long detour home."

"Conceivably," admitted Doc.

"Exactly where were you all these weeks?" Pat demanded.

"Mongolia," said Long Tom.

"China," thumped Renny.

"All over creation," clarified Monk. "And places in between."

"That explains why you all need a shave and haircuts," quipped Pat. "Stop by my place sometime. It will be my treat."

The bronze man began issuing orders. "Monk, prepare our largest amphibian for take-off on short notice."

Monk brightened. "Where are we goin' next?"

"Where we can do the most good. Renny, a fresh crop of graduates will be released from our College with the New Year. Instead of offering them vocational reeducation, we will encourage the abled-bodied ones to enlist in the armed forces. This will speed up the matriculation process and ensure a steady steam of fresh fighting men for the war effort."

"While we're at it," boomed Renny, "I can fly up there and give them a head start on their basic training."

Doc eyed Ham next. "Look into legal matters relating to our international operations."

"Righto, Doc."

As the trio rushed to telephones, Johnny inquired, "How may I help?"

"You are still recuperating, Johnny. Best you get well. There will be enough to do in the weeks and months ahead."

"What about me?" asked Pat eagerly.

"A fresh batch of newspapers would be very helpful," requested Doc. "We are several days behind current developments."

Pat looked as if she wanted to argue the point, but decided against it. The bronzed girl ran out to buy any newspaper she could find, soon returning with one armload, then rushing out to locate any Extras just hitting the streets.

There were a lot of them. Pat distributed these among Doc's men, who had scattered over the vast eighty-sixth floor headquarters, leaving Doc and Johnny Littlejohn alone.

Johnny went over the stories as fast as the papers came in, covering his indignation with a scholarly aloofness.

"Not as bad as might be expected," he admitted grudgingly.

Johnny had carried over some of his disrespect for newspapers from his days as an eminent professor of archeology and geology in a staid eastern university.

"There is no mention of our recent operations," noted Doc Savage. "Nor of your remarkable discovery, which is just as well."

"Indubitably," agreed Johnny. He put the newspapers aside and picked up a notebook on Cadwiller Olden, which Doc stored in the library for convenience. He came to a picture of Olden, which gave the fellow's exact weight, well under a hundred pounds, and his startlingly tiny measurements.

"I'll be superamalgamated!" Johnny remarked. "I fail to understand this fellow. He was tiny. I would think he would try to have someone around him who was near his own size. Instead, he forever surrounded himself with a bunch of giants."

"He was a psychological case," Doc said.

"Obviously."

"Most geniuses are psychological cases, although some of them hide it so well the world never knows," the bronze man remarked. "Something in an otherwise ordinary fellow drives him on and on and he becomes a genius, either at some good profession, or outside the law."

"In Cadwiller Olden's case, it was his size."

"Exactly. He was so small he had become terribly sensitive to it. So he became consumed with the idea of dominating others, of having persons much larger than he completely at his mercy. The quickest way he could get power, evidently he decided, was to turn crook, and do a good job of it."

"The same idea a lot of others have had," Johnny muttered.

"The penitentiaries are full of fellows who got those ideas," Doc agreed.

Johnny continued to read. Then, he put the book aside and went to a large terrestrial globe in the library. A red adhesive marker stuck to the globe at a point where the city of Tokyo lay in the islands of Japan.

"I had not noticed this before," he murmured. "You have been anticipating trouble from this quarter."

"We have our work cut out for us," Doc Savage said grimly.

Johnny took from his lapel his monocle magnifier, and started polishing it studiously. This was a certain sign that the scholarly archeologist had something serious on his mind.

Doc Savage noticed this, and caught Johnny's eye.

"I have been considering all that has transpired in the last few weeks," Johnny declared. "And I cannot help but admit to my shortcomings and outright failures in the lamentable affair of Tamerlane."

"You did your best, as you always do," Doc assured him.

"Perhaps. But many perished due to my overweening thirst for historical knowledge. I cannot ever forget that." The reedy archeologist abruptly pocketed his glass. "I have been considering leaving the Doc Savage organization," he added quietly. "Retiring, actually."

"That does not sound like you, Johnny."

"Perhaps it does not. But I am a changed man. I am thinking of returning to the classroom, where I can do no further harm."

Doc eyed him steadily. "You can do more good as part of our group. Now that America is at war, your expertise will be needed more than ever."

"It is good of you to say that." There was a catch in the archeologist's voice. When Johnny tried to resume speaking, his voice broke. He swallowed several times. "I bungled one of the greatest archeological discoveries in history when I assisted in the resurrection of one of history's worst conquerors. And that was only the beginning of my folly." His voice was warped with emotion.

Doc told him, "Tamerlane would have been discovered by someone at some point, if not during this present century, in a future one."

"Yes, I suppose that it true," admitted Johnny.

"And if you had not summoned me to help, his deferred plans for conquest might have succeeded this time."

Johnny's grave face brightened. "I had not contemplated that eventuality."

Doc added, "Destiny may have placed you in the position to be the man who helped to end the scourge of Tamerlane once and for all."

"Perhaps you are correct," murmured the starved-looking archeologist.

A sudden thought struck Johnny.

"I'll be superannuated!" he said wonderingly. "It has just dawned on me that we have never absolutely determined if the so-called Ice Genius was the actual Tamerlane, or not."

"It seems inescapable that he was," advised Doc.

"Then who is the individual buried in his royal tomb in Samarkand?"

"No doubt he was a Mongol who fit the general description of the true Tamerlane, possibly a blood relative upon whom were inflicted injuries consistent with the man whose secret tomb his advisors hoped to conceal against the day he was revived."

Johnny nodded. "Imminently plausible."

"It is the only explanation that fits available facts," Doc pointed out. "Now, let us get to work."

They returned to studying the globe and began making plans for the battles which lay before them.

About the Author
LESTER DENT

THE LIFE OF Lester Dent spanned only 56 years on Earth. During that time the world changed dramatically. The pioneer West had not completely passed from the American scene when he was born in 1904. At the age of eight, Lester journeyed from Wyoming to Oklahoma in a wagon train, encountering hostile Indians, bad weather and treacherous quicksands along the way.

The son of homesteaders, he seemed destined for the simple life of a rancher or farmer. But young Les had other ideas, in part fueled by stacks of pulp magazines he found in the bunkhouse of the cowboys who worked his family's spread.

As an adult, Lester became a telegrapher and later a telegraph maintenance man—a position that in the 21st Century would be equivalent to a computer technician.

In the 1930s, he went treasure hunting in the Florida Keys with a metal detector he built himself. He learned to fly an airplane during the Lindbergh era, but did not own his own personal ship until 1944. Later, he launched an aerial photography service called *Airviews*, which grew until it had a fleet of four planes.

Taking over his father's dairy farm in the 1950s, Lester brought scientific management to agriculture and Grade A milk to his corner of Missouri and settled down to a life as a gentleman farmer.

An avid ham radio operator, Lester was up on the roof of the house he designed in La Plata, Missouri, fixing the aerial in the Winter of 1959 when he suffered a heart attack. It would later prove fatal.

When he died, the space race has just begun. Lester had once remarked about his Doc Savage novels, "They would be so outdated today that they would undoubtedly be funny. Hell, when I wrote them, an airplane that would fly 200 miles an hour was science fiction. They would be of no interest any more."

On September 28, 1964, two weeks before Lester Dent would have turned 60, Bantam Books released the first American reprints of his Doc Savage novels since the original pulp magazine had folded in 1949. Had he lived to see these books selling in the millions of copies, no doubt Lester would have been both simultaneously pleased and aggravated, since he was not entitled to receive of a dime of royalties, having sold all reprint rights to his stories. He would never have imagined that in the 21st Century his unfinished Doc Savage manuscripts, premises, plots and outlines would feed the latest revival of the Man of Bronze.

But here we are.

About the Author
WILL MURRAY

WILL MURRAY ONCE had a life goal of reading every Doc Savage novel ever published. But a time he was done, he became interested in unraveling the mystery of the many writers who wrote under the Street & Smith house name of Kenneth Robeson. While doing that work, he discovered there existed an unpublished Doc Savage novel, so Murray devoted his time to locating that lost manuscript and getting it into print.

A year before *The Red Spider* was first published by Bantam Books in 1979, Murray visited Lester Dent's widow, Norma, in La Plata, Missouri and discovered the outline to an unwritten Doc novel. The idea of writing it himself crept up on Murray slowly, but by the end of 1979 he was hard at work on *Python Isle*.

He only meant to write that single novel, but one thing led to another and here we are some 35 years later and Will Murray has now written or coauthored 16 new Doc Savage novels, more than any other writer apart from series originator Lester Dent.

How many more Doc Savage adventures Murray will ultimately pen remains unknown, but since the winds of fate appear to be blowing his way, he hopes to remain in the saddle for many years to come as the Kenneth Robeson of the 21st Century.

About the Artist
JOE DeVITO

IN TERMS OF really getting to know the character, I came by Doc Savage late. At least by the standards of most Doc fans. As an artist who grew up in the paperback book era, understandably it was those James Bama covers, as opposed Walter Baumhofer's pulp magazine versions, that first caught my eye. The monumental poses, single light source, limited palette, and the overall simplicity of the compositions, hit me on two levels: they were striking images in and of themselves, and they felt accessible to me artistically when I was just starting out. I thought—I could do this! I would later come to fully understand how complicated it can be to achieve such simplicity, but by then I was already off and running.

Sometime after, there was a fortuitous trip into a Hoboken, N.J. bookstore. There they were: virtually every Bantam Doc edition, all in great shape, for some ridiculously low price—25¢ or 40¢ each. I had never seen them all together before. The impact was immediate. I bought every one on the spot. I moved beyond the covers and actually began to read the novels themselves, starting with the first, *The Man of Bronze*. They were fun reads, clearly of their time, and so evocative, filled with action-adventure, science fiction, over-the-top characters, gadgets and gizmos. One is never too old for that stuff; quite the opposite: it is the kind of thing that keeps a person young at heart in the midst of life's unavoidable realities.

443

More years along, here I am working on Doc Savage covers myself. In part, I think it is the subliminal goal of all illustrators, writers and creators of all stripes in the imaginative arts, to become part of, and contribute to, the fantastic world they grew up in. Working with Will Murray on Doc has certainly helped achieve those ends. We are ever mindful of our good fortune to be in a position to pass on the bronze torch into the future.

www.jdevito.com
www.kongskullisland.com
www.novenaart.com

About the Patron
BOB GASPARINI

LIKE MANY OF you, I was first introduced to Doc Savage and his five aides by reading the Bantam Books reprints that ran from 1964-1990. Whether you became a Doc fan from the original pulps, the Bantam reprints, Will Murray's 1991-93 series or more recently through Will's new Wild Adventures of Doc Savage, all of us who read Doc share a love of adventure, science fiction, suspense and American heroes. The Doc Savage covers have also enjoyed an amazing evolution over the last 81 years, featuring a select number of very talented artists including Walter Baumhofer in the '30s, James Bama in the '60s, Bob Larkin in the '80s, and Joe DeVito since the '90s.

An opportunity to collaborate with Joe DeVito and Will Murray on a classic Doc Savage cover, this time the 50th anniversary cover commemorating the Bantam paperback reprints, was a wonderful experience, and for this I am thankful and appreciative to both of them.

I also want to thank my wife Carlita who has patiently stood by and supported my Doc Savage collecting over the years. I sincerely hope that all who are reading this enjoy *The Ice Genius* and Joe's 50th anniversary cover painting honoring the Bantam paperbacks.

Bob Gasparini
September 18, 2014
Estero, FL

Bob Gasparini is a cancer geneticist who is President and Chief Scientific Officer of NeoGenomics Laboratories, a NASDAQ-listed genetics testing laboratory headquartered in Fort Myers, Florida. Bob lives part of the year in Fort Myers with his high school sweetheart and wife of 39 years. They have 3 grown children, Scott, Lindsey & Connor and 4 other "kids" with fur. When not in Florida, Bob & Carlita can be found in the small town of Sharon Springs, New York, where they enjoy life and the outdoors in a rural American community.

Made in the USA
San Bernardino, CA
10 May 2015